Oil and Water

For my daughter, Jian,
and the future generations

In memoriam:
Christopher and Nancy Evans
Jacqueline P. Evans
Susan D. Arndt

Oil and Water

Mei Mei Evans

UNIVERSITY OF ALASKA PRESS
FAIRBANKS

ALASKA LITERARY SERIES
University of Alaska Press
P.O. Box 756240
Fairbanks, AK 99775-6240

Library of Congress Cataloging-in-Publication Data

Evans, Mei Mei.
 Oil and water / by Mei Mei Evans.
  p. cm.
 ISBN 978-1-60223-200-6 (pbk. : alk. paper) — ISBN 978-1-60223-201-3 (electronic)
 1. Fishers—Fiction. 2. Tankers—Accidents—Fiction. 3. Oil spills—Alaska—Alaska,
Gulf of, Region—Fiction. 4. Communities—Fiction. 5. Restorative justice—Fiction.
6. Human ecology—Fiction. 7. Alaska, Gulf of (Alaska)—Fiction. I. Title.
 PS3605.V3693O45 2013
 813'.6—dc23
                    2012032607

This is a work of fiction. Names, characters, places, and incidents either are the product of
the author's imagination or are used fictitiously. Any resemblance to actual persons, living
or dead, events, or locales is entirely coincidental.

Cover design by Kristina Kachele
Cover art: *Spelunka,* copyright 2012 by John Sokol

This publication was printed on acid-free paper that meets the minimum requirements
for ANSI / NISO Z39.48–1992 (R2002) (Permanence of Paper for Printed Library
Materials).

♻ Printed in the United States on recycled paper

1

One minute he's wielding a sledgehammer under the glare of flood-lights, smashing ice from the steel deck of the Borealis. *The next he's aloft on a wall of water, deposited feetfirst into the storm-tossed Bering Sea as casually as a gust of wind snatches a scrap of paper. Gregg flails in the slushy, half-frozen ocean, slag ice needling his flesh, his cries for help drowned in the pandemonium of crashing waves. He watches the bulky crabber motor away from him, the grinding churn of the boat's engine lost in the gale. He was working alone. Who saw him go over? How soon before they save his sorry ass?*

Not soon enough. Gregg's a poor swimmer at best and now he's drown-ing because he can't draw a breath without inhaling saltwater. Numbed by cold, his thrashing grows sluggish. Soon the shivering is uncontrollable, and his body spasms as if someone were administering electroshock. When his core temperature plummets, his jaws begin to clack involuntarily. Then the shivering stops as suddenly as it began, replaced by one of hypothermia's telltale signs, and Gregg's body flares with inexplicable heat. Fumbling with fingers that barely move to shuck his waterlogged clothes, he wants only to drift, naked as a newborn, into his next life.

Gregg's peering through his army-issue field glasses when Lee clambers up the aluminum ladder to join him on the flybridge. "There's something out there," he says. "Can't tell if it's alive." He hands her the heavy binoculars, pointing into the greenish-gray waters of the Gulf of Alaska, no land in sight. The *Pegasus* bucks against the ebbing tide.

Lee's as slight as Gregg is large, sea otter to his walrus. She widens her stance in an effort to maintain visual focus against the pitching of the boat. "Must be a bird. It's like its wing is broken or something," she says, pulling the binoculars from her face to glance at him. "An albatross?"

Gregg shakes his head. "Dubious." Lee's spiky new brush cut reminds him of the quills on a porcupine. He and she have the same thick black hair, same dusky complexion, same Asiatic eyes: hers Korean and his Alaska Native blood. But now, Gregg thinks, he's the only one wearing a ponytail to the middle of his back.

He rubs his tired eyes and finds himself recalling yet again the winter he fished out of Dutch Harbor. His first time on a crabber, the only time he's ever gone over the side, the ocean so cold it felt hot. He has no recollection whatsoever of being rescued by his shipmates. The mishap has been on his mind ever since he and Lee set out—probably because he has no business fishing over here in the eastern gulf, a district utterly unfamiliar to him.

"You want coffee?" she asks.

"Yeah."

Lee returns the field glasses; Gregg slips their strap over his head as she climbs down to the deck. Why'd she have to cut off all her hair? She already dresses like a guy. Now she looks like one, too.

His concentration veers abruptly. They're closing on the tanker lanes, which is a good thing, because he needs to cross this water as quickly as possible. He's been told that the big ships stray all over the chart out here, paying little heed to the designated corridors, let alone to smaller vessels like the *Pegasus*. To the VLCCs—very large crude carriers—a forty-footer like *Pegasus* is mere flotsam, a literal speck on their radar. In fact, he remembers, one of the first oversized oil ships, in the sixties, actually ran down a Spanish trawler in the Mediterranean without even knowing it. Once back in port, the master of the supertanker apparently noticed some damage to his hull, which led to an investigation. All hands on the fishing vessel, meanwhile, were lost at sea, their lives sacrificed to the big tanker's cargo of black gold.

Gregg scrutinizes the chart again as if hoping to find something printed on it that wasn't there a few minutes earlier. At least visibility is good. Lee returns with his coffee. "What's wrong?" She hands him the insulated plastic mug, and he accepts it without once unlocking his gaze from the water ahead.

"We're in the tanker lanes." Gregg craves a cigarette, trying to remember why he'd thought it a good idea to quit smoking. Neither of them talks while he negotiates the chop, the sea flattening only when they outdistance the tide rip.

"What's that?" Lee cries at the same moment her skipper spots the oncoming enormity. Gregg feels the hair rise on the back of his neck. Son of a bitch. That is one big mother. The black steel-hulled ship ruptures the ocean like a supernatural whale that never stops surfacing, plowing before it a tidal wave of displaced water.

"It's okay." Gregg guns the throttle, spilling hot coffee on the back of his hand. "We're moving faster than them."

"It's so big. How can it be so big?"

The supertanker blots out the sun. And that's only the above-water portion of it, Gregg thinks, the part that's visible.

"Jesus," Lee says. "It's bigger than a cruise ship."

"It's as long as the Empire State Building is tall." Gregg adjusts the course until he's certain the *Pegasus* is out of harm's way. "So they say."

Lee gawks at the huge ship. Strangely, the monstrosity is almost silent as it cuts across their wake. Now they can read the name painted on its enormous snub-nosed bow: KUPARUK.

"What's that mean?" he asks.

Lee squints at the tall block letters. "Isn't it an oil field? On the North Slope?"

The white wheelhouse ascends like a multistory apartment building from the tanker's dark hull. Gregg tries to imagine riding that far up, eighty or a hundred feet above a deck as long as three football fields. Can those on the bridge even see their personnel on the foredeck without using binoculars? He knows supertankers are built to flex against rough seas, in the same way that the Pipeline itself has been built to withstand Alaska's frequent earth tremors and quakes. Maybe, if you have to design something to absorb that kind of shock, you should reconsider building it at all.

The immense ship takes whole minutes to pass. Gregg pictures the belly of the vessel, lying beneath the waterline, out of sight. Like an iceberg. And like an iceberg, hazardous not only to fishing boats but to a whole way of life, *his* life, one dicey enough even without supertankers to fuck things up.

He needs a goddamn cigarette.

Finally, the *Kuparuk* recedes to the southeast, and Gregg feels his heart rate slow.

"It'd be weird to run into Aaron out here," Lee says, breaking the silence.

Gregg grunts. "The tugs only escort these guys as far as Muir Inlet. Three hours north of here. At least." He hasn't seen his son in over a year, hasn't even talked to Aaron by phone since Christmas. As if trying to prove something to his old man, the boy had gotten hired by Stoddard Maritime right out of high school, and now he works the tugs that escort the tankers in and out of the Pipeline port. Gregg takes his first sip of coffee.

Lee draws her own fancy binoculars from beneath the bib of her foul-weather gear and scans the water ahead, no doubt glassing for birds. He casts a glance back; the big ship has vanished more quickly than Gregg would have thought possible. What's he doing out here, anyway? Last year's middling catches had pressured more than a few of them into chancing black cod this spring, but he's the only one who'd geared up for District Five. His mounting debt is beginning to resemble a super-tanker: no end in sight. Fishing never goes well when the stakes are this high.

"Look!" Lee shouts, pointing.

Gregg throws the throttle into neutral, once more splashing coffee on himself. In the distance, two school bus–sized icebergs of blue-tinted glacier ice bob on the swells.

"That must be what we saw earlier," she says. "A growler."

Great, he thinks, rubbing his hand. First tankers. Now bergy bits. Just my friggin' luck.

Dead asleep, giant crab pincers fasten on her shoulder. "Dammit, Gregg," Lee mumbles. Her skipper always wakes her with the same vise-like grip as if, in the effort to keep his touch "professional," he feels he must forsake any semblance of gentleness, too. Lee presses the button on her wristwatch to illuminate the display. It feels like they're riding some swells.

"Why'd you let me sleep so long?" she says to Gregg's receding figure, sliding her long-underwear-clad legs out of the sleeping bag to hunch for a moment on the edge of the bunk. But her hulking boss has already ducked through the companionway, returning to the wheelhouse.

Lee pulls Carhartts over her long johns and insulated socks, slips her feet into deck shoes, and shrugs into a hooded sweatshirt. Still zipping her third layer, a dark woolen vest, she mounts the short staircase to join Gregg at the helm, breathing deeply of the cabin's decidedly fresher air. Even though he's quit smoking, he's got the outside door cracked, as usual.

Lee can see marker lights about five hundred yards ahead. Clear night, or rather, morning. "*American Eagle*?" she asks. The *Eagle* is the tender that will carry their catch, when they get it, to the AlaskaPride cannery for processing.

Gregg nods, jotting into the log that lies open on the console before him. Then he regards her directly, lifting his chin. "Why'd you cut it?"

Lee grins. "I knew you'd say something. Eventually." She runs her fingers through her short-short hair, picturing the black bristles poking straight up like a kung fu action hero's. "Doesn't it look cool? Like a porcupine?"

He snorts. "Hedgehog, more like."

She whacks him with the back of her hand. The sensation's the same as smacking a barn-door halibut.

When she returns from the head, Gregg eases from his perch. As usual, he relinquishes the wheel to Lee only after she wraps both hands around it. "Stay in their wake. Keep her at forty-eight hundred RPMs."

"'Her'?" Lee likes to give her skipper a hard time about the she-boat thing. Slipping onto the swivel seat that's still warm, almost hot, from Gregg's occupancy, she hooks her heels in the metal rung of the chair—an action that unfailingly reminds her of climbing onto a barstool. "Why'd you let me sleep so long?" Lee asks again. It's half past three; he had said he'd wake her at two.

"Because even you need your beauty rest, Princess."

Lee shakes her head.

Gregg chuckles. "Want some coffee before I turn in?"

"Not yet."

Without another word, he's gone.

Gregg can still get a few hours' sleep, Lee figures, his first since they left Selby almost two days ago. She checks the gauge. Holding steady at forty-eight hundred. Settling herself behind the wheel, she pictures again the supertanker they'd crossed paths with yesterday and senses that she'd dreamt of it, although trying to recall the dream now is like grasping at smoke.

She and Jackie had driven into Denali National Park last August, the surrounding tundra already red and ocher from frost. Because it was overcast when they finally arrived at dusk at the end of the park road, low dense clouds shrouding the horizon, they had pitched their tent, cooked supper, and gone to sleep with no clue as to which of the nearby hills might gather to form the base of the highest peak in North America.

Jackie had awoken first, wriggling her long torso out of their shared sleeping bag to pee outside the tent. "Lee! Get out here," she said in a low voice. "You won't believe this."

Emerging on hands and knees, Lee saw at once that the sky had cleared, pink and gold sunrise glinting from countless glacier-hung pinnacles, bathing the entire Alaska Range in an electric vermilion wash. Then she realized that looming head and shoulders above all the other shining summits, more massive and imposing than she could have imagined, reared a showstopper of ice and snow. The massif's frozen ramparts so dominated the landscape as to beg a new descriptor altogether. The sheer bulk and majesty of Denali rendered the word "mountain" a euphemism. Lee and her blue-eyed lover had gaped and clutched at each other foolishly, as if they themselves could claim some credit for The Great One's breathtaking supremacy.

Alone in the wheelhouse, Lee thinks that the *Kuparuk* is like that, too. Not so much "ship" as something in a class of its own. Like the eight-hundred-mile Trans-Alaska Pipeline, which she has heard is visible from space, the gargantuan supertanker strikes her as an astonishing feat of human engineering.

Lee knows better than to express her admiration in front of Gregg, however, since he loathes the oil industry as only a fisherman can. When the Pipeline was first proposed to Congress, in fact, he was one of a group of Alaskans who'd traveled to D.C. at their own expense to lobby for an overland trucking route—anything to preempt industry's plan to transport crude petroleum by sea. The risk of an ocean spill was flat-out unacceptable, these Alaskans argued before federal lawmakers. People in Selby still talk admiringly of how Gregg brandished a king crab on the floor of the U.S. Senate, the giant crustacean's spider-like legs overhanging the edges of the conference table when he finally set it down.

Of course, the Pipeline had been approved anyway, and if not for its construction, people like Lee might not even live in Alaska today, she thinks, since North Slope crude is what greases the wheels of the state's economy. She raises a hand to her head again, the short hairs bristling her palm. She likes how the cut exposes her wide face with its prominent cheekbones, making her look androgynous and, she hopes, faintly threatening. She especially enjoys the fact that she now looks even more Native, and thereby more "Alaskan."

Lee figures their physical resemblance to each other is the main reason she and Gregg get along so well. Friends always express skepticism when she insists that her skipper has never, not once, come on to her. Sure, she's a lesbian and he's old enough to be her father, but neither fact has ever slowed down any other Alaska man for so much as a nanosecond.

Hedgehog. Shit.

Checking the gauge again, she gooses the throttle. Lee likes driving the *Pegasus*. At least, she enjoys doing so under conditions like these: calm seas and the relatively mindless task of following the tender. She can navigate fine in the wake of another boat, but has only a rudimentary understanding of how to chart a course or calculate the readings taken from the array of instruments mounted into the console as well as onto brackets overhead. The digital readout on the fathometer, for instance, jumps all around, sometimes increasing or decreasing in nerve-racking increments. Ditto with the radar, whose glowing amber smudges bleed across the screen, making it look to her like they're always on the verge of running aground.

She's never doubted her ability to learn these things, but as much as she likes commercial fishing, she knows it isn't her life's calling (whatever that might be), so she's reluctant to get too invested in the boat's operation.

Lee checks to make sure the tender's still in her line of sight, then reaches for the hollow glass fishing float that's about the size of a baseball, its surface abraded and weathered to the same shade of green as a frost-coated alder leaf. Gregg's lucky talisman. She presses the cool glass to her cheek before replacing it carefully beside the boxy LORAN, the device transmitting long-range aids to navigation.

8

She glances at the tachometer and leans back, watching the beacon at the top of the *American Eagle*'s mast sway to and fro like a metronome while the *Pegasus* flies into the darkness between them. Relaxing into the seat, Lee pictures the Rufous hummingbird that visits her nectar feeder at home, how the tiny creature hovers motionless in midair, its wings beating so rapidly you can't even see them. Once, the rust-brown-and-iridescent-green bird had brushed her cheek, as if in greeting. Like driving the boat at night, she can't say why the memory makes her so happy, only that it does.

Twenty-six hours later, having worked through the night, Lee massages her throbbing wrists as she watches sunrise burnish the Coastal Range with copper-colored alpenglow. A high-pressure system must finally be pushing out the low. Is that why so many birds are flying west?

The ganions are baited, the longlines coiled neatly in their tubs. Gregg wants to soak the gear all day, so she and he will take turns sleeping. With any luck, they'll wind up with a decent catch. She can see the volcanic range clearly now. In the morning light the snow-covered mountains resemble mythical creatures. The idea of molten lava seething beneath slabs of glacier ice fascinates her, and Lee knows that from the air, as on a topographic map, the frozen spires would appear as flattened, vaguely circular splotches of ice splaying into irregular glacial tongues licking their way to tidewater. When you hike up to one or fly over it in a bush plane, the seemingly smooth surface of the glacier reveals its many corrugations, the crevasses reminiscent of the child-bearing stretch marks on a woman's belly.

Lee shakes her head abruptly and raises the Nikons to scan the open waters of the gulf, spotting a high-flying slender-winged bird on the edge of her field of vision. A tern? This early? She's so tired she's probably seeing things. Arctic and Aleutian terns are some of her favorite birds, not only because of their world-record migrations but because of their quicksilver aerial maneuvers. She remembers how Jackie used to razz her: "They're *all* your favorite!" The creature flits from view before she can make a positive identification, and Lee lowers the small but power-ful binoculars.

"For my favorite birder, for her favorite birds," read the card that accompanied the expensive lenses. The two women were sitting on the small Scandinavian-style sofa they'd bought earlier that day at a yard sale. The perfect piece of furniture for their single-bedroom house. Lee had set the binoculars back into the gift-wrapped package.

Jackie tucked her wavy chestnut hair behind her ear. "The salesman told me you could exchange them if you wanted something different," she offered quietly. "I have the receipt."

"No, it's just—" Lee struggled to speak against the pressure in her throat. "No one's ever given me anything like this."

Her own third-anniversary gift to Jackie had been a sterling silver loon pendant. Not exactly a pair of Nikons, but not too shabby. Lee had chosen it because, supposedly, loons mate for life.

So much for that idea.

Four cormorants squabble off the stern, scavenging the remnants of baitfish she'd hosed off the boat just moments ago. The big birds begin to fight in earnest only yards away, beating their dark wings in an energetic scuffle over a scrap of food. Someone had once told Lee that cormorants are called "shags" in New Zealand, a name she thinks fits the scarecrow-like birds perfectly. Lee recalls the children's book she has sometimes read aloud to Elias and Minke about a boat-dwelling Chinese family who used captive cormorants to help them fish. By tying lines to the birds' feet to prevent their escaping, and by placing metal rings around their necks to keep them from swallowing, the cormorants could still swim and dive but the people could pull uneaten fish from the birds' gullets to sell. It seems like the story described a real custom; she wonders if it's one still practiced in China today. In general, Lee disapproves of people exploiting other creatures for human ends, but then, her work these days is that of killing fish, so who is she to talk?

She raises the lenses again to watch the last airborne birds flicker toward land. Pointed wings, forked tails. Definitely terns. Hallelujah.

Must mean it's really spring. Is Jackie dating? Lee's head jerks, like a dog sniffing the thorns on a devil's club. Enough of this. Time to hit the rack.

She's a lot better off resuming her original contract, "marriage" to Alaska. After all, the Northland is Lee's first love: she's most alive when wandering the tundra, exploring the rain forest, or fishing on the ocean. Wild Alaska is what gives her life meaning, not the struggle to maintain some tired relationship.

Gregg tests the hydraulics, watching Lee shovel crushed ice into the fiberglass totes they've lashed in the transom well to accommodate their overflow of fish. He'd never have guessed the fishing could be so good out here. Shit, it hasn't just been good; it's been un-fucking-believable. A few more trips like this and he might even start to dig his way out of debt.

After two days of busting butt, his deckhand's as stooped as an *aka*, or old granny, doubled over from years of cutting meat and scraping skins. Gregg knows better than to tease her, however; Lee's worked her tail off for him.

At least she'll have a healthy bonus to show for her trouble, even if it comes at the cost of any real sleep and what is doubtless wicked carpal tunnel pain from baiting hooks and pulling skates of gear laden with pop-eyed fish. Does she resent the fact that, in an effort to save money, Gregg hadn't hired another hand? He'll definitely bring others on for herring, then halibut and salmon. Soon enough they'll be fishing non-stop. Time to line up another deckhand.

Is Wassily Chukanok serious about crewing? As far as Gregg knows, his childhood friend hasn't commercial fished for years. He helps Lee shovel ice onto the pale-gray, elbow-length cod that now plug the holds, and together they maneuver the hatch covers into place.

"You smell that?" he asks, sniffing the breeze.

"Forest fire? In the Interior?"

Gregg shakes his head. "Wind's from the east and anyway, much too early for fires. Snowpack hasn't even melted." The trace odor is vaguely acrid. Nothing to worry about, he decides. It's not like the ocean's going to catch on fire.

Everything looks shipshape, the product ready for delivery. They'll spend the night anchored near the *American Eagle* in Beauty Bay, and Gregg figures Lee will enjoy some beachcombing as much as he will before they begin their journey home tomorrow.

He'd like to find another glass float, for Aaron. (Hell, with this haul, he can fly the boy to Selby for a visit. And if they continue to do well, maybe he'll even treat his son to an all-expenses-paid trip to Mexico or Hawaii next winter.) Gregg loves combing the wild coastline for the antique buoys. Some guys collect the handblown glass globes from the ruins of old canneries, cutting them from rotting nets, but he considers that cheating. The real prizes are those found far from human habitation, because it means that wind and currents, not people, have fetched them there, each weathered orb its own unknowable mystery.

He mentions to Lee that the single sideband radio is out of commission. "I'm not worried about it," Gregg adds. "We can always raise Ivan on the CB once we get inside."

"I'll stow the gear, scrub everything down," she says, referring to the after-fishing chores.

He nods. Deckhands like Lee don't come along every day, male *or* female. Ironically, her lack of ambition to advance her fishing career is exactly what makes her so valuable. She glances at him in surprise as he begins to work alongside her, stacking baiting tubs.

"I'll take care of this," she repeats.

"Don't worry about it."

When they move on to coiling lines, she looks at him again. "I got it. Really."

"No sweat," he says. "It's good for me. Keeps me humble."

"That'll be the day."

They work in silence until Gregg asks, "What about Wassily?"

Lee nods. "He'd be good."

It's settled then. Gregg will give Chukanok a shout once they regain radio reception at Cape Shelikof.

2

The ocean has him in its grip, sucking him under, his body trussed in bullwhip kelp or ship's lines and his flesh seared by the winter sea. Gregg gasps for breath, ice-riddled saltwater pricking his flesh.

He wakes in pitch-darkness, his body damp with sweat, thighs entangled in his old flannel blanket, and recognizes the dream-memory before fully awakening, but his breath continues to ratchet, his heart revving like a stuck throttle.

Something's really fucked up, he realizes. A sickening stench of manure, and some kind of fumes. Fuel. Propelling himself from the bunk, eyes stinging, Gregg pushes back panic. In the sightless silence, he tries to identify the danger, but the only sound he can hear is Lee's soft snores from the opposite berth.

The smell, enormous and cloying, assaults him like a physical force. Gregg's eyes stream, nose running. The overwhelming odor calls to mind raw soil, as of earth scraped open by a bulldozer or backhoe, but it also smells like gasoline. Lots of it. Napalm? He flushes with fear, his sphincter clenching—the body's involuntary, instinctive response to danger, the "pucker factor" he remembers all too well. Are they going down? Gregg gropes his way to the wheelhouse.

What's going on? Think, buddy, *think*.

The boat is still. Too still. Fear cools his flesh even as tears warm his cheeks. He wipes away snot and holds his arm before his mouth, breathing through the fabric of his polypropylene sleeve as he stumbles out to the deck as erratically as if he were drunk. What the hell. Has he fallen off the wagon?

No, he's cool. What the fuck is going on? When Gregg steps into the soft glow of the boat's marker lights, the full force of the fumes buckles his knees, stabbing his eyes anew. He grabs hold of the welded metal davit to arrest his fall.

He gasps and tears blur his vision. The frost-covered deck singes the soles of his bare feet, an immediately tactile sensation that helps him to orient, so Gregg focuses on the cold to counter his dizziness, sucking air through his teeth to avoid breathing through his nose.

Lee lurches through the cabin, flashlight beam veering wildly as she joins him on deck. When she directs the light downward, Gregg sees that she, too, wears only long johns, her feet bare. "We're leaking fuel?" she pants.

"It's not diesel," he says softly. They both whisper, as if to speak normally might ignite a spark that would blow them sky high. He takes the light from her, shining it first on the bow, then on the stern, but nothing appears amiss. When Gregg turns the beam onto the surface of the surrounding water and they both step to the rail to look over, however, he can only stare, uncomprehending.

The sea appears dense and opaque, a plastic lifelessness to it that he's never seen before. Even in calm conditions—like here, a protected cove—the ocean is a living entity; it kisses your hull. But something is wrong with the water. It lies inanimate and limp, as if dead.

Handing the flashlight back to Lee, Gregg stretches on his belly to extend an arm through the scupper. When he raises himself, holding his hand in the beam of her light, a shiny brownish-black sludge coats his fingers. They both bend forward to sniff at the same time. The greasy substance smells like bunker oil mixed with shit, he thinks.

"Petroleum, for sure. But not gas. Not diesel," he hears himself say. What the fuck. Gregg stands, his stomach cramping and bile rising to his throat. He holds his soiled fingers before his chest, as if shot in the hand. Movements made stiff by cold, he shuffles back into the cabin, flicking on lights and switching up the radios with his clean hand. Lee follows him robotically, as wide-eyed as a Vietnamese mama-san whose ville has just been strafed. Gregg wants to smack her, snap her out of it.

No reception. Nothing but the chatter of static. The surrounding mountains interfere with CB and VHF reception, and he remembers even as he reaches for the dial that his single sideband's down. Damn. A wave of nausea assaults him, but he catches hold of the seatback and lowers his head, forcing himself to draw deep breaths.

Everything feels dreamlike, hallucinatory. Lee crumples to her knees just inside the doorway, moaning, then struggles to her feet and rushes back outside. Gregg can hear her retching. As usual, he thinks, he's failed to protect someone entrusted to his care.

"You okay?" he calls to her.

"What's happening?" Lee's whimper sets his teeth on edge.

"That's what I want to know." Ripping sheets of paper towel from the roll beside the sink, Gregg swipes at his dirty fingers before peeling back a corner of the Astroturf that carpets the cabin. Where's Aaron? Please, let my son be safe from harm. Lifting out the trapdoor set in the plywood floor, he lowers himself into the engine room.

When Gregg hoists himself from the cramped compartment minutes later, now scrubbing his stained fingertips with a dirty blue rag, Lee's curled up on the galley bench in a fetal position, clutching her gut. "It's not ours," he says. "Can't be." He shoves the fitted hatch back into place and realigns the synthetic carpet with his feet.

"Then what is it?" Lee's saucer eyes remind him of those black-velvet paintings of waifs. This isn't my fault, he reminds himself.

Gregg's stomach rises again, and he wills himself not to puke. He dare not be sickened like his deckhand or they'll really be screwed. Focus, man; use your head. We're due west of the tanker lanes, same direction as the prevailing currents. He's immediately so convinced it's an oil spill that he questions only where. How far away? Entering Beauty Bay last evening, he'd been surprised to find the *American Eagle* already departed and had supposed the tender full, had resented that others might have done as well as *Pegasus*. Now, he guesses that Ivan had learned of the spill and taken the *Eagle* in early to outrun the spreading contamination. With his sideband down, no one could have reached Gregg back here even if they'd tried. "Must be an oil spill," he says aloud.

Lee stretches the collar of her turtleneck until it covers her nose, pushing herself upright on the padded bench, eyes wide with fright. "What do you want me to do?" she asks, her voice quavering but so matter-of-fact that Gregg thinks of the old saw, "When the going gets tough, the tough get going."

He locks eyes with her. "Pull the anchor. Stay up there with the floodlight." He can get them out of the bay, but it's too dangerous to travel any further in the dark. They'll have to wait until daybreak for that.

The radar screen is entirely aglow, as if the *Pegasus* lies atop a landmass. Has the radar crapped out on him, too, like the sideband? Forty minutes later, Lee guiding him from the bow, Gregg has her reset the hook behind Beluga Point. They're pretty exposed here, but at least the air is breathable. Better to risk the brunt of gulf weather than to keep breathing those foul vapors.

From the flybridge at dawn, they gaze upon a vast oil slick, its muddy discoloration extending as far as Lee can see, the rocky shoreline stained brownish-black in both directions from the night's high tide.

Up close, the water surface is gelatinous, clotted, and coagulated like some kind of infernal gravy, complete with giblets of seaweed and driftwood. When the wind blows the fumes directly in her face, Lee's eyes sting and her stomach clenches, but the effect is nothing like it was inside Beauty Bay, where she felt sure they'd been in danger of dying. Would she and Gregg be dead now if they'd stayed put there overnight? She hugs herself, shivering.

As the sun crests the ridgeline of the nearby mountains, prisms of light reflect from the surface of the oily swill, transforming it into swirling bands of rainbow colors. Almost pretty.

Gregg tells her to pull the hook again.

"All the way?" she calls over her shoulder, reluctant to soil the foredeck with the greasy residue that now adheres to the anchor and chain.

"What else?" he barks. Once the equipment clears the bow, he jams the boat into gear. They ride low to the water with their heavy catch, close to the rank effluence that has replaced the shimmering sea. At least their fish are safely stowed, Lee thinks, protected from this toxic offal. Once they're under way, Gregg reduces the boat's speed in order to "keep this shit from splattering her any more than necessary," as he puts it. Then he tells Lee to make sure the black cod are well iced.

"I just checked them," she says.

"Check 'em again!"

By the time they turn into Muir Inlet, Lee paces the cabin wishing she had something, anything, to do. The AM radio startles her with its sudden reception, and she and Gregg learn that just before midnight Thursday—the night before last—the Mammoth Petroleum Corporation's newest, largest, "most state-of-the-art" oil tanker had run aground on Montague Reef, "a well-known navigational hazard."

"That's the one we saw," Lee says, trying to get Gregg to look at her. "The giant ship. *Kuparuk.*"

Her skipper says nothing. Thirty-six hours into what's being called "the Mammoth *Kuparuk* Critical Incident," the amount of spillage has been estimated at twelve million gallons, making it one of the world's largest oil spills, according to the commentary.

"What's that mean?" Lee asks. "How much is twelve million gallons?"

Gregg clenches his jaw, not speaking.

Prevailing currents are bearing the unprocessed crude or "raw" petroleum northwestward. This tidal sequence is the second highest of the year, and oceanographers calculate it's causing the slick to spread faster than it otherwise would. The most recent aerial survey has estimated the size of the oil spill at five hundred square miles.

"Five hundred square miles!" Lee exclaims, trying to equate this area with something she knows, but Gregg only glowers at her.

They learn that the spill is expanding by the hour and that, so far, there's no organized effort to contain it. Residents of the communities lying closest to the grounded tanker have put to sea in their own boats in so-far futile attempts to prevent the oil from washing ashore. Lee's never heard of these settlements—Native villages, she guesses—but judging from the flaring of his nostrils, Gregg has. Someone explains that the "boom" the state requires the oil company to keep on hand for such emergencies had been buried under fourteen feet of frozen snow at the Pipeline terminal. As if a detail from a badly plotted movie, they hear how in the early hours of the "incident," only one person could be found who knew how to operate both the front-end loader and the forklift necessary to extricate the protective material. After working nine hours straight—alternating between the two pieces of heavy equipment—the retired Pipeline worker had been hospitalized with chest pain.

One official after another offers his opinion that it's already too late to contain the bulk of the escaped petroleum. A handful of islands in the nearby sound have been completely inundated by crude oil washing ashore at depths of three feet. Up to my waist, Lee thinks. When she imagines wading through the noxious substance, her stomach threatens to spew again. She wants to cling to someone, to be consoled, but her skipper makes it clear she should leave him alone.

Gregg chews through the ballpoint pen clenched between his molars and, tasting ink, chucks the offending instrument through the sliding

18

window. He wipes his mouth with the back of his hand, only to smell the fetid odor of raw petroleum that still clings to his oil-stained fingers.

The radio reports that "countless" oiled seabirds have washed ashore in "numerous" locations. No one says if the birds are alive or dead. No mention of any attempts to rescue them. Gregg keeps his eyes averted from Lee, who appeals to him with a stricken expression that serves only to make him want to sling her overboard.

Experts seem generally agreed as to the crude petroleum's toxicity, but dispute the amount of exposure constituting a human health risk. The state epidemiologists warn listeners to avoid contact with the poisonous substance.

"But what if you're surrounded by it?" Lee says. "What about breathing it?" She stares at her skipper's hand like it's turning gangrenous before her eyes. "What if you get some on you?"

"Stop," he says, more harshly than he intends. At least Lee quits whining.

Gregg hates driving through what looks and smells like an endless latrine, hates the thought of it defiling his beautiful *Pegasus*. How much sea life has already been taken out by the crude oil, writhing in agony before floating belly up? After many unsuccessful attempts, he finally manages to raise a crab-fisherman friend in Old Harbor on the VHF. Roy promises to get a message to the Kodiak Marine Operator to call Peg, Gregg's ex and Aaron's mother, to find out where their son is. He gestures with the mike to Lee. Anyone she wants to contact?

His deckhand stares at him with tears in her eyes. "I don't even know Jackie's new phone number," she says. "I guess I could try Tess, or, no, she's at a thing. A conference. In Fairbanks." Soon Lee's fretting again, which infuriates him.

In the shadow of the Fairweathers, they lose radio reception for an interminable hour. Thankfully, Lee goes out on deck. While the radio crackles emptily, Gregg considers what he's heard, none of which has mentioned any kind of coordinated oil spill response. Neither the state nor the Coast Guard has yet to mobilize in the face of what is clearly already a full-blown disaster. No mention of industry moving to head off the unspeakable threat posed by an uncontained spill on an unprotected coast. The only ones doing anything are local residents, using their own boats, and responders are rapidly losing the window of opportunity: five hundred is a lot of square miles. Gregg wonders what could have been done in the early hours of the grounding—*if* boom had been readily deployable, *if* contingency plans had been in place, *if* the state and the feds had ever been even halfway serious about holding Big Oil accountable for the risks posed by the ocean transport of unprocessed crude. Almost two days into this thing, there's still no plan. How screwed up is that?

Lee reenters the cabin. "Want a break?"

"Leave me alone," he snarls, trying to soften this with a smile that probably looks more like a grimace.

When they regain radio reception, it's the same pathetic palaver. All talk; no action. A National Oceanic and Atmospheric Administration spokesman projects that "the leading edge" of the spill will reach Selby in approximately seventy-two hours.

"Selby!" Lee looks frantic. "Three days?"

Gregg frowns, trying to focus on matters of navigation. Why must women always be so emotional? When he seizes the opened can of Pepsi she offers him a few minutes later, he squeezes it so hard that most of the soda geysers out the top, spilling onto his leather deck shoes. Lee tries her best to sponge his feet and the floor, but he growls at her to back off.

According to the next talking head, the Mammoth Petroleum Corporation will withhold the names of all tanker personnel until the cause of the grounding has been determined. What else could it be but mechanical failure, Gregg thinks, since the whole point of the supertankers' electronic navigational systems is to *eliminate* the possibility of human error. Besides, Montague Reef isn't exactly the kind of nautical hazard that requires exceptional navigational skills. It's a prominent rock, marked by flashing lights and clanging buoys, flagged red on every chart. It seems to him, in fact, that it would be harder to hit it than avoid it.

Eventually Lee dials in KRBB, Selby's own public radio station. "Daniel!" she exclaims with emotion, and Gregg, too, recognizes the hepped-up voice reading the by-now-repetitive public-health caution regarding the crude oil's toxicity. None other than Daniel Wolff, Aaron's high school wrestling coach, who had coddled the boys so much they lost regionals. After playing Mr. Mom for a number of years while his wife supported them through her job at the hospital, Wolff had recently landed paid work as a news jockey for Rugged Bay Broadcasting. Lee increases the volume, relishing the familiar voice.

Wolff sounds jacked as he announces the governor's intention to establish a disaster-assistance center in Selby. Gregg finds the other man's excitability distasteful but knows Lee is tight with Daniel Wolff, Tessa, and their two young children, so he tries to mask his disdain for this candy-ass. As the radio reporter continues his self-important drivel, however, Gregg suddenly can't stand being cooped up in the cabin and orders Lee to take the wheel.

Stepping outside, he can breathe again. Gregg stares at the seemingly endless expanse of mud-colored petroleum that entirely surrounds them. The Gulf of Alaska's as discolored as the fucking Mekong Delta.

What *does* twelve million gallons mean?

He remembers his first oil spill: the *Torrey Canyon* jackknifed at the mouth of the English Channel, folded back on itself in a V. How many gallons was that? Although he was only a green deckhand at the time, Gregg will never forget the full-page *Life* magazine photos of oiled seabirds, the before and after shots of broad white beaches covered with sticky tar, area residents trying their best to remove the scourge with shovels and buckets. That copy of *Life* got as much scrutiny in Gregg's Alaska coastal village as any issue of *Penthouse* or *Playboy* he and his buddies later pored over in the army. The glossy oversized pages of the European maritime catastrophe had proven especially fascinating to the Native elders, lifelong fishermen all.

He tries to recall particulars of other spills: the *Amoco Cadiz* off France and the *Argo Merchant* near Nantucket, America's hallowed whaling capital. Santa Barbara. The *Erika*. What about that well blowout in the Gulf of Mexico, Ixtoc? How many gallons with each of those? Gregg thinks of all the newspaper photos and television footage over the years of oiled birds, blackened coastline, people everywhere scrambling to clean up the latest contamination. How can it be that just within his lifetime, oil spills have gone from unheard of to practically commonplace?

He knows that up to three tankers a day load at the Alaska Pipeline terminal, somewhere in the neighborhood of eighty a month. And each one has to traverse the North Pacific, which serves up some of the roughest water on the planet.

But the *Kuparuk* is newly built.

So what, dipshit? The *Titanic* was on her maiden voyage.

Gregg stands in the transom well between the two totes of cod, which, true to her word, Lee has kept well iced. Due to the viscosity of the crude oil, the *Pegasus* inscribes no wake; the thick layer of greasy, diarrhea-like raw petroleum flattens even the prop wash. He stares at this unprecedented sight and hears a sound escape his throat. His nose runs again, eyes blinking involuntarily. He feels his eyelid flutter, a tic, and swipes at it repeatedly as though swatting a mosquito.

Gregg looks around for something to hurt, finally seizing a galvanized tub that he crumples against his chest before hurling it over the side. No splash.

The twitching in his eye continues, further enraging him. His throat tightens. He swallows hard. The only consolation—and it is considerable—lies in the bonanza of black cod he carries, the kind of catch you fantasize about, the kind that has you ringing the bell at The Anchor and buying the house a round of drinks. Word is the Japanese are paying top dollar this year for the delicacy, which they call sablefish.

As long as the temperature remains cool and they make it back sometime tomorrow, Gregg stands to clear a lot on this trip. Shit, he'll be rich. For a while, anyway. He can pay off the winter's worth of boat payments. Or settle with Peg for his delinquent child support once and for all, be done with it. He'll buy something nice for Aaron. Lee will get a hefty bonus. Maybe there'll be enough left over for Gregg to pay down some credit card debt. He reaches out to the nearest tote, as if to reassure himself.

One thing he knows for sure. His first expenditure will be at the Mercantile when they reach the harbor: a fifth of Jack D. and a carton of smokes. The promise he made to Aaron to quit drinking pushes its way into his conscience, nagging him as he looks out over the ruined gulf. Fuck it. He tosses his guilt over the stern. Fuck it.

Daniel Wolff finds Tessa huddled on the futon sofa with the kids when he gets home from the radio station. Still wearing the maroon yoga pants she likes to travel in, his wife tenses when she sees him, whereupon Minke starts to cry. An LPN at Peninsula Hospital, Tess was attending a statewide nursing conference when the *Kuparuk* grounded, and although she'd left Fairbanks early the next day, she could fly only as far as Anchorage. With so many people now flocking to Selby, emerging as the command center for the crisis, the airlines had overbooked. Tess had overnighted with her parents and then spent the whole day at the airport, finally getting a seat home this evening when Frontier Air added extra flights.

"Where have you been?" she demands, sweeping flyaway strands of auburn hair from her face. "You said you'd be home hours ago."

Daniel finds himself staring at her mascara and lipstick. She seldom wears makeup in Selby.

"Papa." Elias, their towheaded seven-year-old, plucks his father's sleeve.

"What time is it?" Daniel asks, lifting the boy to give him a kiss. Elias wears his Spiderman pajamas and has a smear of blue toothpaste at the corner of his mouth.

Tessa gives her husband a sharp look. "Almost midnight."

"I lost track. Sorry." He sets the boy down and picks up Minke, wiping away the toddler's tears with his thumb.

"Have you eaten?"

Daniel shakes his head, sensing that Tess doesn't want to talk about the oil spill until the children are in bed.

"Me either." She takes Minke from him and ushers Elias toward the kids' bedroom.

He sets to work making grilled cheese sandwiches and heating up some cream of tomato soup. When Tess enters the kitchen, she sniffs, "Comfort food?" before recanting, "I guess we could all use a little comfort right now." By way of apology, she encircles his waist with her arms, kissing his graying blond hair and leaning her head briefly between his shoulder blades, before plucking the spatula from his hand so he can say goodnight to their children.

Daniel's surprised by how ravenous he is, but then again, he can't remember when he last sat down to a meal. Everyone at KRBB has been grazing on the go—doughnuts, chips, cold pizza—whatever food shows up at the station.

Tess sets her soup spoon down after a single taste. "You should have seen the Anchorage airport. Talk about chickens running around with their heads cut off."

Daniel eats his grilled cheese sandwich in gulps.

"Is it like that here, too?" she asks.

"Probably worse," he says with a mouthful.

"Do you think it's as bad as everyone's saying?" she presses.

He nods at her in surprise as he swallows. "It's bad. They're already calling it The Big One."

"Are Lee and Gregg safe?"

"I don't know."

Tessa stares at him. "They went fishing over there."

"I haven't heard of any boats in trouble. Besides the *Kuparuk*, that is." Neither of them takes the remark as a joke.

"How much are you working?" Tess pushes her food away.

He and everyone else at the station, not to mention more volunteers than he can track, have been working around the clock, but Daniel knows that if he says so, she'll ask how much of it he's getting paid for.

Thankfully, she changes the subject, gesturing toward the children's bedroom. "How are they doing?"

"They're pretty oblivious. Fortunately."

"Have they been with Carla the whole time?" she asks, frowning.

And Tony, he wants to add, but thinks better of it.

"Did you get more hours, at least?"

Daniel's position is technically half-time. In the roughly forty-eight hours since news of the spill broke, he's likely clocked close to forty hours, only twelve of which he'll be paid for. "Malcolm's going to apply for emergency funding from the state."

"Good."

He waits to see if Tess will pursue their familiar argument about finances: her angst over their negligible net worth, the pressure she feels to stay on at the hospital even though she increasingly dislikes her job, and his guilt about how much he enjoys radio work, despite the ridiculously low pay. Especially they disagree about the affordability of another child. He wants one now; she wants to wait. Even if she's still in her thirties, Daniel turns fifty in a few years, and he doesn't like it that people already mistake him for his own children's grandfather.

"How much do you think the kids understand?" Tess asks. "Elias, I mean."

Daniel moves his empty bowl aside. "I told him what happened. They're going to have an assembly about it at school this week. If there is school, that is."

"What do you mean?"

"There's talk of a district-wide closure. Keeping kids home to minimize their exposure to the oil spill."

"If it comes here," she says.

"*When* it does."

Tessa stares at him again.

Despite the hour, her mom calls. Daniel eats his wife's soup and her untouched sandwich, then smears peanut butter on each of two slices of bread and eats those, too. As he does the dishes, he listens to Tessa's end of the conversation: "We're okay. . . . They're okay. For now, anyway." Long silence while she listens to her mother. "We'll think about it. I'll call you tomorrow."

Slipping into bed in an oversized t-shirt, makeup removed, Tess says, "Mom wants us to bring the kids to Anchorage. She says they'll be safer there." She snuggles against him and strokes his jaw, which is stubbled with whiskers. "You look like a movie star," she murmurs.

Touching his own fingers to his face, Daniel remembers the last time he had a beard. Rampant foot rot, too. He puts an arm around her, choosing his words with care. "What do you want to do about Elias and Minke?"

"We need family time. I mean, I've been gone. And you, too, sounds like. They need us right now more than they need Grammie and Gramps."

She grows still as fatigue claims her. Despite the fact that he's scarcely slept in the last two days, all Daniel can think about is returning to the radio station. Just when he supposes Tess has dropped off, she reaches out to him. "I missed you."

They make love more passionately than they have in months. And without protection—an almost unheard-of occurrence given Tessa's determination not to have an unplanned pregnancy. Afterward, she falls asleep at once. "Sleep well, beloved," Daniel whispers, holding her spooned against him as he tries to guess how far the leading edge of the spill has advanced in the last few hours.

When her breathing grows rhythmic, he carefully extricates his body from hers, dresses, and pens a note that he leaves on the kitchen table. Daniel lets himself out of the house quietly, surreptitiously, relieved to be headed back to work. No, not relieved: completely stoked.

3

Lee paces the deck. Traversing the oil spill is like motoring through a boundless sewer. The stench of it scrapes the back of her throat. Oil and water, she finds herself repeating inanely, oil and water don't mix. When they enter the tide rip off Harriman Entrance, where the crude petroleum has mixed with seaweed, drift logs, and rubbish like plastic bags and Styrofoam containers, it resembles some kind of hellish cesspool.

Her stomach still threatens at any minute to ride an express elevator up her esophagus and out her mouth. A jackhammer judders inside her head, and her throat feels inflamed. From exposure to the hydrocarbons? Doesn't that cause cancer? It hurts to speak, and anyway, Gregg's glued to the radio, still not talking.

Lee again offers him relief at the wheel, but her skipper shrugs her off when she touches his arm. Feeling unsettled whether inside or out, she chooses to return to the deck. The ocean with its long horizon, as befouled as it is, nonetheless offers solace. And it keeps her out of range of the radio's incessant yammer, the effect of which makes her want to clap her hands over her ears, like Elias does when Tess scolds him. At first, Daniel's voice on the radio had brought comfort, but now it just weirds her out because he sounds an awful lot like he's enjoying himself.

A following wind pushes them home. The sky is cloudless. The brightness, in fact, feels wrong to Lee—as if it should be raining fire and brimstone instead, in keeping with the Doomsday feel of this event. They are closing on Kennedy Channel and the Sentinels, a range whose sheer snow-drenched flanks plunge directly to waterline, examples of the area's famed "sunken coastline." She can see where oil has stained the hems of the mountains' frozen white skirts.

When they at last reach clean water, she gives thanks and breathes more easily. They pass Baidarki Island, apparently uncontaminated. Lee's heart lifts. Isn't that the half-moon bay where Gregg found his lucky glass float?

Too soon, however, the *Pegasus* reenters the oil, which now appears particularly thick, puddinglike. Lee notices large globs pocking the surface, as if the raw petroleum were coagulating.

A brightly colored, thumb-sized triangle protrudes from one of these clots. A bird's beak, brilliant scarlet and orange-yellow. Now Lee can see the puffin's face, open-eyed but sightless as it lies in its toxic sarcophagus. Dozens—maybe a hundred—of these floating lumps bob on the small waves. She reels backward, bashing into the smokestack.

Gregg slows the engine, sliding open the cabin door. "You okay?" he asks, his tone one of concern but also, unmistakably, annoyance. Why is he so angry with her? Lee gestures helplessly at their surroundings. One of the largest objects moves sluggishly, the bird listing in the crude petroleum, struggling to hold its oil-coated head above the slurry but barely able to stir the surface with its wing.

A cormorant. For the first time all day, Gregg makes eye contact with her, but Lee can't read his look. Maybe she can save the large bird with the dip net. Or, no, better to shoot it with the .22 and end its suffering?

Gregg returns quickly to the wheel, idling the boat. Lee continues to grapple with the problem of the cormorant as the boat glides forward on its own momentum. She notices a flock of perhaps fifty murres flying in low off the port bow. In a second they will do that awkward, comical murre maneuver to slow their flight preparatory to landing on the water.

Gregg reacts more quickly than she, erupting with a shout, windmilling his arms as he crosses the deck bellowing "No!" But the murres ignore his commotion, alighting en masse about a hundred yards ahead. Each bird settles on the spill, its white breast immediately blackened by petroleum.

Lee forgets to breathe. The boat coasts forward, closing the gap between itself and the doomed seabirds. Some of the murres seem to immediately understand their predicament while others take longer to register their fate, but soon all of them thrash, crying out in mounting desperation, straining to free themselves from the dangerous substance. Birds disappear under the bow. Everything seems to be happening in slow motion. Lee stares in disbelief.

When the boat glides into the birds' midst, she hears their panic, sees their frantic efforts to extricate themselves from the cloying crude oil. Turning so abruptly that she slips on the side-deck, Lee seizes the boathook from the rigging and extends it into the water to try to pull in individual murres.

But of course the helpless creatures cannot grasp the extended pole, and her effort only frightens them more. Lee withdraws the now-contaminated aluminum tool, dropping it to the deck.

Some of the birds seem to be trying to gain purchase with their feet on the boat's fiberglass hull. Lee grits her teeth to stop them from chattering, and as the *Pegasus* drifts over more of the helpless creatures, the rest at once stop struggling, as if resigned to their death.

Gregg goes back inside, puts the boat in gear.

What would she have done with them, assuming she could have managed to bring any of the murres aboard? Where would she have put them? Lee snatches the soiled boathook from the deck, brandishing it against an unseen assailant. When she casts it like a javelin into the sea, the dark oil swallows it without a trace. Lee feels herself verging on combustion, flames issuing from her body, her eyes throwing sparks.

The secretary of the interior lobbies for the use of dispersants—solutions and powders designed to scuttle, or sink, floating oil. Gregg listens intently as the cabinet member describes a plan to use crop dusters from the Lower Forty-Eight to deploy these chemical agents onto the spill. However, as some pundit soon comments, the State of Alaska has never before allowed the use of dispersants because of their "known deleterious effects" on marine life. Apparently, in what the National Public Radio commentator calls "an unlikely reversal," a number of environmentalists are arguing that the damage caused by these chemicals might after all be preferable to the toxicity of an uncontained oil spill. Go for the dispersants, Gregg decides. How could anything possibly cause more harm than the lethal hydrocarbons now flooding the sea?

Someone else with a PhD weighs in. This egghead says he doubts that chemical dispersants will dissolve in the North Pacific because the water temperature's too cold. The professor then adds that he can't resist pointing out that Mammoth Petroleum itself manufactures the lion's share of the world's dispersants. What the hell does that mean? That the same company that owns the grounded tanker, the same outfit responsible for this unholy mess, stands to reap a fortune from the sale of its own solvents to clean it up?

Still others urge setting fire to the tanker, to burn off the remaining product rather than let it keep entering the ocean. But the state so far prohibits this course of action, too, proclaiming that fire will only "add insult to injury" by contributing airborne pollution to that already running rampant in the sea. Now Alaska's attorney general excoriates oil company executives for their lack of preparedness in responding to the spill. Gregg can perfectly picture the paunchy, double-chinned white man in a dark suit and tie, puffing out his chest and thumping his fist on a podium in Juneau.

All anyone's doing is pointing fingers, he thinks. Lee stares at her skipper in alarm when he kicks the sheathing under the wheel, leaving a sizable dent.

In fact, the only state-approved response plan so far calls for maneuvering an empty tanker alongside the *Kuparuk* and "lightering" the residual petroleum from the crippled vessel. Talk about securing the barn door *after* the livestock bolt. Talk about too little, too late. It's the goddamn Keystone Cops. Gregg clenches his molars so hard his jaw aches.

They learn next that the Native community of Pogibshi has been "oiled" during the night. Lee's eyes go round, her hand rising to her mouth. She hasn't said a word since they ran over the birds, but now she beseeches her skipper with a panic-stricken glance. Gregg pretends to adjust the LORAN, avoiding her gaze. Marine biologists will soon depart Anchorage on an overflight to assess the impact of oil on Pogibshi's shoreline, cautioning villagers in the meantime not to eat anything harvested from the sea.

"No problem," Gregg says bitterly. "They'll just hop in their Learjets, fly to Anchorage for groceries."

Wassily and Marie are fucked, pure and simple, he thinks. Case closed. So much for their Experiment in Indigeneity. The couple and their brood of three had moved to Pogibshi last year in an attempt to recover a more purely traditional lifestyle. They haven't even had a summer there yet, the only time of year when subsistence comes easy.

Gregg and Lee had motored over to the village of two hundred just a few weeks ago, when he put the *Pegasus* back in the water from her winter dry dock. Clean-shaven and squeaky-clean in a yellow polo shirt, Wassily Chukanok harped jokingly on Gregg to let him crew: "You already got a token female, so why not hire a token Eskimo?"

To which Gregg had retorted, "Hey, man, I *am* the token Eskimo."

"*Avuq*, more like." Half-breed. Wassily grinned. Then he punched Gregg on the shoulder and called him *kass'aq*—the Yup'ik equivalent of "honky." His standard insult.

Marie, too, was decked out in what Gregg thought of as city clothes: khaki slacks and a button-down blouse. The couple made him feel underdressed in his jeans and t-shirt. (Lee, of course, wore her usual threadbare denim overalls and paint-stained Salty Dawg sweatshirt.) While the kids attended school in the one-room building that doubled as Pogibshi's community center, the four adults strolled down to the beach to gather dinner.

At their coaxing, Lee sampled a variety of kelp and popweed from the strand line, but Gregg saw her balk at the pale orange sea urchin roe Marie offered and consumed with relish herself.

"You look like a Native," Marie chided Lee, again extending the spiny green cup of tiny eggs many considered a delicacy. "You should try it." This time, his deckhand gingerly tipped back the prickly container and looked surprised to discover how palatable its contents were.

Back at the house, the kids came home hungry, and everyone feasted on the steamed mussels and Dungeness crabs the grown-ups had found. They all gave Lee a hard time for preferring melted butter to the seal oil the rest of them jostled over. Marie even produced some dryfish, sent by relatives back home, she said. "We'll make our own this year," she added with a wide smile that showed her beautiful teeth.

"Not too long now before we get herring eggs," Wassily said, rubbing his stomach with a satisfied smile. When he again asked for work, Gregg said, "Are you kidding? You're the one who's got it made in the shade. I'm going to sell the boat and move in with you!"

And it was true: the *Pegasus* skipper envied his old friend his family life. In any case, Gregg was too embarrassed to try to explain in front of Lee that, as a cost-saving measure, he'd decided not to hire a second hand for black cod. He pictures the wide beach below the settlement where they'd foraged for dinner. Now buried under three feet of crude oil.

Rounding Shumagin Head, they finally outdistance the spill for good. Gregg draws a deep breath and, for the first time in two days, increases their speed.

Not until they enter the relatively protected waters off Kalgin Slough, however, do they encounter any other boats. Approaching the mouth of Rugged Bay, Gregg sees an armada of about a hundred vessels: everything from crabbers to fishing charters, or "six-packs," tour boats to landing craft. Several floatplanes taxi slowly in the distance.

It heartens him to think of this fleet going out to meet the oil, establishing a defense against its approach, but he soon realizes that everyone's just milling about. He's never seen anything like it. True, commercial fishing periods involve any number of boats, but openers have a frenzied air to them, everyone gunning their engines in anticipation of the starting flare. This gathering, in contrast, feels aimless, like everyone's scratching their asses.

Monitoring the CB chatter confirms his assessment. No one knows what to do. Well, once he offloads his fish, by God, he'll show them.

Show them what, asshole?

"KHL 360 calling KBZ 974. You there, Gregg?"

That inimitable Wyoming twang. "Dusty. Hey." Gregg makes out the seiner *Rodeo Rose* with her distinctive red wheelhouse. And he can tell from the sudden drop in radio chatter that others have likewise tuned in to the call.

"How far away is it?"

Gregg tells his buddy—and everyone else, given the nature of CB radio—where he finally left the spill behind.

"How'd you do?"

"Real good." The words are out before Gregg can stop them. Understatement is the superstition by which all fishermen report their catch, and he knows it will be widely understood by his response that the *Pegasus* has cleaned up. That, and the fact that he's no doubt last to come in.

"Yeah. I see how low you're riding," Dusty drawls.

Gregg rubs his face. Too late now. Good thing Lee's on deck; she'd have given him a tongue lashing for inviting bad luck.

Dusty's next comment affirms Gregg's status: "Welcome home, partner. You're the last one in. Switch to thirteen?"

Unlike the widespread usage of their current channel, thirteen affords at least the chance of a private exchange. Of course, anyone can monitor it who wants to, but most fishermen have enough self-respect not to follow conversations that change channels, if only because no one likes to be caught eavesdropping by his crew.

"Stand by," Gregg says, adjusting the dial. "Go ahead, Cowboy."

Dusty pauses, clears his throat. "Been trying to raise you all day. Had us worried when you didn't show up. Radio problems?"

"Roger that." Gregg knows his fellow fisherman doesn't want to discuss electronics.

"There's talk the cod are contaminated."

Gregg's speechless for a minute. "Bullshit! No way. We pulled the last skate hours before we ever saw any oil, and besides, we fished well away from the reef." Gregg can hear how much he sounds like he wants to kill the messenger.

"Unbelievable how fast it's moving," Dusty says. "Just wanted to give you a heads-up, brother. AP's taking the fish, but they're not paying. Not yet. Maybe not at all."

Gregg feels his stomach somersault. Mistrustful of his ability to speak, he finally clicks the mike a couple of times to signal that he's heard.

"Take care, *Pegasus*." Dusty pauses. "*Rodeo Rose* out."

Gregg stares at the transmitter in his hand, raising his eyes to correct the course. He cranes his neck backward until he hears vertebrae pop. AlaskaPride's not buying?

He'd pretty much kept it together when they discovered themselves surrounded by oil. He'd somehow managed to function well enough to get them this far—including running over those hapless birds, for Christ's sake. No way is he going to lose it now.

There's always herring. Short and furious, but generally lucrative. He and Dusty have plans to joint venture, in fact. Gregg scarcely registers the appearance of the Coast Guard chopper, now hovering above the flotilla. Maybe he should hire an extra hand for herring, gamble on a strong return, and try to recoup his losses if no one's buying cod.

The herring are the first of the open-water species to journey shoreward to spawn at winter's end, a cause for celebration up and down the whole Northwest Coast. He remembers from childhood how, singing and drumming and dancing in their regalia, the entire village would turn out to welcome the shoals of sparkling fish every spring. The shallow lagoon flashing silver with spawners beyond number, the water foaming white as *agutuk* when the female fish released their eggs and the males their milt, all of it whipped into froth by the frenzy of their procreation. By March, Gregg—and every other coastal Native he's ever known—craves the flavorful crunch of fresh herring eggs. Once, when he'd gotten stuck in Seattle doing boat work, Peg had surprised him with a gift of air-freighted hemlock branches coated with the delicacy, convincing him that he'd married well.

Is that a whale breaching dead ahead? Dall porpoises? No, Lee would be jumping up and down at her post in the bow if it were. He rubs his eyes.

Humans are not the only creatures to rely on the herring for nourishment after a long, lean winter. He's been told that humpback whales time their return to Alaska waters to coincide with the arrival of the fertile fish because it guarantees sustenance to the giant mammals and their young after the monthlong migrations from nurseries in Mexico or Hawaii. Now Gregg pictures the blur of shorebirds that likewise always seem to accompany the teeming spawners. Migratory birds, too, must depend on the fish for their refueling needs after flights of thousands of miles. He nods to himself. That's what he'll do. Pull out all the stops, go balls to the wall for herring.

As he threads his way between the idling boats, he sees that the *Mary Jo*, an ancient green-and-white wooden tender, wears a tar-dark scum of oil at her waterline. Only then does it occur to him that, despite his careful piloting, the almost new teal-and-cream-colored hull of his beautiful *Pegasus* must be similarly defiled.

A C-130 rumbles overhead. Lee wonders if the big-bellied plane transports black cod to overseas markets. She hopes they're not too late to sell theirs, which Gregg has told her is hands down his most valuable catch ever. The din of boat and aircraft motors unnerves her, evoking as it does television footage of the war in the Middle East: soldiers in desert camouflage, armored vehicles lumbering across windswept sand, helicopters whipping dust into dervishes. What kinds of tales do the returning troops tell Jackie, who now works as a counselor for the Veterans Administration in Anchorage? The blue-and-yellow state ferry *Nelchina* approaches in the dusk from Kodiak, a reminder that today is Sunday and that Lee and Gregg have been gone exactly one week.

The convergence of boats and aircraft suggests a commercial opener— a fishing session monitored by Fish and Game, when you sometimes have as little as fifteen minutes to make a set. No second chances. With fortunes resting on getting seines laid out "on the money," boats work in tandem with small planes, the pilots spotting schools of fish from the air and directing the skippers below accordingly. When a silver floatplane lands in twin plumes of water behind them, Lee recalls how Mike Delarosa and Kent James had died two years ago, their Super Cubs colliding in midair as both men spotted for herring above the inlet. Suddenly chilled, she shivers.

What are all these boats waiting for? Why aren't they out intercepting crude oil?

As they enter the mouth of the bay, generally referred to as the Gateway because of the rocky headlands that loom on either side, a huge helicopter approaches, its oversized blades whapping the sky like a demonic ceiling fan. Lee's hair is far too short now to be snatched by the vacuum of the rotor wash. In other circumstances, it might have amused her; instead, the noise and pressure make her eardrums ring alarmingly.

Covering her ears with her hands, she can just make out Kittiwake Ledge. The usual spring miasma of countless airborne birds shape-shifts over the rookery and when the helicopter withdraws, Lee studies the scene with her Nikons. Despite the heavy vessel traffic, the kittiwakes appear undeterred in their tireless fetching of nest-building grasses and twigs.

The last time she'd been to the ledge was with Jackie and Tess, about a year ago, during the short break between herring and halibut season. (Neither of which had proven very profitable, she recalls. Please let us be in time to sell our catch!) Lee had introduced her two closest friends to sea kayaking—Tess in a borrowed Klepper and she and Jackie in a fiberglass double rented from 'Yak Treks.

The other two women had enjoyed as much as Lee always did how the kayaks let them experience the marine world "up close and personal," as Tess put it. While the deckhand delighted in scoping the tenements of seabirds nesting on impossibly narrow cliff-side perches, her friends thrilled to the playful otters cavorting in the water nearby.

They'd seen lots of mother-baby otter pairs that day: the adult animal floating on her back with a fluffy youngster riding diagonally across the raft of her body. The three women had also drifted in silence past lone otters slumbering in the kelp beds, and Lee had told Jackie and Tess in a low voice how the marine mammals anchored themselves with the sea vegetation, so they could rest without being swept away. "They never leave the water, not even to give birth," she explained, as if it were a point of personal pride.

It occurs to Lee now that she hasn't seen any otters—or porpoises, seals, sea lions, whales—for the last two days. Hopefully, it's because they've all fled the oil spill. She wonders when Tess will be home from her nursing conference.

Gregg calls her in. Lee joins him at the wheel.

"They're saying the captain was shitfaced." Her skipper turns down the volume on the radio so they can talk.

"What?"

"Some of the crew smelled liquor on the guy's breath." Gregg's outraged. "But the fucking Coast Guard took so long to get hold of a testing kit, the results will be inconclusive. Too much time elapsed." He shakes his head in disgust. "Assholes."

Lee finally finds her tongue. "The captain was *drunk?* That's how come the tanker smashed into the reef? Because *he* was smashed?"

Suddenly, she blushes, as if to say, "Oops. Forgot my boss is a recovering alcoholic," and sees from his scowl that Gregg knows exactly what she's thinking. He turns away from her, resetting the radio volume.

Lee slips back outside. A drunken captain? Impossible. Much too farfetched. Now well inside Rugged Bay, they encounter still more boats and the Coast Guard cutter, *Turnstone*, that homeports in Selby. Dozens of skiffs and inflatables dart between larger vessels. Another sea plane takes off through the Gateway, trailing water from its floats. Maybe it's leading the charge and now people will finally do something.

When Lee, Tess, and Jackie had paddled home in their kayaks that evening, the setting sun ignited a pathway on the surface of the bay, a luminous tangerine-colored track that ran all the way from Kittiwake Ledge to the small-boat harbor. Halfway home, the three women had encountered literally thousands of murres feeding in the tide rip.

"Penguins?" Jackie guessed.

"It's Alaska, Dr. Dermot," Tess smirked, "not Antarctica." She and Lee had a good time ridiculing the learned clinical psychologist for her ignorance of Alaska wildlife.

As the three of them approached in the small boats, the closest of the seabirds would panic and scramble to launch themselves with clownish murre clumsiness, achieving liftoff only with much flapping hullabaloo. For the longest time, a steady percussion of wing beats and worried squawks heralded a seemingly endless procession of the plump, low-flying birds in the shimmering pink light. That night, Jackie had tears in her eyes when she thanked Lee for what she called "the best day of my life."

Right, Lee thinks. Too bad the things and places that gave her the greatest joy weren't good enough for her lover. She remembers the morning's murres, floundering in the oil spill, then run over by the *Pegasus*. Of course other creatures are getting hammered by the spill, not escaping it, she realizes. How could they possibly avoid it, when the contamination already covers hundreds of square miles?

Her face and hands long ago numbed by cold, she remains on deck the rest of the way in. The boat pushes smoothly through the swells, now climbing, now cresting, now coasting down the soft slope of the wave, so rhythmically that it feels choreographed. Riding the steady rise and fall of the bow, Lee tries to think of something to look forward to about being home.

She imagines the spill washing ashore in Rugged Bay in a matter of days, fouling near-shore waters. A pod of glistening black-and-white orcas breaching in its toxic shadow. A pride of sea lions surging through the crude, their stiff whiskers blackened, faces filmed with grease. A siege of herring floating dead atop petroleum-laden seas.

Lee pictures the neon-green beach vegetation—the new shoots of goosetongue and sandwort and lovage that at this time of year, unfurling from winter dormancy, always seem lit from within. Obliterated by a single black tide. The dense, stinking ooze filling once-crystalline tidepools, suffocating delicately tendriled anemones and so many other forms of intricate sea life.

She stands at the rail, staring unseeing at the passing shoreline. When bringing aboard large halibut, fishermen use a murderously sharp steel hook fastened to the end of a stout wooden handle to stab the bottomfish and haul it bodily on deck. This must be how it feels to be gaffed. Could the tanker captain really have been drunk? Feeling her stomach cramp, Lee hangs over the side to vomit. Because she's eaten almost nothing for two days, it amounts to little more than dry heaves, but the pain takes her breath away all the same.

4

Daniel must have moved into the living room to sleep on the futon, Tessa thinks when she wakes. Has she been snoring again?

She checks on the kids, cinching the belt of her bathrobe and feeling the vestiges of last night's lovemaking between her thighs. Minke sprawls on her back, mouth open, her beloved toy panda bear, Pandy, on the floor beside her bed. Elias, as usual tangled in his bedding, lies with a leg overhanging the edge of the mattress. She caresses the head of each sleeping child in turn, inhaling their beloved scents before leaving the room.

No Daniel. Tess sees the note on the table and feels a pang of abandonment that quickly morphs into resentment when she crosses the cool linoleum in bare feet and reads his hastily written message: "They need me at the station." Doesn't he realize his family needs him, too?

The red light blinks on the answering machine. At least he's had the courtesy to phone. But no, it's her mother again, telling Tess the children don't belong in Selby: "The oil's almost there. Do you want them to get sick? Bring them to us."

Flicking on the radio, she stands in the middle of the kitchen listening to what Elias calls "Papa's job voice" intone that the oil spill is estimated to be traveling at the rate of fifteen sea miles a day. "NOAA scientists now predict that it will eventually reach the Aleutians," Newsman Daniel reports gravely.

"But the Aleutians are a thousand miles away!" Tess thinks, while also absorbing her husband's next announcement, that sea otters have been especially hard hit by the spill. Tess pictures a bewhiskered inquisitive otter popping its head from the ocean to check out humans boating by. Or a mother otter swimming on her back, clutching a baby. Daniel informs listeners that a famous sea lion haul-out has been oiled during the night. Biologists question whether the sleek half-ton marine mammals will now seek another location to come out of the water or return to the old one out of habit. Aren't sea lion haul-outs historic, Tess thinks, used generation after generation? Will the exposure to petroleum kill the large animals?

An unfamiliar female voice replaces Daniel's, and Tess slips into a chair at the table, drawing her robe around her, to learn that Selby residents have organized an effort to try to divert the oncoming oil from entering the Gateway, something about using logs to "boom" the bay. A bird-cleaning operation has been set up near the airport. That's where Lee will be, if she's back from fishing, that is. But if Lee were back from fishing, wouldn't she have come by the house or left a message? Lee's cabin is so far from town that it lacks phone service. Maybe Tess will drive out there later to look for her.

She remembers the photographs published in yesterday's *Anchorage Tribune*, which she'd read and reread while waiting for hours at the airport for a flight. The full-page photo on the front page: an aerial shot of the stricken tanker surrounded by its dark silhouette of oil. Inside, a kind of album of the spill that included pictures of a man standing on a beach, thigh-deep in crude petroleum; a close-up of a duck coated in black goo; shots of coastline completely inundated with oil. Tessa's eyes kept returning to the images of oiled birds, photos which, although published in color, all looked black-and-white.

Now someone on the radio is talking about a joint state and federal effort to protect Kittiwake Ledge, Rugged Bay's seabird rookery, and as Tess recalls the shallow nests occupying every scrap of horizontal space on the cliff sides, wheeling birds in constant motion, she can hear the cacophony of shrill bird cries and smell the sharp ammonia stink of guano.

She can't think of Kittiwake Ledge without remembering the kayak trip last summer with Jackie and Lee. And she can't think of the kayak trip without recalling how dispassionately Lee had told them about being molested by her male cousins when she was growing up—something not even Jackie had known.

Only they weren't her cousins, Tess remembers, they were her uncles, because Lee's adoptive mom, Weezie, had two much-younger step-brothers who were only a few years older than Lee. And those boys had abused her more than once, apparently, threatening Lee that she'd be sent back to the orphanage in Korea if she ever told anyone what they'd done to her.

"Mommy." Elias stands in the doorway in his pajamas.

"Hi, honey." Tess invites her son onto her lap. "I missed you." She nuzzles his tousled mop.

"What can I eat?" he says, pulling away from her.

"Don't you want to go back to sleep? It's a stay-home day. You were up really late last night."

When he shakes his head, his flaxen hair flops over his eyes. She should cut it.

"I'm not tired." Smiling impishly, he adds, "Shake a leg. Chop-chop."

It's how Daniel wakes him every school morning, reaching through the bedcovers to give the boy's foot a squeeze.

"Where's Papa?" Elias crouches in front of the cupboard, rummaging through boxes of cereal.

"At work. Listen." Tess increases the volume on the radio, where a deep, gravelly voice provides the day's marine weather forecast and tidal information.

"That's not him," Elias says.

43

Tess turns off the radio, but almost immediately switches it on again, low. "What do you know about the oil spill?" she asks.

"It's killing birds?" The boy wags the cupboard door with his hand.

"Anything else?"

"Selby's going to turn black."

"The beaches might, but town won't. Not the buildings. Not your school or our house." She goes to him, kneeling so they're eye to eye. "Lots of moms and dads are really busy because of the oil spill. That's why Papa's at work."

"I'm *hungry*," Elias whines.

Tessa pours him a cup of milk, sets a skillet to heat, and quickly whisks together a batch of pancakes.

"Can we get Cocoa Crunch? Keith and Kevin have it."

She needs to thank Carla for looking after the kids. Exactly how much time had they spent next door? Tess pours three small pancakes into the heated pan.

When KRBB's local broadcast is replaced by NPR's *Morning Edition*, she learns that the unnamed captain of the Mammoth *Kuparuk* has gone missing. Apparently, no one knows his whereabouts. What on earth. How do you lose someone like that? Hasn't he been arrested? A Coast Guard spokesman explains how the blood sample taken from the tanker captain had tested at twice the legal limit for alcohol, but that the sample had been acquired so many hours after the fact of the grounding as to be inadmissible.

She increases the volume on the radio, unsure how appropriate the content is for Elias. Her need for information outweighs her customary caution, however. As improbable as it sounds for a supertanker captain to have been drunk on duty—after all, he's a white-collar professional paid a small fortune for his services, right?—Tess has the uneasy feeling that this man's inebriation might exactly explain how a ship the size of a skyscraper has come to rest on what everyone keeps saying is a well-known navigational hazard.

"Papa!" Elias exclaims, recognizing the voice that now interviews Mayor Griswold, asking how townspeople can best prepare themselves for the onslaught of toxic oil.

They listen to the radio until Minke wakes, burbling in her bed. Daniel should have talked to me, Tess thinks. She accepts that at least one of them has to work, but this is an emergency, for crying out loud. Isn't being a husband and father at least as important as his pitifully underpaid half-time job? Besides, it's Sunday. He doesn't even work on Sundays. She'd flown home from Fairbanks with the idea of them facing the oil spill together, as a unit. Daniel's always going on about how important family is to him, but now, it seems, he can't even be bothered to discuss his work schedule with her. Minke starts to fret.

When the toddler threatens to howl, Tess tells Elias he can watch TV while she feeds his sister, a permission so unexpected that the boy hesitates to turn on the set.

"Go ahead," she reassures him. "It's okay."

When she gets the chance, Tess tries phoning friends, but even though it's still early in the day, a time when many people would normally be getting ready to attend church, not one of her calls is answered, except by machine. It dawns on her that everyone who can do so is volunteering in some capacity: safeguarding the salmon streams, rescuing oiled birds and otters, or preparing food for those who are. According to the radio, local fishermen are joining with their counterparts in other coastal communities to organize a blockade of the Pipeline terminal. What is that supposed to accomplish? Another group plans to set out into the spill in an attempt to head off the oil before it washes ashore—a far more productive cause, she thinks.

People not only want but need involvement at a time like this, Tess realizes, to relieve their anxiety and help them regain a sense of control. If not for the kids, she would...what? But I've been gone. Elias and Minke need me. Who would care for her son and daughter if she were to volunteer? Surely, tending children is an important contribution to the community, in its own way. Tess recalls her mom's offer—insistence, really—to take the children. Maybe she and Daniel should consider the option, after all.

It wasn't always like this. She remembers that when she first met Daniel he was still mourning the loss of his first wife, five years after her

45

death. He couldn't get enough of Tessa's comforting attentions then. She knows it's no accident she became a nurse; she has always been a sucker for those who are suffering. While Minke eats cut-up pieces of pancake with her fingers, Tess considers once again how much psychic energy she wastes in competition with a dead woman—a contest she can never win.

They're making good progress up Rugged Bay, a long, narrow body of water that some people call a fjord, and will reach the harbor within the hour. Gregg's convinced he can talk the manager of AlaskaPride's Selby plant into taking the fish. After all, he and Fritz are practically related, and the cod are beautiful, pristine. Lee's done a great job keeping them iced. Once Fritz lays eyes on their catch, he'll realize its worth.

Darkness ascends from the surface of the water, the snow on the upper mountainsides reflecting pinkish light. Gregg locates a few homes on shore: Butch and Emily's cabin in Sunshine Cove, the Richardsons' place across the way.

Lee enters the cabin. "Look," she says, and together they study the vessel activity at the mouth of Gold Creek. Gregg discerns a string of white, sausage-shaped buoys lying in a lazy crescent there. Half a dozen skiffs appear to be setting out a second, longer necklace to encircle the first.

"They're protecting the hatchery!" he says. "Finally, somebody's doing something." He turns to high-five her, but Lee appears on the verge of tears. Gregg pictures the rows of black plastic incubators arrayed in the warehouse-like facility set just out of sight beyond the spruce trees. "You worked there, right?"

She bites her lip. "This is the time of year salmon eggs hatch."

Gregg understands roughly how the system works. The pea-sized orange eggs overwinter in the bottoms of the incubators and then, as the minuscule baby fish hatch in early spring, they rise to the surface of each tank to be siphoned off into a network of concrete raceways that wash them into Gold Creek. The creek, of course, eventually carries

46

the salmon fry to the ocean for their first encounter with saltwater. Somehow, along the way, the young fish will imprint the smell of this exact watershed, this particular bay, and will know to return here and nowhere else to spawn and die after their years spent roaming the vast Pacific. What's so sad about that? He searches Lee's eyes.

"What are they going to eat?" she says, and he frowns at her before remembering what they'd heard on the radio about the oil spill wiping out plankton, the principal food source of salmon smolt. And of so much else. He waves her away.

In the twilight, Gregg can see town for the first time. The last of the sun glances off the windows of the hospital, Selby's only three-story building. He looks for Ptarmigan Falls, at the head of the bay. Swollen with spring snowmelt, the hundred-foot torrent plunges over a lip of granite to hurtle earthward with such velocity that when you stand at the waterfall's base, the plumes and sheaves of water look like they're levitating. Two kinds of salmon spawn in the creek: kings in June and cohos in September. Gregg pictures the large silver-green fish making their way shoreward from the open ocean, then finning single-mindedly upstream to hurl themselves almost ritualistically against the cascading water. Tensing his jaw, Gregg steers the *Pegasus* in behind the rock jetty of the harbor, slowing the engine to the required "No Wake" speed.

Where is everybody? The floats are deserted, all the more unsettling considering the time of year. Normally, come spring, the processor and the fishing fleet are gearing up for six months of nonstop activity and the harbor's bustling. Instead, the boat basin resembles a scene in a movie where everyone's been killed by contagion. Ghost town.

Gregg massages his neck, focusing on the task at hand. The transfer of fish to the processor will take some time in light of their bumper catch. But the offload happens quickly and quietly, which speaks volumes to how deeply fucked things are. Instead of having to wait their turn among dozens of vessels queued up at Cannery Row, the usual procedure, the *Pegasus* is the only boat. And instead of the customary chaos of grunts bustling around on the pier like worker ants, a skeleton crew of three—Les Cooper on crane, Tim Arndt on forklift, and JJ O'Connell humping totes—finishes the job in no time, despite Gregg's motherlode. The whole transaction is as effortless as any fisherman could wish, so why is he gnashing his teeth?

Fritz Detweiler, who's married to Peg's cousin, brings the ticket down to the boat himself. In addition to having wives who are related, Gregg and the plant manager have shared a few years' worth of AA meetings. They'd last seen each other in Fritz's cluttered office a few days before Gregg and Lee left and had discussed the likely excellent price for black cod this year—the very consideration that had prompted the *Pegasus* skipper to risk venturing into the eastern gulf. Now, the mustached manager looks like he's aged ten years in as many days, his customarily genial demeanor replaced by something resembling bereavement.

"Donna and the kids okay?" Gregg asks anxiously.

"Good enough." Fritz sounds rough.

Gregg wonders for the first time what he himself must look like, imagining one of those cartoon characters who's so angry that smoke issues from his ears.

"Fish and Game has just canceled herring," Fritz says carefully," because of the threat of oil contamination."

The fisherman peers at the cannery manager.

"They'll likely postpone halibut for the same reason," Fritz adds, avoiding eye contact.

"But the spill's nowhere near the bottom-fish districts," Gregg blurts.

The other man tongues the snoose wadded in his lower lip, then spits neatly over the side of the boat. "So I understand. The problem is Outside buyers who think it is." He glances at the skipper. "It's almost a thousand square miles, still growing. Who knows where-all it'll end up."

"Five hundred. Five hundred square miles."

"Yesterday, maybe. Or the day before. They say it's increasing in volume because of emulsification with seawater. Whatever that means." Fritz clears his throat. "Listen, I can't pay you now. And probably," he gestures with his head to the facility above them, "your catch and everyone else's will wind up as fertilizer. If that."

Gregg searches the other man's eyes. "But they're beautiful fish. They don't get any better. You saw them yourself."

"Quality," Fritz agrees. "And you hit the jackpot, looks like." He coughs again. "I'm sorry."

The skipper feels his pulse surge against the inside of his skull like storm surf lashing a jetty.

"Some are saying the oil will wipe out all the spawners," the plant manager continues. "Herring, salmon, everything. That it might be years, or never, before stocks come healthy again."

"Anyone doing anything?" Gregg finally mumbles.

"The Gibson brothers and others, they're cabling together saw logs to make booms. Plan is to cordon off the Gateway."

"Is that even possible?"

"They want to try."

The fisherman considers all the people he knows whose livelihood depends on the ocean: those who fish or work for AlaskaPride processing seafood—whether full-time or seasonally—and those who sell gear, build boats, mend nets, install navigational aids, and on and on. Altogether, at least half of Selby's working population must be connected to the seafood industry, one way or another. Gregg imagines the oil passing through and the Department of Fish and Game reopening the fisheries in a month or, at worst, in time for salmon. It'll hurt, but salmon, crab, and shrimp might be enough for people to get by on.

"Can't believe the man was soused," Fritz says, regarding the other man directly.

Gregg studies the stain of oil that remains on his fingers. "I thought they said there's no way to know for sure."

"What else could it be?"

Gregg shrugs. What else, indeed?

When Fritz tells him that a boat-cleaning operation has been set up near the fuel station, indicating a newly halogen-floodlit area of the harbor, the *Pegasus* skipper has to wonder at how quickly things are unfolding. It's like someone, somewhere, consults a manual entitled *What to Do in the Event of an Oil Spill*. First, it instructs, "Close fisheries," and next, "Establish a vessel-cleaning protocol." The thought does nothing to improve his mood. It would have been a hell of a lot better for everybody if the effort put into planning what to do in the event of a spill had instead been applied to preventing one in the first place.

Fritz turns to the rusty iron ladder leading up to the wharf. Donna has MS and between her kids from her first marriage and those she and Fritz have had together, the hard-working plant manager has five school-aged children to support.

Gregg remembers when he first started attending AA meetings in the Methodist church basement, sitting in a circle of metal folding chairs with this man and others on an almost daily basis. He flushes, wondering if Fritz, too, has thought of getting down off the wagon. He feels an uncustomary urge to clasp the other man's arm, but clears his throat instead. "Take care," he says.

The manager nods briefly. "You, too." He steps heavily onto the ladder rungs and begins to climb.

Gregg steers the *Pegasus* across the harbor under the glare of floodlights while Lee readies fenders on deck. More boom, the polyurethane buoys this time a fluorescent green, floating in an indolent circle around the fuel dock. A dozen workers stand around jacking their jaws, and as he approaches, Gregg can see that their canary-yellow Helly Hansen rain gear still sports the creases of its recent packaging, but also that shit-colored spatters and smears mar the fronts of the new waterproof jackets and pants. Half of the boat cleaners look like acne-faced teenagers and the rest like out-of-shape housewives. He recognizes no one. All are visibly keen on the prospect of cleaning the *Pegasus*. This is great, he thinks: fishermen are sidelined, our boats contaminated, and these jokers can't wait to profit from our misfortune.

Two of the boys motor out in a shiny new aluminum skiff containing a new fire-engine-red fuel tank, powered by a gleaming new fifteen-horse Mercury kicker. Who's paying for all this? The boys open a gate in the boom to let the *Pegasus* in, releasing a small soapy fuel slick.

"Hey!" Lee hollers at them. "Watch what you're doing!"

The halfwits gape at her as they resecure the boom behind the boat, initially locking themselves on the wrong side of the floating barrier, in fact. More Keystone Cops. Gregg's so angry he wonders if it's possible to give yourself an aneurysm.

Once they've tied down, he and Lee disembark for the first time. Gregg steps onto the planked float to the familiar sensation of legs turned rubbery from days at sea. The crew of eager beavers, meanwhile, having pulled on rubber gloves, grab their push brooms and scrub brushes from vats of sudsy water that smells like citrus fruit. When he notices Lee catch her breath, Gregg turns back to see that the *Pegasus* doesn't just wear a dark band of oil like the *Mary Jo*, but that the greasy residue of the spill coats a good two feet of her beautiful hull, the black tar now riding well above waterline, released from the weight of the catch.

"This one's the worst we've seen," a long-haired kid whose head is diapered in a blue bandana enthuses to one of his cohorts. "We'll never get it clean!" The teen attacks the bow of the fishing boat with his long-handled scrub brush. "More work, more pay!"

The punk wears a gold ring in one ear. Earrings on a guy? Gregg watches the boy go after the worst of the oil and then pause to free a headset from behind the bib of his rain gear. Having affixed the earphones atop his headscarf, he resumes scrubbing with renewed vigor. The skipper tenses; he's worked his whole life for the *Pegasus*, now smeared with toxic scum, and this faggot's rocking out while he ruins her finish.

Gregg crosses to the worker, shoving him so hard with both hands that the young man falls backward onto the float, his broom skidding into the water. One of the women screams. The cleaners freeze in mid-stroke, backing away from the enraged fisherman; the earringed youngster, meanwhile, scrabbles on his butt against the soapy planks, trying to escape his attacker. Lee catches Gregg's arm in both hands in an effort to keep him from landing another blow.

Her skipper locks her neck in the crook of his elbow. Lee instantly goes still. Releasing her with a shove, Gregg brushes past the wide-eyed, speechless gaggle of workers and strides up the ramp that runs alongside the harbormaster's office. His legs feel stiff from disuse, but his breathing steadies as he walks across the empty parking lot in the dark, feet crunching on gravel.

In all his years fishing, even when he made every mistake in the book, he's never before failed to at least recover expenses. And this time, everything had gone like clockwork. Figures. Gregg recalls what he'd estimated to be the worth of the catch, a record for him. So much for highliner fantasies. He should have known better than to count his chickens before they hatched, should have dumped the fish at sea, thereby saving both fuel and time. But no, what was the name of that couple he and Peg had been friendly with, the ones whose first pregnancy had resulted in a stillbirth? Despite the fact that her baby was dead, Cecily nevertheless had to deliver it.

He makes his way to the only lighted building in the harbor. He's let his deckhand down. Lee has worked hard enough for two, but she'll have nothing to show for it. Nada. Good thing she decided against that Bronco someone tried to sell her over the winter—she'll just have to make do with her old ride. The Datsun pickup Gregg's helped her maintain over the years is a jumble of mix-and-match parts, and it will never win any beauty contests, but it runs. Anyway, she has no debt and has only herself to look out for, no dependents. She'll manage. Sink-or-swim time.

It's not that he typically babies his crew, but he does feel sorry for Lee. She deserves better than the crappy childhood she'd had, abandoned to an orphanage as an infant in Korea, then adopted by a clueless American couple who divorced when Lee was still just a kid. No sooner had her adoptive dad left them for another woman than her adoptive mom was diagnosed with some kind of cancer that took her down in less than a year. Or maybe abandonment is the pattern, and it's no accident that Lee and her girlfriend have split the sheets, leaving his deckhand alone once more.

He'd best worry about himself, he decides. If *he* doesn't keep it together, both he *and* Lee will be shit out of luck. Gambling on good fishing forecasts five years ago, Gregg had ordered the *Pegasus* custom built to his own specifications at a cost of nearly half a million dollars. A dream come true after decades of fishing for others, leasing decrepit tubs from the processors. But the fishing has been only mediocre the last couple of years and now the prospects for this one, projected to be a banner season, don't look too promising. Clearly, he's going to have some cash-flow problems.

He knows any number of fishermen who've gained a boat and lost a marriage, but if Gregg doesn't watch his back, he'll lose the *Pegasus*, too. In the meantime, the bell still jangles on the door of the Mercantile, the place still smells like Comet cleanser, and the shelves are still well stocked. All he cares about right now is his immediate purchasing power. Later, he'll head over to the Selby District United Fishermen's office and see what kind of game plan anyone has so far come up with for oil spill defense. Lee will just have to fend for herself.

He leaves the store with his items in a sack. Stepping into a shadow, Gregg twists the cap off the sour mash whiskey, breaking the paper seal, and raises the bottle to his lips for a long, satisfying swallow.

5

Tess must have gone to bed, Daniel decides when the answering machine picks up at home. He leaves a message that he's taking catnaps in KRBB's break room and eating the chili, casseroles, and baked goods that people have taken to dropping off at the station. He probably won't be home for a few more hours, he says.

Daniel's following a lead that directly links the Mammoth *Kuparuk* oil spill with Selby: Aaron Anderson—one of the wrestlers he'd coached on the Seawolves' squad, and the son of Lee's skipper, Gregg Anderson— was on the supersized ship the night it hit the reef. Apparently the young man, a regular employee of Stoddard Maritime, was pressed into service when a *Kuparuk* crewman got injured the day before the grounding and had to be medevacked off the tanker. Daniel's left messages for Aaron at Stoddard and with the boy's mother in Anchorage but has yet to hear back from him.

The only fact so far confirmed by either Mammoth Petroleum or the Coast Guard concerning the still-unnamed *Kuparuk* captain is that he's gone missing, improbable as that sounds. Some accuse the petroleum industry of having spirited the man away so as to prep him for his eventual reappearance before the press.

Daniel has pieced together the protocol attending the departure of loaded tankers from the Pipeline terminal. It is by now common knowledge that on Thursday the transit lanes were unusually cluttered with building-sized icebergs calved from nearby Mandelstam Glacier, thought to be the result of the recent cycle of extreme high tides, so Daniel wonders if the grounding was some kind of reverse-*Titanic* scenario: captain and crew deliberately navigating off course in an ill-fated attempt to avoid collision with what Alaska mariners call "growlers" and "bergy bits."

In any case, the ice in the channel had significantly delayed the *Kuparuk*'s arrival at the Pipeline terminal, placing pressure on captain and crew to begin loading North Slope crude immediately, in order to expedite their departure. Daniel interviews by telephone the guarded harbor pilot and the loquacious pair of men who were on duty that night in the vessel traffic center. Since the sequence of events all three describe to him fall well within the bounds of normal procedure, nothing so far comes even remotely close to explaining the spectacular grounding.

He also learns that, as a cost-saving measure, the Mammoth Petroleum Corporation had recently pruned its supertanker crews worldwide, rationalizing that the big ships' enhanced electronic capabilities eliminate the need for large numbers of personnel. However, Daniel's also heard that those who've survived the downsizing as often as not find themselves working double shifts. Isn't that illegal, or if it isn't, shouldn't it be?

By the time the ship cast off, the weather in the sound offered excellent visibility. Rule that out as a contributing factor. As required by regulation, a licensed harbor pilot manned the helm of the enormous tanker as it wended its way through the Narrows. Nothing unusual there either.

After the pilot disembarked at the customary location, the ship's captain—the still-unidentified Joe who's now AWOL—resumed command, calling the traffic center for permission to change from the outbound to the inbound lane. When Daniel first heard this, he assumed it to be the obvious cause of the grounding: a fateful decision that would all but guarantee a head-on collision. But no one he's spoken with considers the maneuver to have been at all problematic. Turns out it was a fairly routine move in the presence of ice. In fact, the tanker immediately preceding the Mammoth *Kuparuk*, the Exxon *Long Beach*, had made an identical dogleg just hours earlier. At this point, though, things get a little confused, since no one will say who, exactly, was at the wheel of the *Kuparuk* when it "fetched up hard aground."

While others embrace the titillating possibility of the captain's intoxication as the likeliest cause of the disaster, Daniel dismisses the idea as absurd. He instead conjures what seems to him a far likelier explanation: the failure of the supertanker's state-of-the-art navigational systems and the captain, an exceptionally skilled mariner, resorting to heroic manual measures to avert catastrophe. As to the alcohol smelled later on the man's breath, who's to say the captain hadn't done his drinking *after* the collision, while awaiting the arrival of the Coast Guard? After all, who would begrudge you the consolation of a stiff belt or two after such a harrowing ordeal? Of course drugs and alcohol are contraband on the big vessels, but surely many ship personnel have their own stash.

Maybe Aaron Anderson—anonymously, of course—can give Daniel the scoop.

He remembers how, even as paramedics worked frantically to save Elena's life, the police officers responding to the accident had made both him and the truck driver walk the painted line atop the traffic lane to check their sobriety. Distraught over his wife's injuries, Daniel felt humiliated by the order, especially when they declared him clean.

After hours of scrubbing, the cream-colored hull of the *Pegasus* remains banded by a wide, tobacco-colored stain. Using the biodegradable solvents and stiff-bristled scrub brushes available at the cleaning station, Lee does her best to scour the anchor winch and the foredeck, but these, too, seem destined for permanent discoloration. It reminds her of the smoke damage after her family's kitchen fire when she was still in grade school. Before her father moved out, at any rate. Gunther had extinguished the blaze himself, never once losing his cool, even when flames licked across the ceiling and caught the curtains on the other side of the room. The ivory-colored Westinghouse refrigerator turned an uneven rusty gray, and he and Weezie had explained to her that nothing could bleach a smoke stain out of something once it set.

She tries to remember more about that night, which is her only memory of the man she once called Daddy acting heroically. Now she wonders if Gunther's fondness for liquor might have caused the fire in the first place. How much of their lives together had he spent intoxicated? She knows his drinking had contributed to the divorce even though Weezie never talked about it. One day he lived with them, the next he was gone, and Lee didn't see him again until her mother got sick, her beautiful red hair falling out in clumps. Lee had long ago decided that the two of them had adopted her in a last-ditch effort to resuscitate their failing marriage. Obviously, it hadn't worked.

Lee returns the cleaning supplies she borrowed. "Where you from?" she asks the group of workers who, having finished washing the *Pegasus*, now mill in boredom on the soapy dock.

"Anchorage."

"How'd you wind up here?"

"Job Service!" they crow, like the chance to clean oiled boats is the best thing that's ever happened to them.

"Who hired you?" Lee asks.

"Mammoth Petroleum!" It sounds like a pep rally.

Their response catches her off guard. Shouldn't the state be the one hiring boat cleaners? It doesn't seem right somehow that the same company responsible for the oil spill should also be the one to decide who gets these jobs. How much is Mammoth paying them, anyway?

Another sullied vessel motors over, the *Chitina*, and suddenly reanimated, the boat cleaners scurry en masse to the far end of the float to swarm the aluminum bow-picker.

And why bring workers all the way from Anchorage? Why not hire locals? There's a lot of people right here in Selby who could really use the money.

She's never seen the harbor so empty, except perhaps that one winter when it froze solid from boat ramp to jetty. The cleaning station is the only float that hosts any activity. Because no one's around, she sees no need to draw the curtains across the portholes while changing out of her work pants and rubber boots into jeans and sneakers.

Gregg returns to the *Pegasus* with an unlit cigarette in his mouth. Well, better cigarettes than booze, Lee thinks. Her skipper starts the engine, maneuvering the boat across the thoroughfare and into the slip without a word. As she fastens lines, he disappears again.

Lee assembles her possessions, faltering over the murder mystery she'd had a hard time putting down on their way out to the fishing grounds. She'd found the paperback bestseller to be a real page-turner. Then. Now, most of the way through the book, she somehow knows she'll never finish it.

She straightens her sleeping bag on the mattress and tidies her cubby. Other than her wallet, there's nothing on the boat that Lee requires in town. She always leaves her fishing gear on board, keeping another set of clothes and personal effects at home. Since it sounds like it might be a while before they fish again, she figures she can always return to the harbor should she happen to need anything. Not because she's hungry, but because she can't remember when she last ate, Lee forces herself to consume a small bowl of Cheerios and milk, hoping she can keep the food down.

She guesses Gregg will be back because he's taken nothing with him and hasn't asked her to lock up. She knows he's more at home on the *Pegasus* than he is in the near-empty apartment he rents in a fourplex by the hospital. Lee wants to say something to him, to tell him that things will work out, so she tears a leaf from the notepad in the galley and locates a pencil stub in the utility drawer.

They'd had every reason to think this could be their best season yet. Instead, their catch proven worthless, it seems like no one even knows when anyone will fish again. Lee had looked forward to possibly earning enough this year to replace Rainbow; the compact pickup already has a hundred and sixty thousand miles on the odometer and a record-setting number of mismatched body parts. She'd also set her heart on making enough to be able to afford a trip to somewhere—anywhere—warm and sunny next winter.

"Dear Gregg," she writes. From what Fritz has said, her skipper probably won't even recover the food and fuel costs of the trip, let alone moorage fees and insurance. His losses render Lee's trivial. Unable to think of anything worthwhile to say, she finally balls the scrap of paper and tosses it in the trash, returning the pencil to the drawer. Sliding the wheelhouse door closed behind her, she steps onto C float. She'll check on her skipper tomorrow. Anyway, Lee thinks, rubbing her neck, who does he think he is, grabbing her like that?

She discards the notion of trying to hitch a ride into town. Walking will not only return her land legs, but it will calm her. Struck as always by how differently land smells from ocean, she sniffs the damp dead-grass odor of snowmelt and wonders if the temperature in town is still dipping below freezing at night or if spring has arrived in her absence. As she settles into her pace, her heart grows lighter.

But the relative isolation of Harbor Road gives way to an unantici-pated stream of vehicles clogging Seaside Drive, which, a mile later, nevertheless leaves her unprepared for the bedlam of traffic in town. The congestion of cars and trucks resembles the hustle and bustle of midsummer, when twice-weekly cruise ships bring in hundreds of tour-ists, who mob Selby's half-dozen blocks of downtown, thronging to the souvenir shops and art galleries and bookstore. From Memorial Day weekend to the season's conclusion three months later at Labor Day, both in- and out-of-state visitors jam the town—some with recreational vehicles, some pulling boat trailers behind trucks—all in the single-minded quest for fish and fun. Lee has never regretted that she's usually working on a boat during the summer, far from the maddening crowds.

Unlike summer, however, when leisure and relaxation suffuse the vacation air of the coastal community, people loitering over ice cream cones and photo opportunities, a sense of crisis now permeates the darkness. Unfamiliar vehicles snake bumper-to-bumper down Main Street, even though Memorial Day is still more than two months off. Lee's never before associated Selby—a town without a traffic light—with the concept of rush hour, and the unprecedented commotion unnerves her, especially since Sunday nights here are about as quiet as they come.

Many of the vehicles bear official-looking insignia on their door panels, compounding Lee's sense of dislocation because it means they're from out of town. Her pulse quickens when she fails to recognize any of the drivers. Where have they all come from, and how did they get here so fast? She'd assumed that returning home would offer solace, but now she becomes aware of a throbbing pressure beneath her breastbone, which aches as surely as if she's been struck. No, Gregg hadn't hit her before he locked his arm around her throat. Then what? Is it from breathing the fumes from the oil spill?

Lee picks up her step, half trotting. Lights blaze from every business front, figures hastening into and out of buildings with an air of urgency discernible even from afar. All parking spaces occupied, trucks and cars pull over at random, heedless of fire hydrants or pedestrian passage.

On the far side of the street, Stork Stokowski rides past on his old Schwinn, knees jabbing the air. His boyish face radiates the same preoccupation as everyone else's. Lee's expression, too, must look distraught, creased with anxiety. She calls out to him and Stork, himself a deckhand, dismounts, crossing to her when traffic permits.

"You just get in?" He holds the handlebars of the fat-tired blue bicycle with one hand while embracing her with the other. She's glad to see someone she knows and grateful for the hug even if, standing on tiptoe, she barely reaches his chest.

"You cut your hair." He releases her. "No offense, but you stink."

Lee brushes the bristles with her palm. "I guess I haven't showered in a while," she says self-consciously.

He shakes his head, eyes widening as he makes the connection. "No, you smell like a crankcase. You've been in the spill."

She nods. Surprised to feel tears welling, she wills them away. "You?"

"Other way. Port Clark." Stork has yet to take his eyes off her. "How bad is it?"

Lee can't bring herself to meet his gaze. How to answer that question?

"Did you hear they're saying it'll go all the way to the Aleutians?"

Lee gapes at him.

Stork continues, "Can you believe the guy's blood alcohol was twice the legal limit? Is that messed up or what?"

Lee stares at the *Shamrock* deckhand, now tongue-tied for a different reason. So it's true. Hadn't anyone noticed the captain was drunk? Why on earth would they let him have command?

"Wonder if he likes his liquor on the rocks, too," Stork sneers. "Sorry," he adds when he sees the look on her face.

Lee's father, Gunther, always poured his Johnny Walker over ice cubes. She remembers how the ice crackled and tinkled as it expanded in his drinking glass. She motions to the traffic and asks, "What is all this?"

"The governor declared a state of emergency."

"What's that mean?"

"It means we're royally screwed. It means we're eligible for disaster assistance." Stork tells her how personnel from both state and federal regulatory agencies, and from the Mammoth Petroleum Corporation, began arriving in Selby Friday night.

"They knew right away this was a big deal?" she says.

"Yeah. Sucks, doesn't it?" As they walk, Stork pushing the bicycle, he describes how all the VIPs, or what he calls "muckety-mucks," have established "command posts" wherever they can find space. "It's a war. An occupation."

He indicates the shabby old Seabright Motel, where the state has set up shop, a full sheet of plywood leaning against the glassed-in entry with the words "Disaster Assistance Center" hand painted on it in blood-red letters that have trickled and run before drying. Stork next points across the street, to the decidedly more upscale Sheraton, which locals still call the "new hotel" even though it's been in business for almost a decade. In contrast to the state's makeshift sign, a large piece of blue Plexiglas emblazoned with the petroleum company's logo—the orange silhouette of a woolly mammoth—has already replaced the hotel's wreathed "S" in a lightbox beside the entrance.

Gesturing to each headquarters in turn, Lee's companion pretends to be a ringside emcee speaking into a handheld microphone: "In this corner, ladies and gentlemen, the State of Alaska: 'Last Frontier,' 'North to the Future.' And in this corner, the multinational oil giant, Mammoth Petroleum: 'Energizing Your Life.'"

Carl Hatfield, who installs telephones for a living, exits the Sheraton and makes a beeline for the Seabright, coils of beige phone line clutched under his arm, pliers in hand, his trademark fedora riding further back on his head than usual.

"I guess Mammoth got serviced first," Stork observes. "So maybe Big Oil won the first round."

He gestures to the old trading post on the corner of Waterfront and Main, vacant for at least a year but now illuminated by bare lightbulbs hanging from extension cords that dangle from the ceiling. As she stares through the large plate-glass windows that used to display potbellied woodstoves and long-handled gardening tools, Lee sees instead men and women in brown trousers and khaki shirts, black name tags affixed to shirt pockets. Despite the presence of folding chairs and card tables, everyone's on their feet, either pacing with phone receivers pressed to their ears or engaged in tense conversation with one another.

"Fish and Wildlife," she says. Stork nods.

As they proceed, a balding, middle-aged man hails them from a white sedan double-parked across the street. "Fishermen?" he calls, hands cupped around his mouth. His voice seems pitched too high for his portly build. The car has an Avis sticker on the bumper, which means it has most likely come from Anchorage—the nearest auto rental location—a day's drive away. While Lee approaches reflexively, Stork hangs back.

The man extends a business card to her through the open car window. "I'm staying at the Baycrest," he says earnestly. "I can help you."

Does she need help? Up close, Lee observes the fellow's pasty complexion. Perspiration beads his forehead and upper lip despite the cool of the evening. The shiny fabric of his green sport coat tautens across his broad shoulders as he extends his hand to shake hers. His tie looks uncomfortably tight. She glances at the card: "Gerry Gower, Attorney at Law." A Seattle address.

Gower gestures toward the Sheraton. "I'll file suit against Mammoth Petroleum for you, for loss of wages."

Lee calculates the speed at which this man had to have acted in order to arrive in Selby this quickly. "You came all the way from Seattle?" she asks.

He shakes his head, beaming. "No, no. I lucked out. I was already in Anchorage."

"Lucked out?" As Lee backs away, he flings an arm after her, as if to pull her back. "You Native?" he asks hopefully. "Even better!" Lee rejoins Stork as Gower makes one last pitch. "Call any time, night or day. I've got a pager."

"I should have warned you," Stork apologizes. "It's a feeding frenzy. Sharks smelling blood."

"Do we really need lawyers?"

"Who knows? I'm keeping my options open."

They pass the hastily assembled command centers for the Alaska Department of Fish and Game and the Department of Environmental Conservation, operating side by side in a single-story duplex that normally houses a real estate office on one side and an insurance agency on the other.

"What happened to Brenda and Mike?" Lee asks, referring to the husband-and-wife proprietors of the two local businesses.

"Relocated to their home, I'll bet. In favor of leasing out the office space, you think?"

Downtown, so familiar, has somehow been rendered unrecognizable since Lee left to go fishing only a week ago. Her chest feels tight; Cheerios sour in her stomach. The Coast Guard has set up an operations center in the Washeteria. The Environmental Protection Agency now occupies Rugged Bay Books. And something called the Minerals Management Service has taken up residence in what was until recently the Up Bay Café, an establishment of dubious cleanliness but tasty short-order fare that its aficionados referred to cheerfully as The

Upchuck. The state health department, having issued numerous citations, finally shut down the eatery for good this past winter.

The National Oceanic and Atmospheric Administration appears to have one of the larger response teams. They've set up shop in the bowling alley. Lee sees men and women in dark jumpsuits hovering over the scoring tables, looking absurdly misplaced amidst the gleaming lanes, polished pins, and multicolored bowling balls.

"Please tell me it's all just a bad dream," she murmurs.

"It *is* a bad dream," Stork replies. "It's a freaking nightmare." He touches her arm. "People are saying the spill is really a lot more than twelve million gallons."

"What do you mean?"

"They claim it's being underreported, that it's closer to forty million, which would make it one of the largest spills ever."

Lee doesn't know what to say. Two slabs of ceiling tile tent against one another in a crudely fashioned display on the sidewalk before the hardware store, "Oil Spill Public Information Center" penned on both sides in black marker, under the words "Coming Soon," as though advertising a popular attraction. A new splitting maul props open the front door. While an unfamiliar man in denim coveralls installs an enormous photocopying machine in the foyer, another stranger, a silver-haired woman wearing a mauve polyester pantsuit, hovers nearby clasping a Styrofoam cup in both hands.

"I'm going in," Lee says, hugging Stork good-bye.

"See you around. Be careful." He remounts his bike and pedals away into the night.

When Lee asks her how much oil has spilled, the elderly woman nervously pushes the bridge of her wire-rimmed spectacles and explains that she's been told to release only information that's been cleared by the governor's office.

"But the oil spill's *here*, not in Southeast. Juneau's a thousand miles away."

"I'm sorry." The woman avoids eye contact with Lee.

"Is the ship still leaking? How are they going to get the oil out of the water?"

The state employee coughs in embarrassment. "Can you come back in a few days?"

"At least tell me what we should do if we've been exposed to hydrocarbons."

The woman clutches the empty coffee cup, as if for protection. "I don't know," she whispers. "I'm sorry."

Lee decides to hike up the hill to the radio station in search of trustworthy information. She wonders if some agency or other has taken over KRBB's old wood-frame building, too, or if anyone will even be there, for that matter, considering how late it is.

But the building is jammed, as though locals have sought refuge here, driven from the center of town by the occupying forces. At last she encounters familiar faces. No sooner does Lee step through the entrance than townspeople converge to hug and welcome her. "Thank God you're safe," some say. "We were worried." *Now* I'm home, she thinks.

Those seeking information like Lee and those offering their services crowd the front office. Half a dozen people monitor what seem to be incessantly ringing telephones. Lee's landlady and neighbor, with her frizzy halo of fine white hair, catches the deckhand's eye from across the room, blowing her a kiss. "Welcome home," Irene mouths while holding a phone receiver to her ear. The younger woman weaves past others to give the retiree a hug, and Irene pats her tenant on the cheek without once interrupting her phone conversation. "If I were you, dear," she's saying into the mouthpiece in the sweet-little-old-lady voice she uses when most annoyed, "I wouldn't count on getting work cleaning up this oil spill. Alaska's unemployment rate is one of the highest in the nation. You're better off right there in Cincinnati, I guarantee it." She hangs up the phone crisply and reaches for Lee with both arms. "You're back."

"When did you start working here?"

"Not working. Volunteering." Irene gestures to the other unpaid phone operators. "Bruno and I have been worried sick about you," she adds, referring to her large Chesapeake Bay retriever, who spends as much time in and around Lee's one-room cabin as he does at his owner's house next door. "Jackie phoned."

"Here?" Lee asks.

"No, she called me at home. She's worried about you."

"She is?"

Irene regards the deckhand skeptically and hands her the triangular half sandwich sitting on a napkin in the corner of the desk. "Eat this," she says, narrowing her eyes when Lee distractedly sets the food on a file cabinet. "Now."

"Yes, ma'am." Surprisingly, the peanut-butter sandwich tastes really good.

The phone rings again and Irene moves to answer it. "Rugged Bay Broadcasting. How may I help you?"

Malcolm Bradbury, KRBB's rangy station manager, tries with his sonorous voice to get everyone's attention. Lee has always thought his flawlessly enunciated baritone makes him a natural for radio work. "We've been given permission to broadcast 24/7, but we really need volunteers with radio experience," Malcolm beseeches the crowd. "Any experience at all. Please." Several people say they'll help, and the administrator removes his horn-rimmed glasses, nodding gratefully as he rubs his eyes.

Lee's never seen Malcolm other than clean-shaven, but tonight he sports considerable stubble. Unlike most men in Selby, the station manager is always impeccably attired: khakis versus blue jeans, dress shirts versus t-shirts. Malcolm must be going for that unshaven celebrity look, Lee thinks, although what he looks is haggard.

"What's the update, Chief?" It's Leonard Gannaway, who works the counter at Selby Building Supply.

"The spill seems to have split in half," Malcolm says, replacing his glasses. "Some's moving toward the strait. The rest is following Shumagin Passage. Baidarki Island just took the hit."

Baidarki! Lee pictures the crescent of sandy beach strewn with colored glass floats like so many Easter eggs. A surge of dark petroleum oozes over the sparkling buoys, vaporizing each on contact.

"Selby's got another day and a half," Malcolm says. "Port Clark's maybe two days behind us."

The room goes quiet. Volunteers let phones ring until the answering machines engage. Some people wipe their eyes.

"NOAA says the Barriers will be next," Malcolm resumes. Like Pogibshi, the two Chugachmiut villages on the Barrier Islands each house a couple hundred mostly Native residents. The islands also provide nesting habitat for countless murres, whose eggs' food value has enabled continuous human settlement there over hundreds of years. The birds' teeming rookeries, in turn, have made the Barriers a huge draw for sightseers, enriching local economies. Lee pictures the speckled brownish-green eggs, sharply pointed at one end to keep them from rolling off the narrow ledges on which the seabirds roost. Murres. She sees them landing again in the oil off the bow of the *Pegasus* and remembers that the black-and-white seabirds are capable of diving to depths of five hundred feet or more.

The station manager goes on to say that Selby has emerged as the coordination center for oil spill response. "We're well situated." Does Malcolm mean that Selby lies equidistant between Port Clark and Anchorage, or that it stands directly in the path of the oil?

Lee catches sight of Daniel emerging from the soundproof broadcast studio, headphones around his neck. Compact and muscular, Tessa's husband moves like a man with a mission. And like Malcolm and some of the other men here, Daniel has sprouted whiskers, too. Even as she thinks the reddish-blond stubble suits him, Lee realizes that these guys' new facial hair results from lack of time to shave rather than from a sudden shared impulse to grow beards. Daniel's blue eyes come into focus on her from somewhere seemingly far away. He's one of the few good-looking men she knows who doesn't think himself a gift from God. For one thing, his nose was broken as a high-school wrestler, which kind of messes up his face, and for another, there's always been something tentative about his manner. (Because he was the one behind the wheel of their car when his pregnant first wife, in the passenger seat, was killed by a driver running a red light?)

Daniel regards her with a distracted expression, drawing her to him only when she extends both arms for a hug.

"You cut your hair," he says, sniffing it and wrinkling his nose. "You saw the spill. How bad is it?"

Lee shakes her head. She still doesn't have an answer to that question that she trusts herself to speak aloud. "What are you doing?" she asks instead.

He smiles happily. "I'm in charge of hourly updates: location of the leading edge, weather outlook, contamination index, mortality counts..."

There's no mistaking his pride. "'Mortality counts,'" she repeats numbly. "'Contamination index'?" She searches his eyes again, seeking to understand.

"Daniel Wolff! Line five."

He grasps Lee's shoulders hard, kissing her on the forehead as he squeezes past. His enthusiasm confuses her. She wants to ask when Tess will be back, so she follows him into the next room but sees him shake his head at the woman who hands him the phone and hears him say, "Not 'til Wednesday." Lee guesses she will have to wait a few more days to see her friend and wonders who's watching Minke and Elias.

Irene materializes at her side. "A bunch of folk have gathered at Harbor Air, at the hangar," she says. "They're setting up a bird-cleaning station."

Lee squints at her.

"To wash oiled birds," her landlady explains gently.

The deckhand feels her heart race. She tries to picture herself tending an oiled seabird—like a murre—holding its trembling, impossibly weightless body in her hands.

"The Building Supply's providing material for cages," Irene continues. "Hotels are donating towels. The electric association's setting up lights and space heaters. Someone's on their way from California, someone with expertise cleaning contaminated wildlife." She drifts away to answer yet another ringing phone.

Of course, Lee thinks. Irene and Daniel, Malcolm, others—each has a defined role to play in this emergency, a job to do. Their responsibilities no doubt also help them to cope with the stress of the crisis, not to mention the fact that what they're doing helps others to cope, too. She, on the other hand, remains capsized, still just trying to right herself.

Lee needs to get involved—the sooner the better.

Tamara Smith, who'd waited tables at every restaurant in town before being hired as the new radio station's administrative assistant and whom Lee has known since they both landed in Selby years ago, tells her that KRBB has spent a tenth of its annual operating budget in the last three days alone. "We're broadcasting nonstop. And we put in six more phone lines," the capable office manager adds, gesturing around the front room, which, the deckhand now sees, resembles a telethon. "We're getting calls from all over the world."

Lee blinks at her, not comprehending.

"Most people want jobs," Tamara explains, raking a hand through her bangs. "They want to come here and get rich cleaning up oil, like it's another gold rush or something." She shakes her head disapprovingly. "But really," she goes on, brightening, "an awful lot of callers want to help. They want to know what they can do, where to send money. Probably half of the calls are about the otters."

"What about them?"

Tamara gives Lee a peculiar look. "You haven't heard? Otters are getting wiped out by this thing. Hundreds of them have already died."

Otters. Lee stares at the other woman blankly.

"They've set up a recovery center at the high school," Tamara continues. "The first ones came in last night." Her voice trails off. "I don't know. I heard most were dead by the time they got here." She takes Lee's elbow and leads her to an overstuffed sofa in the staff break room. "I'll fix you some tea."

The deckhand sinks into the large cushions and closes her eyes, concentrating on drawing breaths that don't hurt. She puts a hand over her heart, where the pain is. A cube-shaped clock radio on the book-shelf plays the station's broadcast. A Congressman from Indiana wants Alaskans to know the entire nation holds them in its prayers.

Tamara returns with a steaming mug of Red Rose tea, setting it on the floor beside the couch. "Can you believe the tanker captain was blotto?"

Lee shakes her head.

Tamara sits beside her, eyes pooling. "I'm scared. Aren't you? Things are already so crazy, and the oil hasn't even hit us yet."

Lee closes her eyes, wishing she could time travel or something, come back only when things return to normal. Beam me up, Scotty.

Tamara blows her nose loudly. "I should be out front," she says, rising.

The deckhand nods. She remembers Gregg straight-arming the kid in the harbor before clamping his elbow around her own neck. Stork cracked jokes, but you could tell he was upset. Tamara's weepy. Irene, Daniel, Malcolm—they're all focused, busy. In contrast, Lee feels like a sleepwalker. Alone in the small room, she blows on the tea and nudges with her finger the slider that controls the volume on the small boxy radio. Daniel conducts a live interview with Nick Calhoun, apparently on a ship-to-shore radio phone, judging from the time lag in Nick's responses and the clicking in the reception. Lee pictures the wildlife biologist's widow's peak and horn-rimmed glasses. Nick's somewhere near Cape Calliope, approximately two hundred and fifty miles southeast of Rugged Bay, talking about the seabird remains found at Ground Zero.

"We estimate over three thousand dead birds on one beach alone."

"What kind?" Daniel asks. "Could you tell?"

"Every kind," Nick replies, his voice acquiring an edge. "Oystercatchers, kittiwakes, auklets, puffins, guillemots. Lots of murres. A loon."

She winces. In the silence that follows, the biologist adds, "Did you know this is the home of the Alaska breeding population of oystercatch-ers? Or it was." He sounds tense. "Our oystercatchers account for over half the world's population, and we only have about five thousand of them. Or we did, until a few days ago."

Abruptly, Lee switches off the radio and reaches for the *Newsweek* lying on an adjacent endtable. She sips the tea and skims an article about

John F. Kennedy Jr. and his latest romance with some New York social-ite who looks like she's still a teenager. The pundits predict a wedding announcement soon. Lee wonders why she has never before realized that she and John-John were born in the same year.

Which reminds her. How could she have forgotten? It would have been yesterday. Lee hurries to congratulate Tamara.

The administrative assistant shakes her head. "We had to postpone it." She dips her face and adds defensively, "What else could we do? Something like this kind of blows your personal life out of the water, you know?"

"Sorry, Tam." Lee flushes with embarrassment. "I didn't think."

Someone (is it Dorothy Connors from the chamber of commerce?) broadcasts an appeal for clean towels and sheets for the bird- and otter-cleaning operations. "We desperately need volunteers," the spot concludes.

"Did you set a new date?" Lee asks.

Tamara shakes her head. "Not yet. Jake says we should wait until things settle down. I'm thinking that could be a while." She blows her nose. "I've got to stop crying."

"Tell me again where they're washing the otters?"

"At the high school. In the gym."

6

Lee finds that Selby's largest paved parking lot has become a construction zone. Dozens of men and women, many wearing tool belts, assemble wooden frames from piles of lumber stacked at the edges of the asphalt. It cheers her to recognize those laboring under portable floodlights, generators vibrating loudly in the center of their work area. Completed two-by-four cribs and ten-foot-square collars assembled from rough-cut planks lie stacked in the shadows against the long, windowless wall of the swimming pool annex.

Another handful of figures wield acetylene torches by the gym entrance. Clad in leather shirts or heavy canvas jackets, masked by dark-lensed face shields or goggles, they cut fifty-five-gallon fuel drums in half lengthwise, the red-hot incisions smoldering in the wake of hissing blue flames.

Lee notices other spectators like herself. The workers themselves, however, intent on manufacturing, ignore the onlookers. She steps past an insulated semitrailer. Water has pooled on the pavement beneath its refrigeration unit. Does it contain food for the volunteers?

Lee swims at the high school three days a week in the winter, and in fact was last here just a couple of weeks ago to watch a basketball game between the Selby Seawolves and the Whittaker Wolverines. How are schools preparing their students for the spill? She wonders again who's minding Elias and Minke. She should stop by the house tomorrow.

The letter board that normally welcomes visitors to the facility, announcing the week's athletic events, now reads "Marine Mammal Treatment Center." Lee hesitates. Which ocean animals besides otters are at risk? Seals? Porpoises? Whales? Is it even possible to clean an oiled whale? Will the spill eventually travel so far that it endangers walruses? It will, if it goes all the way to the Chain, like Stork said.

The girls' locker room is draped in blue poly tarps; she finds the floor of the dimly lit gym likewise covered by reinforced plastic sheeting and crosses it cautiously. Exposed plumbing runs down the middle of the cavernous room, figures working on hands and knees to fit together lengths of white PVC pipe. Lee recognizes R. J. Carter and Bo Wheeler, both licensed plumbers, and wonders why someone doesn't turn the lights up, so people can see.

Picking her way across the space, she becomes aware of the incongruous odor of dish soap and makes out huddles of workers at the far end of the gym. Are they washing otters? She can't hear anything over the sound of running water and the noise of the building's air exchange system and can't see well in the murky half-light.

As she approaches, Lee counts ten washing stations, with more under assembly. The wooden cribs she'd seen outside now support the halved steel barrels, which serve as washtubs, each surrounded by figures clad either in rain gear or in dark plastic trash sacks that have had arm and head holes cut in them. She has yet to see an otter.

She recognizes Treya Williams first, soon realizing with a tight throat that she knows almost everyone: Jeremy Sloan, Willow Nelson, Margaret from the library, Joel from the *Misty Dawn*, Clayton, Kendra, Annabelle—friends, neighbors, fellow fishermen. No doubt she knows the volunteers at the bird-cleaning operation, too, a thought that reignites the pain in her chest.

At each of the washing areas, a remarkably docile otter forms the hub of a wheel of human beings. The animals lie atop hammocks of seine web that prevent them from being completely submerged in the water in the barrel tubs; Lee soon realizes the listless creatures must be sedated. Additional volunteers circulate with armloads of towels and half-gallon containers of aqua-tinted dishwashing detergent, accounting for the distinctive, if misplaced, smell.

Why dish soap? Then she thinks of TV commercials for dishwashing liquids that boast of their grease-cutting power.

Three pairs of hands hold each animal securely by legs and head, while a fourth person works soap into the wet fur. Every station has a garden hose with a spray nozzle. The larger animals scarcely fit in the metal troughs that Lee now notices, bear Mammoth Petroleum's distinctive orange woolly mammoth logo. These washtubs have been fabricated from oil drums, after all, but the irony of it still gives her pause.

Intent on their work, and no doubt due to the midnight hour, no one's talking much. Those whose hands are occupied nod to Lee in recognition, smiling briefly. For the most part, though, the atmosphere feels somber and tense, like that of a field hospital, she guesses, as she watches Dennis Bailey do his best to mop the tarp-covered floor, while Theresa from the DMV duckwalks behind him, a balled towel in each hand with which she buffs wet spots.

"Can you help me?"

Lee recognizes the son of the couple who own the Mercantile, in the harbor. An only child like herself, Ryan Hanson has grown into a burly young man, acne scattered across his forehead.

"You bet." Lee seizes her chance, eagerly following Ryan outside, where she observes row upon row of the molded plastic carriers used to transport dogs on airplanes. The cages are set haphazardly on the tarmac, some double-stacked, an Alaska Aviation cargo van parked nearby. From the top of the steps, Lee glimpses shadowed movement in some of the kennels.

As Ryan approaches the vehicle, Lee stops to collect herself. How can there be so many? The boy gestures to the white van. "They're waiting for us to unload them."

When she hears one of the animals shriek, it raises the hair on her neck. Lee stumbles on the cement stairs, catching herself on the iron handrail.

"You okay?" Ryan asks.

She inhales carefully. "Just a sec."

"I'll get someone else," he offers, starting back inside.

Lee stands with effort, shaking her head to clear it. "Come on," she tells him. Time to get a grip, she tells herself: you can't afford the luxury of freaking out. Time to get on with whatever needs to be done.

By the time she returns to the gym, Lee's ready to lend a hand with the washing. Her new teammates make her a trash-bag jerkin so she won't get soaked. Camille, a former high-school gymnast who now works for Parthenon Pizza, shows the newcomer how to position herself at the end of a washtub, and Lee takes hold of her first oiled otter.

A thickly bearded man she knows as a fellow lap swimmer stands at the otter's head, wearing waterproof orange bib overalls and thick leather welder's gloves reaching to his elbows. Kurt has a master's degree and works summers on a National Marine Fisheries research vessel. Like lots of others here, he looks beyond tired, holding the bedraggled animal's head in his two gloved hands not only to support it but also to keep it from biting anyone. Lee has inferred from overheard conversations that Kurt is one of the organizers of the otter-rescue effort. Camille helps their fourth, a ponytailed high-school sophomore named Heidi, whom Lee guesses to be around sixteen, to alternately spray the animal with water, drizzle it with dish soap, massage the suds into the thick fur, rinse it all out, and repeat the process over and over again.

As she grips the unconscious animal's limp hind legs, its strong, tapered tail lying between her forearms, Lee finds herself thinking of Bruno, her landlady's Chesapeake Bay retriever. The two animals are about the same size. The otter's hind legs are shorter and both more bowed and more muscular than the dog's, however, and its feet more flipper-like than Bruno's webbed paws.

Lee has never been so close to an otter and has certainly never touched one before. The creature looks like a furry, bewhiskered human, albeit someone very small and extremely stoned. Her eyes keep returning to the mat of coarse hair covering its chest and belly, used to transport crabs and clams from the sea bottom to the surface, where the otter then uses the rug-like mat as a table, cracking food open against itself with a rock. She's seen them do this countless times. Are any of the otters here the same animals she's watched with so much pleasure over the years? How many of those are sick now, or dying, or dead?

Baby otters ride on this mat of thick hair, too. But the animal her team bathes otherwise bears little resemblance to the sea mammals she's seen in the wild. There's a world of difference between those healthy, playful sprites and these sickly, fur-matted creatures.

In addition to the stomach-turning odor of raw petroleum, Lee catches the familiar scent of ocean in the otter's matted fur, a pungent, briny alive smell that the artificial fragrance of the detergent soon masks. Camille instructs her to avoid eye contact with the animal. "We don't want it to bond with us humans," the young woman explains officiously, " 'cause that might ruin its chances of survival later." The pizza deliverer's estimation of herself seems to have escalated in accordance with her new role as a savior of oiled sea mammals.

Selby's lone veterinarian, Ralph Burch, circulates from station to station clutching a loaded syringe, stethoscope draped around his neck, thinning brown hair mussed, mouth set in a grim line. Lee learns from her teammates that more vets are en route from Anchorage and the West Coast, and that additional otter and bird care centers are being assembled in Port Clark and Kodiak in anticipation of the oil spill's continuing devastation. It's the first Lee has heard that Kodiak stands to be oiled, too, a thought that squeezes her heart anew.

Dr. Burch is reluctant to medicate the otters too heavily, for fear of adding to their life-threatening stress, so the marine mammals sometimes awaken in the middle of washing, requiring more sedative. Each time their otter struggles, Lee tightens her clasp on its legs, silently apologizing even as she mentally roots for it to resist her grip. But the creatures' efforts to free themselves cost them energy expenditures they can ill afford, so the veterinarian reminds the holders patiently and repeatedly that they must do their best to completely immobilize the otters—that that's how they can best help the imperiled animals to survive.

Soon Lee is as drenched as everyone else, but still sweating beneath the plastic trash sack. "Why's it so hot in here?" she asks.

"Same reason it's dark," Camille replies. "To keep the otters comfortable."

"But it's not like they aren't used to the cold."

Kurt explains. "They're not like seals or cetaceans. They don't have blubber. All their insulation has to come from their fur. Buoyancy, too. Once they're oiled, they have a hard time swimming and they get hypothermic, so they're going nuts trying to lick themselves clean."

"And the oil's toxic," Lee says, searching his eyes.

"That's why it's so important to capture and clean them as quickly as possible," young Heidi adds earnestly. "Before they eat too much of the poisonous oil."

Kurt tells Lee in a tired voice that otters also absorb toxicity through their eyes and skin. "If they don't die of pneumonia or hypothermia first, they can die of organ failure. Or else starve to death because they're too sick to find food."

The four of them spend almost three hours washing their animal, finally passing it on to a team of workers in surgical masks who towel it dry and blow it all over with handheld hair dryers until the cleaned fur fluffs.

"What's with the hospital masks?" Lee asks.

"The fur gets in your nose and you can't stop sneezing," Camille says, her know-it-all air beginning to grate on Lee.

"Totally," Heidi laughs, exposing the metal braces that band her teeth.

That night, their foursome doesn't lose any otters, but others do. Dr. Burch tells the volunteers that over half the animals surviving the trauma of capture are nevertheless dying in transit or in rehab.

In addition to administering injections, the veterinarian regularly bears away the bodies of deceased animals through the rear door of the gymnasium, returning empty-handed. At one point, Lee finds herself mesmerized by the sight of someone she recognizes as a grade-school teacher, who occupies on her team the same position as Lee: hind-leg holder. The deckhand watches as Sally Ann Fraser's shoulders slump, body sagging, as she collapses in tears. The animal the schoolteacher's team has just spent hours trying to save no longer breathes. Dr. Burch hurries to the site, bending over the unmoving animal with his stethoscope before performing CPR to no avail.

Spellbound, Lee unconsciously eases her grip on their new otter's legs, causing it to buck, at which Kurt frowns, Heidi squeals, and Camille glares.

"Sorry, you guys. Sorry," Lee says, coming back to herself.

"Do you really think the captain was drunk?" Heidi asks.

"Probably," Camille says. "Alaskans drink like there's no tomorrow."

"He's not from here," Kurt says testily.

"How do you know?" Camille challenges him.

"Because none of the tanker captains are."

With a start, Lee remembers awakening one night when she was young and finding all the lights still on in the house. Descending the stairs in her flannel pajamas, she discovered Gunther asleep in his recliner, an empty glass in his lap and an empty liquor bottle on the floor beside him. Not asleep, she realizes now. Passed out. Lee had tried with mounting panic to wake her father, finally creeping back upstairs to hide in the hall closet, heart pounding, terrified that her uncles, Carl and Ben, would somehow find out she was alone and come after her. It must have been one of the rare times Weezie traveled for work.

"Not so tight," Kurt says softly, gesturing at Lee's hands, which are clenched around the otter's legs. "You'll cut off his circulation."

Lee feels nauseous again and wonders if she'll have to dash to the bathroom, but mercifully, the sensation passes.

The third otter her team washes has had half of its face torn away. Where an eye should be, only a swollen socket, raw and bloody, remains.

Lee wonders if, in its weakened state, the creature has been attacked by another animal. Kurt holds the wounded head firmly in his gloved hands, taking care to keep soapsuds from the ravaged flesh.

"Sea lion?" Lee asks.

Freckle-faced Heidi answers, after first glancing at Kurt. "Dr. Burch says they do it to themselves, they're that desperate to get the oil off." The girl's face reddens as she dissolves in tears, suddenly looking half her age. "It's so unfair," the youngster continues, wiping her nose on the tissues Camille hands her. "What did *they* ever do to deserve this?"

Like an animal chewing off its own foot to escape a steel trap, Lee thinks. When had daylight first brightened the skylights of the gym? She feels the pressure in her chest. It hurts to breathe, and something else bothers her. Heidi's too young for this. Where are her parents? Why don't they take her home?

Gregg's so agitated he knows there's no point trying to sleep. By day, he and his fishing cronies subsist on coffee and candy bars while prepping their boats to venture into the spill. By night, they press into Selby's bars, drinking hard.

The protective boom that Mammoth Petroleum had promised to provide the coastal communities never materializes. According to the oil spill contingency agreement the company had signed years earlier with the State of Alaska, twelve miles of boom would be permanently warehoused at the Pipeline terminal. So what accounts for the delay? The media soon reveals that there had never been twelve miles, but only two, all of which was deployed around the crippled tanker on day three. After some of the highest tides of the year had already dispersed most of the oil, of course.

The relatively little protective material on hand elsewhere in the state has been sent to Anchorage for marshalling and eventual distribution to the communities deemed hardest hit by the spill. Meaning, of course, further delay.

"Norway!" Gregg bellows, when he learns the source of the boom ordered for Selby and Port Clark by the U.S. Coast Guard. "*No way! Talk about a state of preparedness!*"

The petroleum industry's two SRVs—spill response vessels—have so far managed to recover approximately one hundred gallons each of the spilled oil. "Only eleven million, nine hundred ninety-nine thousand, eight hundred more to go," Billy Read deadpans with mathematical accuracy that would have been humorous were it not also the calculation of what's beginning to feel like unquantifiable loss. The petroleum giant and the feds have so far spent more time arguing over how to "retrieve" spilled oil than they have actually doing so.

So Selby's fishermen dismantle their purse seines, gear they've spent hundreds of winter hours assembling by hand. Gear that in materials alone cost from fifteen to twenty thousand dollars per seine. Gear that they know will be useless to them once it's contaminated by the oil.

Unlike the wide mesh of gill nets, the fishermen reckon the seine web to be small and stout enough to effectively trap the now jelly-like crude petroleum. They plan to suspend lengths of the tough webbing between pairs of boats working in tandem, and after they've corralled the oil, they'll use brailers to transfer it into plastic and fiberglass totes strapped to their decks, thereby preventing the toxicity from contaminating their holds. (Should the below-deck compartments become contaminated, each skipper knows he might just as well scuttle his boat—because the Coast Guard will never allow it to be fished again.) They'll show the multinational petroleum corporation, with its state-of-the-art technology, the most effective way to contain a spill, by God. Even so, Gregg and his friend Dusty, the devil-may-care cowboy skipper of the *Rodeo Rose*, lock eyes with one another before each draws his knife from a sheath on his hip and slices resolutely through the first woven strands of black nylon seine.

Like the others, Gregg's goddamned if he's just going to roll over, tits up, without making some kind of stand. He envisions himself and his band of brothers transferring the oily excrescence from the surface of the ocean to the Anchorage headquarters of the Mammoth Petroleum Corporation, filling the twenty-story building floor to ceiling with the indescribably foul slime. "Here you go," the fishermen will say to the suits. "Take it. It's yours."

After ninety-six hours of calm seas, perfect conditions to respond to what has by now been dubbed the worst oil spill in North America—perfect conditions, that is, if you have both the resources and the will to do something meaningful—the weather has blown up, threatening as some say, to push the oil to Russia. "The window of opportunity has been lost," officials declare. The hell with that, Gregg mutters, grinding the stub of yet another unfiltered cigarette into a plastic ashtray at the Doghouse. It wasn't lost. It was fucking squandered. "Give me another," he orders the bartender, handing over his empty glass.

Among other things, the storm rips out the log boom that people had worked for days without sleep to get in place across the Gateway, so now stray timbers trailing frayed cable pose a safety hazard all the way to Harriman Entrance. Nonetheless, scores of boats set forth from Selby and Port Clark, a dozen women accompanying a hundred men. Everyone struggles to keep the seine web submerged in the breaking seas, riding up and down the whitecaps at cross purposes to one another, the netting more often out of the ocean than in. As Dusty observes drily to Gregg, the gear's dunked in the oil spill just long enough to ruin it and render it forever useless, but nowhere near long enough to capture even a fraction of the sea-swept petroleum that now blankets two thousand nautical square miles.

Thus forced to abandon the prospect of oil removal on the open ocean, the fleet makes for the protection of Herring Cove, where they discover two feet of crude petroleum standing idly in the shallow water, sheltered from the now-roiling sea. Here, in a single hour, they fill every tote, baiting tub, and utility bucket they have, finally resorting to scooping small quantities of crude into plastic garbage sacks. Although the oil that remains afloat in the sheltered cove is now theirs for the taking, they have nowhere to put it.

In the passion of the moment, some of the guys yank hatch covers from fish holds, but Gregg and Dusty holler at them not to be fools. Gregg sees tears of frustration glistening in the eyes of more than a few of the men but notices that the women look ready to kill. If anyone from Mammoth Petroleum should have happened along, those gals might have done them some serious hurt.

The next day, Gregg, Dusty, and Mark Delacroix share a table at the Downtown Grille. Despite the fact that they've all showered, and that Dusty and Delly have even shaved, Gregg can still see flecks of petroleum on his friends' faces. No doubt the crude freckles his own dark skin. Still on their first cups of coffee, they've already filled the glass ashtray with cigarette butts.

"Captain Richard Aengus. What the hell kind of name is that?" Delacroix says. "And where is the schmuck?"

"Captain Dick," Dusty smirks. "Moby Dickhead. You think Mammoth's shielding him?"

"He's history, wherever he is." Gregg puckers his lips like a pollock, releasing a wavery smoke ring.

"Foundered," Dusty mutters.

"What's that mean?" Delacroix asks.

Gregg answers for the *Rodeo Rose* skipper. "It means 'ruined.' Finished." He draws a finger across his throat. "Kaput."

"Not him. *Us.*" Dusty leans forward abruptly to crush another cigarette. "It means we're fucked six ways to Sunday."

Upon learning that the Mammoth *Kuparuk*'s Captain Richard Aengus has a record of not one, not two, but an unbelievable three DWIs, Gregg decides the son of a bitch deserves his fate. Even at my worst, he thinks, I never drove drunk. Granted, when the *Pegasus* skipper overindulges he usually passes out and therefore *can't* drive. Still, he tells himself, it's a matter of principle.

Aengus is an unusual name. How about anus, or *anuq*—Inupiaq for "shit"? And speaking of bullshit, don't oil companies screen their tanker captains for drunk-driving violations? How'd they manage to miss this asshole's record? Or, more reprehensibly, had they known of his drinking but hired him anyway?

Gregg finally connects with Aaron one night by pay phone from the Sand Bar. The boy, at Peg's in Anchorage, tells his father how he'd been recruited off a tug to fill in for a seaman on the *Kuparuk* who'd trashed his back. How he was standing watch when the tanker struck the reef and got soaked to the skin by the crude oil that fountained overhead, raining back down onto the deck. How it's made him nauseous for days. He says he's been told he'll have to testify.

"Wait a minute," Gregg says. "Let me get this straight. You telling me you were *on* the tanker?" He should have stopped after those shots. His thinking is muddled.

"Yeah, I even talked to Captain Aengus once. Before—"

Gregg hears his son's voice catch. He's not going to cry now, is he? "Pull yourself together," he growls. Goddamn it, Aaron. When are you going to grow up and stop being such a puss?

7

As many of her coworkers at the hospital have done, Tessa uses accrued leave to take time off from work, causing supervisor Donna Wilkinson to grumble about people who shirk their duty. Elias and Minke never even see their father because the only time Daniel comes home now is to grab a few hours' sleep in the middle of the night.

Having learned that the kids had spent essentially her whole absence in Fairbanks next door with Carla, Tony, and the twins, Tess offers to care for Keith and Kevin after school, thereby freeing Tony to work on boom construction while Carla volunteers washing oiled birds. When Tess asks, her neighbor says she doesn't think Lee is volunteering at the bird center, unless it's at night.

"It's open at night, too?"

"Round the clock. Same with otter care."

Maybe Lee's doing something spill-related on a boat, then. Daniel had told her that he'd seen the deckhand at the radio station, and the mother wishes her friend would get in touch since it's not exactly convenient for Tess to bundle the kids into the car to drive all the way out to the remote cabin—especially if Lee's not even there. And with no phone, there's no way to know.

On Tuesday Tess takes Minke with her to buy groceries while Elias is at school. It's obvious Daniel hadn't done any shopping while she was gone, and now they're out of bread, milk, eggs, and anything fresh. She notices herself turn on the car radio before she even secures her daughter in the child safety seat and it occurs to her that KRBB has become her communications lifeline. No doubt the radio coverage proves indispensable to anyone else who's actually—or, like her, effectively—housebound. Tessa now realizes that, among other things, she's jealous of Daniel. His is no ordinary job, especially not under these extraordinary circumstances. Tracking down and making sense of oil spill events no doubt helps him manage the stress of the disaster, and in broadcasting the information, he assists the entire community. By helping others, he helps himself.

No fair, as Elias would say.

So, too, Carla and Tony are handling their distress by volunteering. Tess has never felt so isolated.

She buckles Minke into the seat of the shopping cart. The produce selection is dismal; the only fruit available at Crawford's Market are bruised bananas and dented apples. In the dairy section, Tess encounters Rosemary Mattox, wearing her newborn in a sling, and they both coo and cluck over each other's daughters.

"Daniel's on the radio nonstop," Rosemary says. "He's doing a great job."

Tess acknowledges the compliment. "But it's not official. He's still only half-time. And I'm staying home with this one because he's working so much." We're losing money, she thinks but doesn't say.

"No one's buying fish," Rosemary murmurs. "Dusty couldn't sell his black cod. None of them could." She glances at Tessa. "Fish and Game's already closed herring and halibut. Now they're saying they'll probably cancel salmon, too." Her eyes pool and she ducks her head as if to readjust the sleeping baby.

Tess stares at the other mother. Of course, fishermen stand to lose the most from the oil spill. After all, if this event has turned her and Daniel's lives upside-down, how much more traumatic must it be for those families who depend on the ocean for their livelihood? Unlike Tessa's own ambivalent relationship with nursing, for example, fishing has always seemed to be more than mere occupation to people like Dusty Mattox, Gregg Anderson, and even Lee, for that matter. Fishing isn't just something you do, she realizes; it's who you are. She touches Rosemary on the sleeve as the other woman rolls her shopping cart away.

Minke sleeps hard by the time they reach home. Reluctant to wake her, Tess parks in front of the house, where she can watch the slumbering child from the living room windows. Turning off the engine, she sits listening to the car radio for a moment. Someone who keeps track of these things has pronounced the Mammoth *Kuparuk* the largest oil spill in North America.

This time, when she hears the appeal for volunteers to help clean otters, Tess pictures the pelt that's part of a hands-on display at the Pioneers' Museum, along with skins from a coyote, a wolf, and a beaver. The otter fur is far and away the thickest and softest, which amply conveys to anyone who touches it why Russian and American traders had once hunted these animals to the verge of extinction.

She thinks of the personable otters she, Lee, and Jackie had seen while kayaking around Kittiwake Ledge last spring. Some of the sea mammal mothers, floating on their backs, clutched babies to their chests—exactly the way Tess has nestled her own and her friends' infants.

Lee's sure to be taking the spill hard. She likes to say that when Gunther moved her along with his second family from Indiana to Anchorage, it was the best thing that could have happened. And Tess knows Lee doesn't just mean because it put her out of reach of those predatory boy-uncles who'd terrorized her childhood. Lee's love for wild places and creatures becomes apparent to anyone who spends any time with her. Look at her choice to live so far from town—no running water, no electricity. No phone.

Tess sighs. She'd bet good money that Lee's volunteering at more than one activity. Oil recovery by day and bird washing at night? She herself had better start thinking of some way to pitch in, or she's going be consumed by her resentment of Daniel. The moment she considers the possibility of caring for sea otters, Tess knows it's perfect. If she could do so, in fact, she'd drive to the high school immediately and start tending the furry, childlike animals without further delay.

Instead, she carries groceries into the kitchen, where the red light blinks insistently on the answering machine. Four messages. Daniel has left yet another clipped recording that he won't be home for supper and will work late. Her mom sounds unnerved, insisting that Tessa call her back right away. Her neighbor Carla wonders if the twins can spend the night; a planeful of oiled birds are en route and the center has asked her to stay late. Finally, Jackie, calling from Anchorage, wants to know if they have any news of Lee. Her usually modulated voice, that of the trained psychologist, sounds strained as she explains that she hasn't been able to talk to her ex-lover since before the spill and wants to make sure Lee's okay.

Tess calls her neighbor first, glad to repay the debt of childcare. As usual these days, there's no answer next door, so she leaves a message assuring Carla and Tony that the boys can sleep over.

Bracing herself for her mother's latest petition to have their only grandkids brought to Anchorage, Tessa's surprised and somewhat alarmed to find her mom in tears. "Have you seen the news?" the older woman sniffles.

"What happened?"

"They're picketing the Mammoth Petroleum building downtown!"

"Who is?"

"Everyone! Protesters. They're accusing the company of double dealing, carrying signs with blown-up photos of oiled birds and otters that say 'Right to Life!' Posters with skulls and crossbones. I'm worried about your dad," her mother weeps.

"Why?"

"They might come after him!"

"Who?"

"These people. These fanatics."

"But why would they?"

"Because he worked for Mammoth," her mom shrills, as if Tess is being unfathomably dense.

"He's retired."

"I know, but people have gone crazy. Suddenly the petroleum industry is the Evil Empire. Are the children safe?"

"Mom, Selby isn't like Anchorage."

"*Anchorage* isn't like Anchorage right now!"

When she finally calms her mother and hangs up the phone, Tess replays the conversation in her mind. Like many other Alaska families she knows, construction of the Pipeline had brought Tessa's family north in the first place, when Mammoth Petroleum hired her father to work as a teamster in Prudhoe Bay. He and her mom had driven them from Minnesota to Alaska in a Vista Cruiser, the two adults taking turns driving while Tessa and Susie and Wendell fought for window seats in the back, the cargo space of the station wagon stuffed with the family's most indispensable household goods because they'd been told that whatever they shipped would take at least two months to arrive.

Everyone's always trumpeting the fact that petroleum-related jobs doubled the population of the state in the seventies. The Pipeline was under construction throughout her high-school years, as Mammoth flew Tess's father, like many of her new friends' fathers (and an occasional mother), to the North Slope to work two-week rotations followed by two weeks off. The oil company made it very worthwhile for their employees: good pay, excellent benefits, generous bonuses, and time off. And pensions, she presumes, for although her dad has long since stopped working, her parents still live in their spacious home on Anchorage's upscale Hillside, along with many other well-to-do people connected to the petroleum industry.

Remembering the full-page newspaper photo of the *Kuparuk* surrounded by its expanse of black oil, snow-covered mountains forming a dramatic backdrop, Tess realizes the aerial shot must be recognizable the world over by now. She recalls her parents boasting that construction of the eight-hundred-mile Pipeline was a feat on par with the building of China's Great Wall or Egypt's pyramids. The state has used royalties from the sale of North Slope crude to erect all kinds of public buildings—performance halls, libraries, and no-expenses-spared schools. Like Selby's new high school, in fact, opened just last year. Because it's by far the town's largest, most well-appointed structure, locals have dubbed it the Taj Mahal.

And isn't Alaska the only state without an income tax? Instead of paying out, every resident receives an annual dividend derived from interest earned on the investment of oil revenues. She and Daniel had used their own first Permanent Fund Dividends to help make a down payment on this very house, and every fall they bank the children's checks for their eventual college educations. It seems to her that pretty much everyone in the forty-ninth state has benefited from oil development.

Until now?

Picturing again the bird's-eye photo of the accident, Tess imagines the immense dark blot surrounding the grounded tanker as a kind of Rorschach test: what does it say about the civilization that regularly allows such things to happen?

She glances out the window to make sure Minke's still sleeping and begins to fold the clean laundry she'd earlier heaped on the futon couch. Again, she considers looking for Lee, but isn't sure where to start. Tess must be the only able-bodied person in Selby who's not volunteering on the spill. Once the clothes are folded, she calls Anchorage to leave a message on Jackie's phone that Daniel has seen Lee, that she seemed okay, and that they will try to get a message to her to call Jackie. It's obvious the two women still care for each other. Why don't they just get back together and be done with it?

Elias, Keith, and Kevin burst noisily through the kitchen door, home from school. Tess makes a big bowl of popcorn and pours three cups of orange juice, telling the boys to play in the yard when they finish their snack.

When she sees Minke stirring in her car seat, Tess brings the toddler into the house and feeds her. She puts together two cheese sandwiches and some carrot sticks for Daniel. Then she gets all four kids into the car and drives the short distance to the radio station, listening to what has become her husband's hourly "Oil Spill Update." Daniel has acquired fluency in a new language: "critical incident," "emulsification," "leading edge." Elias listens thoughtfully; Tess thinks their son must understand something of the catastrophe.

"Papa's excited," he says.

"He sure is," she agrees, telling the boys to stay in the car and watch Minke. "I'll be back in a flash." A Daniel-ism.

Momentarily disoriented by the changes to KRBB's front room, the jumble of extra desks and phones, all of them monitored by locals who must be volunteering, Tess finds Tamara now working in the far corner.

"Congratulations, Tam," she says. "Sorry I missed your big day."

The worker smiles thinly. "Thanks."

Tessa looks around the room, shaking her head. "I can't believe this. Can you?"

"Actually, it's starting to feel normal. Isn't that weird?" The phone on her desk rings, so Tamara picks up the receiver, pointing Tess to the production studio, with its large, soundproof window, the speakers throughout the building carrying the broadcast that emanates from the enclosed chamber.

Daniel stands with his back to the glass, wearing what look like over-sized headphones, speaking into a microphone suspended from the ceiling on an adjustable arm. Although he clutches a notepad, he never so much as glances at it. Instead, he gesticulates with both hands despite the fact that no one in radio-land will ever see his forceful gestures.

She can hear the hoarse fatigue in his voice as he describes the imminent approach of the "black tide," but also the unmistakable thrill, just as Elias had remarked in the car. This crisis, worrisome as it is, invigorates him. It turns him on. There's no other way to describe it.

Tessa glances over her shoulder to see if anyone else has observed this. She feels like a voyeur, as though she's witnessing something illicit or indecent. Finally, she turns away, leaving the food with Tamara to give to Daniel later. Malcolm had damn well better pay him for all this overtime. And she had best stop waiting for her husband to check in. Time to make some family decisions herself.

Selby gets greased on day six. Gregg notices that since the town is also the first oiled location that's connected by road to Anchorage, the "critical incident" now assumes heightened status.

Just hours before the spill arrives to obliterate Selby's shoreline, Mammoth Petroleum announces the hiring of unskilled workers for beach cleanup, "effective immediately." Stipulating a flat rate of twenty dollars an hour, the corporation will additionally provide all-you-can-eat hot meals to all workers. The petroleum giant looks to charter boats large enough to house cleanup personnel, as well as smaller vessels to transport said workers to remote beaches. It offers to pay hundreds of dollars a day in leasing fees.

When Gregg catches himself estimating what he would clear if he were to lease the *Pegasus* to the oil company, he thinks, Over my dead body. But some of the Herring Cove fleet members apply for the jobs. Matt Jones gets a contract for the *Coelacanth*. "What else can I do?" he apologizes to Gregg. "I got kids to feed."

Gregg shrugs. No comment. He considers with rancor Mammoth Petroleum's cheesy motto. "Energizing our lives" is right, you mother-fuckers. First you destroy the place we live and wipe out our livelihood, then you offer to pay us so much you hope we won't notice.

Beaches contaminated overnight, the bodies of oiled birds and all manner of dead or dying marine life now begin to wash ashore below town. The state posts notices along the waterfront: "Toxic Substance!" "Health Hazard!" But ravens and foxes, seals and ospreys can't read, Gregg thinks. Just as you can't remove this much toxicity from the environment, so too you can't prevent critters—be they finned, furred, or feathered—from coming into contact with it, ingesting it. What scientists refer to as "opportunistic feeders" are feasting on the unprecedented abundance of tainted food, sickening themselves in turn. And a sick animal is tantamount to a dead animal, since it's one that can no longer fend for itself.

At what point in the cycle does the oil stop being poisonous? Gregg wants to know. What happens to a coyote that eats, let's say, a mink or marten that's been feeding on oiled clams or mussels?

He notices that the petroleum corporation seems to have anticipated every eventuality, hiring what they call "beach patrol" personnel whose job it is to walk the Selby shoreline around the clock and, armed with flares and air horns, try to scare away birds and animals scavenging the remains of the spill-killed. Twenty bucks an hour. It has by now been projected that the crude oil will travel at least fifteen hundred miles, contaminating as much Alaska shoreline as the coasts of Washington, Oregon, and California combined. How many beach patrollers would it take to monitor that entire length of rugged coastline? Gregg knows it can't be done, but observes that Mammoth Petroleum does an excellent job pretending that it can.

When the spill buries Selby's beaches in a foot and a half of toxic mud, even those reticent by nature, the most law-abiding of citizens, storm the oil company's offices in the new hotel to demand action and accountability. As if anticipating the outcry, the petroleum giant promptly announces a "town-hall meeting," to be held that evening at the Taj Mahal.

It may be the first known instance in the history of the small fishing town that an audience arrives not only on time but actually in advance of a scheduled event. When Gregg enters the high-school auditorium at quarter to eight, the crowd's already standing room only, so he joins those sardined into the aisles.

Two conference tables have been butted end to end across the stage, nine metal folding chairs behind them awaiting occupants. Half a dozen microphones in squat metal stands have been set out on the tabletop, their black wires snaking across each other.

The *Pegasus* skipper takes in the scene. No doubt about it; for a place like this, peopled as it is by self-sufficient personalities who want nothing more than to be left alone, it's a historic turnout: parents and infants; grandparents and teenagers; snowy-haired pioneers and tie-dyed hippies; boat builders, deckhands, cannery workers; laborers, business owners, store clerks; women with hairdos, punks with tattoos; Seventh Day Adventists, Latter Day Saints, Jehovah's Witnesses, Methodists, Lutherans, Baptists, Episcopalians, Catholics, adherents of who-knows-what belief systems, and those like Gregg who haven't set foot in a house of worship for years. Those who catch, hunt, grow, and gather their own food and those who routinely buy groceries at the Super Duper. The well-to-do and those down on their luck; military veterans like himself and those who burned their draft cards in the sixties. Really, the only ones missing are those serving in the Middle East, he decides. The oil spill's an equal-opportunity debacle.

Gregg even sees a contingent of villagers, many of the women wearing colorful *kuspuks*. He's never known more than one or two Natives to attend a public event in Selby before. Are Wassily and Marie here?

Doorways filled, people spill into corridors, blocking exits. Robert Morse, chief of Selby's all-volunteer fire department, talks into a walkie-talkie as he patrols the area below the stage. Gregg imagines Rob's torn between the risks posed by the overcrowded space and everyone's right to learn firsthand what's coming at them.

The skipper spots his deckhand at the back of the auditorium. Lee still looks shell-shocked, hollow-eyed, and spooked. Thank God the place is so crowded there's no possibility of her making her way to him. It shames him to think of how hard he'd worked her . . . for nothing.

Everywhere he turns, he sees the same tight-lipped expressions: furrowed foreheads, haunted eyes. There's not a single face that doesn't register alarm. Although people talk animatedly with one another, their passion is that of anxiety, not pleasure. In fact, the atmosphere reminds him of the aftermath of a firefight. Voices charged with the desperation of those who find themselves pinned down without backup.

Mayday. Mayday.

This is one of those defining moments, like JFK's assassination. What were you doing when you heard the news? Life before and life after the spill. It's like finding out that your sister's been shot in a hunting accident and will never walk again. Or learning that the bottom has dropped out of your marriage, your wife's leaving town and taking your son with her.

Reporters and journalists jostle for space before the stage. Gregg spots the familiar logos of the three national networks on the large black TV cameras perched atop tall tripods, but recognizes only KRBB's Daniel Wolff and Malcolm Bradbury in the pool of media types. The two men, both wearing headsets, have arranged their equipment on the left apron of the stage, positioning themselves where they can make necessary calibrations. No doubt Wolff's really getting off on the live feed.

Shortly after the hour, eight somber strangers make their way onto the stage, four men from either side, as if choreographed. The last to emerge from stage right wheels before him a large map of southcentral Alaska taped to a portable blackboard. Once he has it where he wants it, the middle-aged man ducks back behind the curtain to retrieve an aluminum display easel fitted with an oversized tablet.

The ninth figure, a silver-haired gent wearing an expensively tailored suit and fancy tie (a sight approximately as common in these parts as a passenger pigeon) enters from stage left and remains standing behind the center chair, while the other eight men silently seat themselves on either side of him. The Dapper Dan pats his hair once before extracting a microphone from its stand. The audience settles down immediately.

The speaker's tall, tanned, and distinguished looking. "Good evening, ladies and gentlemen. Thank you all for coming out." His voice contains the slightest hint of a Southern drawl, and he's clearly practiced at public speaking, Gregg observes, as their emcee regards the audience steadily and enunciates with care. "My name is Dean Carson. I reside in Houston, Texas. A few days ago, the Mammoth Petroleum Corporation asked me if I'd be willing to travel north to work with you all in responding to this unfortunate accident. I've visited Alaska twice before, so I know how special your state is. Frankly, I jumped at the chance."

Carson smiles and pauses briefly, as if he hopes his remarks will ingratiate him with the crowd, but the audience is noticeably impatient. This dude would be well cast as the kindly but iron-willed grandfather in a family film, Gregg thinks. He also notices that Dean Carson has all the trappings of a successful politician: poised, well-groomed, articulate. He is, in short, precisely the polished sort that many in Selby are most predisposed to mistrust.

Carson explains that Mammoth Petroleum has arranged this town-hall meeting in an effort to inform coastal residents as to what has already transpired, as well as the best "guesstimates" for what the future holds. His calculated folksiness has many in the audience shifting with irritation.

Carson proceeds to introduce the men flanking him, and each stands as his agency affiliation is announced. All of the federal employees, in addition to wearing uniforms, are clean-shaven like Carson: the Coastie in his snappy dress blues, Fish and Fur in its usual lackluster beige and brown, and NOAA in the trademark charcoal-gray *Romper Room* jumpsuit. In contrast, the four state workers on Carson's left all sport some degree of facial hair. Likewise casual in dress, the Alaska employees' preferred attire is variations on the theme of flannel shirt, blue jeans, and leather belt with oversized buckle.

As the eight men stare straight ahead, poker-faced, Gregg comprehends what he should have realized from the get-go, which is that this is nothing more than a staged performance. Mammoth Petroleum has pressed these federal and state reps into service and orchestrated the evening with one goal in mind: to lend credibility to its public relations effort.

Why hadn't the Coast Guard or the governor's office convened the gathering?

Gregg reconsiders the men seated behind the tables. Of course they're all *kass'aqs*, all white. Some things never change. As different as those of us in Selby may be from one another, we still have more in common with each other than we do with any of these bureaucrats. This isn't just the locale of some "freak event," a work-related posting. It's where we live, where we've chosen to put down roots and raise families. This is our home.

And we're not the kind of people who answer to The Man—whether that's Uncle Sam, the governor, or some corporate CEO. We choose self-employment; we take pride in working for ourselves. No, Gregg decides, those in the audience and this panel of experts who won't look us in the eye are as different from one another as oil and water.

8

Lee regards the lineup of seated figures on the high-school stage from her post against the back wall. Why all men and why all Caucasian? Surely the Coast Guard has some women in its ranks, one or two minority officers? The state agencies must likewise employ a mix of people. Probably in this age of affirmative action even the petroleum company employs a few dark-skinned and/or female managers, so how come there isn't a single Alaska Native up there?

The maleness and whiteness of the panel make Lee question how sexism and racism might relate to the fact of the oil spill itself. It's the kind of thing Jackie would notice, and if she were here, Lee's ex would no doubt have already worked out the answer.

Lee's spent pretty much every waking moment washing otters, beating a retreat to her secluded cabin to sleep. As much as she craves information about the disaster, she's also come to dread it because the news so far associated with the tanker grounding—the captain's known alcoholism, the cuts in crew sizes, and the absence of a real-life contingency plan—make her heartsick. How dare Big Business and government collude in jeopardizing the safety and sanctity of all the astonishing creatures who depend on the ocean for life!

Last night, she'd unplugged the radio in her cabin, stowing it under the sink. Sure, it's important to stay informed, but you have to safeguard your sanity, too, so Lee's ambivalent about attending this event at all. She keeps to herself at the rear of the auditorium, close to an exit.

"There you have it," the nattily dressed Mammoth Petroleum spokesman says in his jocular way, concluding his introductions. "These fellows comprise the Mammoth *Kuparuk* Critical Incident Command team. Let's give them a hand." Few join in his applause, however. The mood of the audience is one of skepticism, if not outright mistrust.

Recovering smoothly, Dean Carson says, "We'd appreciate it if you could save your questions for the end of the presentation. Now, let's bring y'all up to date on this thing."

A husky female voice—Lee recognizes it as Rosie Jackson's—yells from the middle of the large room: "It's not a 'thing.' It's an environmental holocaust. The worst oil spill in North America!"

This gets to Mr. Carson. His eyes narrow for just a second before he wills them back to neutrality. He's going to have a hard sell, Lee thinks, and indeed, their host takes a seat, pushing the microphone across the table to the National Oceanic and Atmospheric Administration scientist, who rises. The tall, curly-haired man wears his agency's uniform, a dark-gray jumpsuit giving him the unfortunate appearance of a handyman. The NOAA spokesman seems to be the only one besides the oil company rep who looks even remotely comfortable on stage, but unlike Dean Carson he never smiles.

Lanky and loose-limbed, NOAA draws a jumbo-sized black marker from his breast pocket as he approaches the map that's taped to the portable blackboard. Uncapping the fat felt-tipped pen, he proceeds to shade the blue area of the chart from now-infamous Montague Reef westward to Selby and on toward Port Clark. "This designates the area of the spill so far," he says, X-ing and striping the paper with energetic black strokes, like a kid going to town on a coloring project. He speaks of "prevailing longshore currents," the government's "overflights" and "groundtruthing" efforts. When pressed by audience members, he declines to offer predictions as to how far the crude petroleum will ultimately travel. "It's impossible to say," he states.

"Is it *possible* it'll reach the Chain?" a voice calls out.

NOAA hesitates. "It's possible," he finally admits, and the crowd's agitation escalates in contemplation of the black tide washing ashore as far away as the distant Aleutians. "At this point," the scientist resumes when the clamor subsides, "the light ends of the hydrocarbons—the toxic components of crude oil—have all evaporated. The oil has largely emulsified with ocean water into what we call 'mousse.' Some of you have seen it; it's viscous, and sometimes it's got fucus or popweed mixed in. We estimate the mousse from this particular spill to be composed of as much as eighty percent seawater."

"This particular spill." The phrase jolts Lee, who until now has not considered the occurrence of other oil spills, even though they've been well chronicled over the years. Of course the Mammoth *Kuparuk* is not the first such accident in history, which means only that many other people and creatures—those inhabiting the coastal zones of the world—have likewise had their lives upended. She wonders what the victims of past oil spills now make of this one.

The NOAA scientist continues his explanation, wielding his specialized vocabulary, the effect of which both numbs and perplexes. Like his use of the word "mousse," as if calling crude oil mixed with seawater after some dessert will make the fact of it more palatable?

At first Lee has trouble grasping what this intense specialist seems at pains to explain: that the crude oil has emulsified with seawater to five times its original volume, thereby increasing exponentially. Does this mean that instead of twelve million gallons, the spill now measures closer to sixty million? She notices that others in the audience seem equally bewildered, whispering amongst themselves.

"One last thing," NOAA concludes in a loud, authoritative voice. "I know there's been a lot of concern about the oil sinking as it weathers and possibly contaminating the seafloor. You don't have to worry about that. It has been demonstrated conclusively that crude petroleum *does not sink.*" And with that declaration, he returns to his seat.

Again a voice calls out from the audience. "If the oil doesn't sink, then why has bottom-fishing been suspended until further notice?"

Some of the men on stage visibly stiffen, but remain expressionless and mute. Drawing the mike to himself while still seated, Dean Carson proceeds into a recap of the chronology of the incident, stating that the flow of oil from the tanker was stanched by day three and declaring that there has been "excellent containment" from the beginning. Excellent containment? Lee remembers motoring home through the endless manure-like slime. She pictures Selby's beaches, now deep in toxic muck. By what stretch of the imagination has the oil spill been "contained"? Two of the state reps confer with one another animatedly as the audience grows restless again.

Carson announces that the Mammoth Petroleum Corporation's cleanup effort has so far "recovered" two thousand gallons of oil, asserting that "all of your spawning areas and critical habitats have been cordoned off with either absorbent or deflective boom." He smiles at his audience like a benevolent patron. "Your salmon are safe."

At that, the crowd erupts, those who aren't already standing in the aisles leaping to their feet. Everyone protests at once, eventually quieting enough to let Willy Draper become their spokesman. The NOAA scientist extricates a microphone, bringing it to the front of the stage while Willy threads his way forward.

"Just for your information, Mr. Carson," the balding city council member says, grasping the mike, "the salmon mean a lot to us, it's true. But there are plenty of other wild creatures that live in these waters and along these shores. You people are not even close to protecting all the important habitat because all the habitat is important."

The audience applauds loudly and long. "Most of the protection we do have so far is due to the hard work of local citizens using their own money, their own boats, and their own equipment," Willy continues. "Not to mention their own time and initiative."

More applause and foot-stamping. The hooting and cheering evolve into a standing ovation for the log-boom builders, and several minutes pass before order is restored enough for Willy to speak again. "What little premanufactured boom *is* out there has all come from private sources. We still haven't gotten any of the boom you—or the state—promised us because, well, Norway's a long ways away." His until now evenly tempered delivery trembles with feeling. "And you've only sectioned off the areas that biologists could agree on. What about all the other beautiful"—Willy pronounces the word as two: *beauty-full*—"places? What about all the other wild creatures—not just salmon—that deserve protection?"

The theater has grown quiet. Willy bows his head before raising it to regard Carson directly. "You must have seen by now what the rest of us are seeing, which is that nothing—no amount of boom or anything else—can protect the coastline from this stuff." He takes a breath. "We'd just feel better if you'd quit trying to make it sound like it's no big deal."

Carson listens attentively, but offers no reply.

Gregg steps awkwardly onto the armrest of an aisle seat, gripping Chuck Naylor's shoulder for balance. Lee's skipper points accusingly with his free hand at the Mammoth rep. She wonders if his fingers are still stained with oil from Beauty Bay. "Most of your boom is worthless. The tides are too high. Half the time, it's not even *in* the water." Gregg's voice is taut with anger, his index finger punctuating his remarks. "Fly out there in your company's fancy chopper. See for yourself." Her boss looks like he wants to jab holes in Carson's body, and Lee remembers him shoving the boat-cleaning kid in the harbor, grabbing her neck in a chokehold. His behavior makes her uneasy; she senses she's not the only one who finds Gregg's undisguised hostility a little out of line and breathes more easily when he steps down from his perch.

Carson's expression remains unreadable. When the crowd grows quiet again, he clears his throat to speak, but someone yells, "Quit patting yourselves on the back and clean up your mess!"

More catcalls and jeers.

Carson makes his way to the easel at the side of the stage and lifts the cover on the pad of poster paper, flipping it behind the rest of the tablet to reveal a pie chart, a circle divided into three unequal wedges. He explains that the smallest sliver represents the percentage of crude oil that has been "retrieved." The next largest wedge is the percentage estimated to have evaporated. He doesn't say so outright, but Carson's words imply that the oil company itself is responsible for both outcomes.

Lissa James, who teaches kindergarten at Mears Elementary, rises from her seat. "But isn't it true that the fishermen have brought in many times more oil than you have?"

After another round of hooting and applause, Lee notices Lawrence Michelson crouching beside KRBB's broadcasting equipment on the stage apron. Larry wears black denim logger's trousers, steel-toed boots, and red suspenders over a faded green t-shirt. When he stands, his barrel chest and Popeye forearms bulge like a bodybuilder's even though the only muscle sculpting he's ever pursued is his work as a longshoreman. The men behind the conference tables stir uncertainly at his proximity.

Larry doesn't wait to be acknowledged. He addresses both the panelists and the audience, cupping his hands around his mouth to form a megaphone. "And isn't it true, Mr. Carson, that your background with Mammoth Petroleum lies exclusively in public relations?"

Carson hesitates before responding. "That's right. Now, if you don't mind, we'd like to continue." He turns back to the easel.

But Larry is not so easily dismissed. He pivots toward the audience, raising his voice. "It's also a matter of public record that our master of ceremonies officially *retired* from the Mammoth Corporation three years ago. Which means he has no decision-making authority and will most likely rotate out of here in a couple of weeks. To be replaced by another public relations flack. And so on." Larry gestures for silence. "No skin off *his* nose what happens to *us*."

"There's a possibility I'll be back." You can tell Carson immediately regrets rising to Larry's bait; he makes a delayed, self-conscious gesture with his hand as of shooing away a fly.

The longshoreman persists. "Old Dean-O here's an expert at smoothing ruffled feathers, and he should be. He's got the best training money can buy." The audience rumbles. "I hope you all appreciate as much as I do," Larry now declaims, "that the Mammoth Petroleum Corporation, number two on the Fortune 500, doesn't see fit to send us someone empowered to make operations decisions. To them, Selby's just a speck on the map and Alaska's still the far, frozen north." People rise noisily to their feet again. "Don't let him sell you a snow job!" Larry finishes, springing neatly off the stage.

Carson turns his back on the audience to appeal to his panel of experts, so Lee can't read his expression. Will he have the decency to come clean about his role? Probably not, she guesses, since isn't that exactly what public relations seeks to do, maintain appearances?

Too much talk; way too little action. She should have known this would be an exercise in frustration. Chest throbbing, Lee slips out of the building, retrieving her old three-speed bicycle from the rack behind the school. Her stomach protests the odor of raw petroleum wafting from Driftwood Beach. All she really wants to do is find Tess, who *must* be back from Fairbanks by now, and who she guesses will be home with the kids since Daniel's inside covering this spectacle. Mounting her bike, she sets off in the direction of their house before squeezing the squeaky hand brakes abruptly. If she goes to Tess, Lee will undoubtedly break down. They both will. And if there's one thing Gunther and Weezie had taught her—by example if not by word—it is not to cry over spilled milk. Or spilled oil. Tears are nothing but an indulgence, a waste of time. So instead of riding into town in search of her friend, Lee pedals around the corner of the school to the entrance of the otter center. Thank God there are things she and others *can* do, direct actions they can take to make a difference. In fact, the spontaneous upwelling of volunteerism that's arisen so naturally in response to the disaster is the only thing right now that does offer relief from the relentless devastation of the spill.

"Are all your tanker captains drunks?" Frank Derman yells at Dean Carson. From his vantage point beside KRBB's equipment, Daniel sees that the question from the Crawford's Market owner catches the Mammoth Petroleum rep off guard.

The remark triggers others from angry audience members: "Why'd you hire him?"

"Where are you hiding him?"

"Why haven't you fired him?"

"How'd you lose him?"

The antagonism in the theater spreads like a brush fire. This must be how riots start, Daniel thinks. He pictures Gregg Anderson, a sizable man, teetering on an armrest just moments ago, doing his best to intimidate Dean Carson. Good thing the police and fire department have a presence here. Left to their own devices, men like the *Pegasus* skipper might actually try to storm the stage. As for the public condemnation of Captain Richard Aengus, whatever happened to trial by jury? Doesn't the tanker captain deserve his day in court like anyone else?

Carson hastily turns the presentation over to the state employees. It takes a while for the crowd to settle and Daniel decides people resume their seats only because they still trust their fellow Alaskans to level with them.

The Fish and Game biologist, a graying man who wears wire-rimmed spectacles, rises slowly to his feet and agrees that the boom is not working out as his agency would like: "We tried to boom Kittiwake Ledge, but the tides tore everything apart." He explains the new plan, which they'll execute in conjunction with Fish and Wildlife—acknowledging with a nod his USFWS counterpart at the adjoining table—stationing teams of "boom monitors" in the most critical locations within the next twenty-four hours in order to manually reset the equipment when it fails.

"It's still too early to predict what long-term effect the spill's going to have on our fisheries, but there's a growing perception Outside that *all* Alaska seafood is tainted." The biologist pauses. "You and I know it's ridiculous, but if that's public perception, it doesn't matter whether it's true or not." Good point. Daniel scratches a note to himself on his stenographer's pad, and the audience stirs as people comprehend the dire implications of the statement.

"What about fry emergence?" someone calls. The reporter sees a quizzical expression flit across Dean Carson's face before the Mammoth spokesman can mask his ignorance.

The scientist shakes his head tiredly. "We don't know. We just don't have any data." He explains that the spill has occurred at the height of the emergence of newly hatched salmon fry from streambeds and hatcheries into the ocean. And, he reminds the audience, adult salmon are already returning to spawn. "We do know that the oil is wiping out plankton, so it seems reasonable to conclude that large numbers of fry and smolt will either die outright from toxicity or else starve to death."

Of those salmon that do manage to survive, the elderly biologist continues, no one knows what effect the petroleum will have on the young fishes' ability to imprint their streams of origin, which in turn will determine their capacity as adults to find their way back to reproduce in the future. He says that the only known study of this effect documents the return of mature Atlantic salmon to spawn beneath a fuel dock in Massachusetts. Listeners laugh, until they realize he has simply stated a fact.

The Department of Environmental Conservation representative pulls one of the microphones from its stand. Avoiding Dean Carson's gaze, the long-necked ecologist clears his throat nervously. "I need to correct an earlier misrepresentation: the business about the flow of oil from the *Kuparuk* being stanched by day three." Coughing again, the gawky redhead appears to gain confidence. "We conduct overflights of the tanker twice a day, and I'd just like to say, for the record, that we're still documenting leakage." He finally risks a glance at Carson. "We've got it on video."

The Mammoth Petroleum publicist ignores him, instead introducing the ramrod-stiff Coast Guard lieutenant in his crisply pressed blue uniform, officer's hat set carefully on the table before him.

Just then, there's a commotion at the back of the auditorium. Daniel cranes his neck to see Terri Cronin, one of Selby's three women skippers, pushing through the double doors in foul-weather gear and knee-high Xtratufs, a length of gummy, greasy chain and a filthy angular metal contraption slung over her shoulder. Even as he realizes she's carrying an anchor, Daniel wonders if Dean Carson knows what it is. The crowd in the aisle presses awkwardly to either side to clear a path for the woman fisherman and her hardware, TV cameramen aiming their lenses to record her passage to the stage.

A big woman who's never been known for her delicacy, Terri lobbies tirelessly on behalf of commercial fishing interests at Selby city council meetings. She mounts the stairs to stand before the seated men, dropping her burden in a jangle of metal on metal. The DEC rep extends his microphone to her, and the *Northwind* skipper points a tar-darkened hand at the NOAA scientist seated behind the table.

"You said the oil doesn't sink," Terri accuses him. "Then what the hell is this all over my Danforth?" It's the last straw; the crowd erupts.

As if on cue, the paunchy agent from the Alaska Division of Emergency Services rises in place, waving his arms overhead to get everyone's attention. "The state's accepting applications for disaster assistance," he says loudly into a mike. "Emergency loans, food vouchers, health care, counseling, whatever you need. We're working on a protocol to establish priority, but everyone's entitled to the help." He nods at Terri, who remains standing beside her soiled hardware, and declares, "We'll get you a new anchor."

Terri stares at the rumpled state worker as if he's demented. "I don't want a new anchor," she says, the fight draining from her voice. "I want the old ocean. The one we had before the spill."

Dean Carson glances at the Coast Guard officer, who briefly shakes his head. Leaving her gear behind, Terri descends the stairs and exits the auditorium, collecting pats on the back.

Carson beckons to the trim hawk-like man in the Western-style shirt and cowboy boots who sits at the far end of the feds' table and who has, until now, remained practically motionless. The visibly fit middle-aged man would be well suited for Special K breakfast cereal commercials, Daniel thinks, as the "incident commander" introduces himself.

Keith Tomashaw explains in a hard-edged voice that he's a firefighting specialist from the western Rocky Mountain region, hastily summoned along with his team of near-commandos to coordinate emergency response to the oil spill, since the government lacks anyone or anything better suited to the task. Speaking to Carson directly, this powerfully athletic man warns, "These people see right through your dog-and-pony show, Dean. They know your company has so far done little more than package an environmental and economic disaster into some kind of three-ring circus, with you as the ringmaster. Mammoth Petroleum's already written the oil spill off as a tax deduction." Tomashaw turns to the astonished audience. "Your best course is to demand an operations chief, someone empowered to get things done." That's all. The incident commander sits to stunned silence.

Contrary to acknowledging that he's just received a drubbing, Carson seems eager to take center stage again, like a game-show host who's saved the best for last. In fact, Daniel observes, his demeanor now might best be described as jaunty. Carson proceeds to outline Mammoth's claims process for those whose livelihoods have been "unfavorably affected by this thing."

Indeed, audience members begin to clamor for a different reason. Many demand to know how they can get hired by the petroleum corporation for beach patrol or oil spill cleanup. Fishermen want to know exactly how Mammoth plans to determine the amount of damages, since season forecasts often come in low.

"We're going to sit down with officers of your fishing organizations to figure out a formula that's fair. Don't worry; nobody will be short-changed," Carson says.

"I've got a radar and electronics business," Riley Winchester calls out. "Folks don't fish, they don't need me. What do *I* get?"

"You get to submit a claim," Carson says soothingly. "We'll make things right."

Pamela Leland raises her hand. "My work is hanging nets. If nobody fishes, they don't need me. Can I file a claim?" The coiffured net maker's voice cracks. "I'm a single mom."

"You can file a claim. We will make things right," the oil company rep repeats.

As individuals loudly demand to know how they can get their hands on a portion of Mammoth's wealth, Daniel recalls a Selbyite who'd slipped on the greasy floor of an Anchorage McDonald's a few years back, suffering a concussion. Those who knew Duncan liked to say, "The bad news is that he hit his head. The good news is that it happened at McDonald's." So, despite this being the largest spill in North America, do people think the silver lining is that it's Mammoth Petroleum's? It startles him to realize that the oil company has staged tonight's event in order to promote this very view.

Like a figure biblically empowered, Carson extends both arms to quiet the tumult. Clutching the microphone like Charlton Heston on Oscar night, he draws himself erect and announces, "Mammoth Petroleum pledges to compensate anyone and everyone who shows loss of income." Signaling for silence, Carson continues, "We've got jobs for all who want them, and we'll give preference to local hire." He's got people's attention now. "Just bring a piece of mail with your Selby address on it. Our office is open from eight until eight—seven days a week." The oil company rep pauses dramatically before proclaiming once again, "The Mammoth Petroleum Corporation pledges to make things right."

Daniel watches as old Stanley Nelson, one of Selby's original pioneers, maneuvers his walker to the front of the theater. Stanley bears the distinction of being the area's oldest surviving homesteader. He still lives in the log cabin he built on his allotment; unlike others, he hasn't subdivided or sold off his land. He hasn't moved into the Pioneer Home, nor has he left the state for Arizona, if only during the winter months. No, a half century later, with the help of some grandchildren, he continues to grow melt-in-your-mouth red-jacket potatoes every summer.

The old-timer has to be pushing ninety. If anyone alive can be said to embody Selby's frontier spirit, it would have to be Stanley Nelson.

Someone holds a microphone to the senior citizen's lips while he leans on his walker. "You should be ashamed of yourself, son," Stanley says forcefully, compelling the oil company's front man to pay attention.

Dean Carson cants his head and clasps his hands before his waist in a respectful posture.

Stanley Nelson's labored breathing rasps over the sound system. "I've been told your company's about as rich as Croesus, but that doesn't matter, does it?" He pauses. "You know as well as I do that no amount of money in the world can ever make this right."

The crowd begins to disperse. Dean Carson confers with the Coast Guard lieutenant. Daniel watches as some audience members, subdued and silent, file through the exits into the night like mourners departing a funeral. Others, talking animatedly, make their way to the front of the auditorium, looking for help—or is it handouts?

9

It doesn't take long for Tessa's anger at her husband to reach flashpoint. Not only does Daniel's obsessive preoccupation with the spill keep him from his family, she fumes, but it precludes her own participation in any volunteer activity, like washing otters, that might bring her some peace of mind. She's not sure which consequence she resents most. The night of the town-hall meeting, for example, she has no choice but to stay home and care for the kids.

Carla fills her in on the event the following morning.

"People were ready to use him for crab bait," Tessa's stocky neighbor reports with merriment of the public reception to the Mammoth Petroleum spokesman, whose name she misremembers as Dean Martin. The two women drink coffee and eat store-bought ginger snaps at the kitchen table while the children play outdoors. Sea breezes blow the acrid stench of the oil spill into the neighborhood. Fortunately, Tess thinks, the fumes are no longer toxic. Or are they?

When Carla describes the way people heckled the Mammoth spokesman about the missing tanker captain, Tess decides to keep her thoughts to herself. What a bunch of hypocrites. Everyone reaps the benefit of Alaska's North Slope petroleum, but the minute the oil industry stumbles, they get vicious. Clearly, Mammoth's doing its best to rectify the situation. The company so far has acted generously—there's no other word for it—in accepting responsibility for the accident.

"So anyway," the other mother says, licking her fingertips after inserting yet another whole cookie into her mouth, "I'm thinking Tony should claim loss of earnings from fishing."

"I thought he decided not to fish this year."

"He could have, though. Eric LaChapelle offered him a job."

"But he turned Eric down, didn't he?"

"Yeah, but Mammoth doesn't know that." Carla grins and reaches for another ginger snap.

Tessa stares at her neighbor, more stupefied than outraged.

The district superintendent announces his decision to close all the schools at week's end, which means that in Daniel's absence, Tess thinks bitterly, she might as well be a single parent. When Elias asks her once too often when his father will be home and she hears herself reply, "Damned if I know," she realizes it's time to let her parents have the children. She's always cutting Daniel slack. So what if his first wife died? So what if Elena was pregnant with what would have been his first child when that delivery driver plowed through a red light into the side of their car? Daniel's married to Tess now, and she, Elias, and Minke deserve better from him.

In the face of the school closures, Carla and Tony arrange for Kevin and Keith to stay with Tony's sister in Anchorage, so Carla offers to take Minke and Elias with her, too, when she flies up there with the twins. Tessa's parents will meet them at the airport. As much as she knows that her mother and father overindulge their only grandchildren and that this episode will no doubt become ammunition in her mother's arsenal of criticism aimed at Daniel's and her parenting, Tess also recognizes the arrangement as a godsend. The heck with the expense of the plane tickets; by now she cares a lot more about saving otters than she does about saving money by driving the kids to Anchorage herself.

So it is that the children make their first airplane trip unaccompanied by either parent. Not only that, but Tess can't wait for the kids to go. She never got around to cutting Elias's hair and figures she'll hear about it from her mom that night.

Now she can find Lee. Anyway, she's supposed to relay Jackie's increasingly anxious phone messages. Possibly Tess will change her mind about cleaning otters in favor of working side-by-side washing birds with her friend, so she drives directly from the public airport terminal to the Harbor Air hangar, where scores of volunteers have already washed over a thousand oiled birds, most of which have died anyway.

The airless hangar is oppressively hot, and the stench of wet feathers, raw petroleum, and overheated guano make Tess gag. Wow. The humid, fetid reality of bird rescue bears little resemblance to the romanticized version she's been playing in her mind.

They keep the building well heated, Norma Richards tells her, to protect the frightened creatures from hypothermia. And no, Lee's not among the volunteers. Norma says she hasn't seen the deckhand since before the spill.

Lee could be helping to assemble and deploy boom, or else she might be working with those trying to remove crude oil from the sea. After all, she likes working outdoors, enjoys physical labor, and is good with boats. But Tess will just have to look for Lee later. Right now, she needs more than anything else to roll up her own sleeves and pitch in, so she drives back across town to the high school.

As with bird cleaning, the otter-care effort appears well organized, especially considering how quickly it has all come together. In less than a week. Tessa finds the gymnasium, like the hangar, stuffy and dimly lit.

It takes her a moment to get her bearings before she begins picking her way across the exposed plumbing toward the lighted office. The drowsy wet otters look helpless and pathetic. When she notices a familiar figure working at one of the central washing stations, Tess doesn't at first recognize Lee. The younger woman's eyes are darkly hollowed from lack of sleep, she's lost weight, and when did she cut off all her hair? She looks like a cancer patient. Tess bursts into tears, crossing the room in anticipation of an emotional reunion.

But the first thing Lee does upon registering her presence is to flash a deer-in-the-headlights look of alarm. When she does finally meet Tessa's eyes, Lee's expression becomes fixed and unfriendly, almost hostile, as if she resents her friend for being there or is angry at her for some reason. She never even relaxes her grip on the animal's hind legs. It shocks Tess to realize how much weight Lee has lost. The word "zombie" comes to mind.

Many others have the same aspect, however. The mood in the gymnasium is, to put it mildly, subdued. "You haven't been by." Tess clears her throat when she hears herself whining like one of her children. "I thought for sure you'd be cleaning birds." Suddenly she's stricken with self-consciousness; everyone else is hard at work, everyone except her. She babbles on, unable to stop. "Some of them have pecked holes in themselves trying to get the oil off." To her great embarrassment, Tess starts to sob, at which point Lee asks a young guy with long sideburns to take her place, but not until he comes forward to firmly clasp the otter's bowlegged ankles does Lee step away from the animal. She stiffens when Tess tries to embrace her.

"Daniel's at the radio station all the time," his wife blubbers. "I sent the kids to my folks."

Lee leads her outside into the daylight, nodding in sympathy, but saying nothing.

Tessa blows her nose loudly into the clean blue bandana her friend has produced. "Have you talked to Jackie? She's trying to get hold of you."

"Not yet," Lee says.

"She calls our house every day."

The deckhand shakes her head, distracted. Molly Webster pokes her face out the fire door. "Can you take my place? I need to make a phone call."

"Just a sec." Lee turns back to Tess as Molly withdraws. "There's talk of Mammoth hiring all the volunteers. Boat owners, boom builders. Even the bird and otter people. They want to put everyone on their payroll."

"That's good." Tess blows her nose again. "Right?"

"No!" The younger woman frowns at her. "We have to be free agents. That's the whole point."

"I don't get it. Why not be paid?"

"Because they're making it about money. It has to be something given freely, from the heart."

Tess stops crying. "So why not pay those who want to be paid, and let everyone else work for free?"

Lee stares at her as if she can't believe what the wife and mother has just said.

"I don't see what the problem is," Tess repeats.

"If you don't see the problem," Lee says with surprising rancor, "then that's a problem."

"So explain it to me."

"Forget it. You want rain gear or not?"

The next morning, awakening alone again in a now-empty house, Tessa's smoldering anger at Daniel flares into flame. When she switches on the clock radio beside the bed, a gesture by now habitual, she hears him announce that the oil spill has reached Port Clark. Despite the gravity of the news, she shuts off the radio rather than continue to suffer the affront of his stentorian radio voice.

She showers, dresses, and drives to the station.

It's like a replay of her last visit except that her husband now records instead of broadcasting live. He works alone again in a small studio. Again he wears headphones, clutches papers in his hand that he never looks at, and once again he gestures passionately as he speaks into a suspended microphone. Also as before, he proves completely oblivious to her presence on the other side of the soundproof glass.

Despite her resentment, or because of it, Tess observes Daniel as if he were a stranger. His intensity, the way his whole body coalesces to transmit his words, is mesmerizing. No doubt he has a real gift for this work. Damn him.

Daniel suddenly stops talking, checking his notes. He appears unruffled, but the quality of focused concentration gives way to puzzlement. With a single motion, he slips the headphones from his ears to rest around his neck.

Tess waves her arm to catch his attention. When that doesn't work, she raps on the glass with the back of her hand, her gold wedding band making a tiny, tinny sound. It's unsettling, the way he peers out as if he doesn't recognize her. How is it that Tess has become so inconsequential to everyone? She watches the familiar crease between his graying eyebrows deepen. And then he smiles, the lopsided grin that usually wins her over.

But not today.

He holds up a hand, fingers spread, and looks at her inquiringly. Can Tess give him five minutes?

She leaves the building in a fury.

When he catches up with her just as she turns the key in the car ignition, she can tell he's pissed, too.

Daniel jerks open the car door and they glare at each other, neither one speaking.

"The kids are in Anchorage." Tess watches his face. "They left yesterday. Did you even notice?"

He's speechless for a moment. "You made that decision without talking to me?"

"You're never around to talk to!"

Daniel rubs his eyes. She can see he's upset by the unexpected news. "Where were you last week?" he asks.

"At a conference. But I was working."

"I'm working, too."

"At least I get paid for what I do."

He doesn't bother to dignify this with a reply, but what Tess says next, and the vehemence with which she says it, catches them both off guard. "You never mention the accident anymore, and do you realize you've never, ever, told me anything about Vietnam I couldn't read in a history book? It's like you lead a double life, Daniel. You act like you're having an affair with an oil spill!"

Her husband unclenches his jaw. "Okay," he says slowly. "Can we talk about it tonight?"

"At 3:00 a.m.?"

He ignores the jab.

"I won't be home," Tess says. When Daniel still doesn't reply, she realizes he probably thinks she's trying to retaliate. "I'll be washing otters."

He nods. "That's good."

"I cut back my hours at the hospital." Tessa studies his eyes, which remain guarded. "But I still have benefits, which is more than we can say about your job." She starts the car. Daniel closes her door firmly, and by the time she's backed out of the parking spot, he's already disappeared into the building. Fine, Tess thinks. Have it your way.

In the coming days, she functions as though on autopilot, initially spending twelve hours straight at the otter center, working split shifts at the hospital. Five of Tessa's nursing colleagues have made similar work arrangements—two, like her, to wash otters, three to care for birds. They all work reduced hours at the hospital in order to maximize their time with the wildlife. There's nowhere else Tess would rather be right now than tending sea otters; she has no qualms whatsoever about sending the children away.

Everyone in the community handles the crisis of the spill differently, she observes. Many, like Tess and her coworkers, have thrown themselves into volunteering. Some channel their emotions into protesting the oil industry, for all the good that will do. A number of Selby families—most of them wealthy—have fled town to escape the contamination. People do whatever they can to offset the upheaval in their lives, often forsaking their family's needs.

Some of the otter-center workers engage with one another nonstop, as if the disaster's an unprecedented opportunity to socialize. Some ricochet between extremes of emotion—joking one minute, weeping the next. A few, like Lee, have withdrawn, scarcely talking, their body language defying others to intrude on their private pity parties.

At first, Tess had rejoiced in the prospect of working with Lee, delighting when the center's coordinators assigned them to the same team for a particular shift. But the younger woman keeps her distance, and if Tess persists in attempts at conversation, Lee purses her lips disapprovingly, as if caring for otters is such sacred, somber work that you mustn't derive a shred of enjoyment from it. Is the deckhand's sense of loss more acute than others' because of her difficult childhood? Maybe she feels abnormally bereft because she and Jackie have so recently split up. Whatever the reason, Tess concludes, the younger woman's acting like a real jerk.

Wall-to-wall washing stations fill the gym, but the survival rate for otters improves only incrementally. As much as, if not more than, helping marine mammals, the activity provides necessary therapy for humans, too. This had definitely proven the case for Tess when she finally took hold of her first oiled animal and felt flooded with relief, like someone in free fall whose parachute then opens with a dramatic upsweep.

Perhaps it's for this reason that some volunteers care for otters or birds in the early morning before heading to their regular paying jobs, then return again after the workday to volunteer some more. Others, who can't themselves help with wildlife, can't build boom or scoop oil from the ocean, contribute however they can. People regularly drop off food, for example. Old Lu Chapman takes to baking large batches of peanut-butter brownies that her grade-school grandson proudly delivers to the otter center every afternoon, waiting quietly for the chipped china platter to empty so he can bear it away.

Many of the female otters are near-term pregnant due to the time of year. In fact, it's the preggos and the sickest animals that have shown up disproportionately in the treatment center because they're the ones that are easiest to capture. Tess works the dish soap extra gently into the fur of her first swollen-bellied otter. She can feel the fetus moving within, and her own uterus seems to contract in solidarity.

In the last days of school, children had made pictures of the oil spill, drawings now taped to the walls of the gym. Many of the portraits depict tearful seals, porpoises, whales, otters, and fish. Tess wonders if the crying motif is a case of one child hitting on a successful technique that everyone else then copied, or if maybe their teachers had suggested the theme. On the other hand, perhaps the young artists spontaneously arrived at the identical means of expression. What a sad thought.

Some of the kids have drawn sea creatures, real and imagined, swimming in translucent blue water. From the looks of it, the children had then taken black markers or crayons and smeared their own handiwork, to show the obliterating effects of the oil spill. Tessa doesn't like to think of them defacing their own drawings in this way—not because it isn't an accurate analogy of what's happening to the ocean, but because it is.

She's transfixed by a child's bold rendition of an erupting volcano, one of Elias's favorite themes. Amidst the belching flames and bright orange lava, stick figures of two adults and two children hurtle forth from a fiery cone. From the base of the mountain, a black stain hemorrhages into the surrounding turquoise waters. Various marine mammals float lifelessly, *X*'s replacing eyes. Indeed, the artwork is signed "Elias W." But when she mentions the picture to her son on the phone that evening, all he wants to talk about is his day spent at Alaska's largest shopping mall.

Riding her old three-speed bicycle to the otter center early one morning, Lee decides to swing by Deborah's Meadow in search of songbirds. Unlike sea- and shorebirds, the singers should be relatively unscathed. Shouldn't they?

Lee sees Nick Calhoun before he sees her. The wildlife biologist, too, wears binoculars around his neck and stands just inside the shadow of encircling birch and aspen. She wonders if she can slip away without drawing notice. Too late. He waves a hand in greeting as he approaches.

"Looks like we had the same idea," Nick says, gesturing to her half-raised Nikons. "Thought I heard a Townsend's warbler, but I couldn't scope it."

Lee's not sure what to say. Although they're barely acquainted, she thinks he looks gaunt and troubled.

"Did you know they winter in South America? In the rain forest," Nick continues, "which is getting cut down at some inconceivable rate to create pasture for cattle fated to become fast food."

At first, Lee assumes he's just making conversation. She remembers Daniel's radio interview with Nick, how dismayed the biologist had sounded as he told of the seabird mortalities at Ground Zero of the spill.

"Did you hear that Captain Aengus turned himself in to the authorities?" he asks her.

"No," Lee says. "Where is he?"

"San Diego. Says he's been with his daughter. They're bringing him back to Alaska."

Lee doesn't want to talk about the *Kuparuk* captain. Figuring she might as well look around since she's here, she raises her binoculars to glass the meadow.

"You know, people talk about bird migration as if there's a particular place each species calls home, but the fact is that birds are almost always on the move," Nick says. "Like the so-called Arctic tern," he adds, as if pleading. "True, it breeds in the Far North, but by December it's down in Antarctica. And hangs out there for several months, so it could just as well be considered the *Antarctic* tern, you know?"

Although he glances at her, Lee gets the feeling that Nick just needs to talk, and it doesn't really matter to whom. She wishes she hadn't decided to stop here and tries to think how she can most politely excuse herself.

"The point is," he explains in a tremulous voice, "for birds like terns that circumnavigate the globe, Alaska is a major source of food and nesting habitat. Even though our summer's short-lived, it offers round-the-clock sunlight, vegetation growing nonstop, insects hatching right and left. Good fuel for long-distance flyers, you know?" Nick peers into her eyes. "At least fifty million birds nest here every year."

"Fifty *million?*" Lee recalls the huge flocks of sandpipers and dunlins she's seen on the mudflats at the head of Rugged Bay in fall and spring: how one minute the ground just looks normal, and the next what you thought was beach detaches and lifts off, tens of thousands of individual birds soaring as a single entity, like an unbelievably large flying carpet. Right now, she realizes, those same mudflats are deep in spewage from the spill.

"And did you know that some species—like the bar-tailed godwit— fly continuously for up to a week, sometimes more if they hit bad weather?" Nick's voice cracks.

"Continuously? You mean they don't stop?"

"They *can't* stop. They fly here from Asia, and their plumage isn't waterproof, so if they try to alight on the ocean, they'll drown. They have to eat when they finally make landfall in Alaska, or else they'll die." He searches her face as if a fellow birder will surely understand his anguish. "They feed on herring spawn, on marine organisms, on tiny clams called..."

Nick has tears in his eyes. "Sorry," Lee says, backing away. "Have to go. I'm late for work."

10

The third Sunday of the oil spill, incident day seventeen, snow blows sideways when Lee arrives by bicycle at the otter center. She finds Kurt smoking a cigarette at the entrance.

"I didn't know you smoked," she says, breathing hard as she props her bike against the wall. The swirling snow is melting on contact with the earth.

Her bearded teammate greets her with a nod. "I don't," he says in his deep voice. "Haven't smoked for ten years." He glances at her. "Don't worry. Disasters have to end sometime, right?" After another drag on the cancer stick, Kurt asks, "Did you see the skimmers and dredges in the bay?"

"The what?" she says, wishing she sounded more intelligent. He must think she's a moron.

"Mammoth's spill equipment. Show-and-tell," Kurt says sardonically. "Of course they're not *using* them; they're just making sure the press gets plenty of pictures." He shakes his head. "They're going to pressure wash the shoreline. Then, supposedly, the oil will drain back into the water and they'll skim it off."

"Don't you think it'll work?"

Kurt frowns. "Oh, it'll work, all right. But if there're any organisms left alive out there after the oil, high-pressure hosing will finish them off."

When he's done smoking, he picks up his cigarette butts from the ground and disposes of them in a nearby trash can. They enter the building together to find Camille and Heidi already in their rain gear, studying a neon-pink sheet of paper.

"Look at this, you guys!" Camille hands the flyer to Kurt and Lee before turning to high-five Heidi. The teenager giggles.

The press release states that since the Mammoth Petroleum Corporation already funds the "retrieval, transport, cleaning, and care" of oiled birds and otters, the volunteers staffing both centers essentially amount to employees. Consequently, those involved with these activities "in any part" will be hired by the oil company and placed on its payroll. The rate of pay is twenty dollars an hour. The paper directs "said volunteers" to register on site immediately and concludes with the warning that, effective the next morning, only registered employees will be permitted on the premises of the otter and bird rehabilitation facilities.

"Isn't it great?" Heidi asks Kurt. "We get paid!"

"We'll be rich!" Camille crows.

Lee can tell from his expression that Kurt's as upset as she is.

"What's your problem?" Camille challenges them both. She turns from Lee to Kurt and back again, the ends of her childish pigtails whipping against her cheeks.

Neither Lee nor Kurt responds.

"This whole thing is Mammoth's fault. Why *shouldn't* they pay us?" Camille presses, her dark eyes flashing. "It's not like I'll be working at the cannery again this summer. No one will. And who knows when you're ever going fishing again," she says to Lee. "Why should we lose out even more than we already have? This is one way Mammoth can make it up to us."

Lee stares at her. Doesn't Camille understand it's blood money?

"It's not a handout," Heidi offers tentatively, her freckled face deeply flushed. "We have to earn it."

"But it's not optional," Lee explains, waving the brightly colored piece of paper. "They're not just *offering* wages—they're *requiring* them. No one can choose to not get paid. We won't even be allowed to set foot in here unless we sign a contract." She crumples the flyer and throws it to the floor.

"So?" Camille says, kicking the balled paper. "Why not get paid? What's the big deal?"

"Because it's unethical," Kurt says. "Don't you get it? We'd be benefiting from the otters' suffering."

"Bullshit!" Camille declares. "Mammoth makes beaucoup bucks off Alaska. Now it has to give some back is all."

Their discussion ends abruptly when a lipsticked blonde in a slate-blue trench coat and black heels gingerly picks her way across the tarpaulin-covered floor to ask if she can interview them for *60 Minutes*.

"For a whole hour?" Heidi asks.

"No. I don't want to interfere with your work. Can I just ask you a few questions?"

"It's a TV show," Camille tells the teen.

A cameraman arrives, splaying the legs of his large tripod in preparation for filming, clipping a too-bright light to the apparatus.

"How's my hair?" Camille asks Heidi, primping with a flounce in the sudden glare.

Heidi titters. Lee scowls. Kurt's already gone.

Smiling, the blonde holds a microphone to her glossy crimson mouth and asks Camille, "How does it feel knowing you'll be paid for the same work that you've so far done for free?"

"I like it. It's awesome." Camille gives the camera guy a thumbs-up and a wink. "It's definitely going to help a lot of people."

"How so?"

"Well, like, I usually work the slime line every summer, you know?"

"The 'slime line'?"

127

Lee turns away as Camille explains about gutting fish and crab at the cannery in preparation for their processing.

"How much do you make working on the, uh, slime line?" the woman asks.

"Six seventy-five an hour."

"And how much are they paying you to wash otters?"

"Twenty bucks?" Camille can't keep the note of disbelief from her voice.

"How long have you worked in the seafood industry?"

Camille thinks. "Five years."

"But now the fisheries in your region are closed because of the oil spill, so you're probably out of a cannery job, right?"

"Right."

The microphone swings to Heidi. "What kind of work do you do, and how much are you paid?"

"Um, babysitting. Three fifty an hour."

"I see," says the interviewer, motioning to the cameraman to film Lee. "And how do you, a Native Alaskan, feel about the oil spill?"

Lee stares at the woman. It is of course not the first time she's been mistaken for Alaska Native, but it's the first time she's ever felt like slapping someone for it. Choked by feelings she can't name, she pushes past the cameraman and exits the gym.

Kurt's sucking on another cigarette out front. The spring snow has stopped. "I hope Aengus rots in hell," he says.

"It's not just him." Lee fights back tears. "It's so much bigger than just him."

But Kurt wants someone to blame. "Richard Aengus. Dick. At least the name fits."

Lee pictures her tall, taciturn father with a glass of booze in his hand. The more Gunther drank, the more gregarious he became. She sways unsteadily, causing Kurt to reach out and take her arm. "You okay?"

"I can't believe this," she whispers. "What will we do if we can't help?"

Kurt draws on his cigarette, exhaling a stream of smoke. "Maybe we can sue for the right to volunteer."

"Really?"

"No." He shakes his head. "It's over. We're well and truly screwed."

The ache in Lee's heart blooms throughout her rib cage. She turns away, stifling a cry.

"Sure you're okay?" Kurt says, dropping his cigarette stub to the ground. He steps on the butt, then bends to retrieve it.

Lee struggles for control of her emotions. She goes to her bicycle, pretending to check the chain, making as if to ride. Her teammate bids her good-bye. He crosses the street, turning back once to check on her, so she waves to reassure him. But when Kurt's passed from sight, she replaces her bike against the wall and creeps behind the densely needled ornamental pines that front the building, curling into a ball on the half-frozen woodchip mulch, covering her mouth with both hands, trying not to wail.

Hearing voices approach, Lee holds her breath. She's got to get out of here, but where can she go? When she's alone again, she kneels, brushes herself off, and hurries on foot across the parking lot. Feeling light-headed and exposed in the open, she angles for the spruce forest that lies just beyond the high-school playing field. If only she can make it to the cover of the woods. As she reaches the four-lane running track, however, a honking horn and a car's sudden braking make her stop. Tessa, in their blue Subaru station wagon. Once again, Lee pictures herself melting in her friend's embrace, unleashing a torrent of pent-up tears.

"Wait up! Where are you going?" Tess calls through the opened window before cutting the engine and releasing her seat belt. She gets out of the car and pinches the sleeve of the deckhand's wool jacket, in obvious high spirits. "What's wrong?" she asks, appraising Lee. "Want to sit in the car?"

The younger woman shakes her head, wiping her eyes with her fingers.

"Did you hear how much they're going to pay us?" Tess burbles. "More than I make nursing! Of course, there aren't any benefits, but still—" She stares at her friend. "Oh, I forgot," she then says, in an altogether different tone of voice. "You're not happy about it. You think their money's corrupt."

Incapable of speech, Lee draws a deep breath.

Echoing Camille, Tess says, "It's not that big of a deal. We deserve to get paid for our efforts. Why shouldn't we? It doesn't lessen our contribution."

The deckhand puts her hand to her chest, wondering if she's having a heart attack.

"You didn't get paid for black cod," the older woman goes on. "All that hard work for nothing, and what a waste of fish! Why should you lose even more earnings because of some stupid drunk? At the very least, this'll help you recover your losses from fishing. This and your claim." Tess scrutinizes her. "You are filing a claim, right?" Provoked by Lee's silence, she continues in the same needling voice. "You have only yourself to look out for. I've got two kids. A family," she says, adding drily, "such as it is."

Lee feels herself swaying.

"To top it off, I seem to be pregnant. My period's late. I'm never late."

Abruptly, the younger woman sits on the cinder track, legs splayed before her.

"You know, if we don't take the money, somebody else will." Tess stands over her. "Everyone's headed here now. The stampede is on. Get rich quick."

"Mammoth's trying to buy us off," Lee finally manages. "Doesn't that bother you?" She wipes her nose on the back of her hand.

"That's baloney, and you know it. The oil spill's a tragedy, but luckily for us, Mammoth's rich enough to take away some of the sting." She challenges Lee to contradict her.

"You're compromising your values."

"The heck I am. I'm just being practical. Better than cutting off my nose to spite my face, like some people." Tess looks at her friend meaningfully. When Lee still says nothing, she adds, "I'm taking the money."

The younger woman rests her head on her knees, all fight gone. "You know, it's funny. I didn't blame Mammoth for the spill, but I do blame them for this. A lot."

"Well, I *do* blame them for the spill," Tess counters. "A lot. They had no business hiring a known alcoholic. They owe us."

"Don't you think you're selling out? That it makes you like an accomplice?"

Speechless, Tess gives Lee a shove. "Go to hell." She turns to her car then swings back. "Like you've never spent a Permanent Fund Dividend."

"It's not the same thing."

"Oh, no?" The older woman opens the car door.

Lee hugs herself. "Why do you have to drive everywhere, anyway? Since when is Selby so big that you can't walk a few blocks?"

"Don't you dare. This isn't about my driving."

"Yes, it is."

"And you don't own a truck, I suppose."

"I'm not using it," the deckhand says. "I haven't driven at all since this happened. I might never drive again."

Tessa sneers. "Right. And you'll never ride in a car, or a boat—or a bus, or an airplane—ever again? Sure."

"I don't know," Lee says softly.

When Tess puts the car in gear and drives away to take her shift of otter care, Lee gets to her feet, limping across the grass oval enclosed by the track, hand pressed to her chest. She feels feverish, in need of the protection of the woods. She pictures herself spread-eagled on the reindeer moss and lichen and Labrador tea, breathing deeply of the forest's restorative, smoky goodness.

Making her way along the tree-lined bluff, Lee finally reaches a familiar secluded glade, presided over by an old, bowed birch. The embankment here rises forty or fifty feet above the shoreline, the stooped tree providing a sheltering canopy under which the ground has remained dry despite the morning's snow flurry. She sits with her back against the gnarled trunk.

Gradually, the pain in her chest subsides. She observes cleanup workers on the oiled beach below, white utility buckets in hand. The so-called technicians, hooded and hatted against the chill, all of them wearing rubber boots and gloves, carry what look like cheerleaders' pom-poms, which they use to swipe perfunctorily at oiled rocks the way a housemaid might touch up an already spotless object with a feather duster. The workers are decidedly more animated in their conversations with one another than they are in performance of their beach-cleaning duties. Twenty dollars an hour.

The tide has receded, oil-shadowed ocean undulating far from shore. When did she lose track of ebb and flow? Lee can't even remember what phase the moon is in, waxing or waning, a thought that compounds her misery.

The ground is cold beneath her, but she feels safe here. Relaxing a little, she considers again the latest salt in the gaping wound of the oil spill: Mammoth Petroleum's appropriation of the volunteer efforts. Her earlier need to cry has been replaced by a familiar sense of dislocation as she stares at the snow-covered mountains across the mottled bay. She makes herself small and holds very still, like a rabbit caught in a snare. If someone were to stumble upon her, they'd know right away she'd been violated.

Although Daniel now spends most nights at home, he does so in his son's vacated bed. Tessa rarely sees her husband. Working two jobs herself, she's as likely to be gone from the house as he.

They cohabit like roommates, not spouses. Without the children's daily needs to bind and give purpose to their relationship, they devote themselves instead to their own particular microcosm of the oil spill: otter rehab, broadcast journalism.

Seemingly overnight, morning sickness confirms Tessa's pregnancy. No way will she carry a baby to term in the midst of this madness. Not an option. She's disenchanted with her marriage, for one thing, and for another, how can she and Daniel possibly afford another child? Otter care pays well, but it's hardly a career. Because she'd been so unhappy at the hospital even before the spill, Tess tries not to think about resuming work there full-time. Too bad it isn't her sister who'd conceived. Susie and her husband, Brian, who have been pursuing expensive fertility treatments in California, would rejoice at the prospect of a baby—not wish its conception away.

When Tessa recalls the abortion that terminated her first pregnancy, her final year of nursing school, she remembers how she had cried with remorse for months afterward. She and Daniel both. He would flip out if he knew what she was considering, so Tess thinks maybe she will just have the D&C in Anchorage without telling him. Keep it simple. Avoid the drama.

One rare evening when both are home, they agree to fix dinner together for the first time since the spill.

"I'll defrost some shrimp," Daniel says, as she measures rice and water into a saucepan.

But not until they finish eating and begin to clear the table does either of them speak again, at which point Tessa comments that it might be a long time before they have any more seafood to put in their freezer.

"It's the same for retailers," he says. "All of the frozen supply's going to feed the otters, and nothing new is coming in. Obviously." Daniel pauses. "Mammoth's offered the station a grant, 'no strings attached.'"

"How much?"

"Fifty grand."

"You're kidding."

He draws out a chair for her, and they sit down again. "I don't think we can accept it. The board called a special meeting. They were still at it when I left."

"Why not accept it? You all are working your buns off."

Daniel seems to understand that she's not so much offering a compliment as stating a fact. "Malcolm thinks it's a conflict of interest. We're supposed to be a *public* radio station, not one underwritten by a corporate sponsor. Especially not by Mammoth Petroleum."

"What do *you* think?"

He shrugs. "I don't know."

"These are extenuating circumstances," Tess argues. "Isn't it better to take the money and keep broadcasting than to use up your resources and have to stop? Why should the station shoot itself in the foot?"

"People are starting to question Mammoth's deep-pocket approach."

"So you keep working overtime for no pay?" She uses her voice like a prod. "The moral high ground?"

Her husband presses his lips together.

"You don't think I should take their money for working with otters, do you?" Tess asks.

"I think it's a complicated question."

"Let me ask you this, then," she says. "Something simple. When are we ever going to make enough to start setting something aside?"

Recalling how miserable Lee looked that morning at the high-school track, Tess decides those who've quit the bird and otter treatment centers rather than accept Mammoth's wages need to face reality. Of course no one's happy with the situation, but some of us seem to be doing a better job than others of accepting it. Oil is a fact of life, people. Get a grip.

She's had no contact with Lee since then (not that that has stopped Jackie from calling the house every other day looking for her ex-lover). Tess knows she has not exactly gone out of her way to extend an olive branch to her younger friend, but it offends her nonetheless that Lee never comes by like she used to, all the time, before the spill. Not even to see Elias and Minke. Granted, the kids are in Anchorage, and she and Daniel are never home. But still.

True to Dean Carson's word, the oil company has opened a local claims office, leasing what was until the spill a Montessori preschool. Now, so many households having lost their livelihoods, parents either can't afford instructional childcare or else suddenly unemployed moms and dads find themselves unexpectedly at home all day with their little ones, so they don't need the service. As a result of the precipitous loss of business, Marsha Middleton, the owner-operator of Child's Play, has had no choice but to file for bankruptcy.

So instead of toddlers playing gleefully on the swing sets and climbing structures in front of the colorful building, a queue of hopeful claims applicants winds through the yard to stretch down Alder Street. People stand in line for hours even though Mammoth offers them the option of taking a number to be contacted later at home. Tess supposes that since people can no longer pursue their usual vocations, many of them have nothing better to do than commiserate with one another as they await their turn with one of Mammoth's claims adjusters.

The majority of those now known as "oil spill technicians" are unskilled laborers who'd normally be plying minimum-wage jobs. Not surprisingly, they prefer to work for the petroleum giant and earn the big bucks. And although Mammoth Petroleum's press releases have brought job seekers to Alaska in droves, the newcomers are equally intent on high-paying oil spill jobs, so suddenly no one wants to wait tables or flip burgers in local restaurants; no one wants to work as lowly salesclerks in retail businesses; no one will stoop to changing bedding in area hotels or at the hospital—or to caring for children, the elderly, and the infirm. Unable to compete with Mammoth's wages, local enterprises find themselves facing insolvency. The Super Duper is stretched thin for checkers even though business has increased tenfold.

By mid-April, thousands of job seekers have descended on south-central Alaska. They come from every state in the union, even from overseas. Journalists, photographers, personal-injury attorneys, politicians, and curiosity seekers make steady pilgrimage as well. Property owners rent out accommodations in guest rooms and in parked recreational vehicles; newcomers who can afford it pay good money to sleep on living room sofas and even, Tess learns, in garden sheds. Luanne Fyfe is rumored to have sold sleeping space in her late husband's antique DeSoto, which she'd lovingly had restored in his memory years ago.

Before long, those who've arrived in search of spill jobs grossly outnumber Selby's thirty-eight hundred year-round inhabitants. Many of the new arrivals live in tents and makeshift shelters on the upper beaches, above the reach of the foul petroleum that washes ashore with depressing regularity, twice a day, bearing with it the carcasses of oiled birds and otters. The tent dwellers seem to enjoy themselves; their encampment reminds Tessa of old magazine photos of the Woodstock Summer of Love. But whenever it rains, or if oil spill work is halted for any reason, the campers inundate the library, post office, and any other public space that offers shelter.

Portable toilets spring up everywhere, keeping municipal employees scrambling to maintain them. Between the crude oil on the beaches and the makeshift sanitation facilities, the caustic stench on warm days is truly nauseating. Officials worry about the outbreak of disease. All we need now, Tessa thinks, is a hepatitis epidemic. Thank goodness the kids aren't here.

She watches one night on TV as Captain Richard Aengus of the Mammoth *Kuparuk* is led into an Anchorage courthouse for his pretrial hearing. The middle-aged man has grown a beard since the accident, and he wears a Lakers' ball cap pulled low over his eyes. Even so, there's no disguising his unrepentant—if not downright defiant—scowl. Is it that he considers himself blameless, or that he resents the fact that Mammoth Petroleum has hung him out to dry? Tess wonders if his weakness for liquor was really the cause of the tanker grounding and if the truth of the oil spill will ever be known.

11

Dark greasy smudges mar the formerly unblemished surfaces of the *Pegasus*. It's obvious that Gregg has taken the boat back out into the oil. When Lee notices a new boathook lying on the foredeck, its aluminum shaft tacky with the tarlike residue of crude petroleum, she cringes, remembering her efforts to pull in the oil-soaked murres.

Finding the wheelhouse locked, she sees Stork coiling lines on the *Shamrock*. He tells her that Gregg's been arrested for assault and battery. Stork heard it from someone who'd heard it from someone else, so he doesn't have details. He has other news, too, which he steps onto the float to deliver to her in a low voice: the *Rodeo Rose* is lost at sea. Dusty, the cowboy skipper, and his crew of three have been out of radio contact for over twenty-four hours. Lee blanches when she hears this. The two deckhands embrace hard before she pedals her bike back into town.

She pictures Gregg getting roaring drunk as in the old days, falling or maybe even leaping off the wagon under all the pressure of the oil spill, then brawling with another equally stressed-out fisherman. She wills herself not to think about what might have happened to the *Rodeo Rose*, picturing instead the entire crew raised to safety from the incapacitated boat by a hovering Coast Guard helicopter. As she walks her bike across Glacierview Drive on her way to see her jailed skipper, she encounters Daniel emerging from the public library.

"What's up?" he asks.

"Not much." She's not about to discuss Gregg's business with someone who broadcasts on the radio. Nor can she bring herself to share the other news with anyone who knows little about fishing. "What about you?"

"I've been researching Captain Aengus. The man's a Greek tragedy." As she had been the night at the radio station, Lee's struck by Daniel's enthusiasm.

He tells her how the *Kuparuk* captain still refuses to say what he'd been doing while he was AWOL.

"I thought he was with his daughter," she says.

"Maybe, maybe not. I'd give a lot to know what he was up to, wouldn't you?"

Not really, Lee thinks. She's not sure she can stomach any more of the oil spill's discouraging revelations.

At the time of the grounding, Daniel continues with shining eyes, Aengus's driver's license had been revoked, just as it had previously been suspended, twice, for drunk driving.

Lee frowns. "Everyone in the world knows that by now."

"The guy was a track star in high school," Daniel goes on, undeterred. "All-state. And his maritime academy instructors still talk 'admiringly' of his 'instinctive gift for sailing.'" He uses his fingers to supply the quotation marks. "It's like a Greek tragedy," he repeats.

Lee's more taken aback by Daniel's passion than she is by Richard Aengus's biography.

"It's like his competence and maybe his arrogance led to his downfall," he adds. "Hubris. The Fates zeroed in on him. The guy became a lightning rod."

"He's a scapegoat," she complains, "a distraction from all the other problems with the petroleum industry—like how our government's in bed with Big Oil."

Daniel nods. "You're right, but one way or the other, Aengus screwed up. He was in command. He should be punished."

They both look up then, to watch a bald eagle laboring to gain altitude above them. The bird clutches something limp and obviously weighty in its talons.

"A king salmon?" Daniel guesses.

"Could be."

"'When thou seest an eagle, thou seest a portion of genius,'" he quotes.

Lee shakes her head. "A genius that's feeding on oiled carcasses," she mutters.

Daniel glances at the raptor again, then back at her. "Even if they manage to avoid the oil themselves, they could still be eating things that are contaminated?"

"They *are* eating things that are contaminated," she says sharply. "Depend on it. That's what eagles do."

Daniel clutches her arm, still staring after the bird. "And eating oil will kill them. Sooner or later. Then something else might eat the dead eagle, which is now contaminated, too. And that something else could die. And on and on?" He withdraws his hand to squeeze his forehead. "Jesus."

"Brooding eagles—and other birds—are tracking oil into their nests, onto their eggs. The eggshells absorb toxicity, which kills the embryos." Lee looks into his eyes. "They'll never hatch." She remounts her bike. "It's the worst time of year something like this could have happened," she says, recalling biologist Nick Calhoun's deep unhappiness at Deborah's Meadow. "Everything's either coming out of hibernation, getting born, or migrating here. Everything's hungry, and there's tons of food lying around. Only problem is, all of it's poisoned."

Weeks have passed since they came in from longlining. Having made no effort to check on him sooner, Lee now feels guilty for neglecting her skipper. So she's prepared to find him miffed, but when Officer Curtis Beauchamp shows Lee to Gregg's cell at the police station, her boss is all smiles.

The windowless, unpainted, concrete-block room, no more than eight feet by twelve, contains a lidless stainless-steel toilet and a small, single-tap sink. Gregg sports a scraggly beard, his long hair snarled and matted. He sits on the edge of the narrow built-in bed that's made up with beige sheets and a single putty-colored blanket, the confined space reeking of cigarette smoke, crude petroleum, and the sourness of dirty clothes and human sweat laced with liquor.

"Well, look what the cat dragged in!" Her skipper's a mess, but he's in a jovial mood. Obviously, he hasn't yet heard the news about Dusty. He takes a drag from the cigarette clamped in his fist. "Damn, Lee. You're nothing but a bag of bones. You look like shit."

"Look who's talking," she retorts, but in spite of herself, the deckhand smiles. This is the old Gregg, the pre-divorce skipper of a custom-built forty-footer who thought he had the world by the tail. What's gotten into him?

He chuckles. She's rarely known him to be in such good humor, even under the best of circumstances. Her stomach clenches with what she must tell him.

He beckons for her to sit beside him on the bed, but she opts to stand against the cool concrete wall instead. After all, Gregg smells pretty ripe.

"Aaron was on the *Kuparuk* when it grounded," he says.

"No way!"

He recounts to her what his son had told him about that night.

"Jeez." Lee pictures airborne crude oil careening skyward, driven by tremendous head pressure, then raining down on the deck of that gargantuan ship, showering Aaron in the process. "Is he okay?"

"He asked Stoddard for a leave of absence, and they gave it to him." Gregg shakes his head. "Don't know why he thinks he needs time off." Exhaling smoke, he says, "He'll have to testify at the hearing." He lights a new cigarette from the stub of the old, acting for all the world like he's entertaining her in the privacy of his own home. "What've you been up to?"

Lee hates to see him chain-smoking, but knows better than to comment. She describes cleaning otters, telling him how she quit working at the center when Mammoth Petroleum instituted its no-volunteers policy.

"Why'd you do that?" Gregg asks. "You should've taken the work."

She shrugs.

"You're not thinking we'll be going out again anytime soon, are you? Because I guaran-goddam-tee you we aren't. Nobody is." He sips his cigarette.

"*Rodeo Rose* is lost at sea, boss." Lee bites her lip.

Gregg stares at her, eyes narrowed, as if she's messing with him.

"They're out there right now, looking for them."

Her skipper's eyes bore holes into her. "Where?"

"Amatuli Strait. I guess Dusty thought he'd try out west, since every other district's closed by order."

Gregg continues to glare at her, before swinging his head like a wounded animal. "No. No. *No*. Who's with him? Chris? Doug?"

Lee nods. "And Dave. Dave Brant."

"Don't know him."

"Nice guy. Came up a year or so ago. Used to fish the *Nugget*."

Her skipper shakes his head, the cigarette in his hand forgotten. "How close were they to Cape Chichagof?"

"Don't know."

"When did it happen?"

"Day before yesterday." Lee feels tears welling.

"What're conditions like?"

"Not good. Gale-force."

Skipper and deckhand regard each other in silence, both knowing full well the odds of anyone surviving that turbulent chute of frigid water, even in life rafts and survival suits, and even in what for the strait would be considered calm seas.

The cigarette burns Gregg's fingers, so he drops it to the cement floor, stepping on it distractedly with his stockinged foot. He blinks, gazes at the ceiling.

Lee slides down to sit with her back against the cement wall. She remembers meeting Dave Brant the winter before last, shortly after he'd arrived in Selby. Ironically, it was at a wake, a gathering to mourn the loss at sea of the captain and crewmembers of Selby's last doomed fishing vessel, the crabber *Archangel*. Miraculously, Jared Simpson had been plucked unconscious in his survival suit from the Bering Sea by Coast Guard rescue swimmers. He alone survived; no trace of the big boat or of Jared's shipmates has ever been found.

Maybe at least one or two of the *Rodeo Rose* crew will be saved, Lee prays, her thoughts turning to Dusty's wife, Rosemary, and their new-born daughter—to Doug and Shawna and their teenaged kids.

Gregg stands abruptly, walking to the far end of the confined space, where he ignites another coffin nail with a plastic lighter. "How many other boats do you s'pose had the same idea as Dusty?" he asks.

Lee shakes her head.

"Fucking Mammoth," Gregg mutters. "They might as well have executed those guys, shot them right in the head. Goddamn corporation should be put on trial for murder." He paces the length of the cell. Lee draws up her legs so he won't step on her.

"Did you hear about our oil brigade?" he demands.

With the earlier Herring Cove success to guide them, he tells her, sixty-three boats had set out again from Selby, with more from Port Clark and the outlying villages—in all maybe two hundred vessels. Fed up with Mammoth's lack of initiative in stemming the spread of the oil, the fishermen had decided to keep after it themselves.

"Our first attempts backfired," he says. "We didn't get squat. But when the tide changed, it flattened right out, and we started smokin'." He turns to her with gleaming eyes and tells how they used every method they could think of to get the petroleum out of the ocean. Some scooped it with buckets; some corralled it with seine web. Others used brailers. The oil has weathered to the consistency of Jell-O, he says. "You can practically pick it up with your hands." Gregg pauses to smoke. "We nailed it; it worked great. Only trouble was, once you get it out of the water, the shit starts to melt."

Her skipper describes lining the holds with six-mil visqueen.

"The holds!" Lee interjects.

"Roger. With totes on deck." Gregg explains how they hung lengths of net between boats and, working in tandem, drew the oil into the shallows, where people in hip boots and chest waders used buckets and brailers to scoop and carry it above the high-tide line into pits they'd dug in the beach gravel and lined with yet more plastic. "We filled everything we had." He extinguishes his cigarette against the wall and flips the butt toward the metal toilet, missing the bowl.

"You see any wildlife out there?"

"Nothing alive, if that's what you mean." Gregg tugs his straggly beard and stops pacing. "How's Rosemary taking it?"

Lee shakes her head again. His smoking is making her eyes water and her throat feel scratchy.

"They just had that baby," her skipper says. "Dusty was stoked about finally being a dad." His voice trails off. "We could have gotten even more," he continues in a moment, "but we had nowhere to put it. Even with AlaskaPride donating totes and three of Wally Flynn's barges standing by offshore." Gregg looks at her imploringly. "We filled *everything*, Lee. Hell, we got more in a day than all of Mammoth's skimmers, pumps, dredges, and whatnot have gotten this whole time. Not that it takes any great skill to outperform those numbnuts. But there was nowhere to put it." He hawks and spits into the sink, not bothering to turn on the tap. "We asked Mammoth to come get it, to pump us out so we could refill and keep going, but they 'declined.'"

"Declined! What do you mean?"

"That's what shut us down again," Gregg says bitterly. "No place to fucking put it." He draws on the cigarette, exhaling through mouth and nostrils both. "They claim the EPA and the DEC won't grant permission to bring the stuff ashore, because of its toxicity." He sits down heavily on the bed, his animated retelling giving way to slumped shoulders.

After a minute Lee says, "You still haven't told me how come you're in here."

Her boss lights yet another cigarette. "I lost it," he says matter-of-factly. "When I realized how gutless the state and feds have been in standing up to Mammoth, how little will anyone has to actually *do* anything about the spill, it boiled my blood. I waited for him to show up for work."

"Who?"

"Fuckface. Dean Carson. The emcee." Gregg grins. "I jumped him in the new hotel's parking lot. Got my hands around his starchy button-down collar and told him I was going to squeeze until his eyes popped out of their sockets and rolled down his cheeks."

Lee feels her mouth open; she's as horrified by her skipper's act of violence as she is warmed by the thought of the oil company spokesman losing his infuriating poise.

Gregg chuckles. "Scared the piss out of him. No shit. Guy peed himself."

She stares at her boss's satisfied smile. "Would you really have killed him?"

"Don't know." He laughs.

"You're taking this awfully personally."

"Goddamn right," Gregg says, his expression now devoid of humor. "Aren't you?"

Lee shrugs. She's at a loss these days to describe how she feels.

"You filed a claim, right?"

"Did you?" she replies, deflecting his question.

"Soon as I get out of here. I'm going to sue them for everything, make 'em pay forever. Rosemary should sue. And the other wives and girlfriends, all the children."

He continues after a moment. "You better get your claim in before those fuckers find some loophole that lets 'em skate." Gregg fixes her with his gaze. "You put down for every fishery you can think of. We would have done it all this year: cod, herring, halibut, salmon, crab, shrimp—everything."

Lee's face betrays her skepticism. They never fish everything. No one does.

"Okay," he relents. "Maybe not shrimp. I hate shrimp. But we would've made beaucoup bucks this year, more than ever before. The forecasts were great, remember?"

"The forecasts were decent," she agrees.

"I was going to raise your crew share, too."

Lee studies his face, unsure whether or not to believe him.

"Damn right," he says. "Fifteen percent. Be sure and put that down. You're the best goddamn deckhand I ever had." He pauses. "And don't let them give you any shit about being a girl, either."

"Woman," she thinks, but doesn't say. Would Gregg really raise her share to fifteen? She's never known her skipper to talk so much. When she stands to go, he grinds the latest butt beneath his foot and says, "Dave Brant. He's that guy with the goatee."

"He shaved it, but yeah." Lee glances at him, craving connection, but he's already lighting another cigarette. "How long are they going to keep you here?"

"Don't know." Gregg suffers her hug briefly before pushing her away. "Get me some more smokes, would you?"

Daniel goes home early the night he learns of Gregg Anderson's assault on Dean Carson, the Mammoth Petroleum spokesman. Sitting cross-legged on the futon couch eating a salad, Tessa watches him pace between the living room and the kitchen, his jaw set.

"What's up?" she asks, and he tells her, adding, "I hope he gets hard time for that little stunt."

"It really bothers you."

"Sure it does. Doesn't it upset you, someone from here behaving like that?"

"I don't know," Tess says. "What he did was wrong, but still, he acted on his beliefs. Sometimes actions speak louder than words."

Daniel looks at her sharply, shaking his head. "You have no idea how easy it is to snap a man's neck."

"You're right, I don't. Tell me."

But he's already closed his back to her. He decides to do something so out of character that it takes him a moment to find the knob that turns on the TV. Daniel knows and supposes Tess knows, too, that his fascination with the spill stems from his own life experiences. So what?

A sitcom with a studio audience laughing on cue. Perfect, he thinks.

Tessa continues to care for otters six days a week. Tuesday through Thursday and again on Sundays, she also pulls shifts at the hospital. Of all the spill-related jobs offered by Mammoth, bird and mammal care are the most coveted; the waiting list of those wanting this work now contains over a thousand names.

Port Clark and Kodiak have also established wildlife treatment programs, taking some of the pressure off Selby. All three sea-mammal facilities begin to receive orphaned otter and seal pups—none of which generally survive. Selby even acquires two young sea lions, but they, too, die shortly after they're brought in.

The administrators of the local bird and otter treatment centers keep careful records, storing the bodies of the dead in first one, and then a second, and now a third freezer van parked in the Selby High School parking lot. Only the veterinarians and U.S. Fish and Wildlife personnel have access to the padlocked semitrailers and the legal "evidence" they contain of the petroleum corporation's negligence.

The recovering otters are kept under lock and key as well, four of them having mysteriously vanished from the center. Tessa hopes the animals' abductors have released them into the wild—preferably somewhere far from the spill, wherever that might be. Whether foolish or heroic, the downside of the action is that currently all of the center's employees are regarded with suspicion.

Mostly, Tess works with the juvenile males, which, happily, have started to outlive their injuries. In the beginning, the work had depressed her: oiled animals arriving at all hours of the day and night, many of them perishing within hours. Eventually, however, their survival rate has come to offer hope. As the weather warms, she helps to transfer recovering otters into what was until the oil spill a storage yard behind the school. Here, safeguarded behind chain-link fencing, grouped according to age and sex, the animals can swim in large fiberglass tanks and enjoy fresh air. The creatures take childlike pleasure in each other's company, cavorting under, around, and beside one another, as lithe and nimble in the water as they are halting and clumsy out of it.

As they regain strength, the otters also recover their appetites, requiring regular feeding, five ounces at a time of frozen fish or shellfish. Initially, AlaskaPride and even locals had donated frozen seafood for the marine mammals, but Mammoth Petroleum now purchases the fare from processors as far away as Russia and Japan, having already exhausted the Pacific Northwest's supply.

Center employees carefully thaw, weigh, and record the portions of food. Tessa's challenge is to present the meals to the otters without interacting with them, to discourage as much as possible their habituation to humans. She's supposed to leave the aluminum pie plates of food where the wild creatures can approach at their leisure once she has withdrawn. However, as the social otters recover their health, they use various strategies to attract their caretakers' attention. One sunny afternoon, Tess notices how rank the outdoor compound smells in the heat of the day. She peels off her sweatshirt to hose everything down, relishing the uncustomary warmth on her bare arms. If there had to be an oil spill, she thinks, at least it happened when milder weather can cheer the spirits of people and animals whose lives have been thrown into chaos.

Tessa thoroughly sprays the enclosed area through the fence, the young otters lifting their whiskered faces to the water. Then she coils the hose back onto its reel and retrieves the plastic milk crate containing the animals' food. Letting herself into the compound, she's as usual both thrilled and intimidated by the otters' proximity. Averting her eyes as she sets out aluminum pie plates of pollock, she senses rather than sees one of the young males approach. The bold creature stops about six feet away, vocalizing; it sounds like a stage-whispered "Psst!" When she glances at him, he stares back at her and, Tess could swear, nods in approval. She hurries from the pen, afraid that if anyone has observed her making eye contact, she'll be reprimanded. Too many reprimands and you're asked to leave.

While the otters feast, gulping their meal in a fraction of the time required to prepare it, Tess records notes on a clipboard regarding the animals' eating, grooming, sleeping, playing, and swimming. The record keeping is exactly like jotting chart notes for hospital patients. She then reenters the enclosure to gather up the empty pans and to begin the task of disinfecting the large tank.

It astonishes Tess how quickly the initial emergency of the oil spill has been rendered routine. Most of the original volunteers have left the treatment center, too proud to accept Mammoth's nonnegotiable wages, she supposes. The paid replacements tend on the whole to be less committed than their predecessors, but whether it's the composition of the workforce or the passage of time, something resembling levity replaces the tension of the early days, as workers (now referred to as "sea-mammal specialists") bond with one another, sometimes squirting each other with water. What began as a mission of mercy has turned into a job, and like every other job Tess has ever worked, she settles into its rhythms, arranging the rest of her life around its demands.

One day, a hugely pregnant otter is brought in with scarcely any oil on her. The female's belly is so distended that when she lies on her back, she cannot raise her head high enough to see over her stomach. Tessa dubs her "Girtha," prompting a protest from self-important Camille, whom Tess increasingly finds insufferable.

"You know we're not supposed to name them!" the sanctimonious young woman complains.

But the nickname sticks and soon even the veterinarians use it.

Everyone's thrilled when Girtha delivers not just one but two pups, in a corner of the darkened wrestling room. According to the marine mammal biologist who conducts research on otters, twins are extremely rare. Mammoth's public relations department has a field day, and while some of her coworkers grouse about the oil company "exploiting" the event for its public relations value, Tessa sees little harm in the company's desire to celebrate something positive.

The two otter pups thrive, providing welcome distraction for several days. However, unbeknownst to their caretakers, the U.S. Fish and Wildlife Service makes arrangements for Girtha and her babes to be shipped to SeaWorld. The workers take it hard. These animals have already been victimized by an oil spill; why should they now be sentenced to lifelong captivity? Tess joins with like-minded employees to urge the Department of Fish and Game, the center veterinarians, and even Mammoth Petroleum to intercede.

But federal agents transfer the animals in the middle of the night, when only a skeleton crew is on duty in the gym. Cowards, Tess thinks. When she arrives the next morning and discovers the otter family gone, she finds some of her coworkers sniffling and dabbing their eyes with tissues.

Tess feels bad, too, but tears? Like the fact of the tanker grounding itself, what's done is done. No use crying over it.

The issue of Mammoth money continues to fragment relationships within the coastal community. If anything, Tess observes, the acrimony between people becomes more pronounced as time goes by, not less. Working for the oil company versus not doing so is a wedge dividing Selby. The rift between her and Lee, for example, has become a commonplace. Neighbors stop speaking to each other; longtime relationships disintegrate. Tess even hears of domestic partners who've split over the difference of opinion. Another pattern involves the distress of parents like Heidi's, the high-school student with whom Tess washes otters. Heidi's mom and dad, like those of other young spill workers, are themselves products of the sixties who long ago turned their own backs on materialism, but now they find their progeny seduced by the prospect of becoming "spillionaires." In short, mistrust and criticism separate those perceived of as profiting from the spill from those who refuse to do so. The *Selby Sentinel* runs a front-page headline that salts the wound: "Do-Gooders Do Well."

She and Daniel treat one another with elaborate courtesy, but neither remarks on the fact of their tenth wedding anniversary in early May. Tessa decides her marriage and friendships will either withstand the tensions caused by the spill, or they won't. What will be, will be. What she finds harder to understand is the bewildering necessity she continues to feel to care for oiled otters while simultaneously neglecting her own children. It's a paradox she's at a loss to explain.

She talks to the kids by phone every evening. From the sounds of it, Grammie and Gramps are spoiling their grandchildren rotten.

When officials call off the search for survivors of the *Rodeo Rose*, the community holds a traditional memorial service. Oil spill cleanup technicians do their best to decontaminate a section of Picnic Point so that people can gather on the beach below town. Volunteer firefighters heap together a bonfire of driftwood and scrap lumber, to be lighted at dusk.

Tess and Daniel both go to pay their respects, of course, but as with most things now, do so separately. Even if they had been disposed to attend together, Tess thinks, they couldn't have: he's on assignment for KRBB and *Alaska News Nightly*.

She spots Gregg Anderson right away. Lee's skipper looks shaggy and wild. Word has it that he's been released from custody for the evening, and from what Tess can tell, he arrives inebriated and does his best to maintain the condition with a flat glass bottle in his hip pocket. Despite her still-frosty feelings, she's surprised and disappointed not to find the fisherman's loyal deckhand at this important community event. Tess has heard at the otter center that Lee and others have started an all-volunteer effort to clean spilled oil from Nevada Cove, an enterprise completely independent of the resources that Mammoth Petroleum has brought to bear on beach cleaning—and one that therefore strikes Tess as a complete waste of time. Lee must not be here this evening because she's out on the gulf coast dabbing at oiled rocks with a kitchen sponge. Well, it's the deckhand's own loss.

Although it's always been customary for the community to gather when boats go down, there's never been a turnout like this. People crowd the beach and line the adjacent bluff, and from the number of unfamiliar faces, Tessa guesses that many of the job seekers who've come North in the wake of the spill have joined the occasion. A variety of national media people show up; supposedly, there's even a reporter from the *New York Times*. Family, friends, and neighbors eulogize Dusty, Dave, Chris, and Doug over a portable loudspeaker. Four lives have been lost at sea—fathers, lovers, sons, and brothers who can never be replaced. Tess watches with a heavy heart as, huddled together, the men's bereft partners, parents, siblings, and children cling to each other. When darkness comes on, wreaths of flowers and sprigs of greenery are tossed upon the ebbing tide, which runs like a river past Picnic Point. One by one, hundreds of candles flicker to life behind the shelter of paper cups. Local musicians take up instruments, and Phil Castner, the longest-serving member of the fire department, lights the bonfire, its crackling heat soon pushing everyone back.

Many townsfolk surrender to grief. It's as if they've all just been waiting for a chance to mourn the sickening losses of the spill, Tess thinks. Some people embrace in clusters while others wander singly or in pairs by water's edge. Some sink to their knees in the gritty sand, crying. Dry-eyed, Tess nevertheless feels wrenched by the widespread display of emotion and realizes that no matter how you might feel about what Daniel calls Mammoth's "deep-pocket" response to the disaster, a unique and precious way of life has been lost. *Our* way of life, she corrects herself. "Not lost," she then hears Lee's voice in her head. "Obliterated."

When Tess and Daniel began dating, he downplayed the tragic death of Elena and what would have been the couple's first child. "Things happen," he said, shrugging. Noticing Tessa's shocked expression, he added softly, "Not a day goes by that I don't think of them and wonder what might have been."

12

Back in jail after the *Rodeo Rose* memorial, Gregg's drowning dreams become a nightly event. He wonders what Curtis Beauchamp, the police deputy most often working graveyard shift, must think of his flailing and groaning. The affable Southerner always has a cup of freshly brewed coffee ready for the *Pegasus* skipper in the morning, a kindness the fisherman acknowledges only by castigating the young man for not also bringing him steak and eggs, a Bloody Mary.

Gregg tries to imagine Dusty's final moments. He knows his friend would have remained in the wheelhouse until the last, working the radio even as the boat listed, rolled, and began its watery descent. How many fathoms deep is Amatuli Strait?

Gregg recalls those lost over the years— on the *Archangel*, the *Patricia V., Winged Mercury*, the *Chinook*. There are more. Too many. "Lost at sea" is an especially apt phrase for those whose bodies are never found, he thinks.

The *Pegasus* skipper has two problems, both of which feel equally critical. He needs money, and he needs for the sake of his sanity to leave town. Like everyone else, the fishing closures have left him in a bind, with no foreseeable prospects, and although he promptly files a claim for lost livelihood, he knows better than to assume it will ever be honored by the petroleum corporation. According to local attorneys, Mammoth can be relied on to balk at settling with individual fishermen, and Gregg will have to join with others to sue the company. Pointing to the recent Amoco *Cadiz* settlements, which had taken two decades to resolve, the lawyers counsel the fishermen that Mammoth *Kuparuk* spill lawsuits will almost certainly remain tied up in court at least that long while the oil giant finesses legal challenges. "Don't count on anything," they caution. "More than a few of you will die before this thing settles."

Like everyone else's, Gregg's boat and truck payments, rent and harbor fees, are all long past due. And like any other commercial fisherman the world over, he grows uneasy whenever he finds himself stuck on shore during fishing season, so having now been landlocked for over a month, he actually feels queasy. At this point, no one even bothers to speculate about when they might fish again. Won't be this year, anyway. If he doesn't find something else to do, and soon, he's going to be in a world of hurt in more ways than one.

After Police Chief Abbott releases him from custody with a lecture, Gregg observes that Mammoth's inflated wages have effectively squelched the noble upwelling of volunteer fervor that had characterized the early weeks of the spill and lent a redemptive air to the nightmare. Now, instead of locals working round the clock to rescue oiled creatures and fabricate boom from logs, carpetbaggers overrun the town in their pursuit of oil spill wealth.

He remembers a television special about the Amazon that showed a wild boar falling into the fabled river. Within seconds, hundreds of razor-toothed piranhas attacked the panic-stricken animal, and when the water stopped churning only minutes later, you could see how the bloodthirsty fish had reduced the hapless pig to bones and tusks, picked clean. Exactly the way get-rich-quick hopefuls now make a beeline to the pork belly they smell in the oil spill. Just as uncontained crude oil has proven fatal to the wild coast, he decides, a second wave—of unleashed greed—now toxifies the coastal community.

From the earliest days of Russian incursion, Alaska has hosted a sequence of economic booms: the fur trade, logging, gold and copper mining, fishing, Pipeline construction, petroleum extraction. Now it's an oil spill: environmental holocaust turned growth industry.

Before Gregg got sprung, Curt Beauchamp had told him that Mammoth was still leasing boats. So upon gaining his freedom, the *Pegasus* skipper saunters over to the oil company headquarters in the new hotel, where he enjoys himself shooting the shit with other out-of-work fishermen who mill about the thickly carpeted lobby, savoring the complimentary Kona coffee and the fancy pastries Mammoth has flown down from a French bakery in Anchorage every morning. Some of his cronies congratulate Gregg for his assault on Dean Carson while high-liners like Lance Figueroa and Billy Joe Norton regard him askance. Fuck you, too, the skipper thinks.

The young Mammoth Petroleum flack sitting behind a desk in the hotel's conference room wears reading glasses perched on the end of his nose. He peers over the half lenses, his brows knitting. "Gregg Anderson. Your name sounds familiar."

"I'm a local hero," the fisherman says.

"Well, then," the man replies genially, "I guess we'd better put you to work."

Just like that. Gregg laughs aloud. The left hand has absolutely no clue what the right hand's doing. Here he's been busted for assaulting the oil company's main man on scene, only to now be hired by the corporation for something called "wildlife retrieval." Are these people stupid or what?

The purpose of wildlife retrieval is twofold, the flack explains: to remove as much contamination from the food chain as possible because every conceivable form of life now feeds on "spill-kills," and to help the government build its case against Mammoth Petroleum. Like the carcasses accumulating in freezer vans from the bird- and otter-rescue efforts, the remains of dead animals recovered from the outer coast will help to document the oil company's culpability.

"Let me get this straight," Gregg says, looking the neatly attired employee in the eye. "You're hiring me to go out there and gather evidence against you?"

"That's right," the man replies levelly. "Is this a great country or what?"

When the rep tells Gregg that Mammoth will assign him a crew, the skipper shakes his head. "No, you won't," he says. "I'll get my own."

Gregg's apartment smells about the way he'd expect it to after weeks of nonuse, musty and stale. The landlord has slipped a half-dozen rent demands under the door. Gregg draws back the drapes and louvers open a window. Then he calls Peg in Anchorage and asks to speak to Aaron. "I've got some work for him," he says to his former wife, thinking as how their son is almost twenty but still living with mama. High time to cut the apron strings.

"What do you mean?" Peg asks. "You're not going fishing, are you?"

Gregg tells her about the wildlife recovery contract. "This could be a valuable experience, a historic event. Educational."

"Transporting dead bodies? Sounds gruesome to me."

Exactly why Aaron *should* go, Gregg thinks. His ex is turning their son into a pansy. The boy and his father are overdue for some male bonding. He says only, "It's good money, Peg."

"How much?"

When he tells her, she exclaims, "I'll get him."

Gregg takes a deep breath. Don't blow it, he tells himself; easy does it.

"Hello?" Aaron sounds wary.

"Hey, son." Gregg explains why he's called. "What do you think?"

"When would we leave?"

"Tuesday. We'll fly you down, take it out of your pay."

156

"Teklik Lagoon?" the boy asks.

"You bet."

Aaron whoops. Gregg smiles, picturing his kid pumping his fist, maybe doing a victory dance. All right, he thinks. Some good might come of this godforsaken abomination after all. Unlike the last time his son had fished with him, Aaron's old enough now to pull his own weight, and he's no doubt learned a thing or two working for Stoddard Maritime.

Peg wants to talk to him again. She lowers her voice. "You're still clean and sober, right?"

"Right," he says. Then again for good measure, "Roger that." Can it really be that she hasn't heard of his recent notoriety?

He drives out to Lee's, feeling good. Almost eight o'clock, the sky remains afternoon bright—a reminder that Alaska's getting on towards solstice and a summer's worth of nightless nights.

When his deckhand steps out of her one-room cabin onto its tiny deck, Gregg sees that she's developed raccoon eyes. He also registers the fact that she's lost an ungodly amount of weight. How had he failed to notice this when she came to see him in the holding cell?

"Hey, beautiful."

"I can't believe they let you out already," she says.

He shrugs. "Carson dropped the charges. He's gone back to Houston. Poof."

Lee shakes her head. "You're lucky."

"It's good to see you, too." Gregg sits on the edge of the little porch, taps a Camel out of a new pack and ignites it with a flick of his butane lighter. "So, what's happening?"

His deckhand sits beside him. "We've organized an all-volunteer thing in Nevada Cove. The *Sentinel* calls us the ICE squad: independent cleanup effort," she tells him excitedly.

Gregg regards her with interest as he exhales smoke.

"People are coming from all over the world to join us. Europe. Australia and New Zealand. Japan. Others are sending money."

"You're shitting me," he says with genuine surprise. "What do they want to do that for?"

Lee's pumped. "I know," she says. "It's pretty amazing. One of the things about the oil spill is that people everywhere are outraged—not just here, not even just in the U.S., but all over. It's like Alaska matters to them, even if they've never seen it."

Gregg frowns. No way would he travel all the way to New Zealand just to help Kiwis mop up spilled oil. "You really think you'll be able to clean the cove?" he asks. "I hear the oil's leaching down deep."

"It's symbolic," Lee says earnestly. "This is a way we can respond to the spill ourselves, without Mammoth calling all the shots."

"Who *is* paying for it?"

"The labor's volunteer, and we're getting food and equipment donations. You should see our camp, on that grassy bluff."

Gregg nods. "Sweet. So long as the wind's not out of the southwest."

"Yeah." Lee laughs. "And we just got a grant from the Greatland Conservation Fund. Looks like the Sierra Club and some of them might pony up, too."

Gregg stubs his cigarette against the sole of his deck shoe and flicks the butt into the yard.

"Hey!"

Her skipper looks at his deckhand with amusement. "Okay. Okay." He makes a big show of getting to his feet with a groan to retrieve his litter, miming a sore back when he leans over to search through the grass. Gregg holds up the cigarette butt for her to see before flicking off the remaining ash and dropping it into his shirt pocket. "Sounds like you might be too busy to come with me."

"Where?" Lee says, startled.

He tells her of his wildlife retrieval contract, how he's already hired Aaron and Wassily Chukanok. "But neither of them knows jackshit about the boat, so I was hoping..."

"Where would we go?"

"As far as Glory Point."

"I've always wanted to go there! What about Teklik Lagoon?"

158

"That's what they're paying us for."

"I wouldn't even have to pack!" she exults. "I left all my stuff on board. As usual."

"There you go," Gregg says, feeling expansive. "Piece of cake."

Lee hesitates. "There's just one thing."

Her boss raises an eyebrow.

"I'm not taking their money."

"What are you talking about?"

Lee crosses her arms across her chest. "I don't want any part of their blackmail. I don't want to profit from the spill in any way, shape, or form."

"Damn it, Lee. You know I've got to do a payroll."

"No," she says again, shaking her head.

Gregg's temper flares. "I'll get someone else then. God knows, plenty of hands are looking for work right now."

As he strides angrily to his truck, Lee follows like a puppy. "Wait. I know: I'll turn my wages over to ICE."

"Suit yourself." He opens the vehicle door. "But you better start thinking about putting something aside for winter."

"And no booze. Right, boss?"

"Scout's honor," Gregg says, holding up two fingers.

He drives away shaking his head. Lee's such an idealist, always wanting to believe the world better than it is. When's she going to learn? She said the volunteer cleanup effort was independent of Mammoth, but if she turns her wages over to it, isn't that a lot like ICE getting direct funding from the multinational giant? Oh, well; not his problem.

As he turns onto the highway, Gregg hears on the truck radio that the Alaska Public Radio Network has started compiling eyewitness accounts for a documentary of the oil spill, so Rugged Bay Broadcasting is appealing to boat owners involved in spill activities for a berth for its investigative journalist, Daniel Wolff. They offer to pay a ludicrously small stipend.

What the hell, the fisherman thinks. More money for Greggie. Wolff can sleep on the fold-out galley bench. It's uncomfortable, but then, the radio station is only offering a pittance. His sole acquaintance with Wolff was when the man volunteered at the high school as a losing wrestling coach. He guesses the broadcast journalist has spent little to no time at sea. Gregg chuckles aloud as he drives to Quincy's Saloon to celebrate his good fortune. Lee will definitely have her hands full with this crew.

On the six-week anniversary of the tanker grounding, the leading edge of the spill crosses the Gulf of Alaska, funneling overnight through Amatuli Strait and blackening the coastline of two national parks in the process. Those who'd held out any prayer of containing the rampant crude oil now abandon all hope.

So long, Cowpoke, Gregg breathes, imagining how crude oil must shade the depths where Dusty and the *Rodeo Rose* have come to their final rest. Peace, brother. Gregg probably should have gone ahead and strangled Dean Carson while he'd had the chance. An eye for an eye.

His orders are to cruise westward for up to ten days, comb as much shoreline as possible, and recover the carcasses of every oiled bird and animal they can find. Under no circumstances should Gregg or his crew tamper with the wildlife remains they retrieve, but only transport them back to town, to be immediately relinquished to Fish and Wildlife.

The Mammoth Petroleum Corporation has by then hired over ten thousand "oil spill technicians" to clean beaches, has leased hundreds of boats, small planes, helicopters, and all-terrain vehicles. Another five hundred workers have been put on the payroll for bird and animal rehabilitation in each of three coastal communities. The company has contracted with boat owners to ferry cleanup personnel and to retrieve oiled wildlife. In short, any Alaskan who wants spill work can have it, although a surprising number of people still refuse these gigs. It's as though the petroleum company can't come up with enough ways to hand out money, Gregg thinks. As if it's counting on all those greenbacks to magically soak up the oil—if not in the real world, then at least in everyone's imagination.

Despite widespread efforts to normalize life in the wake of the spill, many in Selby suffer symptoms of posttraumatic stress. Indeed, on day forty-eight, the state announces a series of free "Critical Incident Debriefing" workshops, open to all. Reportedly, though, the sessions get few takers. That's the problem with things like this, Tess decides: those who'd most benefit from counseling are those most unaware they need it. Which is exactly what Jackie says of her VA casework with war veterans in Anchorage.

Tess has for weeks been teamed at the otter center with Camille, Heidi, and a lumbering sad-eyed retiree from Connecticut named Bernie, who'd come to Selby expressly to wash oiled otters and who in fact reminds Tess of a Saint Bernard.

One morning, by way of greeting the others as they prepare to wash their first animal of the day, Camille announces that it's the silver anniversary of her family's arrival in Alaska.

"Twenty-five years ago today," the brassy young woman proclaims. "Same age as me, so I figure Mom was already mucho preggo when they hit the Alcan."

Bernie remarks quietly that, although a newcomer to the Last Frontier, he nonetheless feels that Alaska's his spiritual home.

"I was born here, too," Heidi says. "I'm never leaving."

Tessa agrees. "Alaska's been good to all of us."

Camille regards her teammates sternly. "You know, the Great Land's not so great—not all it's cracked up to be. Even before the spill, I mean."

"What are you talking about?" Tess says irritably, working dish soap into the animal's wet fur. Sometimes Camille really gets on her nerves.

The former high-school gymnast tells them about growing up in Kalifornsky, a sprawling inland settlement west of Selby, the first place in Alaska to be pioneered for its petroleum deposits, and where development in the 1950s had been an unregulated free-for-all. In fact, Tessa's sister had lived in Kalifornsky for several years while working a desk job for Arctic Oil. Tess remembers visiting Susie in her little company house and how the faucets hissed and spurted convulsively because of methane gas in the plumbing or something. The water tasted bad enough that many in the makeshift community paid to have drinking water delivered, but everyone there used well water for bathing, for washing clothes and dishes, and for watering gardens.

"About ten years ago," Camille continues, "my family was one of twenty-seven households to document benzene in our wells." She looks at Tessa. "You know what I'm talking about?"

Tess stares at her. "Why should I?" she says.

"It causes cancer." Camille looks at each of them significantly, although Tess refuses to meet her gaze. "It was in our water," she explains. "We drank it, cooked with it, bathed in it, washed our clothes with it." The young woman appeals to Tess again, as if expecting her, at least, to understand, but Tess does her best to ignore her.

"First us kids started to itch after our baths," Camille goes on. "Then we noticed that our tongues felt like they were on fire whenever we drank the tap water. Skin started peeling from the roof of our mouths."

"Gross," says Heidi.

Tess feels her pulse race. Hadn't Susie said something back then about her tongue tingling, her mouth going numb? Some months ago, the *Anchorage Tribune* had published a series about contaminated drilling mud left behind, unmonitored, at the abandoned Kalifornsky pits. Tess had set the articles aside, meaning to read them soon.

Bernie, looking mournful, shakes his head.

"Every female in my family has miscarried at least once," Camille continues, again glancing pointedly at Tessa.

She hears the anger in the younger woman's voice but wishes Camille would quit trying to engage her—because Tess is the only one with children? Or is it because she's a nurse? "How do you know there's a causal relationship?" Tessa challenges her. "What's your evidence?"

Her coworkers draw back in surprise. Tess returns her attention to the otter.

"That's really too bad, Camille," Heidi soothes.

"Our families filed a class-action lawsuit," their teammate declares defiantly. "It's tied up in litigation. I'm not even supposed to talk about it since the company wants to settle out of court."

So stop talking about it already, Tess thinks. She wishes the self-important young woman would quit blabbering. Tess doesn't want to think about benzene or miscarriages, or to wonder if Kalifornsky's groundwater is the reason why her sister can't carry a baby to term. It causes an uncomfortable sensation in her own womb. No one had *made* Camille's family live in Kalifornsky, she decides. If they were so unhappy there, they should have moved.

The day before departure, Gregg assembles his crew and the radio reporter, to give everyone the low-down on their mission. Daniel observes the pride with which the skipper shows off his impressive boat, and he can tell it really bothers Gregg that crude petroleum streaks and stains the exterior of the *Pegasus*. The wheelhouse, on the other hand, somehow remains spotless, and in fact, the fisherman warns them that he will dock the pay of anyone who fails to shed his or her protective gear before going inside. Since Gregg basically resembles a vagrant with his unruly long hair and untrimmed beard, his fastidiousness amuses the journalist.

Aaron's a half foot taller than Daniel remembers and now looks down on him. The youngster's gangly, all elbows and knees; even his ears jut out from his head, an effect no doubt exaggerated by his seaman's buzz cut. He's trying without much success to grow a mustache and has a nervous habit of rubbing his index finger along his upper lip, as if to make sure the facial hair is really there. "Double A," Daniel greets him, as the others follow Gregg to the stern of the boat.

"Hey, Coach." The clear-eyed young man pumps his hand, smiling. "Sorry I never returned your call, but they told us not to talk to anyone."

"I figured," the older man says. "Don't worry about it."

Aaron seems happy to be here, bouncing on the balls of his feet. "I'm still getting tons of calls. *Rolling Stone, Esquire,* you name it. I'm glad we'll be out of phone range."

Daniel hesitates but in the end can't help himself. "Did you see the captain that night? Was he—"

Aaron looks startled, glancing around to see who might be listening. Taking a breath, he says in a lowered voice, "You know how with some people, you can't really tell when they're under the influence?"

"Why do you say that?"

"Because of how much he drank before we cast off."

"You were there?" Daniel presses. "At the Pipeline Club?"

Aaron looks unhappy. "He had three doubles, at least. Seemed like a lot to me." He rejoins the others as they enter the cabin.

Far from taking any pleasure in the scoop, Daniel's shocked. So it's true, and Aengus really does deserve to be pilloried. It makes him want to confront the man himself, ask him what the hell he was thinking.

Shaking it off, he joins the others inside, where he observes that Aaron and Gregg are the same height, but that the father easily weighs twice as much as the son. The boy and his dad seem awkward around one another, making Daniel wonder how long it's been since they last saw each other.

In contrast to his reserve around his father, however, Aaron falls immediately into a familiar and affectionate routine with Lee.

"Pipsqueak," she teases him, although she barely reaches the boy's collarbone. She throws her arms around Aaron's waist in a heartfelt embrace that he returns unselfconsciously.

When the youngster musses her spiky hair with both hands, Lee cuffs him. "Hey! Respect your elders!"

Not only do they act like siblings, but they resemble each other physically as well, sharing skin tone, dark hair and eyes, Daniel thinks. Both could stand some more meat on their bones and, in fact, Lee is going to be in trouble if she doesn't stop losing weight. Since her short-short hair and dramatic weight loss have left her looking androgynous, she could easily pass for Aaron's sister *or* brother. To a greater degree than anyone else Daniel knows, Lee has acquired a tragic air since the spill—like Maria Falconetti playing Joan of Arc in the classic film.

Gregg's childhood friend, Wassily Chukanok, stands a little apart from the rest of them. Wisps of black facial hair sprout from his otherwise smooth-skinned cheeks, a thick head of jet-black hair topping eyes that seem to absorb everything. Daniel offers his hand and introduces himself when Gregg fails to do so. "How are things in Pogibshi?"

"We're hurting," the Native man says, so simply that the journalist chides himself for asking such a thoughtless question.

It surprises Daniel to realize he's the sole Caucasian here, and it reminds him of Vietnam, when he and Declan Moore were the only white members of their platoon.

"Listen up!" Gregg commands. "Lee's in charge. Do what she says. She knows the *Pegasus* inside-out, so if you have any questions, ask her. She'll show you where to stow your gear."

When they come up from the fo'c'sle, Aaron's captivated by the glass fishing float that rests beside the steering wheel, staring fixedly at the frosted green buoy as Lee points out the features of the kitchen, or galley. The young man asks his father where he got it.

"Beachcombing on Baidarki," the skipper says. "You've seen these before." Gregg lobs the baseball-sized keepsake to the boy, who flinches as he catches it in both hands.

"Never."

His dad laughs at him. "It's not going to break."

"It's glass!"

"Even so, that sucker's been bobbing around in the North Pacific. It'll probably outlast us both."

Aaron traces with his finger the pattern of rhomboid shapes etched onto the float's surface by the fishing net that had once encased it.

"Maybe we'll find one while we're out," Lee tells him.

"Really?"

"Why not?"

As prearranged, a U.S. Fish and Wildlife Service representative comes aboard to brief them about their responsibilities. Khaki uniform shirt, brown slacks, black plastic name tag, brown hair pulled back in a severe bun, matronly Abigail is all business. Daniel flips open a new stenographer's tablet to take notes.

"The agency would like you to retrieve the remains of all oil spill mortalities you can find, but you're forbidden from disturbing anything that's still alive."

"What if we find dead things that don't have any oil on them?" Lee wants to know.

"It takes very little petroleum to kill a wild creature," Abigail says primly. "A dab the size of a dime can kill a seabird. And lots of animals are dying from ingesting it, so you might *not* see any oil on their bodies. Just bring in everything. I mean, make sure it's dead first."

"What if we find things that are oiled or injured but still alive?" Gregg asks. "You want us to perform mercy killings?"

"No!" Flustered, Abigail hastens to explain that only trained "handlers" have the authority to capture live wildlife. She warns the *Pegasus* crew that they can be arrested for violation of this policy. And, she emphasizes, addressing the skipper directly, the fishing vessel will be seized and impounded by the Coast Guard while the matter is under investigation—a process that could take a year or more to complete.

Abigail instructs them to work in tandem with a Port Clark boat called the *Joanna*, which has trained handlers on board. "It's not your job to try to clean up the oil, either. The cleaning crews will be right behind you, but the agency hopes to recover as many mortalities as possible before workers go in with high-pressure hoses and dispersants." She regards each of them in turn. "Any questions?"

No, no questions, so Abigail disembarks.

Impatient to set out, Gregg gives Lee his truck keys and tells her to take everyone grocery shopping. "Mammoth's got a line of credit at the Super Duper. Here's the purchase order number," he says, handing her a scrap of paper as he regards Daniel steadily. "I suggest you eat on Mammoth's tab, too. It'll make my life easier."

The journalist hesitates, nods. "Sure." He worries that if he eats food purchased with oil company funds, he'll cross some kind of ethical line, but he also recognizes that he's essentially Gregg's guest.

"No restrictions attached," the skipper tells Lee, "so be sure you buy plenty of New York steak and lobster tails. Get whatever your little hearts desire."

Aaron grins when he sees that his father's not joking. "Microwave corn dogs!"

"What about herring eggs?" Wassily says plaintively. "Or stinkheads."

"And don't forget to pick up a few cases of beer, some whiskey, and schnapps," Gregg adds, prompting a glare from Lee.

"I jokes," the skipper says, using the expression familiar to bush Alaska, but no one seems very amused.

Selby's merchants have never had it so good, Daniel thinks. Only two months earlier, most businesses were toughing out a lean winter. Now they can't stock their shelves fast enough to keep up with Mammoth-underwritten purchases. It should have been great news for the local economy, right? So why does it feel so bad?

13

L ee."

The deckhand's just exited the Super Duper, leaving the guys to finish the shopping. She whirls around to face Jackie. Her ex-lover's wavy chestnut hair is swept back, its red highlights gleaming; she's wearing city clothes— dark skirt and periwinkle blouse, and her smile's still a thing of beauty. It galls Lee that Jackie looks completely unruffled, especially when Lee herself is so thrashed. "What are you doing here?" she asks.

The other woman peers into Lee's face, trying to make eye contact. "The Division of Emergency Services is 'borrowing' me to help with critical incident debriefing—counseling," she says, following her when the deckhand pivots abruptly and heads for Gregg's truck. "After Selby, I go to Pogibshi, then Port Clark."

Lee pauses with her hand on the door handle. "Where are you staying?"

"With Tess and Daniel. Well, with Tess, since Daniel's going out with you and Gregg, right?"

Lee nods. She opens the door to climb in behind the wheel. "So. You need a ride?"

"No. I've got the Subaru." Jackie gestures to their friends' blue station wagon. "How are you doing?"

Lee sits with hands gripping the steering wheel, staring straight ahead. "How the hell do you think I'm doing?"

Jackie says nothing.

"You moved away just in time," the deckhand says. "Before the spill whacked us upside the head."

"Can we talk about it?" Jackie asks. "Sometime when you're not so busy?"

Lee sees the men waiting for her to pick them up in front of the store, all three laden with double sacks of groceries. She turns the key in the ignition. "Don't know when that will be," she says. "Unless you're still here when I get back."

"You can always call me."

"I'll think about it," Lee says, reversing out of the parking spot.

Daniel observes the oily scum they motor through, clotted with everything from dead birds to seaweed to litter. "It's almost impossible to describe in words how horrendous this is," he says to Lee, covering his mouth and nose with his hand. "Like the stench, for instance."

"This is nothing," she warns him. "It gets worse."

"And our captain acts like we're on a pleasure cruise," he complains, indicating the flybridge, where Gregg and Wassily survey Rugged Bay together, the skipper pointing out sights to his old friend.

"He hates being sidelined during fishing season," Lee says. "All fishermen do." She hands Daniel a pair of work gloves and he helps her stow the greasy fenders. The two shake their heads over the boat's pretty teal trim, now smeared and blotched with crude oil.

"He's worked his whole life for this boat," she says.

"It's a real shame," Daniel agrees.

Approaching the Gateway, the mouth of Rugged Bay, they encounter Mammoth's barge-mounted skimmers and dredges pressure-washing

Thompson Cove, which, because of its orientation, has been only lightly oiled. A crew of perhaps a hundred works the rocky beach.

"What's the deal?" Lee says. "There's no oil there. Why don't they take their equipment out into the gulf where it might actually do some good?" She surveys the skiffs and cabin cruisers that hover offshore of the cleaning operation like worker bees servicing a hive. The smaller boats carry photographers and film crews, all of whom appear to be busy recording the scene.

"Oh, but the light's good here," Daniel says sardonically. "It's photogenic. And with such convenient access to town."

Lee gives him a piercing look. "Doesn't it bother you?"

"You mean, the way Mammoth Petroleum's manipulating reality? It's not the first company to do so, and it for sure won't be the last."

She raises her binoculars to scan for birds.

Ten minutes later, having cleared the Gateway, they hit the chop that heralds the incoming tide and Daniel lurches unsteadily.

"Landlubber," Lee teases.

He raises his arms in mock surrender. "Never said I wasn't." He calls to Aaron, who strolls the deck and in fact appears to be practicing dance steps. "Yo! What's your secret?"

"Skateboarding, dude. Snowboarding. " The young man extends both hands in imitation of a high-wire artist, tiptoeing away from them gracefully even as the *Pegasus* stutters through more whitecaps that keep Daniel staggering.

Once Aaron's out of earshot, he says to Lee, "I can't believe this is how I finally get on a boat. Chasing an oil spill." He shakes his head. "With someone whose judgment I seriously question."

"Gregg's better out here than he is in town," she replies. "And oil spill or not, we'll get to see some amazing places."

When they hit the gulf, water begins to break over the bow, and the color drains from Daniel's face. He creeps inside to stretch out on the galley bench.

"Try to stay upright," Lee urges, following him in.

He raises himself with effort. "Now I get that saying," he pants.

"Which one?"

"How first you're afraid it'll kill you, then you're afraid it won't." He crosses his arms on the table and lays his head down again.

"Keep your eyes open. Focus on the horizon line."

Daniel moans.

"Want some ginger tea?"

"God, no. Does it help?"

His stomach finally settles when the seas do, and Daniel returns to the deck an hour later to find Aaron sitting atop the main hold, clutching his stomach.

"You, too, eh?" the older man says, covering his mouth and nose again with one hand. Something smells hugely, unimaginably foul.

"It's the smell," the boy replies miserably, gesturing beyond the boat. "Makes me heave." Daniel stares. The expanse of raw petroleum here has turned the entire ocean, or so it would seem, the color and consistency of greasy diarrhea. The oil spill that lies before him is of an entirely different order of magnitude than that which he has witnessed immediately around Selby—and that was alarming enough, he thinks. *This* scene, however, is like the End of Days. Apocalypse now. He notices the giant bathtub ring that blackens the rocky shoreline as far the eye can see. Good God.

He knows the state DEC is tracking the oil spill's movement along the coast, but as far as he can tell, no one—not NOAA, not the Coast Guard—is monitoring its journey on open water. Unless the "product" washes ashore, nobody seems particularly concerned with it. Out of sight, out of mind? Daniel makes a mental note to consult wildlife biologist Nick Calhoun about the long-term threat to pelagic sea life.

Lee joins him at the bow. As if reading his mind, she says, "No one's paying any attention to the stuff that's washing out to sea or sinking. Oh, excuse me: according to the experts, oil does not sink."

"Do you think it'll eventually wash ashore in Russia or Asia?" Daniel asks her. "Or drift into the middle of the Pacific and create a giant dead zone?"

"There's already a giant dead zone," she says. "But yeah, it for damn sure won't just vanish."

"Did you know they can ID oil, tell exactly where it comes from? It's called 'fingerprinting.'"

Lee laughs harshly. "They come up with all this ingenious stuff, so why can't they come up with a way to prevent a spill in the first place?"

She hands Daniel her Nikons and he scans the poisoned, discolored ocean. There really is no end to it.

"Back there, at the Gateway?" Lee says. "Where it got rough and you got sick? We call that 'confused waters.' 'Mixed-up seas.' But here's what's really confusing: everybody wants something from Alaska. Furs. Gold, copper, zinc. Fish. Oil or timber. Hunting trophies. The 'pristine wilderness experience that renews your spirit' blah blah blah. But whatever it is, everyone's taking something; no one's giving back."

He glances at her. "How about you? What do you want from it? Are you taking or giving?"

"Fishing's all about taking," she says unhappily. "That's what I mean."

Daniel points skyward, seeking to distract her. "What kinds of birds are these?" He returns her binos and cranes his head back until he gazes directly overhead, neck stretched taut, picturing his son Elias in the same sky-gazing posture.

Lee scarcely glances at the birds flickering above them. "Arctic terns," she says dully.

"Look how fast they move. Are they rare?"

She waits until Daniel lowers his head and looks at her. "They have the longest migration of any bird in the world, from Antarctica to the Arctic, and back. Almost twenty thousand miles a year."

He whistles appreciatively.

"Yeah," she says in a small voice. "How'd you like to fly from one end of the earth to the other, only to end your life in an oil spill?"

The first place the *Pegasus* crew puts in is Mallard Cove. While Gregg anchors the boat offshore, Lee ferries everyone to the beach in the inflatable skiff. She feels a warm breeze on her face.

Surveying the shoreline from the bow of the Zodiac, Aaron exclaims, "No oil!"

Wassily, Daniel, and Lee glance at each other. Is "no oil" even remotely possible at this juncture? But as they draw closer, she can see that, except for some isolated blobs of petroleum that look like stranded black jellyfish, the beach does indeed appear to have escaped the spill. Go figure.

Lee cuts the motor and raises the outboard, leaving the small rubber boat to coast the rest of the way in, gently scraping bottom in the shallows.

"I don't get it," Wassily puzzles, pointing to the rocks and boulders and exposed tree roots that form a low wall at the back of the cove, all of which are heavily stained with petroleum, while closer to them the gentle slope of sand and gravel appears almost completely uncontaminated. With Aaron leading the way, the four clamber out of the Zodiac in their new Mammoth Petroleum–issued hip waders and carry the empty craft above the tide line.

Bundles of sea vegetation as big as rolled carpets line the shore. When Lee comments on them, Wassily says he's never seen so much kelp in one place.

"You think it's because of the spill?" Daniel asks.

Wassily shrugs.

Lee remembers a conversation she'd had with Kurt, when they both still worked at the otter center.

"Ever wonder what the oil's doing to the ecology of the ocean?" he'd asked her on one of their breaks.

"What do you mean?" She was, as usual around him, flustered by her own ignorance.

"You know how otters were hunted so heavily for their fur that they nearly went extinct?" He hunched his back against the wind to light a cigarette.

Lee did know a little about that. (And knew also that Russian fur traders had customarily held Aleut wives and children hostage until the male hunters delivered the requisite number of pelts. Humans do some really inhuman things, she thought.)

"Otters are what's called a keystone species," Kurt told her. "You remove them from the equation and everything else collapses." He exhaled a stream of smoke. "I know you're a lap swimmer. Do you dive, too?"

Lee shook her head.

"But you've seen kelp beds?"

"Sure."

"Did you know that in the summer here, with all the nonstop sunlight, bull kelp can grow two to three feet a day? It's like time-lapse photography." Kurt smiled. "Anyway, kelp beds are special marine habitats, sort of like underwater forests. My favorite place to dive." He took another drag, exhaling slowly. "For one thing, the stipes—or stalks—offer protection from predators, so lots of species like to hang out in kelp beds: porpoises, sea lions, all kinds of fish. They use them as nurseries." He turns to her. "Urchins proliferate on the seafloor underneath because kelp is their main food source. They actually threaten their own habitat by eating through the holdfasts that anchor the stipes to the bottom." Again he draws on the cigarette. "Guess who keeps the urchins in check."

"Otters."

"Exactly." Kurt nodded. "Otters live out their entire lives in and around kelp beds. They're the only marine mammal that never goes ashore, not even to give birth. Which is one reason they're getting hammered by the spill."

"I knew that," she exclaimed, immediately regretting how childish she sounded.

"So you know that without them to regulate the urchin population, urchins could easily kill enough kelp that the ecosystem will actually implode." Kurt sighs, dropping his butt on the ground and stepping on it. "When otters were hunted so heavily a hundred years ago? Urchins devoured so much kelp that it was like underwater clear-cuts. Those beds still haven't recovered."

Lee stares at the oversized rolls of sea vegetation that surround her like so many giant cigars. Is that what's happening right now, an urchin population explosion because so many otters are dying? How many other ecosystems will go haywire as a result of the spill?

Despite the inexplicable absence of petroleum on the beach itself, Daniel quickly counts almost forty stranded bird carcasses and about half as many more waterlogged corpses bobbing in the shallow waves that lap the shore.

Wassily pulls a carton of plastic trash sacks from his knapsack, distributing handfuls of the folded black packets to his coworkers. They all don the elbow-length rubber gloves that Mammoth now orders by the gross—making some manufacturer rich beyond its wildest dreams, Daniel guesses. Because everyone feels squeamish about handling rotting creatures coated in toxic slime, they start by working in pairs, one partner holding open a trash sack while the other gingerly gathers seabird remains, depositing them carefully into the bag. Disturbing the bodies—or body parts—releases the sickening odor of decomposition. It helps to breathe through his mouth, Daniel discovers, wishing someone had had the foresight to provide them with respirators.

Decay and predation have taken their toll on the bird corpses, rendering them all but unidentifiable. Those that aren't already decapitated almost always have their eyeballs plucked out, for some reason. And many have been eviscerated by scavengers. But no matter their condition, Lee has an uncanny knack for recognizing different species, some of which she has never even heard of before. Phalaropes. Whimbrels. Scoters.

"There must be plenty of sick animals in there," Wassily comments, gazing into the dark spruce woods. "Sick from eating these guys."

At first, it unsettles Daniel to handle the remains of the dead. It feels sacrilegious to disturb the bodies of wild creatures that, after all, have probably lived out their lives doing everything they could to avoid contact with humans. Still, it isn't long before he and the others become habituated to the grisly activity. Half an hour, more or less. Since Daniel's experienced something like this before—in war—he wonders if human beings' capacity to normalize horror is, in the end, an asset or liability for the species.

He and the others try out different words for the bodies: Remains. Carcasses. Corpses. Victims. Mortalities. Soon enough they settle on "carks" and "morts."

Gooks, Daniel thinks. Charlie.

Once they've gotten the knack of collecting, each begins to work alone, preferring solitude for the task of grim reaping. An hour later, he notices Lee and Wassily lingering in the same location, apparently picking up globs of emulsified oil and dropping them into their collections bags.

"The cleanup crews are behind us, remember?" he calls.

"But it's melting," Lee shouts back. "Might as well get what we can."

Daniel considers the effort impractical, if not futile, since the incoming tide will just bear with it more oil, as well as more morts. But he too now labors to remove gelled petroleum as best he can.

Aaron spots their first oiled mammal at the back of the beach, calling Daniel over. Something with sharp teeth and claws has already fed on the bloated, toddler-sized seal carcass, and it teems with maggots. The older man watches his face as the boy struggles to compose himself. Aaron's too young for this; what was Gregg thinking?

Wassily fetches two flat shovels from the Zodiac and, holding their breath, he and Daniel manage to transfer the remains of the seal into the triple-layered trash sacks that Lee holds open for them, her head twisted away from the sight and the smell. Aaron wanders off in the direction of the beached inflatable.

When they finish with the seal, the three adults look at each other. "Unbelievable," Wassily says, shaking his head.

"You guys! Look at this!" Aaron hails them from where he's used an entrenching tool to dig a hole near the Zodiac. When the others join him, they see that Aaron's excavation has puddled with not water but dark, glistening petroleum.

"Oh, no." Lee stares into the depression as the young man fingers his upper lip.

"Should have known it was too good to be true," Wassily says.

Scraping sand and gravel back into the hole, Aaron mutters "Sorry," as if he's to blame for exposing the truth of the seemingly unsullied beach.

Daniel slings an arm around the boy's shoulders. "Let's get out of here," he says. Aaron reminds him of himself at that age—old enough in years, perhaps, but still sorely lacking in life experience.

Gregg curses and grumbles about the "toxic crud" they track onto the *Pegasus*. The gray-and-yellow Zodiac, too, soon wears its own mantle of raw petroleum, which, Lee still thinks, resembles nothing so much as baby shit. Except that it doesn't ever wash off.

As daily temperatures increase, the cloying smell of decaying flesh on the coast mingles with the nauseating stink of warmed-over crude oil. In the absence of breathing masks, Lee and her shipmates tie bandanas over their faces, resembling bandits. Do they still risk health hazards from breathing fumes?

She and Wassily line the boat's main hold with a double layer of thick-mil poly and dub it the Mortuary, filling the storage space not with flopping fish or scrabbling crabs but with the bagged remains of what Aaron calls "deadlife." Fortunately, the ocean's cold acts like refrigerant, delaying decomposition. Gregg watches Lee closely one evening as she lowers the day's bagged collections through the hatch. "Not what I had in mind when I had her built," her boss grouses. "She's supposed to be a fishing boat, not a goddamned crypt."

Gregg takes obvious pleasure in having Wassily on board, but Lee hates the way her skipper ignores his own son. Aaron mostly spends his time when they're not working listening to his Sony Walkman, sometimes practicing dance moves. Lee herself does whatever she can to stay occupied. When not ashore bagging morts, she coils lines, scrubs the galley and the head, and washes the boat's windows daily. She does most of the cooking, too, for something to do, and when she runs out of ideas for activities, she plays cards with one of the men or lays out serial games of solitaire.

She also revisits the encounter with Jackie more than once. Her ex-lover's capacity for calm detachment (even in the midst of an environmental disaster!) offends her, suggesting as it does that Jackie's unaffected by the spill. And why—since it was Lee who'd instigated their breakup—does she continue to feel as if her lover abandoned *her*?

Unlike the two-day boat ride home after longlining for black cod, this time the *Pegasus* never outdistances the oil spill, encountering every iteration of ocean-borne crude that has so far been classified: spatter, stringer, slick, tar, tar mat, tar ball, asphalt, mousse, patty, loaf, film, stain, coat, and cover. Lee observes that just as there's an entire lexicon to describe different states of spilled petroleum, so too no bay, cove, cape, arm, sound, strait, passage, point, inlet, channel, entrance, or narrows has escaped contamination.

The beaches they visit at low tide trail ribbons of iridescent sheen over their temporarily exposed expanses. As everyone now knows, the petroleum percolates up from the substrate to ooze back into the sea, only to wash ashore again on the next incoming tide. Lee wonders how many hundreds or thousands of ebb-and-flow repetitions it will take before the spill's residue is completely washed away. But washed away to where? At what point does crude oil finally break down completely and stop posing risks?

The intertidal zones smell worse and worse as the sun's increasing warmth cook both the crude and the organisms it has smothered. Limpets, periwinkles, barnacles, clams, and mussels lie upside-down and inside-out, the lives normally protected by shells and carapaces now decomposed, sometimes liquefied. The single large lopsided claws of dead hermit crabs make them look like miniature boxers who've been KO'd. Lee's stupefied by the almost complete absence of life along the usually teeming shore. Nothing moves. No red-legged oystercatchers stilt-stepping into the surf; no shrilling peeps darting into the lace of foam at water's edge; no crabs zigging and zagging, their busy legs

179

stitching tiny footprints into wet sand; no countless microscopic cope-
pods spritzing about your feet like carbonation.

Now nothing moves except the gulls and crows feeding opportunisti-
cally and gluttonously on the tainted flesh of the spill-killed. Lee soon
gives up trying to scare the scavengers from their poisonous banquet, as
the plump birds merely lift lazily into the air when threatened, to alight
again only yards away, where they continue to forage on the seemingly
inexhaustible supply of carrion.

How long before anyone will once more enjoy steamed clams and
mussels? How long before fish and shrimp and crab are declared edible?
What must it be like for the Chukanoks and others who rely on subsistence, for whom the gathering and eating of wild food is not just
occasional novelty but the very means and meaning of existence? Lee
pictures Wassily's wife, Marie, holding her hair away from her face
with one hand as she lifts a sea urchin to her lips with the other, only
to discover its spiny cup brimming with black oil.

Lee knows she'll never forgive those like Tess who've prostituted
themselves, welcoming Mammoth's hush money. After all, if everyone
had refused payment, the oil company would have had no choice but to
let them all continue as volunteers. And she blames Gregg for bringing his son out here. Wildlife retrieval has proven not merely R- but
X-rated, and Aaron is clearly too young for it. Even so, Lee's glad for
the boy's company. He alone among them remains upbeat, the spill
so far seeming more of a curiosity to him than a full-blown tragedy.
Aaron makes no secret of his desire to find a glass float like his father's,
beachcombing at every opportunity. Maybe teenagers are hardwired
to be hopeful, she thinks, remembering her own middle-school years
when Weezie's illness and death followed so swiftly on the heels of her
parents' divorce that for a long time Lee believed the dissolution of a
marriage would kill you.

In addition to land-based mortalities, they encounter waterlogged
carcasses floating just beneath the ocean surface, often so saturated
that when struck by a boat or nudged by an oar, the sodden bodies
sink. Between the tendency of dead bodies to submerge and the fact of

predation, Lee can easily understand why Fish and Wildlife has estimated that a mere five to ten percent of all oil spill fatalities will ever be documented.

One morning the *Pegasus* comes upon an oiled otter floundering in the tide rip, its fur tufted with putty-like petroleum. Lee grabs the dip net, capturing the sick animal easily and pulling it alongside the boat.

As Wassily helps her lift it on board, the creature thrashes and bares its teeth. Lee wishes they could somehow sedate the otter so it wouldn't waste precious energy trying to defend itself against them. Gregg gets on the horn immediately to raise the *Joanna*.

"Goddammit," the skipper fumes, clicking the transmitter repeatedly. "Where are you guys?" They'd seen the wildlife handlers in Neptune Cove just an hour earlier.

Stricken, Aaron's finger goes automatically to his fuzzy mustache. "It needs help. We have to get help."

Gregg glares at his son. "Shave that thing off, or I swear I'll do it for you!"

Lee and Wassily leave the animal in peace in the transom well, tangled in the dip net. It lies on its back hyperventilating, too exhausted to move.

"Maybe we should put it back in the water, let it die in peace?" Aaron searches the adults' faces.

Wassily, Daniel, and Lee look at one another uncertainly. No one knows what to do. If it's going to die anyway, Lee thinks, then Aaron is right; surely the otter would feel more secure in the element it knows best. Is death by drowning preferable to organ failure? Maybe it would be most humane of them to shoot it.

Gregg drives the *Pegasus* at full speed until he overtakes a small vessel named the *Sea Sprite*, traveling east. Lee knows the skipper, Liz Connelly, and her heart lifts with the good fortune of encountering a rare woman boat captain, whom she thinks more likely to be receptive to helping the otter than a man might be. The *Sea Sprite* slows to allow the *Pegasus* to draw alongside.

Liz, wearing a hand-knit hat, smiles in greeting from her flybridge. Her lone deckhand, whom Lee recalls to be Liz's nephew, catches the line Wassily tosses him, wrapping it handily around the cleat.

"We've got an otter that needs to go to the rehab center ASAP," Gregg tells the other skipper, indicating the terrified marine mammal, now backed against the transom, trying to gnaw its way out of the net.

"We're not supposed to handle live animals," Liz says, eyes wide.

Lee steps closer to the gunwale. "It's really sick."

"We could both lose our contracts." The other woman, ignoring Lee, addresses Gregg. "Could lose our boats."

"It's really suffering," Aaron pleads. "It'll die if we don't help it."

Liz tells her deckhand to free the line. She puts the *Sea Sprite* into gear. As her vessel picks up speed, the young man's voice drifts back to the *Pegasus*: "You going to report them?"

Lee tastes blood; she's chewed the inside of her cheek. Gregg gives the *Pegasus* throttle, in pursuit of the wooden boat, she thinks at first. But as they pass the older vessel, Lee realizes her skipper's decided to transport the otter himself. Aaron squeezes the rail with both hands. Wassily and Daniel confer briefly before Wassily goes to check on the sea mammal.

"It's dead," he reports loudly. "We're legal."

Lee climbs to the flybridge to inform Gregg. He doesn't say anything, swinging the boat in a wide arc without decreasing speed to resume their original course. Aaron stumbles into the wheelhouse, leaving his coworkers to free the animal's body from the dip net, but after struggling for ten or fifteen minutes to disentangle it, Lee finally resorts to cutting the mesh with her fishing knife. Wassily double-bags the dead otter, placing it atop the growing collection in the main hold.

When she goes in search of him, Lee finds Aaron in his bunk, curled on his side, facing the wall. He's burrowed into his sleeping bag, headphones not so much conveying stereophonic sound as shuttering him from the rest of the world. She withdraws in silence.

14

Lee spreads newspaper over the floor of the galley and brings the dip net inside to clean and mend. Daniel scribbles into his spiral-bound notepad at the table while opposite him, and every bit as intently, Wassily studies his red leather-bound Bible. Lee observes her own hands unspooling hanging twine and thinks: if we just keep busy enough, maybe we can pretend that things aren't as hideous as they really are.

"It's a wonder no one's died from this," Daniel says.

"You mean, only thousands of otters and tens of thousands of birds?" Lee responds drily.

"I mean, Mammoth's done nothing to protect its workers—excuse me, 'technicians'—from exposure. No face masks, no respirators, no meaningful health precautions whatsoever."

Wassily clears his throat. "Yeah. Some of the villagers have gotten real sick since the oil came."

"The stuff is toxic, for Christ's sake," Daniel says, at which Wassily flinches. "Sorry."

"Imagine if the holds were full of body bags—I mean, human body bags," Lee says. "This would be like a war."

Daniel snorts. "This is nothing like a war, believe me. Not even close."

Wassily shakes his head but says nothing.

"Why not?" Lee insists, tying off a knot. "If oil wiped out people the way it's wiping out everything else, they'd shut down the petroleum industry in a hurry. Probably we'd be using renewable energy by now."

"I don't know about that," Wassily scoffs, bookmarking his place with the thin gold ribbon attached to the Bible's binding and setting it on his lap. "Do you realize how much money there is to be made from fossil fuels?"

"It's nothing like a war," Daniel repeats stubbornly. "No resemblance whatsoever."

"Sure it is," Wassily says. "It's the same war *kass'aqs* have been waging against Mother Earth and her creatures, including us original people, since time immemorial."

"*Kass'aqs?*"

"White people. Western uncivilization."

Daniel's visibly taken aback.

"Just ask the Ogoni, in Nigeria," Wassily continues. "Or the tribes of the Oriente, in Ecuador. Ask what's left of the Osage, right here in the good old U.S. of A. They'll give you an earful about what it's like to go head-to-head with oil companies in defense of your life, your land."

Daniel flushes, though whether with anger or embarrassment, Lee can't tell. Wassily resumes his reading, turning another tissue-thin page. In a moment, she sets her net-mending down and slips outside to escape the tension.

Scanning the horizon with her Nikons, Lee seeks a glimpse of something living. Anything. As if in response to her wish, a wavering V of migratory birds appears against the high clouds. Lee watches the skein draw closer and recognizes the familiar languorous wing beats and extra-long necks. Trumpeter swans. She offers a prayer of thanks.

But then her heart sinks. It might after all have been better not to see them. What if the swans land in the oil? Shit, they *will* land in the oil because, hungry from their long flight across the gulf, the shore is exactly where they're headed in search of the next meal. Her eyes well with now-familiar frustration and despair. She recalls again her encounter with Nick Calhoun at Deborah's Meadow and wishes she'd been capable of acknowledging the biologist's heartbreak.

Lee thinks of Aaron burrowed in his bunk and remembers how before they left the harbor, now encircled by protective boom, she'd led him to J float and had him lie face down beside her, to view the marine creatures clinging to the sides and undersides of the dock: sea stars ranging from gold to blood-red, urchins like green-needled pincushions, beige barnacles feeding with their pulsing feathery filters, frilled anemones in opalescent shades of white—even a foot-long rust-colored gumboot chiton, which, she explained to him, Russian settlers had eaten and which some people still harvest for food. An entire thriving, silent world, one thankfully uncontaminated by crude oil. At least so far. The boy's smile had stretched from ear to ear.

Daniel appears beside her on deck, looking weary. She offers him her binoculars, which he declines with a shake of his head. "Why's Gregg so hard on Aaron?" he asks.

Lee lowers the lenses. "It's always been like this. As long as I've known them, anyway. I think it might be why Peg divorced him. Well, that and Gregg's drinking." She hesitates because she doesn't want to be disloyal to her boss, but it also occurs to her that Daniel might be able to shed some light on the father-son dynamic. "The last time they fished together was in Bristol Bay three—no, four—years ago. My first summer with Gregg. I thought it might be my last."

"What happened?"

"Aaron was fifteen, I think. Gregg was afraid his son was too young, wouldn't measure up, and he probably had his doubts about me, too—me being female and all—so he hired Royce Harding at the last minute."

Daniel reacts with surprise. "The biker dude?"

"Yeah. Thing is, Royce's redeeming feature, he's a teetotaler—never touches alcohol, and Gregg was trying to clean up his act. Since Royce had never worked on a boat before, Gregg didn't have to pay him full share. I think the way he saw it, Royce and Aaron and me, the three of us, equaled two experienced hands. But Gregg got us at discount." Lee looks at Daniel, aware of the unflattering portrait she's painting of her skipper. "Anyway, he and Royce got into all this competitive BS: who could go with the least amount of sleep, who could go longest without shaving, that sort of thing."

"A pissing contest," Daniel says.

"Exactly."

"At least you and Aaron had each other."

"That was part of the problem," Lee says. "Gregg thought I babied Aaron or something, so he got down on both of us." She pauses. "When we fished Ugashik, a dogfish got caught in the net. You know what that is?"

Daniel shakes his head.

"It's a shark. This one was maybe three feet long, not real big, but still, razor-sharp teeth. You have to pay attention." Lee presses her lips together. "I was all set to throw it back, like we always do, but Royce declares that shark meat's a delicacy. He says we should cook some up. Gregg doesn't skip a beat. He orders Aaron to kill it and butcher it into steaks. Tells me to back off, let Aaron do it himself." Lee glances at Daniel, who listens intently. "When Aaron balked, Gregg threatened to withhold his crew share." She shakes her head at the memory. "So Gregg and Royce have got the shark immobilized, it's suffocating, and they're waiting for Aaron to kill it and prove his manhood or something. Aaron, meanwhile, is freaked. Gregg tries to force his knife into Aaron's hand, but ends up nicking himself instead, so now there's blood, too."

"Jesus."

"I screamed at them, kicked Gregg in the shin. Then I grabbed the shark by the tail and threw it overboard."

"Way to go."

186

"Gregg was *pissed*. I was sure he'd fire me." Lee laughs uncomfortably. "He wouldn't talk to Aaron or me for the rest of the trip. Instead, he'd tell Royce to tell us when he wanted something done. Real mature." She regards Daniel again. "The thing is, I just know it wouldn't have been so bad if Royce hadn't've been there. It's like he brought out Gregg's dark side."

"We men sometimes have that uplifting effect on one another. What did Aaron do?"

"Avoided all of us."

"Smart kid." Daniel smiles. "Well, I guess he got over it, because it's obvious how much he loves you."

Lee turns away to hide her sudden emotion.

"That must've been the same year I coached Aaron," he goes on. "Before he moved away. Gregg came to all the meets, but he never said 'boo' to me."

"Man of few words."

Daniel hesitates. "So how was it seeing Jackie?"

Tearing up, Lee fits the binos to her eyes, immediately blurring her field of vision. "Fine." She aims the lenses at the horizon and asks him how Tess is, to change the subject.

"To tell you the truth, we're not getting along too well."

Lee risks a glance at him.

"When I told her I was doing this and asked if I could borrow her sleeping bag, she threw it at me." He shrugs. "She hates it that I find the spill so interesting."

"If she really hated you, she would have thrown something at you that hurts." Lee titters, amused by the image of Tess in a frilly apron, indignant housewife with one hand on her hip, the other wielding a rolling pin. But Daniel's too preoccupied to share her amusement.

"She's not real happy with me right now, either," Lee offers.

"How's that?"

"A little difference of opinion about getting paid to clean otters." She feels a sudden sharp lump in her throat. "How're Eli and Minke?"

"Still in Anchorage," he says.

"You miss them?"

"Not really. Too much going on; I don't have time to miss them. Besides, they're way better off in Anchorage right now." Daniel sounds defensive. "Tess wants me to feel guilty about it, but I don't. I talk to them on the phone."

"What a time for her to get pregnant," Lee murmurs, turning out to sea and raising the Nikons again.

Daniel pulls her around roughly by the elbow, so he can see her face. "*What?*"

"I think she said she might be," Lee manages, gazing into his startled eyes. "Maybe not?" Then she adds, "Shit."

Once he registers the possibility of Tessa's pregnancy, Daniel feels reinvigorated, a deflated helium balloon exposed to heat and thereby restored to buoyancy. The prospect of another baby fills him with joy. Like a phoenix rising from the ashes, he thinks, this could prove to be the oil spill's gift to their family.

The crew of the *Pegasus* makes ready to ride the tide into Teklik Lagoon. Despite the omnipresent devastation of the spill, Daniel looks forward to the destination. He's heard larger-than-life fables about the hidden estuary for years: how the water is the same color as the South Pacific, how so many spawning salmon congregate there in the summer that you can walk across the water stepping only on their backs.

Gregg, with what Daniel now considers characteristic lack of dignity, complains loudly of having to miss the excursion. It has so far been their modus operandi for the skipper to remain on board while the others go ashore in the Zodiac to make the collections, but now that he thinks about it, Daniel supposes there's no reason Lee couldn't be the one to stay behind, as she seems perfectly capable of keeping the *Pegasus* safe. Not that Gregg Anderson would ever relinquish that much control to either a deckhand or a woman, let alone to someone who happens to be both.

But just as they prepare to lower themselves into the inflatable, the skipper emerges from the wheelhouse, zipping his red Mustang jacket. "Hold up," he says happily. "Ron's on his way over with the *Joanna*. Forecast calls for calm seas; we'll raft the boats. I'm going in with you."

Although new to nautical affairs, even Daniel can see this is a big deal. Obviously, Teklik means something special to Gregg, too.

When they settle into the Zodiac, Lee offers her skipper the tiller of the twenty-horse Johnson outboard, but Gregg declines, his hands deep in the pockets of his float coat. "Go for it," he tells her. "You're the skiff man."

"Woman," Lee growls. "Watch it, bub."

Low-hanging alder boughs sweep out over the water, concealing the entrance of the lagoon. Daniel would never have guessed there was a passageway through the vegetation and the cliff. The channel itself, scarcely thirty feet wide, is accessible only by skiff and only on the flood of high tides. This very feature has kept Teklik unspoiled, Lee had explained to him, although its protection has also been assisted in recent years by both state and federal legislation declaring the estuary off-limits to all fishing—sport, commercial, *and* subsistence.

Lee has also told him that once they enter the lagoon, they'll have to remain there for the day, until the next high tide enables their departure. "Of course," she smiled, "I can't think of a better place to be stranded." As usual, they have one of Fish and Wildlife's handheld VHFs with them as a safety precaution, although Daniel wonders how, if they can't leave the estuary, anyone else could come to their rescue.

As it does everywhere else, a band of glistening crude darkens the rock walls on either side of the narrow channel. Passing below the black stain, twice his height, Daniel observes its top edge to be as level and precise as if it had been spray-painted on the rock surface with the aid of a huge stencil. Of course: "Water seeks its own level."

Gregg expels his breath. "Why couldn't it spare just this one place?"

The canyon encloses them as Lee expertly maneuvers the small craft between jutting rocks and overhanging branches, the whine of the outboard reverberating loudly in the ever-shrinking space. Daniel can feel the current surging beneath them like whitewater, tugging and shoving the inflatable. When the cliff walls draw together above their heads, all but blotting out the light, he breaks into a sweat; one too many tunnels in Cu Chi years ago had left him with a bad case of claustrophobia. The passageway continues to constrict and darken while the clamor of the outboard shrieks in his ears. As Daniel tightens his grip on the Zodiac's vulcanized rubber handles, he feels Gregg's eyes upon him. Keep breathing, he tells himself. Deep breaths, Danny Boy.

Just when the clamorous darkness seems about to swallow them completely, they pop into pure sparkling blue, the spaciousness of the estuary absorbing the noise of the engine. The sunlight's so sudden and bright that they all blink and laugh aloud. Catching his old wrestling coach's eye, Aaron winks. Lee opens the throttle and the boat beats rhythmically across the turquoise water.

This is definitely one of those Sistine Chapels of nature, Daniel decides. No wonder everyone wants to protect it. The color and clarity of the oval lagoon is unusual for Alaska, where glacial silt tends to make water murky and opaque. He's glad he can't see any oil. Is it too much to hope that the narrow channel has somehow kept the pollution at bay?

The morning sunlight pulses with golden haze, the mountainsides neon with new greenery. "Awesome!" Aaron whoops. "Totally rad!" He clutches his dad's field glasses in one hand while kneeling in the bow.

Gregg and Wassily exchange grins, signing each other with thumbs-up, and Daniel understands perfectly the skipper's longing to accompany them to this enchanted place.

"What's that?" Aaron hollers, pointing across the water.

Lee immediately shifts into neutral, the boat coasting on its own momentum. The boy raises the binos. A couple of small, khaki-colored domes float about a hundred yards ahead.

"I can't tell," Aaron says, handing the lenses to his father as Lee re-engages the engine and pilots them slowly forward again.

The objects appear padded, like sofa cushions. In a minute Daniel can tell they're animals, but not what kind. Lifeless, in any case, unmoving.

190

"Deer!" says Aaron. "They're deer." His voice drops. "They must be dead." Once again, the youngster looks more like a child than someone on the cusp of manhood, and once again Daniel's reminded of himself at around the same age, shipping out for his tour of duty.

Lee brings them alongside the pair of animals, which prove to be a knobbed buck and a somewhat smaller doe, half submerged. Both animals bob face-down, but the female lies lopsided, her distended belly acting as flotation. She must be pregnant, Daniel realizes. Neither animal appears to be disfigured in any way, and neither one's got any oil on it that they can see.

"I wonder if somebody shot 'em," Gregg says.

After Wassily and Gregg attach lines to the animals' hindquarters, Lee carefully works the doe hand over hand around the outboard's prop. Father and son draw the buck up beside them on the port side, while Daniel and Wassily do the same with the female on starboard.

Lee eases the motor into gear once more and they complete their journey to shore, slowed now by the drag of the waterlogged animals. She guides the boat in close to the mouth of a small creek and, since the tide's ebbing, leaves it where it fetches up, the deers' hooves bumping bottom.

"Is she pregnant?" Aaron asks, as they all step out into the shallow water.

"Looks like it," Wassily says. "I sure hope her baby's dead, too."

Daniel sees the expression that flits across the boy's face and feels a flash of anger at the other man.

"We'll get a better look when the water goes out," Gregg says. He unzips his float coat and drops it into the boat. "Time's a-wastin'. Chop-chop."

"Aren't you going to help us?" Lee says, unsnapping her flotation vest.

"Hell, no. It's your job, not mine." Once again, only Gregg seems to find himself amusing.

While they set off in pairs toward opposite ends of the crescent beach, the skipper uses the entrenching tool to dig into the sand near the boat.

Pausing along the strandline to watch him, Daniel and Aaron see Gregg stare into the hole he's dug, examine the tip of the collapsible shovel, and angrily throw the tool down.

"He must not have believed us," Aaron says, walking on.

"Guess not."

"What do you think killed them?"

"Don't know," Daniel says. "It's a shame, though. They're beautiful animals."

The youngster clears his throat. "Someone told me the deer is my totem." He laughs self-consciously.

"Totem?" The older man gestures to a bedraggled bird carcass and prepares a trash sack to receive its first offering.

"My medicine animal. That's what she called it."

Daniel doesn't know what to say; he's not very up to date on this kind of thing. "Something to pay attention to, I guess."

"She said that, too. That anytime a deer crosses my path—not just a real deer, but even, like, a deer on TV or a picture of one in a magazine—I should pay attention to it, ask myself what it means."

"So what do you think it means?"

"I don't know. But it can't be good, since they're dead, you know?" Aaron laughs again.

Daniel wishes he could think of something to say, something to make amends to the young man not just for dead deer, but for all the carnage they've encountered, for the oil spill itself. For the ill-treated world his generation is leaving to Aaron's. He rolls up his shirt sleeves before pulling on the rubber gloves. "Could be a scorcher," he remarks, to change the subject. "For the 'far, frozen North,' that is."

As if to one-up his partner—after all, it's not *that* warm—Aaron pulls both his t-shirt and hooded sweatshirt over his head in one motion, tying the sleeves of the now double-layered garment around his waist. He examines his bare arms, mocking himself for the goose bumps that immediately pimple his flesh. "Not exactly deerskin," he says. "More like chicken skin." Warming up with a couple of jumping jacks, the boy darts in front of Daniel to seize the remains of the first oiled seabird in his bare hands.

"Wear your damn gloves! I'm tired of telling you."

"But my hands get too hot. They cook, man."

"Trust me. Better hot hands now than cancer later." The Vietnam veteran explains about Agent Orange—and Agents Green, Blue, and White—and their aftereffects for vets and villagers. "If I could survive a war without getting sick from defoliants, I am definitely not going to let North Slope crude get me now." He peers at Aaron. "Or you, if I have anything to do with it."

"Okay." The young man looks contrite and does his best to clean his hands on the sand before donning a pair of gloves.

Although Teklik has not been completely spared the scourge of the spill, casualties here still number far fewer than any other place they've been. Daniel tallies only eight birds, no mammals. Nor does he see much evidence of oil, though the morning sun already works to melt some of the isolated tar balls that pock the beach. They finish their work quickly, at which point Aaron wastes no time in once again removing his gloves, tossing them onto his collections sack, and making a beeline for the upper shoreline to beachcomb for a glass float. Daniel decides he might as well do his best to remove gelled petroleum before it melts in the heat of the day.

By the time he's worked his way back to the Zodiac, the tide has receded and the two dead deer lie fully exposed. The animals still appear normal to him, no gunshot or other wounds, no traces of oil or any other telltale evidence as to cause of death. From the size of her swollen belly, Daniel guesses the doe's near term and remembers a photo he'd taken of Tess, hamming it up in the last month of her pregnancy with Elias. In the picture, his wife stands naked, splay-footed and large-breasted, hands on her enormous belly, laughing. He remembers how exhilarated they both felt in the days leading up to their son's birth. Daniel smiles.

"They look healthy," he remarks to Gregg, who sits on a driftwood log nearby, smoking a cigarette.

"They look terrific. Sterling. Too bad they're so dead." The breeze carries the fisherman's exhaled smoke right into Daniel's face.

Leave it to Gregg Anderson to spoil the moment. But despite his dislike of the skipper and the incontrovertible tragedy of the oil spill, Daniel feels deeply content. Teklik's enchanting and the day is fine. Most of all, though, he has ample reason to rejoice. Another child!

Sheltered from sea breezes, the lagoon radiates warmth. Wassily and Lee return with only a single trash sack apiece, setting their collections beside the skiff. When Wassily kicks off his rubber boots and peels off his socks, Lee and Daniel look at each other as if to say "Why didn't we think of that?" and promptly follow suit.

Lee breaks out the food she'd packed into a small cooler that morning, handing around peanut-butter sandwiches, setting out packages of chocolate-chip cookies and pretzels followed by apples and oranges, cans of pop, and a thermos of coffee.

"Picnic!" Wassily announces.

"Where's the beer?" Gregg wants to know. Lee shoots him a dirty look. Why does she bother rising to her skipper's bait? Daniel's decided that the key to coexisting with this clown is to ignore him.

"She's worse than a wife," Gregg complains to Wassily.

Daniel calls to Aaron, a hundred yards away. "You hungry?"

"In a minute," the boy replies, raising alder branches to peer beneath them.

"I sure hope he finds one," Wassily says.

"He's going to be majorly disappointed if he doesn't," Lee observes. "But then, he could find a beauty. That's the thing."

"Life's full of disappointment," Gregg remarks. "He might as well get used to it."

Typical Gregg comment. Lee pulls on her socks and boots, gathers her lunch items, and sets off alone down the beach—either to escape her skipper's cynicism or to seek some relief from the tiresome company of men. The guys, on the other hand, predictably fan out around the grub. The sun's directly overhead, so they all shuck their shirts.

194

Aaron flops down beside Daniel, reaching for a sandwich. "I give up," he complains.

"They've gotten scarce—scarce as ptarmigan teeth," Wassily chuckles. "Elusive as razor clams. But that's what makes 'em collector's items, right?"

After eating, his companions nod off one by one. Daniel watches Lee comb the far end of the beach, maybe trying to find Aaron a float? He lies back, enjoying the warmth, and realizes this is the first time he's felt truly relaxed since the beginning of the spill. He should probably put his shirt back on, though, to protect himself from sunburn, but decides it's too much trouble.

Closing his eyes, Daniel supposes you might after all compare the oil spill to a war, insofar as both are acts of annihilation instigated by humans. Both create powerful vortices that destroy everything in their path, as surely as tornados consume whatever they come into contact with, mangling and mutilating beyond recognition. And isn't modern warfare, like an oil spill, a human act of aggression against nature, too? Defoliants. Bomb craters. "Scorched earth." One of the objectives of war is the destruction of habitat, to render it useless to human beings, which of course renders it useless to other life-forms as well. Has anyone ever tried to calculate the damages inflicted on nonhuman species by mankind's armed conflicts?

He's heard how those working the land in western Europe continue to unearth live ordnance from both world wars. Land mines everywhere threaten the life and limbs of innocent people—and animals, he realizes—even in places where hostilities have long since ceased. So, too, the effects of the spill are likely to have consequences for years and years. But unlike Vietnam, for instance, an oil spill doesn't involve human beings deliberately and systematically pursuing ever more ingenious ways to grease each other. (Funny about the colloquialism, though.) And he, Daniel Waverly Wolff, isn't right now spending every waking moment in fear that a single lapse of attention will get him splattered a quarter mile in all directions.

Tess accused him of never talking about the war. No shit, sweetheart. Not only are his memories intensely private, something to hoard, but his recollections of the terror, degradation, and heroism—well, he both resents those who've never experienced it and pities them. Daniel considers the troops now defending U.S. interests in the Middle East: women soldiers, and different terms of engagement, but still war.

He wakes with a start. Did he really nod off? In the way of a catnap, Daniel feels momentarily disoriented, vulnerable, so he holds very still. Aaron snoozes on his side, hands folded between drawn-up knees. Wassily and Gregg snore loudly on their backs.

If Tessa has in fact conceived, she'll want an abortion. He's certain of it. Daniel pulls his boots on, grabs his shirt, and walks unsteadily to the water's edge. It's not my place to judge her, he tells himself. A woman deserves to choose what happens to her body.

He squats to dip his hands in the crystalline lagoon, splashing his face. What could he say or do that would make her change her mind? Daniel feels a flush of fever and notices that his stomach's gone sour. He must be coming down with something.

15

Gregg lies still, watching Daniel Wolff pace beside the lagoon. Strange dude. Aaron and Wassily continue to sleep, the boy twitching a bit, the way he had as a child. When did his son get so goddamn lanky?

The skipper stretches and puts on his shirt, snapping the buttons. Wolff now stares across the water to the channel entrance, apparently thinking deep thoughts. The man thinks too much, in Gregg's humble opinion.

The fisherman heads for the woods to take a leak. Aaron hasn't combed this section of beach yet. Maybe Gregg will get lucky and find his kid a float.

As he pisses into the sphagnum moss beneath a cottonwood, he notices Lee snoozing against the storm berm a hundred yards away. No doubt about it: she looks like a POW. She'd better start taking care of herself if she wants to score a new girlfriend.

Gregg pokes the strandline with a stick of driftwood, turning over tangles of dried kelp, wondering when he himself might hitch up with someone. Peg may not have been his first love, but she was the first he felt drawn to go the distance with. Her dad had seen combat in the South Pacific; maybe that was why Gregg's idiosyncrasies hadn't fazed her. Not at first, anyway. He recalls their courtship, how he'd brought her here to woo her, dropping to one knee to propose marriage on this very beach— and remembers how she'd rapped him on the head, told him to quit horsing around.

At least they can both take pride in their son. Aaron's a little soft maybe, but he's basically got his head screwed on right. The kid should start working out, though; he needs to bulk up. Studying the water level in the lagoon, Gregg decides that although the tide's seeping back in, it'll still be a while before there's enough water in the channel for them to leave. Sometimes it's hard to gauge the depth accurately because of the holdover from the bottleneck. Not that he minds the delay. Far from it. No better place to be marooned.

When a movement catches his eye, the skipper turns carefully to watch a tawny shape emerge from the forest. A young stag, antlers still covered in brown velvet. The buck waits as three more deer—all does— join him, and the four animals pause above the beach cobble before stepping forward in synchronized movement to the edge of the stream, where they lower their heads to drink. For a second, the fisherman has the crazy notion that the two dead deer they towed to shore behind the Zodiac have somehow come back to life. Wolff stands stock-still fifty yards away, eyes trained on the streamside creatures, which have yet to notice either man. Gregg wishes that Aaron could see this, could witness something alive for a change, but knows if he tries to wake his son, the deer will bolt.

The antlered male leads his harem across the shallow water, and they pick their way delicately onto the beach to forage along the tide line, stopping to nibble here and there. What the hell are they eating? They don't like seafood, do they? Maybe it's something about salt.

Talk about graceful. The animals pull with their teeth at the tangles of dark, leathery kelp, extricating the vegetation from other debris the tide has washed up, taking their time to chew the leafy tatters they tear off.

After several minutes of this, the deer suddenly lift their heads as one and freeze, ears flicking nervously. Neither Gregg nor Wolff has moved a muscle, and the others are still asleep. The wind hasn't shifted, but something frightens the wild creatures. They gather themselves and bound into the trees, seemingly in a single leap.

Air Jordan, the skipper thinks with a smile. He glances at Wolff, who raises an arm, so Gregg waves back.

As if their sleeping potions have worn off simultaneously, Aaron and Wassily awaken near the Zodiac, yawning and stretching. Lee joins her boss at the back of the beach, rubbing her eyes.

"I just had a wild dream," she says.

"Yeah?"

"We were fishing sockeyes. Plugging the gear, like we did that time in Kodiak." She smiles at him mischievously. "It was flat calm and we were the only boat. That's how I knew it was a dream."

They laugh together. "Hang on to that memory," Gregg says. "We'll plug the nets again someday." He tells her about the deer.

"Wish I hadn't missed them. It'd be a treat to see something alive for a change."

They join the others, whom Wolff has led to the spot where the deer were grazing.

"Kelp," Wassily says, reaching for a sheet of the bronze-colored sea vegetable.

"It must have nutrients they crave," the journalist comments, ever the analyst.

"Health food," Gregg quips.

Wassily stretches the kelp between his hands, as if to show them how the animals' teeth have scalloped the edges. He shakes his head. "Definitely not healthy. More like, from hell."

Now Gregg can see the dollops of crude petroleum that spatter the shiny plant, or algae, or whatever the hell it is. "This is what nailed them?" he says, turning toward the two dead deer, beached near the boat.

"They ate oil?" Aaron asks. He looks not to his father, but to Wolff. "What did they do to deserve this?" his son whines, setting Gregg's teeth on edge.

"It's an oil spill," the fisherman says gruffly. "It sucks. Get over it."

"You suck!" The youngster spins away, loping across the packed sand.

In a temper, his father moves to pursue him, but Lee and Wassily block Gregg's way. He tries to push past them. "It's time he learned."

"Learned what?" Wolff says. "That his old man's a prick?"

Gregg wheels on the reporter, eyes flashing. Lee and Wassily tense. Then the skipper laughs. "Damn. You people are touchy." He returns alone to the Zodiac, sitting on the inflated gunwale to light a cigarette. He'll deal with Aaron later. Glancing at the dark oil that has pooled in the hole he dug earlier, he wonders what would happen if he tossed in a match.

The tide floods quickly now. Time to roll. The afternoon sun illuminates a rainbow sheen of petroleum on the surface of the incoming water. Figures, the skipper thinks. Nothing good ever lasts.

That night, the *Pegasus* and the *Joanna* lie at anchor almost within hailing distance of each other, awaiting morning and the resumption of collections in Crooked Cove. No one talks much; Gregg's crew does their best to avoid him.

So he's glad when they all turn in early, enabling him to start drinking at sunset, which comes around ten these days. Gregg settles into his nightly perch in the stern, where he has plenty of time to stow Jack in the event that anyone comes calling. Not that he really gives a shit at this point. He makes himself comfortable on the lazarette, pours a long drink into his coffee mug, and raises it in a silent toast to the molten disk of sun that's inserting itself into Hinchinbrook Arm.

It really isn't his day. Gregg never even hears Lee, who suddenly appears at his elbow.

"You promised," she gasps, looking as shocked as a little girl who's just discovered that Santa Claus is really her dad. She seizes the square bottle by its neck and, before he can stop her, heaves it into the sea.

"Son of a bitch. What'd you do that for?" Gregg watches the bottle upend itself and, taking on water, slip from sight. Too bad he hadn't screwed the lid back on; he could have motored after it.

"Fuck you," Lee hisses. "You're a liar!" She seems almost as surprised as he is when she punches him in the face.

It bloodies his lip, but he locks eyes with her and catches her wrist before she can land another blow, giving her arm a serious twist. "Leave me alone."

She spits at him before leaving in a huff, the spittle landing on his beard. Gregg wipes it off with his hand.

Now he's down to two bottles. Better go easy if he wants them to last. It takes him a while to recover his former good mood, whereupon Wolff shows up. Has Lee sicced the radio reporter on him, too?

But no, the news jockey carries a plastic cup. It's empty. He wants a drink!

"Help yourself," Gregg says, producing more whiskey from the storage unit.

Wolff twists the cap, breaking the seal, and pours himself a healthy slug.

They drink in silence, staring at the glowing light of the fading day, the spruce trees in silhouette on the ridgelines to the west like punk-rock haircuts. It feels congenial enough, given how different the two men are from one another. Hooray for booze.

"E-E-N-T," Wolff comments. End of evening nautical twilight. Military speak for time to dig in.

"What part of country?" Gregg asks.

"Bien Hoa. Tay Ninh."

"Cambo border."

The reporter nods, sipping from his cup.

"ROTC?" the fisherman asks.

"Not me," Wolff laughs. "I joined up so I could get my education paid for."

"When?"

"Seventy-two. You?"

"Quang Tri. Khe Sanh. Sixty-eight." Gregg watches the other man's eyebrows lift. Can it be the journalist is actually at a loss for words?

Wolff pours them both another few fingers of sour mash. "You're a hero." He salutes the skipper.

"We should have a drink some time," Gregg says as he tips the mug to his mouth.

Daniel Wolff offers a thin smile. "No time like the present. Cheers."

In the morning they meet up with a black-and-orange inflatable scudding toward Teklik on the incoming tide. The Avon bears the insignia of the U.S. Forest Service and carries a middle-aged white couple, both wearing brown float coats and Smokey the Bear hats.

When they draw alongside the *Pegasus*, Gregg tells the two government employees about the pair of dead deer he carries. "You want them?"

The woman has dark circles under her eyes, like she could use some sleep. "No, take them in, she says. "We've got others awaiting necropsy results."

"Must be hard on you seeing your purviews desecrated like this," Wolff says, gesturing toward the blackened shoreline. Leave it to the college grad to use fifty-cent words when nickel words would do, Gregg thinks.

He notices that the male ranger looks as haggard as the woman. Sallow-faced, the man glances from his partner to the rest of them and back again, as if he can't make up his mind whether or not to spill the beans. Then he spits it out. "All NPS—Park Service—staff in Alaska got a memo from Interior two days ago. Then we got ours from Agriculture yesterday. Anyone who spends monies on the spill that aren't already in the year-end budget will be held personally liable." The guy's so upset he stammers.

It takes a minute for this to register. The skipper sees the puzzled look on his deckhand's face. After their encounter last night, Lee has so far today refused to acknowledge Gregg's existence. "You mean, you're not supposed to do anything about the oil spill?" she asks the rangers.

"Not unless we want to pay for it ourselves," the man says.

His partner tosses her head, too upset to be discreet. "The government decided not to federalize the spill. They claim they lack funding, but what they lack is balls."

"I thought they sent in the Coast Guard," Wassily says. "Didn't they?"

"No. Haven't you heard?" The man looks at each of their faces. "The government ceded authority to Mammoth Petroleum, so now the oil company has nearly complete oversight." He looks whipped, miserable.

"But that's like the fox guarding the hen house," Lee blurts.

"Worse than that," Lady Ranger snaps. "It's like having a known child molester babysitting your kids."

Lee recoils at the words. Toughen up, baby, Gregg thinks. He catches Daniel Wolff's eye. "Snafu."

"Gesundheit," Wolff responds absently to the tired army joke while jotting into his ever-present notebook.

As the Avon motors away from them and Gregg resumes driving, he recalls with shame his giddy relief at scoring this wildlife retrieval contract—like dropping out of freefall into a feather bed, the answer to his prayers. Now he knows he's as guilty of magical thinking as everyone else: we told ourselves that if only we boomed the bay, if only we rescued the oiled creatures, if only we scooped the crude from the water or removed spill-kills from the food chain, everything would eventually come around right. If only we kept the faith and didn't sell out too bad, we could fix this. Then we'd resume our real lives, not so much the worse for wear. Like him and Wolff enlisting for Vietnam. Hip hip hooray. What a crock of shit.

Whenever Gregg has something dicked, he thinks, that's exactly when it falls apart. He always runs the same pattern, like that old Joni Mitchell song. He never knows what he's got 'til it's gone.

Their last stop, Glory Point, consists of a hook-shaped isthmus, a rocky promontory extending almost five miles into the Gulf of Alaska.

Lee's never been ashore here. On charts, the point resembles a finger beckoning, a miniature version of Cape Cod. She remembers the location as one besieged by breakers, described in nautical language as "maximum turmoil" because it's where two tidal systems collide.

Ron will again stay with the two boats rafted together, while Gregg shuttles crewmembers of both vessels ashore in the Zodiac. Based on how long collections have taken elsewhere and on the fact that there will be almost twice as many of them working this site, Lee figures they'll be finished in a few hours. The sooner they complete these final retrievals, the sooner they'll head home, and the sooner she will never again have to have anything to do with Gregg. He's pulled some crap in their time together, but as far as she knows, her skipper's never before lied to her. Ironically, the night Lee discovered him drinking, she was looking for him to say how sorry she was about the loss of his friend Dusty. She knows she'll never forgive him for lying about the alcohol. They're through.

Gregg still sports a fat lip from where she slugged him, Lee notes with satisfaction when she and Daniel, having elected to go ashore first, join him in the inflatable.

It soon becomes evident that Glory Point's leeward landfall is impassable due to a miles-long morass of drift logs that form a seemingly impenetrable barrier, so they're forced to make for the exposed, windward side of the hook instead. But here, despite the placid day, the long beach draws a thundering surf.

Daniel yells to the skipper above the noise. "Calm seas, my ass!"

"This *is* calm," Gregg shouts back. "For here. Day breezes haven't even come up yet."

The skipper hangs off shore, timing the swells before darting in behind a breaking wave. "Go! Go!" he orders, and his two passengers slip over the side of the Zodiac into chest-deep emulsified oil, which immediately fills their hipboots, causing the rubber footwear to balloon around their legs. Gregg's already sped away. The cold water drives the breath from Lee's lungs as spray from the noxious surf showers her and

Daniel. They reach for one another reflexively, struggling for balance and, locking elbows, press forward together toward shore.

"Gross. Me. Out," Lee pronounces through gritted teeth, tasting the foul spray.

"Nasty," Daniel agrees.

When she catches her breath, Lee sees that what looks like an immense sheet of rubberized oil coats the entire beach, like some kind of horribly misguided paving project. "Look," she tells Daniel, who's trying to wipe his face clean but just smearing grease around.

He studies the scene and, meeting her eyes, expels a long breath while shaking his head. Gregg returns with Aaron and Wassily. Again, he times the waves and zips in as close to shore as he dares, whereupon the two new arrivals lower themselves feet first into the drink. The skipper throws the outboard into reverse, turns in a tight arc, and scoots back out to deeper water, the front of the Zodiac at one point pitched nearly vertical by an oncoming wave, threatening to flip. But he guns the motor and the bow comes down with a slap.

Gregg may be an asshole, Lee thinks, but he can definitely handle a boat.

Just as she and Daniel have, Wassily and Aaron clutch one another for balance, spluttering through the surf that likewise soaks them to the skin, droplets of crude oil clinging to their faces and hair. Their expressions, too, reflect revulsion, and Aaron looks a little pale.

Daniel and Lee move to meet them, the four linking arms to shamble together from the ocean surge. The seas are building, oil-laden waves pummeling the beach with growing force, visiting yet more windblown spray upon them as they await the arrival of the crew of the *Joanna*. Lee should have realized the sickle-shaped peninsula would prove a natural catchment for oil, making Glory Point more polluted by far than anywhere else they've been.

"Unbelievable," Wassily mutters.

Aaron noisily hawks up gobs of phlegm, spitting repeatedly.

Gregg ferries in the other crew—stout, blond-bearded Dylan, from England; freckle-faced Jerry, from Wyoming; ponytailed Debbie, who can only be called petite, from Delta Junction, Alaska—none of whom had ever set foot on a boat before the spill. These three stumble to shore as soaked and spattered as the *Pegasus* crew, their expressions similarly incredulous. Because Debbie's Mammoth Petroleum–issued hipboots are many sizes too large for her, Jerry and Dylan hoist her through the drenching spray while she clutches the tops of the waders to keep them from sliding off completely.

Once well away from the surf, and now only knee-deep in the emulsified muck, the seven help each other to remove and pour water from their boots before tugging the wet footgear back on. As they begin the long, taxing slog up the beach, Aaron strikes up a conversation with Dylan, asking him what he's doing so far from home.

"You've heard of the *Torrey Canyon*, yeah?" the Brit says in his rich accent.

"The what?"

Whigs and Tories? Lee wonders.

"You Yanks," Dylan scolds. "Who was it who said, 'Those who ignore the past are condemned to repeat it'?"

"George Santayana," Daniel says irritably. "An American philosopher."

"Right you are, mate." Dylan looks surprised.

Lee decides she will have to ask Daniel later about Dylan's "Tory canyon." Right now she'd better focus on walking, as each step requires planting a foot carefully while breaking the suction of the one before. The last thing she wants to do is to trip and fall into the septic goo.

Dylan and Jerry take turns piggy-backing Debbie. Aaron pushes ahead, as if it is a point of pride to be first up the beach. When the oil is only shin-deep, he tries to run out of it, instead pitching forward with a cry. Breaking his fall with both hands, he manages to stop himself short of a face-plant, but his forearms, stomach, and thighs are now plastered with greenish-black slime. Getting up carefully, Aaron stands with hands held out from his sides like a chagrined scarecrow.

"I told you not to fart around with this stuff," Daniel says sharply, using the edge of a gloved hand to squeegee the putrid mud from the youngster's body.

As she resumes step-sliding forward, Lee feels her ankles brushing and dislodging buried objects.

"What are these things?" Jerry asks, trying unsuccessfully to lift one with his boot.

"They feel like little bumpers," Lee says, referring to the cylindrical rubber fenders used to protect boat hulls when docking. But when she steps directly on top of one of them, it collapses with a brittle sensation beneath her foot, so she reaches down with gloved hands to extricate the thing, thinking it roughly the same size and heft as a small coil of lashed line.

The bird releases with a sucking sound. When Lee holds the eider out before her, Jerry reaches over to spread its wings. Astride Dylan, Debbie squeals, covering her mouth with a manicured hand.

"Blimey," says her porter.

Wassily and Daniel exchange a look.

The workers turn their heads in unison to gaze down the length of beach where, as the contamination grows shallower, hundreds, perhaps thousands, of mounds protrude. Lee lowers the sea duck to the ground. Cemetery, she thinks, but can't press a hand to her throbbing chest because both gloves are fouled.

16

Basalt cliffs bookend the isthmus that the workers predictably begin to refer to not as Glory but Gory Point. The enormous jumble of drift logs that lie tossed helter-skelter like a giant's game of pickup sticks essentially walls off the whole eastern side of the thin extension of land.

When they at last reach the uncontaminated upper beach, Jerry calls Ron on the handheld radio to alert him and Gregg to the fact that collections are going to take them not hours but days. The group sets to work gathering carcasses until the cresting tide gives them an excuse to rest. When the surf finally flattens at sundown, Gregg returns in the Zodiac with sleeping bags, food, and other supplies, including plastic tarps and a spool of poly twine with which they fashion shelters. One benefit of the point's exposure is that a near-constant westerly keeps mosquitoes and other insects at bay.

Lee soon loses count of the number of times she trudges the shoreline, lugging an oil-soaked mort in each hand. Her arms burn in their sockets; her legs ache with the strain of slogging. The workers collect wildlife remains when the ocean withdraws, breaking for rest and meals when the tide floods back in or it becomes too dark to see.

Lee knows they'll never gain the upper hand in removing the dead, since every high tide bears with it at least as many new fatalities as they've been able to collect in the intervening amount of time. Oil spill casualties will continue to wash ashore here for a very long time.

"Why bother?" Wassily complains the second morning, as they pull on boots and gloves. "This is a waste of time."

"Maybe Fish and Wildlife can establish a camp here," Lee replies. "Maybe they can bring in a Bobcat. Maybe that would keep spill-kills out of the food chain." Her voice trails off when no one responds.

Because she lacks proper footgear, Debbie has no choice but to work alone above the saturated beach, near the small hemlock forest. In sneakers, she becomes the custodian of what they now refer to as the Morgue. Using blades of driftwood, the conscientious blonde scrapes each carcass that the others bring to her as free of weathered petroleum as she can, creating an orderly display of the oiled bodies on the strip of wild grass and sedge that runs along the spine of the beach. Debbie also separates the birds from the otters, seals, mink, and other mammals they find. And she keeps a running tally of the dead in a waterproof yellow notebook. In the end, the pages hold so many penciled tick marks that it reminds Lee of how children draw rain.

Debbie's also the one who most often finds the deadlife that have been dragged up the beach by predators. When the young woman surprises a large brown bear burying its face in the bloated belly of an oiled river otter, her staccato shrieks bring the rest of them running in panic. She tells them through tears that the bulky carnivore seemed as startled as she was before it heard the other workers coming and barreled away into the trees. Jerry promptly nicknames his coworker "Bear Bait," but they immediately adopt a buddy system whereby the rest of them take turns working with Debbie and no one now goes into the woods alone.

That night, Lee dreams she's a hibernating bear, holed up for half a year when spring's warmer, brighter days urge her into wakefulness. She hears the steady drip of melting snow, smells new vegetation and thaw-ing earth. Nudging her young cub before her, the gaunt mother bear emerges from her mountainside den and its stale, close air. She and her male offspring sniff the salty breezes wafting from the ocean to discover that this year there's a new smell, one that promises to fill their empty bellies, so the two animals follow the tantalizing scent down to the shore. It feels strange to the female to walk again, the pads of her paws grown soft from disuse, atrophied muscles protesting exercise.

Soon the bears come to a beach strewn with dead birds and animals, all coated with something like mud. The taste of crude oil is neither repellent nor appetizing to them. The spoiled flesh, on the other hand, provides an unparalleled feast.

Lee wakes with a jolt, pinned on her back by despair.

The monotonous futility of the work wears everyone down. As with all the other locations they've put ashore on this so-called mission, Daniel knows their efforts will do little to stem the spread of contamination. Except that here at Gory the attempt seems laughable.

He hates the scourge of gummy oil that clings to his skin from their surf bath of the first day. Despite washing in a nearby creek, scrubbing arms and neck with a spruce branch until his body stings, the water is just too cold to cut the grease. He's going to have to buy Tess a new sleeping bag. Daniel had taken Aaron in hand after the boy's fall, lead-ing him to the glacial creek to strip and bathe, and Gregg's son told him through chattering teeth how he'd been showered with crude petro-leum the night the *Kuparuk* drove into the reef. "It smelled really evil then," the boy said, attempting a joke. "Now it just smells like poo." The youngster's skin remains tacky with the crude's residue. They all need hot showers. Lots of them.

When Aaron complains of not feeling well, Daniel attributes his malaise to the demanding, demoralizing nature of the work. The boy sleeps sixteen hours that night, prompting Jerry to remark that he, too, had been a champion sleeper in adolescence. "Let the kid rest," the good-natured Westerner says. "He's still growing."

Checking on him at midday, Daniel finds Aaron awake but feverish, shivering in his sleeping bag.

"I'm a big help, huh?" the youngster croaks as Daniel spreads his own sleeping bag on top of him.

"Don't worry about it. You hungry?"

Aaron shakes his head, coughing.

"How about some tea?"

"Thanks, Coach."

The workers collect hundreds of carcasses, but know it will be impractical if not impossible to follow the letter of Fish and Wildlife's instructions to bring in each and every spill-kill, for between the surf on one side and the extensive tangle of drift logs on the other, Gory Point will be as difficult to depart as it was to access. Not only that, Daniel thinks, but it would likely take dozens of trips in the Zodiac just to transport all the dead.

Since Lee's still not speaking to Gregg, Wassily and Daniel place the call to the *Pegasus*.

"What's the body count?" the fisherman wants to know.

"Almost two thousand. So far."

Daniel hears Gregg whistle through his teeth.

"What do you guys think we should do?" the skipper asks.

"If we leave them here, other animals will have a feast," Wassily says into the mike. "You should see it. Debbie's got 'em arranged like an all-you-can-eat buffet."

"Can we bury them?"

"Not without a backhoe," Wassily replies. "And you'd have to go real deep or they'll just get dug up again by predators."

"So what do we do?"

"Burn them," Daniel suggests. "We're not exactly short on fuel with all of this driftwood."

Gregg's silent again. The radio clicks. "Okay," he finally says. "I'll talk to Ron. We have to run it by the Fish and Fur. We'll get back to you."

"One other thing, Gregor," Wassily adds. "Aaron's kind of under the weather."

"Make sure he pulls his weight," the father retorts. "Tell him he won't get paid."

Hours pass before the call back. Ron, this time, explains that the feds have categorically denied permission to destroy what they refer to as government property. A protection officer has reminded the two boat owners in no uncertain terms that the agency will impound their vessels should they violate this directive.

Even so, both skippers agree with their crews that while it may be impossible to remove the bodies, they can't just leave them behind for other animals to eat. They've decided that Ron will come ashore with his video camera to film the burning. With good documentation, they figure, no one can accuse them of either shirking their duty or of trying to conceal anything.

Because of the relentless surf, even on this windless day, all except Aaron and Debbie wait at water's edge to receive the *Joanna's* skipper. Ron, in a wetsuit, navigates the Zodiac as close to the rollers as he dares, cuts the engine, and quickly unscrews the outboard from the transom. Hoisting the motor into the inflatable, he bags it in extra-large trash sacks, which he then ties off. Pulling on the oars, he maneuvers the buoyant craft to face the beach. Finally, shipping the sweeps, he fits his diving mask over his face and kneels in the bottom of the boat, clasping the handles on either side.

Within minutes the breakers push him toward shore. "Cowabunga!" he hollers, surfing in on the crest of a wave.

The landing party presses into the surging ocean, and just before the inflatable overturns, Dylan seizes the double-bagged outboard, heaving it onto his beefy shoulders. Wassily and Daniel grab the boat while Lee and Jerry clasp Ron by his backpack, hauling him upright. In his oil-slimed blue-and-gray neoprene wetsuit and streaked diving mask, the *Joanna's* skipper looks like a navy frogman emerging from a sewer.

Spitting and gagging, Ron tears off his face mask.

"Greetings, mate," Dylan grunts under the weight of the motor. "Welcome to our little paradise."

Debbie narrates while Ron films the array of bodies in the Morgue. She's arranged the ninety-three sea otters from largest to smallest, the dead pups looking particularly pitiful at the end of a long row of sea mammal corpses.

"And here we have over a thousand murres, most of them decapitated by predators," the young woman says helpfully.

Daniel decides that Ron's video will resemble some kind of macabre television entertainment, with Debbie as the charismatic hostess. He helps the others to gather first dried grass, then kindling, then armfuls of driftwood, and finally larger timbers for what they intend to become a raging funeral pyre. When they have all the wood assembled, Aaron scrambles around the base of the structure, eagerly reaching in with lighted matches to ignite the tinder. So. Maybe the boy's not as sick as Daniel thought.

Soon the blaze crackles and the flames reach for more fuel. They've built the fire just below the high-water line, so the incoming tide will eventually douse it. Once Ron has finished documenting what he calls "Morgue Smorgasbord," they all begin to throw carcasses onto the large pyre, but it isn't long before the heat drives them back and they instead hand the dead bodies to Jerry and Dylan who, with high-school-quarterback and rugby-player throwing arms, respectively, pitch them into the inferno from a distance. They work together to transport and sling the bodies of the larger animals into the flames, the *Joanna* skipper filming it all.

The scene at first reminds Daniel of the beachside memorial bonfire for captain and crew of the *Rodeo Rose*, but the smell of burning feathers and flesh soon triggers unwelcome memories of the scorching of Southeast Asia, too. He raises his eyes to the black smoke now polluting the sky. Nazi crematoriums. Carpet bombing. Hiroshima and Nagasaki. It seems to him that a recurring theme of his own life has been not just loss but needless destruction. Soon he stops toting and tossing morts altogether and wanders away.

Lee finds him sitting against a large driftwood log. "Can I talk to you?"

"Have a seat," he offers.

"No, thanks. I want to apologize for my big mouth," she says.

"It's okay." Daniel avoids her eyes.

"No, it's not. I'm really sorry."

Neither speaks, watching the bilious black smoke pluming overhead.

"I'm going to quit fishing," Lee says.

"Because of Gregg?"

"And because I don't want to make a living from anything's suffering—not if I can help it."

"Good luck with that." Daniel tries to soften the harshness of the remark by asking, "What will you do instead?"

"Who knows." Lee wanders away down the beach.

Of course, the same tide that quenches the fire delivers more oil spill fatalities during the night. And in the early morning darkness, before the seas build, still more deadlife bobs in the shallows, bumping everyone's legs as they labor to launch the Zodiac. Only with great group effort do Ron, Debbie, and the gear get out at all.

The rest of them figure they can make their way over the massive logjam to the leeward, surf-free side of the isthmus, where the boats can more easily pick them up. They've urged Aaron to ride out in the inflatable, but the boy insists he feels well enough to hike. Packing up, Wassily observes that at least as many carcasses now litter the beach as when they first arrived. "Someone should bring in a D9 Cat," he says.

When Aaron laughs, it triggers such a fit of coughing that Daniel again questions the boy's ability to make the trek. They'll have to take it slow. Once they start out, however, it becomes obvious that the youngster's real motivation lies in his continuing hope of finding a glass float—especially since this is his last chance before they head home.

Daniel's surprised when he himself makes an unexpected discovery. As they all clamber over the storm-tossed timbers, he comes upon a dead bald eagle, the first they've encountered. He stoops to examine the noble bird, emotion welling not only because the creature looks formidable even in death, but because it is the national emblem, after all.

The large predator lies crumpled beside a bleached stump, a single dark streak of oil striping its white head, regal even in death. Dylan says it's so bloody big they might as well forget about fetching it out, but whether because the man's a foreigner or because of some other stubbornness in himself, Daniel knows he'll never leave the eagle behind, abandoned. It would be like seeing the colors on the ground and not doing everything in your power to try to raise them.

He lifts the stiffened raptor, guessing its weight at ten pounds or more, and tries for a while to carry it upright, for the sake of decorum. In the end, though, he accepts Lee's offer of duct tape from her backpack, with which she helps him truss the legs. Another long strip of tape binds the bird's wings to its body and keeps them from flopping outward when he hoists it upside-down by its feet, taking care to avoid the sharp talons.

A half hour later, negotiating a particularly challenging section of crisscrossed logs, Aaron yelps, "I found one!"

Daniel sets the eagle down carefully before joining the others. Beneath a welter of weathered timbers, he can just see a sky-blue buoy the size of an orange. "Nice one," he congratulates the young man.

"It can't be intact," Jerry says. "No way."

Dylan adds, "We'll never get it out of there."

Aaron sets his jaw, looking very much like Gregg in that moment, Daniel thinks. Lee already strains to shift a ten-foot log. "Hang on, love," Dylan says, inserting a stout plank as a lever. They all collaborate to move wood and before long Aaron is able to reach his arm into the newly created cavity. "It's not broken," he exults.

So they keep working and finally Aaron fits his body into the enlarged space. The look on his face when he frees the float and raises his prize for all to see makes the effort worthwhile.

"It's got water in it!" Lee exclaims.

Sure enough, the globe sloshes with liquid. The boy's face falls. "It must be cracked," he says, examining the surface closely, touching it all over with his fingertips. "Bone dry." He sounds perplexed.

"I'll be darned." Jerry takes the buoy.

"It's a mystery," Dylan pronounces.

Lee corrects him at once. "You mean, a miracle."

Aaron smiles. He moves extra cautiously after that, carrying his treasure as if it were made of, well, glass.

17

Back on the *Pegasus* Gregg shakes his head over Daniel's eagle. "No comment," the skipper says, meeting his fellow veteran's eyes. He enthuses over his son's find, declaring the cerulean glass float a beauty. Gregg tries to explain the phenomenon of the water inside: "When one of these gets submerged deep enough—say the net gets dragged to the bottom of the ocean—the pressure forces seawater through the glass. Then let's say the thing works itself loose, pops back up to the surface. That's when it seals up again, trapping the water inside. Something like that." He thinks he sounds good, like he actually knows what he's talking about.

Aaron's coworkers usher him into the shower, tossing a coin to determine who gets the luxury of bathing next. Wassily wins. Lee cuts Gregg a wide berth, apparently still nursing her grievance despite their days apart. "Lighten up, baby," he mutters under his breath.

Later, when the skipper finds Aaron lining a plastic milk crate with laundry, making a padded nest for his precious trophy, he gives his son a hard time. "It's not going to break. That thing's tough."

"I don't care," the boy says, hacking with the ratcheting cough that even Gregg has to admit sounds like something that could tear your throat out. Wassily keeps saying how some of the villagers have exactly the same cough.

It's just a wicked cold, the father tells himself. Something that's going around. The kid's young; he'll shake it off. But Aaron spends the entire inbound trip in his rack, emerging only to use the head or to slurp the canned soup the others heat up for him.

Thankfully, the journey home proves uneventful. Gregg considers using some of his earnings to head out of state and wonders what Cabo's like at this time of year.

They part ways with the *Joanna* just before Port Clark. Soon thereafter the *Pegasus* encounters Mammoth Petroleum's traveling show: skimmers, dredges, high-pressure pumps—everything on parade for the boatloads of paparazzi that swarm alongside the equipment barges like flies on roadkill. Predictably, Gregg notices, they only encounter cleanup activity upon returning to well-traveled waterways. After all, that's where Mammoth has concentrated its media-relations effort.

Having passed through the Gateway, the skipper hears his call letters pronounced carefully on the CB. Tom Hagedorn's distinctive locution. Wolff stands beside him at the wheel, scanning Rugged Bay with the old military binoculars.

Gregg reaches for the mike. "*Pegasus* here. What's up, Harbormaster?"

"Be sure you consult with the attorney general's office before you talk to anyone," Hagedorn says in a strangely clipped voice.

Gregg swivels in his seat to engage Lee, who's playing solitaire at the table. "He sounds weird, don't you think?"

But his deckhand declines to look at him, let alone reply.

So the fisherman addresses Wassily, who studies his Bible on the other side of the table. "Something's up." He depresses the button on the side of the mike. "What's shaking, Tom?"

"Can't talk," Hagedorn replies tersely. "Keep your lips buttoned is my advice." With that, the harbormaster signs off.

Someone cuts into the call, a husky female voice saying, "... on assignment with *USA Today*. We're offering each of you a thousand dollars for exclusive interviews." Wolff regards the skipper quizzically.

The Lauren Bacall soundalike is in turn preempted by an adenoidal male voice whose name gets garbled. "—CBS News. May I board when you reach the harbor, or better yet, come out in a motorboat to meet you?"

"A 'motorboat'?" Gregg says to no one in particular.

On top of *that* call comes yet another: "Vice Admiral Steven Whitney, United States Coast Guard, serving you notice that the F/V *Pegasus* is under seizure."

He switches the radio off and strokes his wispy beard, grinning at Wassily and Wolff. "Sounds like we're in deep doo-doo." The fisherman rather relishes the prospect of going head-to-head with ... whomever.

"We had no choice," Wolff protests. "We couldn't carry the morts out, and we couldn't leave them there. The only solution was to burn them."

Has the *Joanna* met with a similar reception upon her return to Port Clark? Gregg knows better than to try to raise Ron on the VHF.

They motor steadily up the bay. "There they are," Wolff says, handing him the binoculars.

A crowd of maybe a hundred people throng the ferry dock. "Is that a movie camera?" Gregg returns the lenses to Wolff. "It's a big sucker."

"More than one, wouldn't you say?"

Wassily and Lee join them before the windshield, sharing Lee's smaller Nikons. "Fish and Wildlife, a state trooper, police ... and lawyers," Wassily says.

"How do you know?" the skipper asks, slowing the boat to reach for Lee's more powerful glasses.

"They're wearing suits. And carrying briefcases," Wassily snickers. The two men catch each other's eyes and burst into laughter. When they notice Lee and Wolff exchanging bewildered looks, it busts them up even more.

"Maybe you'll get arrested," Wassily says when he catches his breath.

"Again!" Gregg crows, and they double over with renewed hilarity, slapping each other on the back.

The ruckus draws Aaron from his bunk. "What's going on?" he asks hoarsely, looking rumpled and red-eyed.

The father passes his son the binos. "It's a posse."

While the boy absorbs the scene on the pier, Lee clears her throat and says, "If we're going to be the focus of all this attention, we should take advantage of it."

The men regard her expectantly. She outlines her idea.

Wolff nods. "I'm in."

"Me, too," Wassily agrees.

"I get one of the deer," Aaron says.

"Shit. Who'm I to go against the flow?" Gregg laughs. "Dibs on the swans."

It doesn't take long to prepare. Everyone dons their foul-weather gear, and Wassily and Wolff uncover the holds, releasing an ungodly stench that takes a long time to dissipate, even with the stiff northerly. A mirage-like haze wafts from the open hatches, concentrated fuel vapors from the petroleum residue inside. *My catch from hell*, the fisherman thinks bitterly.

Once they lay their selections on an outspread tarp, he gives the *Pegasus* throttle and quickly closes the distance to the harbor. Gregg can see the film crews and photographers capturing their approach. A light rain has begun to fall, so some of the suits lift their fancy attaché cases over their heads like umbrellas, threatening to ruin the expensive leather finish. *Serves 'em right*, he decides.

As they pass the jetty, the waiting crowd surges as one from the ferry dock to the adjacent harbor floats and presses toward his slip. *Talk about lemmings.* Even before they've gotten fenders over the side, let alone tied up, a barrage of shouted questions assail them:

"Is it true you burned thousands of oiled birds and animals?"

"How much did Mammoth pay you to destroy the evidence?"

Gregg watches the peninsula's lone state trooper and the entire five-member Selby police department (including Ben Peebles, the longtime dog catcher recently redubbed "animal control officer") link arms to prevent anyone from boarding the *Pegasus*.

Wassily and Lee return to the wheelhouse from securing the boat. Gregg eyes his crew. "Ready?" he asks. Nods all around. "Let's do it."

Each emerges single file from the cabin and, taking up his or her prop, crosses the deck in slow, silent procession. The skipper leads the way, gripping in each hand the long white neck of a dead trumpeter swan. Despite his considerable height, the birds are so large that their webbed feet trail the ground. To its credit, the crowd hushes and stills, watching the spectacle in near silence while camera shutters whirr and click without pause.

Aaron pulls the Teklik Lagoon buck across the deck, dragging the animal's stiffened body hind-feet-first down the gangplank. It would have been a chore even if he'd been feeling well, Gregg thinks, applauding his son's pluck as the animal's antler-knobbed head bumps over the frets of the ramp.

Wassily goes next, cradling the body of a dead baby otter in the crook of each arm.

Wolff balances the stiffened torpedo-shaped carcass of a small harbor seal on his shoulder. Much of the animal's face has been chewed or scraped away, lending it a ghoulish appearance.

Finally, Lee steps forward with what proves to be the first documented bald eagle casualty of the spill. She holds the Glory Point trophy with wings outspread so they extend on either side of her torso, the raptor's body crucified against her own. The bird's large snowy head with its lone stripe of black oil flops against her collarbone, the hooked golden beak resting on her shoulder and lethal-looking yellow talons catching against her jeans.

Once they've stepped down onto the float, each of them is besieged despite law enforcement's efforts to maintain order. Police Chief Abbott gives Gregg a sour look. Deputy Curt Beauchamp, still just a kid, appears to be pretty freaked out by the whole thing. The *Pegasus* skipper and his crew lay their props at the feet of USFWS agents and beat a retreat back to the wheelhouse.

After the police and Trooper Rinehart succeed in dispersing the mob, or at least in relocating it from the harbor to the parking lot, a young Coast Guard lieutenant in his dress whites—for improved photogenics, Gregg guesses—boards the *Pegasus* and serves him papers, ordering everyone off the boat. The officer declares that his cadets will unload the vessel. The fisherman shrugs. "Suit yourself." He thrusts a gallon container of Pine-Sol into the Coastie's hands. "See that they scrub everything down. And I mean spotless, Mister. I'll be back to make sure you didn't miss anything."

"It's your lucky day," Gregg tells the others. "Someone else is going to unload and disinfect her." He looks around for his son, who's back in his bunk. "Come on, Aaron!" he calls, impatient to get the hell out of there.

First Wassily and then Wolff give the boy a hug. "I want you to meet my kids sometime," Wolff says.

"Go see a doctor," Wassily urges.

"You're leaving that float with me when you fly home, right?" Lee teases.

"No way!" Aaron musters a smile.

Lee gives him a kiss on the cheek. "Get well." To Gregg's surprise, Aaron kisses her back. The boy has indeed had a bonding experience—with everyone except his old man. Lee says nothing at all to her skipper by way of farewell, packing into her duffel all the items she normally leaves on board. It's lucky they're not going fishing anytime soon, he thinks, since it looks like it might take her that long to get over her fit of pique.

Gregg decides that if Aaron doesn't feel better after a good night's sleep in a real bed, he'll take him to see Doc Scott in the morning.

He unlocks his apartment. More rent demands from the landlord have been pushed under the door, along with an application for disaster assistance from the state Division of Emergency Services addressed to "Occupant." Gregg opens a few windows to get some air circulating then asks his son if he'll be okay alone for a few hours.

"I'm wiped," Aaron says thickly. "Think I'll go to bed."

"Good idea. I'll pick up some Pepsi, get a few groceries. You want anything special?"

"No thanks." The kid sounds spent.

As he drives back toward the harbor, Gregg tries to remember the last time he'd set foot in The Anchor. It's been a few years, anyway. The bar has been on his mind for days now. It isn't the drinking, exactly. After all, you can buy alcohol anywhere. It's more the memory of another time, when getting wasted wasn't a character flaw.

Sure enough, his favorite bartender, Margo, greets him like a long-lost friend.

"Wipe that shit-eating grin off your face," Gregg teases her, even as she slips a steaming-cold Corona across the bar to him, followed by a shot of tequila.

"On the house. Welcome back, stranger," she says warmly.

Fritz Detweiler, sitting alone in a booth, brings his Michelob to join Gregg at the polyurethaned spruce-plank bar. Clinking beer bottles, the two men shake their heads in acknowledgment of all the AA meetings they've shared.

Gregg tells the AlaskaPride plant manager and Margo about the wildlife retrieval mission. "What a mistake," he concludes. "I will never pimp my boat like that again, so help me God."

When Margo moves off to tend other customers, Fritz quietly fishes in the breast pocket of his denim shirt, handing Gregg a Polaroid snap-shot. "It's from Seattle," he says. "Pike Place Market."

The skipper tips the photo to get better light. Blue-tinted, it portrays a half-dozen whole king salmon laid out on crushed ice, a hand-lettered sign picketed above the display. "CLEAN, SAFE & DELICIOUS," it says. "NOT FROM ALASKA."

Gregg stares at the picture. Handing it back without comment, he signals Margo and says to Fritz, "Double shots? I'm buying."

By the time he wakes up on the banquette of a booth, sun streams in the windows. Margo finishes her shift and offers Gregg a ride home. Only then does he remember Aaron.

Shit.

Throwing water on his face in the men's room, Gregg catches a glimpse of himself in the frameless round mirror mounted above the sink. He's getting too old for this. He decides to run into the Kwik Stop for coffee, orange juice, and donuts, at least. The only food in the apartment is some cellophane packets of soup crackers. Aaron's sure to be hungry when he wakes—if he hasn't already, that is, wondering where in hell his father is. Gregg doesn't even know if his son has any cash on him with which to buy himself breakfast at the Sea View.

Peg could get a lot of mileage from this.

But when he lets himself into the apartment and calls Aaron's name, there's no reply. Possibly he's lucked out and the boy's still asleep? Gregg finds the door to the small bedroom ajar. "Aaron?" He steps inside. "Hey. How're you doing?"

His son lies in the bed, but not asleep, as the father soon realizes. Unconscious.

If Tess is surprised to find Daniel sitting at the kitchen table that night eating a grilled-cheese sandwich, she doesn't let on.

"Care to join me?" he offers, setting his food down and wiping his lips with a napkin. She wears a baggy green Selby Seawolves sweatshirt; he can't tell if her belly bulges or not. How far along had she been with Elias or Minke before she started to show? He searches her face for clues, but Tess won't meet his eyes.

She sits across from him. "How was it?"

"Depressing. In a word." Daniel tries to hold her gaze, but his wife seems to be appraising the condition of the cupboards above the sink. "How are you?"

She glances his way then, or rather, glares. Silence.

"I talked to the kids. I want to bring them home," Daniel says, but the words provoke the opposite of his intended effect.

"Everything's at your convenience," she says heatedly, pushing away from the table. "When you get tired of playing reporter, then and only then do you come home. When *you* decide it's time for the children—"

He cuts her off. "We're a family. We love each other. That's got to be worth something. We can't let the oil spill break us. Please."

Tess goes to the sink, where she runs herself a glass of water and speaks without turning around. "Did Elias tell you he's been wetting his bed?" In a moment Daniel hears the glass set down on the counter, followed shortly by the closing of the bedroom door.

In the morning Tess, in her long bathrobe, brings Daniel, in his boxers, a cup of coffee. Is she offering a truce? "Thank you," he says, shifting to one side of their son's mattress to make room for her to sit.

She chooses Minke's bed, however, and lowers herself so deliberately while holding her mug of tea that Daniel thinks she *must* be pregnant. He ducks his head lest she see the hope that flares within him.

"You don't think I should be taking their money to care for otters, do you?" Tess asks.

The question catches him off guard. "Can we please start putting all this behind us?"

"You think their money's corrupt."

"I'm in no position to judge," Daniel says.

"But you do judge," she insists.

He swings his bare legs over the side of the bed to face her, weighing what he wants to say against the harm it might cause. "How much has Mammoth spent on otters so far?"

"I don't know. Millions." Tessa's tone is defiant. "They say each one that survives will be worth almost a hundred thousand dollars."

An even higher figure than Daniel's predicted. "How can they justify spending that kind of money when human beings are starving—including children right here in the U.S.?"

"How do you justify not doing everything you *can* do, no matter how much it costs, to alleviate suffering?" she counters. "And how can you place a greater value on people than on other species, when we couldn't even survive without them?" Tess peers at him. "I thought one reason we moved to Selby was to live closer to nature. Now you're saying it's not worth protecting?"

Daniel sets his coffee cup on the small dresser between the two beds. "A lot of wild creatures would be a lot better off without us," he agrees. "It's just that Mammoth Petroleum is so wealthy—richer than entire nations, in some cases. If you're a Fortune 500 corporation desperate for good public relations, I guess a hundred grand per otter is pocket change."

"Does that make it wrong?" she persists. "Would it be better if they couldn't afford to at least try to undo the damage?"

Daniel holds his wife's gaze. "I guess I think washing oiled birds and otters isn't as much for the sake of the creatures themselves as it is to appease our own guilt, to make us feel better about how badly we've screwed up this planet."

"Exactly. Something wrong with that?"

He shakes his head. "No. Maybe the oil spill will show us once and for all that we can't have it both ways. Can't enjoy the benefits of resource extraction without any downside. Americans in general—and Alaskans in particular maybe—have grown so accustomed to entitlements that we're completely unwilling to pay the true cost of our lifestyle."

Neither speaks for a few minutes. "Gregg's a piece of work," Daniel comments.

"What do you mean?"

"Arrogant but insecure. Capable but careless."

But Tess isn't interested in Gregg. "How's Lee doing?"

"Hurting."

"Yeah, well. Aren't we all." His wife looks and sounds sullen, like the kids when they're pouting.

"How about you? How are you doing?" he asks, but Tess still won't answer him, so he tries another tack. "How long's Elias been wetting the bed?"

"It started last week." Now she sounds worried.

"Every night?"

"No. Three times so far." Tess clasps her favorite, almost-round ceramic mug, reminding Daniel of Aaron's glass float—and of a pregnant woman's belly. He wants to embrace her, draw her to him, but knows it's not a good idea.

"I'm driving up to Anchorage today," she announces.

"I'll go with you," he says, thinking she means to bring the kids home.

"No, I'm going alone. I'll be gone a few days."

Daniel waits for the shoe to drop, but she doesn't volunteer more. "I'll look for a new job," he says, trying to catch her eye. "Something with more hours, better pay. Benefits."

Tess rises from Minke's bed to leave the room.

When he returned home the previous evening, Daniel had showered for so long that the hot water ran out, scrubbing his body with a stiff-bristled brush until his flesh felt raw. Now he thinks he should have left himself a thicker skin.

18

Daniel observes that although the U.S. Fish and Wildlife Service has threatened to arrest the captains and crews of both the *Pegasus* and the *Joanna* and to impound the two vessels, the agency in the end merely takes possession of the video Ron filmed at Glory Point and quickly drops the matter. The feds must realize that even though many Americans have come to question Mammoth Petroleum's motives, they're still less inclined to side with government than with what remains of the wildlife.

He learns that while he was documenting deadlife retrieval on the coast, the press has been having a field day. It's been well established by now that not only had the petroleum industry lied about its preparedness for a major spill, but state and federal agencies had likewise utterly failed to ride herd on the oil producers. "Broken Promises!" headlines blare.

Town life seems to have returned to a semblance of normalcy, except that "business as usual" now means the daily demands of responding to an ongoing crisis. When Daniel observes his coworkers at the radio station heading home again at the end of the usual workday, he realizes people are capable of maintaining focused intensity for only so long before they begin to burn out. Having reached its third month, the Mammoth *Kuparuk* Critical Incident is clearly a marathon event, not a sprint, and everyone has had to pace themselves accordingly.

He discovers that Dean Carson's replacement, the new Mammoth Petroleum PR point, is in every way a clone of his predecessor, a retirement-aged WASP male who's neatly groomed and well spoken, but lacking in any decision-making authority whatsoever. This gent, too, takes to parroting what seems to have become the corporation's mantra: "As unfortunate as this event may be, we do well to remember that it's also the normal cost of doing business." The rhetoric of "acceptable risks" sounds too much like Vietnam to suit Daniel.

When he hears stories of cleanup workers afflicted with symptoms like Aaron's fever, cough, and lethargy, the reporter tries to locate medical data concerning human exposure to raw petroleum, only to find that none exists. Incredibly, no one's even monitoring oil spill worker health. What are the long-term risks? What about his own exposure? Daniel decides to interview those who've gotten sick from the oil. He'll talk to Aaron, of course, and ask Wassily for Pogibshi contacts.

Jackie, now counseling the residents of other oiled coastal settlements, calls one night from Port Clark, asking for Tess. After Daniel explains that she's gone to Anchorage (to fetch the kids, he says), the psychologist tells him that all the spill communities are following the same pattern as every other place in the world that's ever suffered a man-made disaster: rates of domestic violence, alcoholism, and drug abuse escalate predictably, taxing and then overwhelming existing services.

"Makes you wonder if Alaska's long winter will make things even worse," Daniel says.

"It's guaranteed," Jackie says, sounding surprised that he hasn't already figured this out. When she asks after Lee, Daniel tells her he hasn't crossed paths with the deckhand since they came in from the coast.

The state has closed area fisheries until further notice, the result of its new "zero tolerance" policy to ensure that not a single instance of contamination mar the reputation of Alaska seafood. At the same time, however, officials repeatedly assure coastal residents and Alaska Natives that subsistence foods are "probably" safe to eat. Are they kidding? Daniel can exactly picture Wassily narrowing his eyes in skepticism and distrust. How must it feel to be among the nth generation to inhabit Alaska continuously for millennia, only to have the same people who overran your land and dispossessed you of your aboriginal rights now tell you what you can and cannot eat?

Mammoth Petroleum Corporation continues to post profits, but has already retooled its brand, forsaking the blue-and-orange woolly mammoth logo in favor of a starry red, white, and blue design sporting only the acronym MPC. With its money sustaining the community, those who don't curse it have come to worship the oil giant. No doubt some are even convinced they've never had it so good. But how long will oil spill prosperity last, and what happens when the bubble bursts?

One afternoon, Daniel finds himself transfixed in his cubby at work by a black-and-white press release photo of a lone cleanup worker—a woman dressed in rain gear, her hair in a long braid—dabbing with what looks like a hankie at a boxcar-sized cliff face blackened by crude oil. He tacks the photo above his desk because the image captures so perfectly the futility of the entire enterprise. You *can't* spot-clean spilled petroleum. The only guarantee against its toxic effects is to keep it out of the environment in the first place.

Since Tess has taken their car to Anchorage, Daniel hitches a ride to the harbor to fact-check the documentary he's preparing on wildlife retrieval. He'd love to see Aaron but assumes the young man has already returned to Anchorage. He should call him, see how he's feeling.

Daniel finds the *Pegasus* empty, the wheelhouse locked.

A clean-shaven young man scrubbing an oil-streaked cabin cruiser in the adjacent slip calls over that Gregg's in Anchorage, "at the hospital."

"What happened?"

"His son was medevacked. Gregg's with him. That's all I know."

Daniel runs up the ramp to the general store with the thought of using the pay phone to call Tess at her parents'. But she doesn't even know Aaron. Who does? Lee has no phone. Should he try calling Anchorage hospitals, asking for Gregg? Daniel stands in the store entry, breathing hard, unsure what to do. Is Aaron's medical emergency the result of his exposure to the oil?

He hasn't been in the Mercantile for years, certainly not since the spill. The profusion of Mammoth *Kuparuk* merchandise on display inside takes him by surprise: sweatshirts, coffee mugs, baseball caps. A wire rack holds some of the bumper stickers that have appeared recently on vehicles around town, reflecting the wide range of sentiment concerning the event: "Boycott Mammoth Petroleum" and "Tanker from the Black Lagoon" but also "Alaskans to Big Oil: THANK YOU" and "Our hero, Captain Aengus!"

Daniel finds himself staring at a hand-lettered sign on poster board that solicits submissions to a Mammoth *Kuparuk* cookbook, a joint project of the Mammoth Petroleum Corporation and the Selby Chamber of Commerce. Recipes. Really? What's Aaron's prognosis? Maybe Daniel should try to get a ride to Anchorage.

He recalls his favorite t-shirt slogan, although it now assumes an altogether new connotation. The garment represents Attu, the island at the farthest tip of Alaska's thousand-mile Aleutian Chain. "It's not the end of the world," the t-shirt says, "but you can see it from here."

Lee discovers that while she was on the outer coast bagging spill-kills, swallows and sandhill cranes have returned to southcentral Alaska. These winged harbingers of summer have never before failed to delight her. Now, however, grief eclipses joy. She worries that harm will befall the migrants, as it has so many other birds. For the first time since coming North, the deckhand thinks about leaving, but has no idea where she'd go. Labrador, maybe? Is it polluted there? She'd like to start over again somewhere new but also knows it would be a good idea for her to finish college, and staying in Alaska is by far her most affordable option.

She hopes never to see Gregg again, and thinking of Tess fills her with so much frustration that her chest hurts. Jackie feels like unfinished business, but who knows what it would take to finish that. Lee leaves her cabin only to wander the surrounding woods and muskeg meadows with Bruno, her landlady's Chesapeake Bay retriever. The reddish-brown dog makes an ideal companion because he can't talk and is always so ecstatic to see her.

One afternoon, a few days after returning from Glory Point, she hears a vehicle approaching. Outside on the porch, Bruno erupts into frenzied barking, his afternoon nap disturbed. Too late for Lee to draw the curtains or hide in her sleeping loft. When she steps to the kitchen window to peek out, she fails to recognize the battered orange Jeep bouncing to a stop in the overgrown grass.

Braking so suddenly that the engine stalls, Daniel springs from the driver's seat, leaving the car door to flap open behind him as he jogs toward the cabin. "Lee!" he calls. "You in there?"

She opens the top half of the Dutch door and tells the dog to shush. Bruno obeys, sniffing Daniel's legs.

"Aaron's in intensive care in Anchorage." Daniel tells her the few details he's been able to confirm: Gregg drinking to the point of passing out at The Anchor, the evacuation of the comatose boy by helicopter, and Gregg and Peg now keeping bedside vigil at the Anchorage hospital. Daniel speaks in a rush, jittery with the news, and then, to Lee's consternation, he begins to weep.

So she opens the lower half of the door, too, and leads him to a chair at her small drop-leaf table, where Daniel cries in earnest into the sheets of paper towel she tears off the roll for him. His loss of control unnerves and then angers her. Lee wants to tug him to his feet and ask him to leave. She draws a breath to give him a piece of her mind, reaching a hand to her chest at the ensuing pain. Suddenly, like a punctured tire, she simply deflates, sinking into the wooden rocking chair and closing her eyes. Aaron. Pipsqueak.

Daniel sniffles a while longer, blowing his nose and blotting his eyes. "It must have been his exposure to crude oil, don't you think?"

"Is that what the doctors say?" Lee asks with alarm.

"I don't know."

"But we all breathed it. We all got sprayed by the surf. No one else got sick," she says.

"Not yet," Daniel agrees. "But remember how he fell and ended up wearing it the whole time we were at Gory?"

They stare at one another then, each recalling with horror how Aaron got drenched with raw petroleum the night the *Kuparuk* struck the reef. Unadulterated crude oil, undiluted by seawater. Daniel weeps some more.

Lee pictures Gregg drinking alone atop the lazarette while they lay anchored off Hinchinbrook Arm. "Gregg was drunk?"

"I guess so." Daniel inhales deeply and rubs his face. "I wonder if we'll all get sick—sooner or later."

Surely her skipper's beside himself... Lee trembles as she rises. Fuck him! She can't breathe. She has to get out of here. Now.

"Speaking of getting sick," Daniel is saying, "when was the last time you ate?"

Lee shoves open the top half of the Dutch door again, gulping fresh air. Outside, Bruno whines, scratching the door with his paw.

"Do you even have any food here?"

"Ramen." Lee speaks without turning. "Peanut butter."

Daniel raises his head. "You probably feel like there're more pressing issues than taking care of yourself."

"Irene's been hospitalized for exhaustion," Lee says of her elderly landlady and neighbor, who in the early days of the spill had volunteered practically around the clock to answer phones at KRBB. She keeps her hand on the door sill in case she needs to flee.

"That's what I mean. Don't you become a casualty, too." Daniel blows his nose again. "So you're caring for her dog?"

"Me and her sister." Lee inclines her head next door. "Daphne's staying at the house."

"I can't believe this," Daniel says. "Aaron." His eyes overflow again. "Double A." He rises heavily to his feet. "Did you hear Fritz Detweiler almost died from an overdose of sleeping pills?"

"The AlaskaPride manager?" Lee shudders. Then, upon considering the news, she says indignantly, "How could he do that to his family? His wife has a disability; they've got five kids."

"He might have done it for the life insurance."

Lee gapes at Daniel. Now she feels like crying, too.

"Do you want to drive to Anchorage with me to see Aaron?" he asks.

"Can he have visitors?"

"Not yet," Daniel admits. "But as soon as his condition improves."

"When would we leave?" Lee's olive-green duffel sits in the corner, still full of her fishing gear.

"I need to arrange some things at the station and throw my stuff together. Can your truck make the drive?" Daniel runs his hands through his hair, making himself presentable again.

"I think so," she says. "If I can start it. Want me to pick you up in town?"

"No. I'll drive back out. That way, we can take the Jeep if your truck won't start." Daniel pulls open the lower half of the door and steps outside.

Lee accompanies him onto the porch, gesturing to the rusty orange vehicle. "Whose is it?"

"One of the volunteer's. Some guy from Kansas. He donated it to KRBB." Daniel hesitates. "Tess took our car to Anchorage. To get the kids." He looks like he might break down again, so she quickly thanks him for coming and pats him on the back, urging him on his way.

"See you later," she says. "I'll be ready."

Lee walks Bruno next door to leave a note for Daphne explaining her departure for Anchorage. Bruno looks forlorn when she clips him to his line outside the two-story house, howling mournfully until she's out of sight.

Alone again, Lee empties the duffel onto the floor and assembles things for the road trip. She knows it will do her good to get away, if only for a little while. And she looks forward to seeing Aaron, of course, even if it's in a hospital, remembering his look of triumph when he found his glass float. She'll ask Daniel to keep Gregg out of the way when she has her visit with his son. She crawls up into her windowless loft to nap, even though she had already slept almost twelve hours the night before. As she lies waiting for sleep's merciful amnesia, Lee remembers the images that used to greet her closed eyelids after a day of fishing: bright silver salmon flopping onto the deck as the gill net grows taut over the drum, longlines strung with pop-eyed cod, crab pots crawling with pincered crustaceans. Now, closing her eyes brings with it only memories of oiled birds and animals, blackened beaches, decomposition and death. Finally, she recalls the silent undersea life she'd shown Aaron in the harbor, the wafting flowering tendrils of pale-green anemones, the miniature pulsing featherlike filter of barnacles. She remembers his excitement. "What's that thing?" he'd asked, pointing to a small crimson sponge. "What about this?"

Daniel returns in the Jeep at dusk, this time remaining in the vehicle while it idles in the drive. Lee pulls the cabin door closed and makes sure it's latched, shouldering her bag. Bruno appears out of nowhere and follows her across the yard. She'll have to clip him to his line again and tie a knot in it for good measure.

"Aaron's gone." Daniel's voice is hoarse, his eyes red.

Lee searches his face, pain piercing her chest.

"He died about an hour ago. Never regained consciousness." Daniel reaches through the open car window to take her hand.

Lee continues to stare at him.

"Gregg's a wreck."

"You talked to him?" She withdraws her hand.

"I'll see him tomorrow," Daniel says. "I'm driving to Tessa's folks' now. You still want to come?"

Where was Gregg when his son needed him, Lee wants to know. Hunched over the bar at The Anchor, downing shots? Bruno nudges

Lee's knee with his big head, whining softly. Had Aaron cried out for his father while he was alone in the apartment? "No. You go ahead," she tells Daniel.

Aaron is dead? How could this have happened? Lee waits for tears but is aware only of the clenching pain around her heart, which continues, somehow, to beat.

When the Jeep's taillights vanish, she looks at her closed-up cabin. Wrestling open the stiff passenger door of the Datsun pickup truck, she sets the duffel on the floor and climbs across the bench seat to the driver's side because that door hasn't opened for years. The cab smells musty. Grass has grown up through the radiator grille, but despite not having been driven for months, Rainbow's engine turns over on the first try. Bruno leaps into the gateless truck bed as she backs from the parking place and lurches headlong down the drive.

Lee will call Daphne from a pay phone somewhere, to tell her she's taken the dog with her. She drives north, propelled by emotions that threaten to drown her like a storm surge if she doesn't outrun them. She wonders if Aaron died from exposure to hydrocarbons, if his death is God's way of punishing Gregg. Will the rest of them sicken, too? At Winter Creek, Lee brings Bruno into the cab with her, and he stretches out contentedly on the long seat. She's comforted by his animal presence, his warm head butted against her thigh.

Lee's never felt so bereft. Her Korean birth parents, whoever they were, had abandoned her in infancy. Then Gunther betrayed both Weezie and Lee with his alcoholism. She knows his nightly drinking had contributed to the severity of Weezie's cancer somehow, making her more susceptible to the disease. Jackie has let Lee down by moving away, as have Tess and all the others who've sold out by working for Mammoth.

Gregg had lied not only to Lee, of course, but to his own son. How is he going to live with himself after this? Better that Gregg should have died and Aaron live.

Just like her skipper's drinking, Captain Richard Aengus's alcoholism had caused a catastrophe. But Mammoth Petroleum, the state, *and* the U.S. government have also failed not just Alaskans but all Americans, as well as people everywhere who love wild nature, by their failure to take adequate precautions to protect it.

The last time she'd seen Gunther was just before he moved out of state several years ago, when his second marriage fell apart. He'd visited Lee and Jackie in Selby, and she remembers how old he looked, his gauntness and receding hairline making her uneasy despite the fact that he'd long ago quit drinking. Jackie, meeting Gunther for the first time, had pronounced him kind. Still, Lee was relieved when her father left town after only a few days, and although he sends her postcards periodically, inviting them both to Spokane, Lee never writes him back.

She drives north in a hurry, leaving the coast behind. The sooner she can outdistance the oil spill, the sooner she will recover from the shock of Aaron's death. Really, her only regret is the fact that her truck's spewing out carcinogens in its exhaust. After a couple of hours, Lee pulls into the gas station at Nellie's Landing where she customarily refuels on long trips. The isolated pumps carry an unfamiliar brand of gas, something sporting a shimmering red, white, and blue logo. The smell when she inserts the fuel nozzle into Rainbow's gas tank makes her stomach seize. Handing the grizzled proprietor a twenty-dollar bill, he assures her of the gasoline's quality as he makes change and closes the drawer of his till. "MPC," he says. "It's still good gas, still Mammoth Petroleum. They just changed the name is all."

Would it really have made any difference if she had purchased another kind of fuel? Aren't all oil companies alike? Lee scans the redesigned gas station. Star-spangled Mammoth. Show your patriotism by buying our product. How shameless can they get.

And what is wrong with her that something like this reduces her to tears when Aaron's death does not?

19

Seated on a stool at her parents' breakfast bar, Tessa studies the cover of the new issue of *Time*, the words "America's Glory?" emblazoned in red across the outspread wings of the dead bald eagle Lee clasps as she descends the ramp from the *Pegasus* in Selby harbor.

She looks like she could be Native, Tess thinks, confused by the photo caption, which identifies "Lee Chukanok," as "an Alaska Native betrayed by government's failure to hold Big Oil accountable."

"Why would she tell them that's her name?" Tess asks Daniel, who's fixing the kids lunch. "Why pretend to be Eskimo?"

"Maybe the photographer screwed up, confused her with Wassily. Assumed they were related? The same last name?" He cuts Elias's peanut-butter-and-jelly sandwich in half and Minke's into quarters.

Tess remembers Lee once sheepishly confessing how she liked it that so many people mistook her for Alaska Native. "It makes me feel like I belong here," she said.

Tess scrutinizes her friend's emaciated sexless figure, which makes Lee look as if she could be male *or* female. Has the younger woman become anorexic? What's not ambiguous about Lee's appearance is her haunting expression of injury and overwhelm, for her eyes in the picture look directly into the camera and burn with feeling. She's the perfect poster child for the Mammoth *Kuparuk* oil spill, Tess thinks, blinking back tears. Poor Lee. Poor all of us. What an unholy mess.

While the kids eat, she and Daniel scan the cover story, which describes the events of Glory Point, illustrated by frames from the documentary video the *Joanna* skipper had made of the wildlife burning—the filmstrips reminiscent of the Zapruder footage of JFK's assassination. "'How do you think it makes me feel?'" Gregg Anderson is quoted as saying. "'I fought for my country. Come to find I'm still fighting for it.'"

"He sounds good," Daniel declares. "Patriotic."

Her husband has already told her how Gregg cut his hair, shaved, and donned a dark suit and tie for his son's funeral. How bewilderment and grief have replaced the fisherman's customary cockiness. "He looks smaller, like he's literally shrunk," Daniel said, recounting the way the *Pegasus* skipper had wandered unsteadily from the chapel immediately following the service. According to Wassily, Gregg was headed for the southwest Alaska village where the two of them had grown up.

When they return home with the kids, Tess discovers that, as measured against their makeshift growth chart on the kitchen door frame, Elias has grown a full inch.

Minke's clinginess is such that Tess nicknames her "Velcro," but this isn't, after all, new behavior. Their capable son, on the other hand, who before the oil spill had not only asked to but insisted upon doing everything himself, now whimpers and demands help with even the simplest task. And Tess herself, who a few months earlier couldn't wait to send the kids away to her parents, wants only to dote on them, to breathe deeply of their sweet milky smell. Accordingly, she gives notice at the otter center in favor of returning to regular shifts of nursing. However, having lost seniority at the hospital when she requested reduced hours

242

to do otter care, she has no choice but to work graveyard shift until she's accrued enough hours to negotiate a better schedule.

Daniel arranges his job at KRBB around hers, so that one of them is always at home with the children. They resume sharing a bed, but due to their opposing work schedules, usually occupy it at different times. Which suits her just fine.

When her husband told her of Aaron's death from pneumonia, he asked Tess if she thought it could be the result of exposure to hydrocarbons. How would you even begin to prove cause and effect, she wonders. She, in turn, had explained her last-minute change of heart in the waiting room of the Anchorage family planning clinic, a decision prompted less by unbounded desire for another child than by aversion to repeating a painful mistake. Daniel sheds tears of gratitude, promising that he will do whatever he can to make things easier for her. "Too bad you can't be the one to give birth," Tess replies.

She learns that Mark Raynor, the ER doc, has filed for divorce from his wife, Barbara. Sharon Branch and *her* husband have split up. Tony, next door, has gone to work for Mammoth Petroleum, driving the press corps in an oversized van wherever it needs to go. He and Carla have brought the twins home, too, but Tony's moved out to live with Jack Vance until, as Carla tartly puts it, he can figure out how to balance work and family. Tess hears of more folks forsaking Selby. Not a bad idea, she thinks, but Daniel and she lack the resources for such a move. Besides, where would they go? She doubts there's any place left—anywhere she'd like to live, anyway—that isn't already or won't eventually be as contaminated as everywhere else, given ocean currents, wind patterns, and human behavior.

The Alaska Mental Health Association receives a grant to hold workshops with children in each of what are now called "the spill communities." At Jackie's urging, Tess and Daniel register the kids to attend Camp My Turn. Every morning for a week, Minke and Elias play in the basement of the Methodist church, grouped with others their age, drawing pictures, making colorful masks, telling stories of their experiences of the oil spill—experiences that of course have little to do with crude petroleum and everything to do with the frightening conduct of the adults in their lives. The facilitators, licensed child psychologists who've volunteered from all over the state, listen gravely to each tale. It must do some good because Elias stops wetting his bed.

When Lee opens her eyes, she has no idea where she is. Tubes and wires connect her very sore body to softly pulsing electronic monitors, to an IV drip. Is she sick like Aaron, she wonders groggily. Will she die?

The next time she wakes, the hospital room is dark except for the glow of electronics and the light wedging in from the corridor. She discovers her right arm in a cast that includes her elbow. A woman with dark hair sleeps on her side in a reclining chair beside the window. A nurse? At the far end of the narrow room another bed lies partially curtained off. More equipment monitoring whomever lies there.

When she awakens again, Lee finds Jackie standing in the doorway, talking in a low voice to a short male nurse who, upon discovering her conscious, springs into action to check readings on the various instruments beside Lee's bed.

Jackie smiles happily. "Hi," she says, dark circles under her eyes. "How're you doing?" The nurse departs.

"What happened?" Lee's tongue feels thick and dry, her throat raw.

"You rolled Rainbow." Her ex-lover holds a pink plastic cup beneath Lee's chin, bending the flexible straw to her lips. When Lee sips the water, it hurts to swallow. Something prevents her from turning her head. A neck brace. When she tries to lift her casted arm, it's too heavy to move.

"You were driving," Jackie says gently.

She remembers the gas station then, how something about it upset her. "Tired," Lee says, dropping off again.

"What happened?" It still hurts to speak. "Where are we?"

It's dark beyond the window. Jackie sits in the recliner writing on a legal tablet by the light of a floor lamp. She looks over the top of her reading glasses, setting her work aside and standing up. "We're in Anchorage. You were driving Rainbow; you hit a moose."

Lee remembers nothing, which frightens her. "Did it die?"

"The trooper shot it, put it down." The other woman indicates the edge of the bed. "May I?"

Lee can't nod because of the cervical collar. "Yes," she says in a feeble voice.

When Jackie sits beside her, taking hold of her good hand, Lee feels tears on her chin, trickling down behind the neck brace. "Where's Bruno?" she suddenly blurts.

Jackie squeezes her fingers. "He's okay. He fell out when the truck rolled, but he's okay." She hesitates. "They had to amputate one of his legs, but the vet says he'll be fine."

"Amputate? Where is he?" Lee begins to cry in earnest.

"In an animal hospital. Not too far from here, as a matter of fact."

"Will he still be able to walk?"

Her ex offers her a tissue from the small box on the swing-arm table that's attached to the bed. "Apparently three-legged dogs do just fine."

Lee's blinking and breathing rapidly. Jackie does her best to enfold her in her arms without disconnecting anything, and the deckhand leans into the shelter of the other woman, sobbing and gasping for breath like a baby. She pictures the inlet in winter, locked shore to shore in ice many feet thick. Come spring, the frozen slabs, some as big as ice rinks, heave against one another violently, with cracking explosions and harsh scraping sounds, jousting in a crazy polar geometry until one day an unusually high tide lifts them apart and floats them out to sea. Finally, she lies back with swollen eyes, tears continuing to eke down her face. "Aaron's dead."

"I know." Jackie never lets go of Lee but now dabs at her own leaking eyes. "Daniel told me. He and Tess came to see you before they went back to Selby, but you were asleep."

She hit the moose just north of Nellie's Landing, the other woman tells the deckhand, and the state troopers had tracked the psychologist down because Lee had a card in her wallet on which she had designated

Jackie as her next of kin. Lee suffers from whiplash, her right arm is twice broken, and her body's mottled everywhere by bruises large and small. Jackie keeps telling her she's lucky to be alive, that the seat belt saved her life. She whispers that the elderly woman in the other bed of the shared hospital room has terminal cancer and can no longer speak.

"Do you know how Gregg's doing?" Lee asks.

"No."

"Does Irene know about Bruno?"

"Yes." Jackie squeezes Lee's hand again.

"Is she still in the hospital?"

"No, but I guess she's pretty fragile. Her sister's caring for her at home."

The deckhand thinks for a minute. "Daphne."

Jackie nods.

"Did you sleep here last night?" Lee asks.

"Last two nights, actually."

Lee can't quite meet her ex's eyes. "Thank you."

"You're welcome."

Later, Jackie shows her the issue of *Time*. "How'd they come up with 'Chukanok'?"

The deckhand sighs. "The photographer thought I was related to Wassily." She glances at the other woman defiantly. "I didn't bother to correct him."

Jackie's too much of a professional to betray her surprise. "Why?"

"Because I wanted them to take us seriously," Lee says irritably. She picks up the magazine and studies the cover. "Cool picture, don't you think?"

Her ex-lover gives her the psychologist look but doesn't comment.

Irene calls, sounding frail, and the two commiserate over all that has befallen them. When Lee keeps repeating, "I'm sorry," Irene replies, "Bruno has a wonderful life, thanks in large part to you," which makes the younger woman cry again.

Tess calls several times, offering her a place to stay until she mends. "I'm home during the day," she says. "The kids would love your company." Despite the generosity of the offer, Lee's not sure she wants to return to Selby. She's also uncertain about forgiving Tess, although from the vantage point of this hospital bed it's hard to remember exactly why she has felt so adamant about disavowing her friend.

Upon learning of Lee's accident, Daniel thinks, *Something had to give.* The bottom has fallen out for the deckhand just as it has for her skipper—and so many others.

Sometime in late summer, he sees from the legal listings in the *Sentinel* that the *Pegasus* has been repossessed. The list of repo boats, grown longer with each passing week of the spill, now fills an entire page. Daniel makes it a point to check in regularly by phone with Gregg, who's living in Anchorage. The fisherman's as likely to be monosyllabic as he is to be eager to talk. He tells Daniel that following Aaron's funeral, he had spent two weeks in the village, taking long steam baths with the male elders who, Gregg says, always outlasted him in their ability to withstand the searing heat of the homemade saunas. He says he thinks the time out there had done him good, but that even though the community is technically "dry," the availability of bootlegged booze had soon undermined his attempts to get sober. So the fisherman has entered a VA-sponsored residential rehab program, attending twelve-step meetings every day.

The two men seldom mention Aaron by name. "You raised a beauty boy," Daniel says in one phone call. "You should be proud."

Gregg's quiet. "He stuck with things, didn't give up," he says finally. "Like finding that float. Did I tell you we buried it with him?"

As with the growing list of repo boats, every week since the Mammoth *Kuparuk* grounding, Fish and Wildlife publishes the running total of known bird and mammal oil spill fatalities. By summer's end, the agency announces it has so far documented the remains of nearly seventy-five thousand oiled birds, over twenty-five hundred otters, and a variety of other marine and land mammals. The weekly press release routinely notes that the figures likely represent fewer than ten percent of actual spill mortalities.

Daniel does the math. At least three-quarters of a million dead birds and counting? Over twenty-five thousand otter mortalities? Daniel knows Aaron and Lee would vehemently protest how the federal Fish and Wildlife Service and Alaska Department of Fish and Game now add insult to the wildlife's injuries. Of the otters surviving the spill, which are being held in a saltwater holding facility in Alexi Bay, over half have been surgically implanted with radio transmitters in order to monitor their movements upon release. In another experiment, government workers capture a number of mink and marten in live traps, then feed the animals crude oil in an attempt to determine exactly how much petroleum it takes to kill an individual mustelid. As well, the state and federal agencies now net live seabirds, kill them (who knows how), then coat the birds' bodies with crude petroleum and set the carcasses adrift in various ocean locations in order to track where they wind up. Finally, federal employees shoot twenty oiled harbor seals and ten sea lions for dissection and study—animals that might otherwise have survived their contamination.

All are efforts to generate additional data for the government's lawsuit against Mammoth Petroleum, all are performed in the name of science, and all of them reek of bad policy. Daniel records a scathing commentary for KRBB, subsequently broadcast nationwide. Animal rights activists immediately contact him to join their crusade, but as much as he deplores the agencies' experimentation, neither can he see himself embracing the platform of an outfit like PETA. To be anti-fur is essentially un-Alaskan, especially when you consider the extent to which Native folk rely on wild food, skins, antlers, ivory, and every other part of the animal.

He wonders what statistics, if any, might one day be available for workers injured by exposure to petroleum. When Daniel inquires of the oil giant, he's told they keep no such records. And it's impossible at this point even to guess who might be suffering spill-related health effects, since Mammoth Petroleum early on had offered a one-time payment of a thousand dollars to those who signed a release for "indemnity from adverse health effects from cleanup work." As the simple, two-paragraph contract stated, it "ABSOLUTELY AND IRREVOCABLY" (this text was capitalized on the form) "releases and discharges the Mammoth Petroleum Corporation from any and all claims." Most of the new oil spill workers had happily signed the contract, regarding the money as a freebie.

How many of them will one day regret having done so, afflicted weeks or months or even years from now by unspecific symptoms, their health "ABSOLUTELY AND IRREVOCABLY" compromised?

Members of Congress travel to Alaska to hold oversight hearings for a House Interior subcommittee on water, power, and energy. Daniel notices that disenchanted Alaskans view the hearings as little more than a taxpayer-funded fishing junket since it's scheduled for the height of silver salmon season. Alaska Public Radio Network broadcasts the proceedings live from Anchorage, and the journalist listens with mounting unease as the participating legislators monotonously interrogate oil company executives: "Did you think the contingency plan you signed offered adequate protection in the event of a major oil spill?"

Time and again, the same response: "The State of Alaska approved it. The state signed off on it."

"That's not what we're asking. We're asking if *you* felt it was good enough."

"The state did not require us to do more."

Patience stretched thin, the congressmen press on. "Did you think this plan would truly defend against a major spill?"

Long pause. Finally, "No."

"And you yourself felt no responsibility to improve its measures? Did you ever consider your obligation to the American people?"

No response.

So emerges the three-part picture of the Mammoth *Kuparuk* oil spill: the unrestrained greed of the petroleum industry, a state government afraid to bite the hand that feeds it, and a make-believe system of federal oversight.

Gregg decides some fuckups are beyond forgiveness. His with Aaron is one. Richard Aengus's with the *Kuparuk* is another. Apparently, the two of them share more than just an addiction to alcohol; each man has also managed to detonate the warhead of his own life.

The Mammoth Petroleum Corporation adopts the legal stance that insofar as Captain Richard Aengus had command of the supertanker, he alone bears responsibility for its grounding. For his part, Aengus refuses interviews—on the advice of counsel, he says.

Gregg wonders if the disgraced captain has entertained any thoughts of suicide. The fisherman has yet to bring himself to contact Fritz Detweiler, who's still recovering from his overdose, but he sympathizes with the cannery manager's attempt to off himself. Gregg knows he has a debt to repay Aaron before he can contemplate the luxury of ending his own worthless life, so he's diligent about working the twelve steps with his new sponsor, while simultaneously doubting he could possibly live long enough to ever look himself in the eye again. Nothing has prepared him for the turmoil he feels—not the death of his mother in a house fire when Gregg was five, or the crippling of his only sister seven years later in a hunting accident. Not Vietnam. Not the divorce. He's lost his boat. Lost his boy. He himself is lost. "At sea." He pictures the hole in his heart as an actual suppurating wound.

Why can't Alcoholics Anonymous carry some guarantee of success, such that if only you make a sincere effort to work the steps, you can be assured of turning your life around? When Daniel tells him of Lee's accident, urging Gregg to get in touch with her at Jackie's, the skipper's far too ashamed to do anything of the sort, and anyway, he knows Lee wants nothing more to do with him. With his program sponsor's encouragement, however, Gregg writes her a letter in which he tries his best to honestly make amends.

The *Pegasus* skipper wonders if Daniel Wolff guesses his debt of gratitude to him. As the fisherman continues to pitch and yaw between self-loathing and self-pity, the radio journalist continues to reach out with regular phone calls.

In one of them, Daniel tells him of his own experience of tragedy: how he and his first wife were on their way home from dinner one night in Boston when a produce delivery truck ran a red light, T-boning their VW Rabbit and killing his wife, six months pregnant with their first child.

"Was the guy drunk?" Gregg wants to know.

"No. Just speeding."

"I'm sorry, man."

"I still feel like it was my fault," Daniel confides. "Like I should have seen him coming, should have gotten out of the way. Survivor's guilt, I guess."

Was the radio reporter suggesting that others bore some responsibility for Gregg's destructive behavior, too? He knows that nothing anyone could have said or done would have kept him from The Anchor that night. And as much as the fellow veteran's story affects him, Gregg considers his own situation to be completely different than Daniel's because he *is* to blame for his son's death. If he'd stayed at the apartment that night like he should have, maybe Aaron would still be alive.

Daniel seems to have compensated for his earlier loss by remarrying, having kids, doing his best to live a productive life. On the one hand, given enough time, maybe it's possible for Gregg to make some kind of atonement, after all. On the other hand, aren't some transgressions so egregious they can *never* be absolved, so there's no point in trying? He has yet to cry for his son. But something about the note he gets one day from Lee, scrawled almost illegibly with her left hand, triggers a welling of emotion.

"I know Aaron would want me to forgive you," she has written, "so I'll try. Anyway, I'm guessing you're already doing a good job beating yourself up."

Throughout the summer months, the so-called cleanup of the oil spill continues. Eventually, authorities abandon the term "clean" in favor of "treated," then relinquish "treated" for the phrase "environmentally stable." Whatever it's called, the response in most locations renders more harm than the oil spill itself. The high-pressure hot-water applications, especially, have effectively sterilized large portions of the upper shoreline while smothering the lower reaches with toxic runoff. In many places, Mammoth Petroleum's cleanup workers unwittingly track oil from the intertidal zone into areas previously uncontaminated. Experts generally come to agree on the impossibility of "cleaning" a cold-water oil spill, concluding that the shoreline is best left to recover on its own. Even so, Mammoth Petroleum, the State of Alaska, and the federal agencies all persist in the motions of "treatment" because none of them wants to risk a public perception of doing nothing.

In addition to the ecological damage and social disintegration of the coastal communities, spill-related activities have caused incalculable damage to early archeological remains. Daniel pictures the collection of yellowed ivory harpoon tips and old wooden visors displayed in glass cases at the Selby Museum. In some instances, oil spill workers trample the fragile traces of house and burial sites; in others, they steal artifacts—perhaps to keep as souvenirs, perhaps to sell illegally. On Kodiak, members of the island's tribal associations link arms to form human chains, in a successful effort to bar work crews from coming ashore onto their lands. They'd rather have the pollution, they say, than the adverse effects of so-called remediation.

At the height of its spill response, Mammoth Petroleum employs twenty thousand workers. The corporation reports having removed over a hundred thousand tons of "mousse and oily debris" from the Alaska coastline, most of it transported by barge to the Lower Forty-Eight for "disposal." Whatever that means, Daniel thinks. Has it been burned? Buried? He wonders if the residents of the disposal sites Outside are aware of what's been imported into their midst. The *American Eagle*, a large fishing tender leased by Mammoth for the transport of cleanup workers, strikes a submerged rock near Port Clark, spilling two thousand gallons of diesel fuel. Which is worse, everyone now asks, the environmental destruction caused by the original flood of millions of gallons of crude oil, or the havoc wreaked by its "cleanup"?

Instead of traveling to Alaska himself to witness the ravages of the oil spill, the president of the United States sends the vice president in his stead.

"Well, it *is* the VP's job to attend funerals," Gregg quips to Daniel in their next phone call.

Accompanied by a Coast Guard admiral in his dress whites and gold braid, the vice president is televised wearing hip waders on Wallace Island, near Ground Zero of the spill, on a stretch of beach "treated" no fewer than a dozen times. When journalists from the world's leading media ask him to do so, the obliging veep steps down off the prepared boardwalk, crouches, and inserts a rubber-gloved hand into the sparkling gravel. Seconds later, holding up fingers dripping with glistening black oil, the vice president's shock is visible. The startled look on his face and the way the impeccably attired admiral beside him recoils serve in a matter of seconds to collapse the illusion of "clean" that Mammoth Petroleum and the government have spent months painstakingly constructing. Alaska television stations broadcast the loop over and over again.

"We could have told him that would happen," Daniel comments.

"Candy asses." Gregg says nothing more for a minute, then tells the other man he's been approached by an activist group, the Petroleum Reform Organization, or PRO, a Seattle-based coalition of Northwest tribes, fishing interests, environmentalists, educators, artists, and others who've joined together to redress the way the government does business with Big Oil. "They want me to be one of their commercial-fishing liaisons," Gregg says shyly. "I'm supposed to go to D.C. with them to lobby for double-hulled tankers."

"That's great," Daniel says. "Congratulations." Maybe this will give Gregg the lift he needs, the reporter thinks.

On day 153 of the spill, in late August, Mammoth Petroleum announces plans to scale back its oil spill response in anticipation of deteriorating fall weather. The company has decided to shut down its cleanup operations over the Labor Day weekend, to resume them in the spring. In reaction to Mammoth's decision, the all-volunteer Independent Cleanup Effort—the thing Lee had helped organize— issues a press release proclaiming that ICE will maintain a year-round presence in Nevada Cove "until the last drop of oil is removed from the shore." Brave words, but Daniel seriously doubts that anyone should be out in the gulf much past September when, as Gregg has told him, storms typically turn life-threatening.

20

Residents of the coastal communities habituate to what will in the end amount to fifteen summers of remediation, traditional seasonal pursuits like fishing and sightseeing replaced by oil spill mitigation. Significant quantities of oil remain buried in the substrate or solidified into thick mats of tar. Hundreds of attorneys both in and out of state organize thousands of people into "injured parties," the largest classes of which are fishermen and Alaska Natives, but as the lawyers portend, Mammoth Petroleum skillfully keeps the lawsuits tied up in court for almost a quarter century.

The oil company restores and refits the *Kuparuk*, renaming it *Adriatic* for its European trade. Daniel remains fascinated by Captain Richard Aengus, who steadfastly declines interviews and refuses to elaborate upon the laconic responses he'd given at the pretrial hearings, leaving it to others to interpret the events of the tanker grounding however they will.

Daniel's own version of those events, based on public testimony and conjecture, goes like this: *Having had to pick its way through the warehouse-sized icebergs choking the entrance to the Narrows, the Kuparuk had arrived at the Pipeline terminal that March day well behind schedule. Faced with the necessity to make up for lost time, captain and crew began loading North Slope petroleum immediately—a lengthy, carefully calibrated process of replacing ballast water with crude oil, maintaining equilibrium in all compartments at all times. Due to recent personnel cuts, many of the crew worked back-to-back shifts.*

Captain Aengus wants to be well rested by the time they cast off, especially since they will once again have to thread a course through the ice. With the tanker secure in port, he is able to nap briefly that afternoon and sees no harm in joining some of his men for predeparture drinks at the Pipeline Club that evening.

Unlike the rest of those granted shore time (all of whom have made a beeline for the bar), the newbie, Aaron Anderson, chooses to use his leave for sightseeing, joining the rest of them at the club only at nightfall. In fact, Captain Aengus himself buys Aaron his first pair of Pepsis, for which he's amply rewarded by the young man's lively account of the herring spawn in a nearby cove. Aaron describes the seething shoal of fish that churned the sheltered waters. He tells the captain how the herring worked themselves into a frenzy upon reaching shore, the females extruding eggs and the males releasing sperm. By sunset, the enthusiastic young seaman claims, the water in the small cove foamed white as milk. How had Aaron described the wheeling birds jockeying for position overhead, diving on the flashing silver fish? Raucous? No, he'd called it a ruckus.

Apparently, Aengus had envied Aaron the spectacle. The captain said it was a phenomenon he'd long wished to see. It sure as hell would have been a more constructive use of his time than throwing back scotch and sodas at the Pipeline Club, Daniel thinks.

Returning to the ship at 2120, Aengus meets with the no-nonsense shipping agent, who boards to go over documents with him. When she leaves, the talkative harbor pilot joins him on the bridge, and at 2210, many crew-members having already put in a full day's work, Aengus gives the order to

256

cast off. As required for departure, the pilot has command, and Kuparuk is under escort by the tug Intrepid.

Second Mate Peter Janacek shares navigation duty with the captain. Despite the other officer's ill-concealed dislike of him, Aengus considers this a stroke of luck. Of all his staff, he feels most confident in the second's abilities and looks forward to leaving Janacek in charge of the bridge shortly so that he himself can go below to his quarters to complete more paperwork.

When the ship emerges under escort from the Narrows, Aengus resumes command, ordering the engines reduced from half ahead to slow ahead. The captain feels the vise-like tightness of his shoulders, the first signs of one of his increasingly frequent headaches gathering at the base of his skull.

Once the harbor pilot has disembarked, the captain calls the traffic center to report the tug's departure and to request permission to move from Outbound to Inbound. He speaks briefly with Janacek, agreeing on a hundred-and-eighty-degree course change that will swing them out of the lanes altogether and allow wide berth in the event of ranging ice. Both men know that the tanker that preceded them, the Exxon Long Beach, has made a similar maneuver. "Bring her down abeam of the reef and then return to the lanes," Aengus instructs the mate. He says it twice. A simple course adjustment, ten-degree rudder right. "Phone me when you begin the turn," he adds, before directing that the engines be placed on load program up. With a vessel as ponderous as Kuparuk, it will take three-quarters of an hour to attain sea speed. Janacek steps into the chart room to plot the course, returning within minutes.

A. B. Rodriguez, a competent seaman, and Aaron Anderson, their temporary hand, share watch.

In the privacy of his stateroom, the captain thinks he might lie down for a few minutes before resuming his assault on the numbing sheaf of documents he must process. His cabin lies at the bottom of a single flight of stairs leading directly to the bridge, placing him but a phone call away from those above. For that matter, they could always holler for him down the stairwell. It's such an unthinkable breach of shipboard decorum that Aengus smiles as he stretches out on his bed.

From the first scrape of the hull, Captain Richard Aengus knows exactly what has occurred. It's not merely a question of tracking the ship's movements even in sleep, as any experienced mariner would do, but a matter of meeting his destiny.

Barefoot, in trousers and t-shirt, he bounds to the bridge for the fourth, fifth—six collisions in all. Each impact, Aengus notes, feels cushioned, no doubt due to the lightness of the ship's steel. He pictures Kuparuk crumpling like a soft-drink can. Neither he nor Janacek say anything for the long minutes that pass before the tanker comes to its final shuddering rest; by then the chief engineer and the third mate have joined them, both men in white athletic socks and seemingly identical gray sweatpants and t-shirts. "What the hell," Henderson demands, taking the aft stairs in leaps, headed for the engine room.

Janacek steps aside, as courtly as a dancer in a minuet. Aengus can read nothing on the second's face. By now, Third Mate Abernathy pores over the chart, glancing frantically and repeatedly at the instrument panel to check coordinates. Although he knows precisely where they've fetched up, the captain nevertheless leaves the third to his efforts. It's good practice and besides, there's nothing else for the man to do. Someone switches on the exterior floodlights, and in their colorless glare the dark oil, driven by the stupendous head pressure of tanks extending sixty feet above waterline, jettisons skyward to plume overhead before cascading back down onto the foredeck.

Aengus orders the engines from stop to dead slow ahead and for the next half hour tries his best to stabilize the vessel, headache all the while thundering behind his eyes. Forward at half, then forward again at full—not to free the supertanker but to further and fully strand it on the reef lest they capsize. The tide is falling, which might mean a reprieve, or not, depending on how quickly the water recedes. This sequence of vernal tides, after all, marks the second most extreme of the year, in a place already boasting some of the highest tides in the world.

The fumes from the crude oil, stringent and raw, make everyone lightheaded. Aengus's eyes water, blurring his vision. The question's not if, but how many, compartments have been breached. Too bad they hadn't grounded while inbound, the captain thinks, empty save for ballast water, rather than fully loaded with fifty-five million gallons. It would have gone better for sea and shore. Aengus watches the product continue to boil from the ship's bowels and hears Aaron Anderson tell Janacek through chattering teeth how he'd gotten showered on deck, thus explaining the greasy trails on the young man's frightened face, the oily saturation of his clothes, and the nauseating stench of unprocessed petroleum.

The chief engineer makes his report: a large amount of product has already escaped. "We're recording movement in over half the tanks," he says. Aengus orders the engineer to perform stress tests to determine stability.

How will the leakage affect the vessel's balance? How quickly will the tide ebb? Might the Kuparuk roll onto her side? Aengus continues his efforts at the conn for another fifteen or twenty minutes. Only when assured that they are well and truly grounded does he at last stand back and order the engines shut down.

The crew musters in the mess hall, where the captain has Abernathy order all hands into survival suits. The chief approaches him again, reporting that they've already lost a hundred thousand barrels and that the oil is now exchanging with seawater within the ship.

Aengus makes his way downstairs to his quarters, head throbbing. Perhaps he glances at his bare feet padding along the carpeted corridor and notices that his yellowing toenails could use a trim. How does he feel about the fact that his career is finished?

He shaves, brushes his teeth, and dresses carefully. If he were Japanese, he would now fall on his sword, but as an American, of course, he's under no obligation to do so. He combs his hair and checks his teeth, then uncaps and takes a pull directly from the bottle of his most expensive scotch, Royal Salute, replacing it in the reaches of the closet.

When the captain returns in his dress uniform to the bridge, he stands for a moment staring east-southeast into darkness. Finally, pressing a clean handkerchief to his face against the noxious fumes, Aengus picks up the handset of the radio to notify the Coast Guard that the Mammoth Kuparuk has fetched up hard aground on Montague Reef.

Founder, Daniel thinks. Said of a ship when it fills with water and sinks. Of course, the word also means to fail.

The Alaska Press Club nominates Daniel's oil spill work for a national journalism prize, and a member of the board of KRBB hosts a reception for him. Her three-story, glass-and-steel house perches on a rocky outcrop overlooking a small estuary on the outskirts of Selby, accessible only by a winding, miles-long road that's been blasted out of the surrounding rock. Daniel remembers having heard rumors of the home's excessive construction costs but has never seen it, let alone been inside. The palatial, high-end dwelling has triple-paned windows, heated tile floors, wide marble countertops. He would not have guessed that anyone in the rough-hewn fishing town enjoyed such an upscale lifestyle. Surely the cost of road construction alone—or of bringing electricity to this remote site—exceeds most locals' lifetime earnings.

Since the board member lives by herself and doesn't work, Daniel supposes her to be an heiress. Wearing faded jeans and a thrift-store Hawaiian shirt, he feels underdressed when he arrives, to be greeted warmly by her in a black cocktail dress, a string of pearls around her neck. But other than station manager Malcolm in his pressed slacks and oxford button-down, everyone else is casually attired. It is Selby, after all.

Daniel wonders what their middle-aged hostess does with her time. Someone whispers to him that she has similarly well-appointed homes in Vail and San Francisco and that she divides her year between the three residences. When he takes his empty wineglass into the cavern-ous kitchen to rinse and refill it with water, he notices a small piece of paper taped to the oversized and otherwise unadorned stainless-steel refrigerator: "A society based on the acquisition of wealth is not a society at all, but a state of war." The quote is attributed to William Morris. Is the board member chastising herself, or does she somehow perceive her own standard of living to be one that eschews "the acquisition of wealth"?

Daniel thinks of Tessa's recently published letter to the editor of the *Anchorage Tribune*, on the occasion of the one-year anniversary of the oil spill. "Enough *is* enough," she'd written. "The real question is: can we learn to live with less?"

To have or to be. Is that the question?

It's not lost on Tess that Selbyites on the whole come to feel discouraged rather than buoyed by the annual reappearance of Mammoth Petroleum in their midst. She herself maintains a belief that the oil company owes it to the spill communities to continue cleanup efforts, but even she begins to worry that what's offered does more harm than good as acrimony persists between those who work seasonally for the oil giant and those who don't. She's not sorry that she's no longer in Mammoth's employ. Belatedly, Tess has realized that one of Selby's greatest strengths was the tolerance most people routinely extended to one another: "Live and let live." Now, the community's so divided that it's hard to imagine it ever recovering its former unity. She and others press their elected officials to hold quarterly town-hall meetings to rebuild a sense of cohesion. "Tell us what's on *your* mind," the public-service announcements say. "We want to hear from *you.*"

Tessa's relationships seem to have entirely reconstellated since the spill, due in part to politics and in part to people moving away. Jackie and Lee are still her closest friends, and she wishes they lived closer, but Tess understands that for Jackie, counseling veterans offers greater personal and professional challenges than her former job at Selby Community Mental Health—notwithstanding the traumatizing effects of the oil spill on coastal residents. And she supports Lee's desire to finish her schooling at the university in Anchorage. Tess knows, too, that the former deckhand hasn't entirely forgiven her for her stint of work for the petroleum giant but trusts that the passage of time will help to heal the wound to their friendship. Maybe, for her part, the younger woman will learn that to err is human.

The deckhand has enrolled as a full-time college student, waiting tables at a popular vegetarian restaurant. Although she and Jackie have reconciled, Lee apparently opposes their living together for now, so she shares a three-bedroom house with a couple of roommates while her lover lives alone in a duplex a half-mile away. Tess assumes Lee's just being difficult, but the couple seems happy enough, so she keeps her mouth shut. She looks forward to seeing them both in August, when they plan to vacation together in Selby. It will be Lee's first trip back.

Tess keeps in touch with the two women by phone. Just yesterday, Jackie had called with the news that's now grabbing headlines all over the world: how the Arab troops, in retreat from the Persian Gulf, have opened the valves of the world's largest petroleum terminal, unleashing the contents into desert sand. They've also punctured the hulls of their own tankers, to drain the crude into the sea. Both are measures to keep America and its allies from appropriating the Middle East's wealth of oil. "They've torched the production wells, which are surrounded by land mines, and anyway, the fire's burning so hot that no one can get close enough to fight it," Jackie said. "It's the mother of all oil disasters."

What is it about petroleum, Tess wants to know. Why do we humans sell our souls for the stuff?

Baby Emily—already six months old—had been born to Tess and Daniel on January 2, winning them the thousand-dollar savings bond put up annually by the Bank of Alaska for the first birth of the New Year. Emmy's a gem, the easiest-going of the three children with her sunny disposition. Daniel's so smitten with his new daughter, so thrilled by the addition to their family, that Tess has warmed to him again, but life with a newborn still seems to her a step backward, especially when she continues to go through the motions of work she finds increasingly demeaning and unrewarding. The male doctors socking away wealth while the female nurses take blood pressures and empty bedpans. Even though Daniel still doesn't earn very much, Tess envies him his career. All she has is a job. She finds herself thinking with discouraging regularity, This is not what I signed up for.

One night, before she leaves for work, Daniel tells her something he's heard at the station. "Supposedly, if you put a frog into a pot of water and heat it slowly on the stove, the frog won't move. It'll just stay there until it gets cooked. But if you bring a pot of water to a boil and try to put a frog in it, it jumps out right away. No problem."

"Are you saying human beings are on the slow-cook track?" Tessa frowns. "Who wants to live like a frog in any kind of hot water? What kind of choice is that?"

The only thing for which she feels unreserved enthusiasm is the garden their family has planted, intending it to be their biggest ever. Tess figures they'll save money by producing some of their own food, and she also hopes it will help to ensure the quality of what they eat since you can never be certain anymore of exactly what's in and on the food you buy.

She's incredulous that the sole penalty Captain Richard Aengus will have to pay for his drunken tanker driving is picking up litter along the Anchorage roadside.

When Daniel wins the national journalism award in his category, he calls Gregg to suggest they travel together to D.C. "The American Press Club is paying my way. Does this Petroleum Reform outfit still plan to use you for lobbying?"

Gregg's leery. He hasn't left Anchorage for almost a year, having no better destination in mind. "How's your old lady feel about you leaving her alone with three kids?" he asks.

"Her parents will come down and lend a hand. Anyway, I'm thinking about maybe taking Elias. You and I can show him the Vietnam Veterans Memorial—the Wall." Daniel's got it all planned.

"Whoa there, partner," Gregg laughs. "That'll never fly with the wife."

It takes him a minute, but Daniel laughs, too. "You're right."

Gregg changes the subject, to give himself time to think. "I finally worked up the nerve to call Lee. She looks good."

"How's she doing with school?"

"Says she wants to keep going after she graduates," Gregg says proudly. "A master's degree in marine biology."

"She and Jackie doing okay?"

"Still not living together, apparently."

Daniel chuckles. "Maybe that'll be the secret of their success."

Gregg tells the other man how Lee rides her bike everywhere, occasionally taking the bus, but never driving. "She's way fit," he says. "Gave me a hard time for letting myself go."

"She might be the most principled person I know, but I guess I don't think everyone suddenly riding bikes is the answer to our energy problems."

"Still, it's a step in the right direction." Gregg admires Lee for the purposeful changes she's made. "You've got to admit it's better than doing nothing." He wonders about his own next steps. His boat's long gone, and anyway, most of the fisheries remain closed. Fish and Game wants to play it conservatively in coming years, in what the agency hopes will prove a successful long-term effort to restore ravaged stocks. Gregg lacks the desire to retool his life in Selby, but where else can he go?

When he and Daniel travel to D.C., they do indeed visit the Wall, running their fingertips over the engraved names of boys they'd known. It's there in the angled vale of polished black granite that Gregg encounters a ponytailed Chumash Indian who tells him about an enterprise American veterans have undertaken in Vietnam.

As the trim former Marine describes the work he and others do with injured and maimed Vietnamese children at Brotherhood and Sisterhood Village, Gregg sees himself joining their effort. What better way to honor Aaron's memory?

"You guys have any meetings over there?" he asks.

"Every day," the brother replies. "The coffee's good, too."

Lee maintains a 3.8 GPA. Calculating she can finish her prerequisites in another year and possibly earn the master's in three more, she decides she'd like to do her research on pelagic birds. She hopes to get hired by the university as a lab assistant, which will help her application to the graduate program, and she welcomes the assigned papers, midterms, and finals. Without the imposed deadlines, she knows she'd still be floundering in a confusion of emotion. Mixed-up seas. Despite Jackie's admonitions that she's got to "feel her feelings," Lee chooses instead to enroll in extra courses and to take classes year-round.

She and her lover seem to have found the middle ground that earlier eluded them. Maybe it was a good thing they'd split up because in a weird way, the oil spill has brought them back together stronger than ever. Unlike Lee, Jackie's outrage at the oil spill is not so much fueled by the agonizing deaths of countless creatures and the devastation of habitat as from concern for the toll it has taken on people. "Damage to the environment exacts a price on human beings, too," she says with feeling. "We can't afford the kinds of psychic wounds something like an oil spill inflicts, so unless and until that changes, we have no business taking those risks."

Even after Tess and Daniel went in to her little cabin and boxed up her things, now stored in their garage, it had still taken Lee all winter to convince Irene she wasn't moving back to Selby. Perhaps someday, with luck, and armed with her fishing experience and an advanced degree, she can get a berth on a research boat. It might even be one that home-ports in Rugged Bay.

Having met the baby when Tess brought her to Anchorage in March, Lee can't wait to see all three kids again. She and Jackie are Emmy's godmothers—the "fairy" godmothers, Tess likes to joke. Lee wants to spend time with Bruno, too, whom Irene declares is "as good as new" despite the fact of his missing leg. And Gunther's coming to visit over the Fourth of July weekend. He'll stay at Jackie's, where there's an extra room. Lee's nervous about her father's visit but proud of herself for issuing the invitation, which he'd immediately accepted.

Since the oil spill, she sometimes has trouble sleeping, awakening in the middle of the night with the incapacitating smell of crude oil in her nostrils and throat, stomach tense. Lee pictures hosts of poisoned sea life and remembers holding the limbs of lethargic otters. She thinks of her new career path as a way to pay homage to Aaron and to make amends to both Bruno and the moose she'd hit with her truck. She's haunted by all the wild lives lost in the oil spill and frets that human beings have already run out of time to make things right.

Often while tending the saltwater aquaria in the biology lab, Lee has imaginary conversations with Aaron. He tells her when she's neglecting her health and when she should have greater faith in others. She keeps asking him the same thing: what do you do if you love nature more than people, but people are destroying nature? So far, all he's told her is that it's not the right question.

"Nothing's going to change until people do," she hears him saying, and Lee wonders if humans are really capable of change.

"Look at you," Gregg's son says. "You've changed. How about giving others the benefit of the doubt?"

But I'm not a joiner, she thinks.

"Now would be a good time to start," he adds.

Acknowledgments

So many forces assisted me in the writing of this book that it would be impossible to mention them all. But I would like to express my appreciation to those of you who rendered invaluable assistance ranging from critique to child care, from filial support to friendship, and who supplied me with information and/or inspiration: Marilyn Barry, Rose Beck, Jean Bodeau, Sis Bolivar, the members of the Book Club, Terri Bramel, Ginny Carney, Steve Clark, Marjorie Kowalski Cole, Joan Connors, Amanda Coyne, the Dahl family, Joan Daniels, Ellyn Derman, Trang Duong, Nelta Edwards, Claudia Ehli, James Engelhardt, Jeffrey and Dian Evans, Owen and Jean Evans, Racie Evans and Steve Julius, Mark Faller, Rona Florio, Libby Hatton, Linda Hogan, Carrie Holba, Marybeth Holleman, M. E. "Pete" Isleib and Brina Kessel, MarBeth Johns, Seth Kantner, John Keeble, Greg Kimura, Maxine Hong Kingston, Tom Kizzia, Jen Kohout, Mary LaChapelle, Debbie LaFleiche, Norma Leland, Birgit Lenger, Nancy Lord and Ken Castner, Dawn Marano, John McKay, Elizabeth McNeill, Sally Mead, Liz Meredith, Jeff and Janet Middleton, Gina Miller, Pamela Miller, Deborah Miranda, Sue Mitchell, Mavis Muller, Richard Nelson, Doug North, Susan Olsen, Mike O'Meara, Riki Ott, Rosanne Pagano, Lynn Paulson, Debi Poore and Charlie Gibson, Bill and Sherry Poplarchik, Joy Post, Tim Rawson, Susan Read-Brown, the Read-Brown family, Jeff Richardson, Libby Roderick, Andromeda Romano-Lax, Ned Rozell, Steve Rubinstein, Bill Sherwonit, Peggy Shumaker Sharon Sibbald, Larry Smith, Cody Sontag, John Sroufe, Rachel Stein, Esther Beth Sullivan, Toby Sullivan, Peter Thielke and Ellen Sklarz, Mary Thompson, Joanne Townsend, Deb Vanasse, Heather Waddell, Deb Ward, Bob Wilkinson, Leland and Pamela Williams, Hope Wing, and Martin Zeller.

In addition, I'm deeply grateful for the support and sustenance I have received from the following: Alaska Pacific University, the Alaska State Council for the Arts, 49 Writers, Hedgebrook Cottages, the Rasmuson Foundation, and the University of Alaska Press.

Thank you.

Other Books in the Alaska Literary Series